THE DEAD SHALL BE RAISED

THE MURDER OF A QUACK

GEORGE BELLAIRS

With an Introduction by

MARTIN EDWARDS

This edition published 2016 by
The British Library
96 Euston Road
London
NW1 2DB

The Dead Shall Be Raised was originally
published in 1942 by John Gifford Ltd

The Murder of a Quack was originally published
in 1943 by John Gifford Ltd

Cataloguing in Publication Data

A catalogue record for this book is available from the British Library

ISBN 978 0 7123 5652 7

Typeset by Tetragon, London
Printed and bound by
CPI Group (UK) Ltd, Croydon CR0 4YY

CONTENTS

THE MURDER OF A QUACK

INTRODUCTION

The Dead Shall Be Raised is, in more ways than one, a story about a cold case. The year is 1940, and it is chilly and Christmas. Carols are sung in Hatterworth, a small Pennine town, as Scotland Yard's Thomas Littlejohn is reunited with his convalescent wife for a short period of leave. But soon the festivities are interrupted by news of the discovery of human remains, buried long ago on nearby moorland. The dead man is quickly identified as Enoch Sykes, who went missing in 1917. Littlejohn is happy to be pressed into service as the police investigation causes skeletons to rattle in several of Hatterworth's cupboards.

The wartime background gives the book at least as much flavour as the seasonal touches. Members of the Home Guard—"Dad's Army"—are responsible for the gruesome find on Milestone Moor, having discovered Sykes' skeleton while digging a trench. The dead man was suspected of having murdered his workmate and former friend Jerry Trickett, and of having fled from justice during the confusion of the First World War. Now the police have a double murder on their hands, and Littlejohn and his new colleagues need to explore feuds and betrayals of long ago in order to uncover the truth about the crimes. When a key witness is murdered, it becomes apparent that a killer continues to stalk Hatterworth.

The story moves at a brisk place, while benefiting from George Bellairs' characteristic quiet wit. The small town and the bleak moors are well rendered, and it seems likely that Hatterworth is a fictionalised version of Saddleworth, not far from where the author grew up. In a tragic and macabre twist, more than twenty years after this book was written, Saddleworth Moor became the scene of a gruesome search for human remains in real life, when it emerged that victims of the Moors Murderers, Ian Brady and Myra Hindley, were buried there.

The Dead Shall Be Raised, which is also sometimes called *Murder Will Speak*, first appeared in 1942. The second short novel in this book, *The Murder of a Quack*, was published the following year. Again, Bellairs wastes little time in plunging his readers into the action: P.C. Mellalieu discovers the corpse of Nathaniel Wall in the first chapter. The dead man, who was in his seventies, has been murdered in an odd fashion; someone half-strangled him, but he died as a result of being hanged from a contrivance of ropes and pulleys that he used in his work. Wall was a "bonesetter", a skilled homeopath who had built up a good practice in the village of Stalden, provoking the enmity of a qualified doctor called Keating, who regarded him as a quack, but could not match his popularity with patients.

The local constabulary promptly calls in the Yard, and Littlejohn takes over the investigation. The dead man's estate passes to his nephew, a qualified doctor, who appears to have a cast-iron alibi. There seems to be no compelling reason why anyone would want to kill Wall, but Littlejohn is intrigued by a collection of press cuttings in the dead man's possession which relate to criminal cases of the past. Might they suggest a motive for murder?

Littlejohn is a diligent detective, of whom his creator once said: "he had no brilliant accomplishments and no influential pals… the marvellous powers of Sherlock Holmes and the techniques of Dr. Thorndyke were denied to him". His strengths are "sheer patience and tenacity of purpose". These qualities, so valuable in real-life police work, do not necessarily make for breathless excitement, but Littlejohn is a genial fellow, with whom readers can empathise.

The murder mystery plots are competently put together, but Bellairs was not aiming to write complex puzzles of the kind so fashionable during "the Golden Age of Murder" between the two world wars. At a time of national crisis, he concentrated on producing mysteries that would distract his readers from the horrors of the war; his books are as notable for their humour and humanity as they are for their plots. In both these stories, his harshest words are reserved for people who exploit others. His brisk characterisations suggest an astute observer of human nature. Probably this came from experience gained in his day job, as a bank manager.

Bellairs' real name was Harold Blundell (1902–1982). He was born in Heywood, just across the county border from Saddleworth, which was part of the West Riding of Yorkshire prior to local government reorganisation in the seventies. He started work in a bank at the age of fifteen, and remained with the same employer until retiring forty-five years later. His literary career lasted nearly four decades, and throughout that time he stayed with the same publisher. Such loyalty tells us something about the personality of a modest, decent man whose affability and sense of humour are mirrored in Littlejohn. Writing was for him an enjoyable sideline; he was not as ambitious in his work as, say, Dorothy L. Sayers or Anthony Berkeley, two Golden Age superstars who had run out of steam as novelists by the time Bellairs started writing. Bellairs may have lacked their flair, but he had greater staying power, and Berkeley (who reinvented himself as a crime reviewer) became both a fan and a friend.

After his retirement, Harold Blundell and his wife Gwladys moved to the Isle of Man, and his love of the island is apparent in various novels that he set there. He continued to write Littlejohn novels for the rest of his life. Rather poignantly, the title of his last book was *An Old Man Dies*; it was published shortly before his death, one day short of his eightieth birthday.

With the methodical habits of a good bank manager, he kept detailed records of his work as a writer, including correspondence, contracts, and press cuttings. Happily for researchers into the genre, Gwladys presented his archive to the John Rylands Library, a neo-Gothic architectural masterpiece in Deansgate, Manchester, which now forms part of the University of Manchester Library. The material in the archive gives a fascinating insight into the career of a "mid-list" writer of the mid-twentieth century, an author who was never a bestseller, but who for half a lifetime worked hard to entertain his readers.

MARTIN EDWARDS
www.martinedwardsbooks.com

THE DEAD SHALL BE RAISED

For Gwlad

with Love

CHAPTER I

The Singing Policeman

"When the day's work was done, o'er a pint of home brew,
He would sing by the hearth the old songs that he knew."

AMMON WRIGLEY

ON CHRISTMAS EVE 1940, DETECTIVE-INSPECTOR LITTLEJOHN, of Scotland Yard, stepped from the well-lighted London to Manchester train into the Stygian darkness of the blacked-out platform of Stockport. Passengers and ticket collectors climbed furtively in and out of the train, anxious to keep all its light bottled-up within it. Dim forms, like the shades of the underworld, fumbled about the station. Piles of boxes, mail-bags, platform-trucks and the hundred and one benches, baskets, lamps, cans, brushes and the like which clutter up such places strove like living things to make progress a vast and ghastly obstacle race. The detective, after extricating himself from a pile of parcels, destined to arrive at their goals well after Christmas, dropped his bag and waited for something to turn up in the shape of a railway official, from whom he might take his bearings. At length, a peaked-cap silhouetted itself against a thin streak of light emanating from a luggage van.

"Porter, where can I find the train for Waterfold?" asked Littlejohn.

"I'm a Salvation Army man, but I think I can tell you," came a pleasant reply from the night. A firm grip was taken on his arm and he was piloted to a shadowy train, waiting, without lights, in a nearby bay.

"This is the train. I've just come in by it. It leaves in half an hour," said his guide and with a cheery good night, left him to his own devices.

Littlejohn stumbled into a carriage, groped for the rack, tested its capacity by gently swinging on it, and slung his suitcase upwards. Then, he slumped on a hard seat, sucked the dying embers of his pipe into activity again and settled to wait patiently for something to happen.

No-one but his wife could have persuaded Littlejohn to make such a trip on Christmas Eve. One November night, he had arrived home to find all the windows of his Hampstead flat smashed and the roof blown-in. Far worse, his wife, Letty, was a casualty at the local hospital. Luckily, the worst that German frightfulness had done to her was to cause superficial cuts and slight concussion, but the detective, tied as he was to duty owing to the stress of official work, did not feel happy until he had packed her off to a quiet area. He had the greatest difficulty in persuading her to visit an old friend of her schooldays, whose cottage, high on the Pennine backbone which separates Lancashire from Yorkshire, afforded not only quiet nights but strong moorland air, a tonic for overwrought nerves. So, to Hatterworth, the village, or town, or whatever it was that held his wife, Littlejohn went to spend Christmas. He had ten days' well-earned and long postponed leave on his hands and until he stepped into the inky depression of Stockport, he had been as high-spirited as a boy on vacation.

The jolt of an engine being violently connected with the train shook Littlejohn out of his reverie. A streak of light from a passing goods-train illuminated the compartment for a moment and it was then that the Inspector perceived that he was not alone. Another dark figure was sitting huddled in the opposite corner, apparently asleep. Littlejohn was not in the habit of inflicting his company and talk on strangers, but from sheer desolation he addressed his fellow-traveller.

"Am I right for Waterfold in this train?"

No answer.

Asleep, thought Littlejohn, and yet he had the vague feeling that he was not right. Somehow, he felt that the eyes of the stranger were open in the dark. Be damned to you then, old curmudgeon, muttered the detective inwardly. His own voice had sounded eerie and hollow in the strange atmosphere of the black carriage. He felt quite detached from the living world, the thousands of people all around him in the town below, people making merry for the season as best they could under the circumstances, in their isolated, well-illuminated little communities, each shut-off from the other by the pitch-darkness of the black-out night. By some strange association of ideas, Littlejohn recalled reciting at a Christmas party when a boy, some lines very apt under the present conditions. In spite of all the years between, he remembered them pat, and glowed with pleasure in doing so.

O solitude! where are the charms
That sages have seen in thy face?
Better dwell in the midst of alarms
Than reign in this horrible place.

The irony of it tickled Littlejohn's fancy. He even chuckled and felt better for it. Let's see… what else?

I am out of humanity's reach,
I must finish my journey alone,

Never hear the sweet music of speech;
I start at the sound of my own.

"Was you sayin' somethin'?" came a thin, old voice from the corner.

Littlejohn started. He wondered if in his enthusiasm he had been declaiming aloud.

"If you were, yo'll have to speak up. You see, ah'm a bit deaf," went on the voice.

"Oh! I'd just been asking you if I was right for Waterfold in this train."

"Eh? You'll 'ave to speak up."

Littlejohn repeated his query, fortissimo.

"Oh aye, ye'r all reet for Waterfold. Ah say, ye'r all reet. Ah'm goin' to th' station beyond that, so ah'll tell you when we're theer. Ah say, ah'll tell you when we're theer."

The stranger kept repeating himself, as though proud of his utterance and taking relish in quoting his statements over and over again.

With a jolt, the train started. They bumped over points, halted for signals, stopped at what seemed to be an unending succession of stations. The harsh clanking and snorting of the engine indicated a continuous gradient.

"DON'T THEY LIGHT THESE TRAINS?" bawled Littlejohn.

"You needn't shout so loud, mesther. Ah can 'ear you all right now that train's started. Funny, isn't it? When there's a row goin' on, ah can 'ear what folk says to me."

Littlejohn agreed that it was very funny indeed.

"They don't light these trains, because they've forgot there is a railway to Waterfold and sich like places. An' judging from th' lights they've put in some o' the local carriages round Oldham way; they might as well save theirselves th' trouble wi' these. Noborry can see their way into 'em, let alone read or see chap's face next to you. Where you come frum, mesther?"

"London."

"Oh, aye. Bin havin' a rough packet there with bombin' 'aven't yer, mesther? We've had our share 'ere, too, though. A redler blitz we 'ad one night about ten days ago. Two land-mines, we 'ad! They fell on th' moors just a mile or two out o' th' town, but they give us a rare shakin' up, I'll tell you." And he repeated himself several times with obvious pleasure.

The stranger suddenly retired within himself, either sleeping or meditating on his recent news, leaving Littlejohn to his thoughts. "You change to the Waterfold train at Stockport," Mrs. Littlejohn had written, "and from Waterfold there's a 'bus to Hatterworth. They only run once every hour and I hope your train's in time, because you've only a margin of ten minutes. The distance by 'bus is seven miles, right into the hill country."

The train stopped and started again with monotonous jolts and tugs. Station after station. Sometimes there would be the sound of lonely footsteps on a platform; at others, utter stillness and silence, as though men had scornfully packed-up and gone home, leaving the forlorn train to fend for itself. Now and then, a gloomy signal cabin seemed to sail past the window, or a green or red signal light. Not a sign of habitation on either side of the line, which apparently ran through a succession of tunnels, making mighty yawning sounds, or deep cuttings which flung back the rattle of the train, the clank of the engine and the rhythmic clicking of the wheels on the rails. At one station, Littlejohn lowered the window and looked out. A vociferous porter was incoherently yelling the name of the mysterious place to nobody in particular. "Iggle-oop, Iggle-oop," he screamed, and then, "FARAWAY!" Whereat the train crawled off.

The night was bright with stars and the air was cold and as invigorating as wine.

"Poot up th' window, if you doan't mind, mesther," said the shadow in the corner, suddenly stung to life by a draught of fresh air. "Ah'm bad on my chest and it's cowd enough in 'ere, without lettin' any more of it in."

No faces or knowledge of what was going on. Only voices and noises. Depressed, miserable, Littlejohn wondered if the journey would last for ever.

"Waterfold next stop, mesther." Blessed relief! The train slowed down, braked hard, and seemed to totter into the station. Littlejohn bade his companion good night and a Merry Christmas and received a thrice-repeated reply.

Waterfold station was utterly desolate. A cold wind blew through it, stinging the cheeks and ears, but filled with the fresh scented breath of moorland. A porter shambled past.

"Where can I get the Hatterworth 'bus, porter?" called the Inspector.

"It went a quarter of an hour since," came the reply.

Littlejohn cursed under his breath. Never again! If his luck continued in this fashion he would probably meet his wife somewhere about New Year!

A cheery Yorkshire voice broke the gloom, speaking from the darkness somewhere to the left.

"That you, Inspector Littlejohn?"

"Yes," replied the detective, surprised that in this forsaken spot somebody should know him.

"I'm Haworth, Superintendent Haworth, of Hatterworth..."

Littlejohn's spirits sank momentarily. Just his luck to be recalled after his endless treck!... He pictured a call from The Yard to the local police to pick him up and turn him back to duty.

"...Mrs. Littlejohn and my wife are friends and I promised to run out and meet the train. We'll get along better in my car than the 'bus. Glad to meet you, Littlejohn, and a Merry Christmas to you."

Two cordial hands met in the darkness and Littlejohn was glad he had come after all.

The little car sped swiftly over the moorland road, now climbing, now coasting easily downhill as the country undulated. The season had made local traffic all the busier and passing cars were frequent. Haworth's dimmed headlamps illuminated the white stone landmarks, erected by the roadside to indicate the route. There was a heavy, healthy smell of peat on the air and the wind hissed in the heather. Littlejohn could make out none of the details of the country through which he was passing, but had a feeling of being amid vast, open spaces. His companion concentrated on driving and said little. The Inspector did not even know what his friend looked like, except that he was medium-built and broad and he spoke with a crisp Yorkshire accent.

"We're crossing Milestone Moor and soon we'll drop into Hatterworth," said Haworth. "Sorry I can't be a bit more sociable at the moment, but this driving in the black-out is the very devil."

"Don't you worry, Haworth. I'm enjoying this. It's nice to sit beside a companion, even if he's not saying much, after the lonely journey I've had! Since dark fell at about Stafford, I've been playing a sort of blindman's-buff. I've just been borne along by vehicles, seeing nothing of the countryside. I've not the faintest idea where we are or what the landscape looks like, and that'll be a surprise for to-morrow morning."

"Yes. You'll not find it too bad here. Our town's the centre of a moorland area of hundreds, nay thousands, of healthy acres. We've about thirty thousand people in our district and in the town itself, farmers, woollen mill operatives, iron workers; and the rest are shopkeepers, policemen and the like, to look after them. Here we are… Hatterworth. Mrs. Littlejohn's spending the evening at my place, which is only a couple of hundred yards from where she's staying. It won't be long before we get indoors, with a warm fire, lights and something to appease our hunger and thirst…"

"Yes. It's a night for a fire, and as I've not had a bite since Crewe at a little after five, a bit of food and a drink won't come amiss."

The car halted and, with the help of their torches, the two men groped their ways into Haworth's home, a neat, detached house on the edge of the town. The night was still crisp and frosty, with stars bright like jewels. In spite of the black-out, there were plenty of people astir in the darkness. Sounds of merry voices, shouts of goodwill and here and there groups of boys carol-singing at the doors of dwellings and holding noisy discussions concerning the alms doled out by their patrons in between their wassailing.

In the bright light of the hall, the detectives cheerfully regarded each other. The darkness had been a barrier between them and now, aware of each other's physical appearances, they greeted one another again, shaking hands and exchanging Christmas greetings, more from shyness than necessity.

Haworth was a sturdy, pink-faced, smooth-shaven man, with a bald head and keen blue eyes. His chin was square and determined, but his whimsical smile and twinkling eyes gave relief to an otherwise stern face. Littlejohn realized that when the merriment died from his face, the Superintendent would be a difficult man to deal with, especially if his antagonist were on the wrong side of the law. They entered a cosy room. Mrs. Haworth, a buxom, homely woman came smiling to greet them, with Mrs. Littlejohn hurriedly making up the rear. The spirit of Christmas and homecoming met them at the door. For Littlejohn the long journey was forgotten.

After the pleasures of re-union, the comfort of warmth and a meal of Christmas fare, the little party settled down for a spell of sociability round the fire. Cigar smoke thickened the air and Littlejohn found his host's whisky to his taste. They talked of many things, including the Littlejohns' adventures in the London bombing, but the session was shortly interrupted by the sound of tramping feet in the garden outside. Almost before Littlejohn had realized that an unexpected invasion had occurred, there was a great burst of music. The Hatterworth Methodist Choir was in first-class voice and loudly serenaded the Haworths, who were respected members of the congregation. *It came upon the Midnight Clear*, *Christians Awake*, and *Once in Royal David's City* were reeled off in rapid succession and then the front door was flung wide and a chattering crowd of carollers surged in and were given the freedom of a larder which, in spite of wartime restrictions, seemed to hold a goodly supply of mince-pies, parkin, plum-cake and ginger wine. Invaders and invaded shouted seasonable greetings at each other, private jokes were bandied about, especially among the bright-cheeked, unmarried choirgirls and then the Reverend Reginald Gotobed, resident minister and master of ceremonies of the troupe, called for silence.

"And now, Superintendent, for your *quid pro quo*. A song to pay for a song, eh?" The parson tittered and bared his teeth genially.

Littlejohn thought that, judging from the amount of food polished-off by the visitors, they had been very well paid indeed, but was curious to know what the parson was getting at. He received a surprise. With a deprecating gesture, Haworth strove to avoid the issue, but the choir would not be gainsaid. A tall, cold-looking man emerged from their body and sat down at the piano in the corner.

He massaged the blood back into his blue fingers and waited expectantly. "Little Cattle, Little Care", demanded the choir. Whereat, Superintendent Haworth of the Hatterworth Police rose from his chair by the fire and sang. His was a robust, well-trained baritone voice and it warmed Littlejohn's heart to hear it. The song, which was apparently an annual institution, was a north-country one, written by Edwin Waugh, and carried a chorus which the choir sang in harmony after each verse.

"Laddie, good dog, the day-wark's done,
The sun's low in the west;
The lingering wild birds, one by one,
Are flitting to the nest:
Mild evening's fairy fingers close
The curtains of the day,
And the drowsy landscape seeks repose
In twilight shadows grey."

The choir chanted the refrain:

"Little cattle, little care;
Lie thee down, Laddie!"

Soon, Littlejohn and his wife were carried away into joining the chorus.

"Well," said Littlejohn to his colleague, when the singers had departed to carol and merrymake and refresh themselves elsewhere, "I've heard of policemen being first-class boxers, footballers, long and high jumpers, and even darts champions, but you're the first real singing policeman I've met."

"Oh, there are plenty of them in the force, Littlejohn. It was just by chance you heard me to-night. I used to do a lot, but now I'm too busy to make a proper job of it."

"If Philip Grisdale doesn't turn-up to-morrow, you'll be busy again, too, my lad," interjected his wife, and Littlejohn regarding her with a puzzled look, seemed to detect in her voice a hope that Grisdale, whoever he might be, wouldn't put in an appearance.

"O, he'll be here all right, never worry," said Haworth. And turning to Littlejohn he explained.

"You'll no doubt have heard of Philip Grisdale, the big London singer. Well, he's a local lad, who's made good and risen to fame, but he never forgets the old place. He used to attend the Hatterworth Methodists when he was a boy and every Christmas Day, he comes back to sing in *The Messiah* which is always given there in the evening. This year, he wrote to say that he was laid-up with tonsillitis. That was last Wednesday. He advised them to find a deputy, but he'd come if he possibly could. *I'm* the deputy. He'll turn up right enough. Folk'll be disappointed if he doesn't."

Littlejohn wondered.

The Littlejohns got to bed about three o'clock on Christmas morning. Somewhere in the distance, a choir was in full spate and the strains of a brass band in full blast, with a euphonium freely improvising in the bass, could be heard. Littlejohn felt full of the spirit of Christmas as he climbed into bed. He was wearing gaily-striped pyjamas, like the colours of some football team. He had once bought them himself and was proud of them.

"You've surely not brought *those* with you again!" laughed his wife.

"Why not? They're jolly nice. I bought these the night before I ran Tossy Marks to earth at Cardiff..."

"Put out the light, Tom, before anybody sees them."

"Do you know, Letty," ruminated Littlejohn irrelevantly, "I hope that Grisdale chap doesn't turn up tomorrow."

"So do I."

"If he doesn't, we'll go to church, eh? It's not once in a lifetime you hear a policeman, and a Super at that, singing in *The Messiah*."

"It's a bargain, then."

The brass band, playing *God Rest You, Merry Gentlemen*, with the euphonium rioting all over the shop, drew dangerously near, but before it arrived under his window, Littlejohn was deep in a sleep from which the last trump itself would only have roused him with difficulty.

CHAPTER II

"...And the Dead Shall Be Raised"

"Dreadfully staring
Thro' muddy impurity."

TOM HOOD

THE REVEREND REGINALD GOTOBED, PASTOR OF HATTERWORTH Methodist Church, gazed with mixed feelings from his pulpit at the crowded congregation assembled to hear *The Messiah*. He was delighted because the collections from such a vast concourse would keep the place free from debt for months to come; but he sighed regretfully as he compared the numbers with those, a mere handful, who normally gathered to hear his sermons. To-night, he was not preaching, but merely acting as chairman at the choir effort. He beamed down at the treasurer, sitting at the back of the building with a stack of collection boxes on a shelf beside him, and he smiled at the faces in the body of the church and in the crowded gallery. The young men of the church were even bringing-in wooden benches and chairs from the nearby Sunday School and crushing them in the aisles, for the pews would not hold all those who clamoured for admission. The fact that, at the last moment, Philip Grisdale had telephoned apologies and regrets at not being able to turn-up did not deter them. Frank Haworth was a good substitute and when the change of singer was noised abroad, no-one worried. From five until six o'clock, the starting-time, a steady procession wound up the hill to the chapel and those from the neighbouring moorland who could not get to town by 'bus were enthusiastic enough to walk there, for the night of Christmas was fine, sharp and clear and many of them would not feel that a proper Christmas-Day had been spent if it did not end at the chapel *Messiah*. Here and there in the crowd could be seen the healthy, honest face of a policeman, off duty and in plain-clothes, who had brought his family to hear his chief sing and, in one pew at the back, sat two local ne'er-do-wells, with several convictions for poaching. They had paid the man who almost made a habit of running them in, the singular compliment of washing their faces and putting-on their best suits and neckcloths to hear if he could sing as well as he could execute the law. The chairman of the local magistrates was sitting uncomfortably beside them. He had arrived late and found a vacant place at the end of their pew; but he had been prevented from keeping a respectable distance between himself and his regular clients by the press of further newcomers.

A stage, like a huge staircase, covered in red baize, rose all round the pulpit. As Mr. and Mrs. Littlejohn, with their hostess, Miss Stalybridge, and Mrs. Haworth entered, the choir were just taking their places on the red steps. The modest trebles who had to climb to the top struggled to mount with decent strides; the more flighty ones displayed a wealth of limb and lingerie. The chorus had been considerably re-inforced by friends from other church choirs. In the two front pews, the orchestra were tuning-up. Programmes fluttered in the audience and those who would appear more scholarly ostentatiously fingered the copies of the oratorio from which they proposed to follow the work from end to end.

The four soloists mounted the first step of the red stairs and seated themselves on bentwood chairs; Mr. Gotobed rose, prayed briefly, handed over the meeting to the choirmaster and subsided.

The choirmaster, a burly, elderly man with a bald head fringed with curly, grey hair, hoisted himself on to his rostrum. He was wearing an out-of-date tail coat and in his hand was a heavy ebony baton with silver mountings, a presentation from the choir for long service. He opened his copy of music, pored over it and closed it again to show that he knew it all from start to finish. Then he tapped his rickety music-stand. The orchestra was composed of men from near and far. Many of them had for many weeks tramped to rehearsals through all kinds of weather in their enthusiasm. There was a predominance of strings and rather a dearth of woodwind, but the conductor must have known his job, for the amateurs played well together and he kept them rigidly under control.

As the lovely overture filled the air, Littlejohn was transported from the hall filled with strangers to the little chapel of his childhood. In his mind's eye, he saw the singing-pew filled with old familiar faces, many now long dead; the amateur organist with his work cut-out in keeping up with the choruses, missing notes, furiously trampling the pedals; the unpretentious but worthy soloists. The ghost of Christmas Past stood by his shoulder. He was roused from his reverie by the tenor solo, which slid easily into its place from the introduction. There was not a vacant seat in the church, the walls streamed with moisture, the place was like an oven. The busy chapelkeeper opened one of the doors leading from the vestibule into the main street and the exquisite aria floated out into the still Christmas night and seemed to ring across the moorland beyond. "Every valley shall be exalted and every hill laid low" echoed challengingly in the quiet hills and valleys of the watching Pennines. Littlejohn remembered his Manchester days when, leaving the police-station at the Town Hall, he had slipped into the Free Trade Hall to hear Frank Mullings sing the same songs, with Norman

Allin, too, and Hamilton Harty conducting the Hallé Orchestra and Choir. The news had not yet reached him that in that very Season, the ravening Hun had, by fire and explosion, reduced that place of happy memories to ashes.

The choir roared its way through *The Glory of the Lord*. Haworth was on his feet vigorously shaking the sea and the dry land. His rich, mellow voice rang round the church to the delight of both the law-abiding and the few malefactors there. Passers-by in the street halted and formed a little group near the open door. "That'll be Frank Haworth," said someone. A heavy, homely woman seated behind Littlejohn murmured in a stage-whisper, "Eh, but it's luvely." That expressed in simple terms the whole experience.

The telephone bell rang in Hatterworth police-station and Inspector Ross answered it. He was rather annoyed at being on duty at a time when his chief was singing and was wondering if he might not just pass the chapel in the course of duty with a view to seeing how things were going.

"Yes…?" he said peevishly to the instrument.

A voice began to tell a tale and the Inspector's face grew gravely interested.

"Right. Hold everything until I arrive. Enoch Sykes did you say? How do you know? A ring on his finger with his initials? Right. We'll be along."

Hastily, Ross scribbled a note. He rang for a constable and handed it to him.

"Take that to Superintendent Haworth at the Chapel," he said. "Now don't go and upset him in the middle of *Why Do the Nations*, but give it him as soon as you can. I'm off to Milestone Moor and you get back here as quickly as you can, because we've a busy night before us. The Home Guard have dug up Enoch Sykes's body on the moor and we'd better be getting on the job. Be off, and don't stand gawking..."

P.C. Joe Shuttleworth made a hasty exit and almost ran along the darkened streets to the Methodist Church. He found George Woodroff, the chapelkeeper, standing at the open door of the dark vestibule. A sweet voice was singing within.

"He was cut off from the land of the living...
But Thou did'st not leave His soul in hell..."

P.C. Shuttleworth shivered.

"I've got to get a message to th' Super, George," he said. "What's best way of doin' it?"

"Best way of doin' it, owd chap, is to wait until he's finished and then catch him as he comes out. Why, what's th' matter, Joe?"

P.C. Shuttleworth lowered his voice into an awful, confidential whisper.

"Th' Home Guard were diggin' a trench on th' top of Milestone Moor just before dusk and they dug-up a skeleton. There was a ring on its finger with th' initials 'E.S.' As like as not, it's Enoch Sykes. So I've bin sent to get Superintendent Haworth right away, *Messiah* or no *Messiah*."

George Woodroff's jaw dropped. "No, Joe! You don't say." The chapelkeeper made excited gestures with his hands and arms and trod the floor like a soldier marking time. He struggled with his feelings. He was not, if he could help it, going to allow anybody, not even a skeleton, to disturb the annual treat now in progress. He closed the door between the vestibule and the main body of the church, as though protecting the interior from evil.

"Tha'll 'ave to wait, Joe lad. You can't disturb 'im at present. Enoch Sykes must 'ave bin restin' on yon moor for twenty years, or more. He can bide another half hour or so, till Mr. Haworth's at least finished *Th' Trumpet Shall Sound*. Then ah'll hand him a note."

"Now, look 'ere, George..."

"If tha want's 'im before, tha'll 'ave to go and fetch 'im off th' platform, then," said the caretaker, his little pointed chin jutting with determination.

P.C. Shuttleworth hesitated. His boots creaked badly. He was a shy and self-conscious, though diligent officer, who came in for a lot of chaff locally on account of his habit of blushing on the slightest provocation. The thought of noisily running the gauntlet of the congregation assembled behind the closed door filled him with such terror that he broke into a cold sweat and his knees knocked together. He, who would without hesitation wade into a public brawl, knock out its toughest participants with relish and haul them singly or in a party to the lock-up, paused in dread at the task before him. Among the sopranos now shouting in chorus inside, was a certain lady whom he one day hoped to make Mrs. Shuttleworth when he could pluck up the courage to broach the proposition.

"All right, George. But I'll get into a row with Inspector Ross for this."

"Tha'll get into a worse bother if tha interrupts the Super. So tha met as well choose th' less of two evils, Joe. By the way, Enoch Sykes's mother's in th' church, too. We'd better tell 'er as well when th' time comes."

Woodroff opened the vestibule door again and there, in the dark, the two sat side by side waiting for their cue. Now and then, they forgot everything as the music ran its course. Applause at the end of the solo parts was not considered proper in the church, but an atmosphere of unbounded approval seemed to float into the anteroom and enfold the two on their vigil as Haworth sat down after a spirited rendering of *Why Do The Nations*. Their throats grew dry as the lovely strains of *I Know That My Redeemer Liveth* wafted gently to them and encompassed them with sad memories. The choir rose and chanted the eerie opening chords of the following chorus, *Since By Man Came Death* in an awful, incoherent pianissimo and the two men, remembering the purpose of the constable's visit there, felt the hair rise in the napes of their necks.

Littlejohn, almost roasted in the hot atmosphere, was enjoying himself immensely and now and then he and his wife exchanged delighted glances. A spirit of ecstatic goodwill filled the place. Glowing, homely faces met his gaze wherever he looked. The weariness of everyday things fell from the countenances of the poor and overworked; the harassed grew calm; the stiffnecked and starchy seemed to relax and shed their pride; and the humble held up their heads. A cornet-player scrambled from the orchestra and self-consciously established himself at Haworth's side. They were an ill-assorted pair: the singer, spruce, well set-up and aglow with energy; the instrumentalist, small, bow-legged and pale. The orchestra played the opening bars of *A Trumpet Shall Sound*, and the couple got into their stride. The cornet, second-best for the silver trumpet of full-dress performances, spoke with precision and the little man blowing it was transformed. Not one out of place, not a second behind-hand, the notes came forth like bubbles of iridescent sound and seemed to burst over the heads of the congregation. It was with difficulty at the end of the solo, that the audience refrained from bursting into delighted clapping.

Just as the choir was preparing to rise for a further outburst, little George Woodroff walked down the aisle with determination, his boots squeaking and tapping on the parquet floor. First, he went to a shrivelled, weary-looking, elderly woman dressed in black who was sitting in a side-pew parallel to the main aisle. He whispered in her ear and she, glancing nervously at him and then at the door, rose and awkwardly made her exit to receive the awful news from P.C. Shuttleworth. Woodroff continued his way to the platform, gestured to Haworth and handed him the note. The Superintendent, rather astonished, opened and glanced at it. He spoke to the tenor at his elbow and then hurriedly descended from his perch. He deliberately chose the aisle beside which Littlejohn was sitting at the end of a pew and, as he passed his friend, he touched him on the arm and signalled him to follow. The congregation whispered, looked anxiously curious and seemed about to rise and accompany them. Then, the choir broke forth and the commotion was stilled. The burst of *Worthy is the Lamb* followed the detectives far down the main street.

"Here's a pretty kettle of fish, Littlejohn," said Haworth as they strode along in the crisp night. "I thought you'd perhaps like to be in at this. Of course, you're on holiday, but, if you're like me, you'll be challenged by this business that's just cropped up."

"I'm with you, Haworth. If I can help, count on me."

"Well, this note says that the body of Enoch Sykes has been dug-up on Milestone Moor. That's a corker for the police and no mistake! We'll be at the police-station in five minutes, but I'll just outline the story briefly. It refers to a murder committed in 1917, during the last war!"

"Good heavens! Talk about shades of the past."

"Yes. In October, 1917, Jeremy Trickett, a local ironworker and, incidentally, a poacher as well, was found murdered on Milestone

Moor, the lonely spot we passed through last night and which you can see stretching right to the skyline from the front bedroom of the house where you're staying. There had been bad blood between him and Enoch Sykes, also an iron worker and poacher, about a girl and when Sykes couldn't be found after the murder, which had been committed with a shotgun, naturally, the thoughts of the police turned to him. I was a constable in Huddersfield at the time, so I had nothing to do with it, but it was the talk of the countryside for months. You see, Sykes was never found. The theory was that he'd either got abroad, in spite of the difficulties due to war, or else managed to enlist and been killed. After a search throughout the length and breadth of the country, the case just had to be put in the unsolved files. This afternoon, the Home Guard were on manœuvres on the moor and, digging a trench, unearthed a human skeleton, which they'd the sense to leave as it was when they found what they'd turned-up. But not before they'd found a ring with Sykes's initials on the hand of the skeleton. So there we are. Sykes must have been there some time and it looks as though somebody committed a double killing to throw the police off the scent. A cunning trick, eh?"

"If your surmise is right, the murderer was cold-blooded and unscrupulous and sheer accident has laid bare his scheme years after the event."

"Yes. Twenty-three years is a long time and a lot of water's gone under the bridge since 1917. The murderer might be dead or have disappeared."

"So the case re-opens?"

"Yes. With a trail as cold as mutton. Still, there it is and we've got to start all over again and do our best, digging in the dead past. Something quite fresh in my experience."

"And in mine, Haworth. I'm in this with you all the way, if you'll have me, unofficially, of course."

"Nay. You're not getting away with that, Littlejohn. If this isn't solved before the end of your holiday, I'm seeing the Chief Constable and we're asking Scotland Yard for a man, with a suggested name to accompany the application. Then, perhaps we'll have you with us for a bit longer."

"Good!" said Littlejohn and the pair of them turned into the dimly-lighted entrance of the police headquarters.

The parish church clock struck nine. In the distance a brass band, with bombardon and bass trombone rampaging deeply, stumbled through its final rendering of *Beautiful Zion* before refreshing itself on the proceeds of its day's efforts at its favourite taproom.

CHAPTER III

Milestone Moor

O, the famous Duke of York, he had ten thousand men,
He marched them up yon hill, and he marched them down again.

OLD SONG

ON THE MORNING FOLLOWING THE DISCOVERY OF THE CRIME of more than two decades since, Haworth and Littlejohn eased their large bodies into the police-car and as the church-clock struck ten, started on their uphill journey to Milestone Moor. The day was crisp and clear and early sunshine brightened the streets of the town and shone cheerfully on the surrounding countryside. The cobbled thoroughfares and stone buildings of Hatterworth were soon left behind and the car cruised easily upwards along the well-surfaced moorland road. A great, quiet wilderness soon spread all around the travellers. Whin and heather, their knotted, clinging roots showing in the peaty soil, swayed like the waves of a brown sea as the keen wind teased them hither and thither. A verge of fine turf, punctuated by white stones with black caps to mark the road in the dark or through the snows, stretched on either side of the route. Huge white clouds, sailing majestically, floated across the blue wintry sky.

The view was superb. On one hand, the moor, unbounded, reaching right to the horizon, decked in the browns and reds of winter. Pools of water, covered with thin skimmings of ice, dotted the wasteland. Moorland brooks rattled to join a stream which gurgled beneath a frozen film along the side of the road. On the other hand, a steep slope of mossy turf, gradually changing into grassland where man had set about and conquered it. The valley beneath, with Hatterworth nestling in it beside its fast-flowing River Codder, and beyond that, gradually rising ground, terminating in another boundless stretch of hills. Hatterworth, built of local stone, seemed to fit snugly in the general scene. Its long rows of three-storeyed cottages, its public buildings, chimneys and towers and its open-spaces were ranged along a lower highroad which, from the hillside, seemed a mere thread winding into the distance. Between the high Milestone Road and the town, the wilderness had been tamed to man's uses. Rough, dry stone walls divided it like a great chessboard. Cattle and sheep in the sloping fields. A labourer slinging lime on the green grass of a meadow, the powder flying like steam. The eternal battle between man and the moor to hold it in check. In the distance, the white smoke of a train, laboriously mounting the ridge into the heart of West Riding.

The car climbed gallantly. Telegraph poles, heavy-laden with wires and in close formation against the weather, like an army with ranks closed against an enemy, swept past the policemen. Across the open moor, the Home Guard were deployed and busily manœuvring. Having laid bare the problem of the skeleton and turned it over to the proper authorities, they had now returned to more important and urgent tasks than those of the dry bones of the past. The place was dotted with khaki-clad figures, running, leaping, stumbling, attacking, earnest in their mock-battling. The "enemy" from West Riding was attempting, with little apparent success, to wrest Hatterworth and its upper and lower roads from the native volunteers.

The car pulled-up at a spot by the road and the two officers climbed out. At this place a rough bridge spanned the wayside stream and thence a path struck across the moor. The track had been almost obliterated by time, but had apparently, at some distant date, been used by vehicles for carrying stone from a small disused quarry on the hillside. About fifty yards from the highway along this rough road and beside a shrivelled gorse-bush, stood a small knot of men. Two were in their shirt-sleeves, digging; the others consisted of two policemen, a rough-looking fellow who seemed to be a moorland farmer or hired-hand, and a member of the Home Guard. The policemen saluted as the newcomers arrived; the men with the digging-tools followed suit, proving also to be constables.

"Well, boys," said Haworth good-humouredly. "Found anything?"

"We've got up all the bones, sir," replied one of the excavators, passing his hand over his sweating brow. Dr. Griffiths has been up but said he couldn't do anything until we'd finished and found the lot. We're to take them to the mortuary for him when the job's done. There they are."

He indicated a tarpaulin sheet on which were spread a motley assortment of dirty bones, browned and fouled from the action of the damp peat in which they had for so long lain. A brown skull leered from among them. There were shreds of clothing adhering to parts of them and old, rotten leather indicated that the corpse had been shod when buried. A twelve-bore shot-gun, its barrels caked with rust and earth, but its stock remarkably well-preserved, also reposed on the waterproof sheet. Haworth touched it gingerly.

"Buried him with his weapons like a chieftain, I see," he said. "No doubt we'll be able to identify and trace the gun, too."

One of the policemen was, with great thoroughness, passing the earth through a number of sieves and extracting small articles from the residue. Haworth turned to him and smiled.

"A nice job you've got there, Hickling. Have you found anything worth shouting about?"

The constable raised a youthful, rosy face and grinned in response.

"Some coins, sir, a watch, a clasp-knife, pipe, baccatin, and about ten pellets, lead ones, which have probably fallen out of the body as it's decayed. Dr. Griffiths was most particular about finding those if we could."

"Good. Carry on, Hickling. Fiddling work, but very important. Gather all the stuff together when you've finished and bring it down to the station. We'll go through it thoroughly there. And now, Littlejohn, as far as I can, I'll show you where Trickett's body was found. As I said, I wasn't here at the time, but I've had the spot pointed-out to me. It's across here."

Haworth led the way from the rough road, across the moor for about fifty yards. A dry wall, tumble-down and neglected, had at one time marked off a small intake or holding, the farmhouse of which now stood a gaunt ruin on the farthermost boundary. Half-way along the off-side of the wall was another stunted gorse-bush, tortured by wind and weather. Haworth pointed to it.

"That's the spot. You see it's not far from where they've found Sykes. The old theory was that the first was killed by the second, who made a clean getaway. Now, with the discovery of the other corpse, that theory—a score of years old—is exploded. We've to begin again, probably with all the clues gone and the bulk of the useful witnesses dead."

Littlejohn puffed vigorously at his pipe and glanced around.

The vast, cold moor was a rare place for holding secrets. A silence seemed to brood over it, punctuated now and then by the cries of birds or the shouts of the Home Guard, still manœuvring vigorously.

Even the presence of so many men over the wide expanse seemed powerless to dispel the loneliness. The elemental seemed to hang over the scene. The creeping fingers of the powers of destruction worked unseen, twisting and stunting the vegetation, tearing down the boundaries erected by man, shattering his habitation and sliding relentlessly over fields he had cultivated, dragging them back to the wilderness.

"I think it'll be a good idea, Littlejohn, if we call on the man who was in charge of the crime at the time. He's the man I followed, Superintendent Pickersgill. His house is on the outskirts of the town. There'll be flesh and blood in his tale, if we can get him talking, and an account from him will fill-in the dry bones of the report on the files, which should be here later in the day."

"Good idea. We've time before lunch, if you like."

"Right, Littlejohn. We'll be off then. Funnily enough, the chief before Pickersgill, Inspector Entwistle, is still alive, too, and living with Pickersgill and his wife. His father-in-law. Between them, they should be able to give us a tale. The old chap's about eighty, but very full of beans. The pair of them are mad on hens. We'll probably find them in the hen-run."

The pair of detectives made for the highroad and entered the car. The air was cold and clear. Leaden clouds showed in the distance.

"Looks like snow," said Haworth, adjusting the rugs round their knees.

Gently they coasted down to the valley. On the way, they passed the victorious Home Guard, mustered and marching smartly back to town.

Littlejohn glanced back and, through the small rear window, saw the police, their task finished, gingerly carrying in a tarpaulin all that was left of Enoch Sykes and a tragedy of years long gone.

CHAPTER IV

Conference in a Hen-Pen

On then, on and away, ere the sun be set!
Ere on the moorland, the evening mists enfold me,
And my chattering teeth and feeble, tottering limbs
Presage the end...

GOETHE

THE CAR HALTED BEFORE A NEAT BUNGALOW, SET BACK ON A bank overlooking the road. The detectives climbed out, mounted the gravel path, and Haworth rang the doorbell.

The face of a shrewish-looking woman was thrust round the curtains of the front room, rapidly withdrawn and, a moment later, the door flew open.

"'Morning, Mrs. Pickersgill. Is Charlie at home?"

"Yes. He's with my father among th' hens. They spend all their time there nowadays."

No wonder! thought Littlejohn.

Ex-Superintendent Pickersgill's wife looked a tartar. Quite obvious that she wore the trousers. A thin, masterful-looking woman of medium build. Long, thin nose; sharp, grey eyes. Hair gathered in a tremendous grey bun and held rigidly in position by what looked like a fish-net. A look of perpetual, meddling curiosity. Evidently a native of those parts, for she spoke broadly and with little evidence of polish.

When Pickersgill was a sergeant under Inspector Entwistle, his ambition led him into marrying his chief's daughter, who had already set her cap at him. He admired her cooking and thrift, and the partnership had proved a success. Mrs. Pickersgill was reputed to be the brains of the show. It was said that her husband had got on at his job through working-off on his men and his cases the energy which he was forced to repress at home. Their five children—all girls—took after their mother in thrift and forthrightness, but their father was their favourite. They formed a bodyguard round him, protecting him from the horrors of being totally henpecked. The last of his daughters was married a month before the Superintendent retired on pension. The situation was saved by his wife's father coming to live with them. Ex-Inspector Entwistle, who was a widower, took fright at the overtures of his housekeeper, who was beginning to make matrimonial passes at him in spite of his great age. The old man brought his hens with him. The ex-policemen thereupon formed a partnership, built the most sumptuous runs and scratching sheds, and spent all their time in the company of their birds.

"Can we come through and have a word with him? This is Inspector Littlejohn, of Scotland Yard; Mrs. Pickersgill."

"Good mornin'." Scotland Yard and its famous personnel left the stern-faced woman unmoved. She had lived with policemen all her life.

"Aye. You'd better come through. Wipe your feet."

She led them through a narrow hall into the dining-room, which overflowed into the back quarters. The place was so full of furniture that it seemed to leak at every entrance. In passing through, Littlejohn got a photographic impression of the place and a sense of constriction. He was a north-countryman himself and had seen some strange households in his own parts of Lancashire; but this beat the lot!

Stockings on the table-legs to protect them from unruly feet! Coconut matting on the floors, for the best carpets were only unrolled and used at week-ends, when the best fire-irons of shining brass were also laid-down at the hearth. The furniture was of highly polished old mahogany. A fine mule-chest served as a sideboard. A number of uncomfortable chairs precisely placed about the room. On the walls, two framed pictures from Christmas almanacs and depicting strangely dressed characters indulging in "Love's Young Dream" and "The Tryst", respectively. A large steel engraving of Derby Day and a laborious fretwork plaque announcing "East West Homes Best". A mantelpiece full of brass candlesticks of all shapes and sizes, fussily arranged in order of height. The whole place shone with elbow grease. Too clean and prim to be cosy! No wonder the men preferred the hen-cotes.

Haworth and Littlejohn followed the woman through a scullery in which were standing a number of uncooked apple-pies waiting to be capped with pastry and put in the oven. The fruit looked meticulously chopped and arranged. Mrs. Pickersgill indicated the largest of a number of solid-looking sheds, spread in a tidy, grass-covered plot about twenty yards or so from the back-door.

"You know where to find them, doan't you, Mr. 'aworth," she said and returned indoors. Littlejohn, from the corner of his eye, saw her seize a carpet-sweeper and begin vigorously milling over the matting on which they had trodden in passing through.

At the bottom of the garden, a saucy-looking stovepipe emitted a trail of smoke. Haworth made for it and knocked on the door of the shed, where the occupants were evidently enjoying the warmth of the furnace and immunity from feminine chatter.

"Come in," called a hearty voice.

If Littlejohn expected to see a timid man, decimated by years of nagging and domestic dragooning, he was mistaken. Haworth introduced him to a tall, heavily-built fellow, with a large, grey moustache. Bald head, surrounded by a fringe of silvery hair. Twinkling, brown eyes under shaggy brows. His companion was a stocky old man, with slightly protruding blue eyes, a shock of white hair and a torpedo beard to match. An aged edition of the legendary Captain Kettle. His knotted, dark-veined hands spoke of great age. Both ex-policemen had healthy, red faces.

The pair were seated side-by-side on a wooden bench, rendered comfortable by a long cushion. They wore cloth caps. The younger was smoking a long, curved pipe with a large reservoir attached for straining-off the liquid by-products. His aged companion had a battered, foul little briar wedged between his few remaining teeth.

The warm shed was apparently the headquarters of a complicated system of hen rearing and egg producing. In one corner, a large incubator. Bins of foodstuffs all over the shop. Pot-eggs on shelves. Two rat-traps, an old birdcage and a storm lantern hanging from the roof. All around were scenes of feathered activity. Hens rooting for grain in the dry chaff spread ankle-deep on the floors. Their owners were watching them with dreamy ecstasy when the visitors entered. The business of laying eggs was, judging from the cries of triumph and quarrelling, going on enthusiastically in the neighbouring nesting-houses. A cock was strutting among his hens and gave a throaty, growling cluck as the intruders arrived. To make himself the centre of attraction, the great bird was pretending to find scraps of food and continuously calling his protégées to come and get it. They ran to him eagerly each time, only to return empty, but hen-like repeated the caper indefinitely. One white hen monotonously leapt at a hanging cabbage, pecking-off bits at each jump, like a little clockwork toy.

Now and again, the old man spoke to the hens, calling them by their names and during the ensuing conference, punctuated it with a running commentary on the behaviour of individual fowls. He was a curious mixture of dotage and shrewd intelligence. With the exception of the poultry, he appeared to have little interest in current topics. He lived in the past and his memory in this respect was wide, precise and boring.

"Glad to meet you, Mr. Littlejohn," said Pickersgill, smiling a welcome and drawing-up another wooden bench to accommodate his guests. Littlejohn and Haworth took their seats and filled their pipes.

"Never called-in Scotland Yard in my day and not so many wrong 'uns got away from me, ah can tell you," said ex-Inspector Entwistle.

Pickersgill winked at the visitors.

"Nothing but drunks, poachers and petty larceny when you were in collar, dad… Now, what about a bottle of beer?"

The old man's eyes glistened and he forgot to pursue his argument.

"I'll not be a minute," he answered, and stumped off to the house to return with four bottles, glasses, and a large slab of parkin on a plate.

"She's dustin' in the front, so ah've got away with some tar-cake as well," he chuckled, like a boy playing a prank. "There'll be hangment to play when she finds out, but it'll be safe in our bellies by then."

They filled their glasses. Mrs. Pickersgill could make cake if nothing else!

"So you want to know about the murder of Jerry Trickett, eh?" said Pickersgill, wiping his moustache on the back of his hand. "Well, I remember it as if it were yesterday. I've good reason to. It was the first murder case I ever had, and blow me, if the murderer didn't give us the slip, or rather, we thought he did. But from what

I can gather, the whole thing's altered now and our old theories are blown sky-high. Funny thing, that."

"Nowt funny about it," chimed-in the octogenarian, mopping the beer and crumbs from his beard. "I always told you, facts is what you want, not theorisin'. A bird in the hand's worth two in the bush… Hello, Biddy's gone lame again. That means she'll lay a double-yoked egg to-morn. Always goes lame when she's goin' to drop a double-yoker."

He indicated a hobbling Rhode Island Red with the stem of his pipe.

"Now, dad. Don't you keep putting-in your motty about things that doan't matter. We've only half an hour to dinner time and Alice'll play hell if we're behind-hand. So let's get down to business."

"Yes," interposed Haworth. "Perhaps you'll tell us, as far as you can recollect, what happened and how far the police investigation went."

"Good job Home Guard dug-up Enoch Sykes when they did," chipped-in the irrepressible old man. "Many as were involved in that enquiry have gone uphill to Hatterworth cemetery and a lot more of 'em have one foot in the grave. Twenty or more years is a long time. Come to that, ah've not got much longer to go myself. Ah'd like to make this th' last of my cases. So hurry-up before ah'm carried-off, too. Ah always told Charlie there that he was barkin' up the wrong tree huntin' far and wide for Sykes. Look nearer home, ah says, look nearer home, and he can't say ah didn't. Now it's up to you chaps to settle this once and for all, and show ah was right before ah die."

"We'll be glad of your help, Mr. Entwistle," politely interjected Haworth. "But, as time's short, perhaps Charlie had better be getting-on with his tale."

"Well, in October, 1917, the body of Jerry Trickett was found on the moor. Early in the morning it was, and a farmer passing in his milk-cart spotted him and gave the alarm. Doctor said he'd been killed about dusk the night before. Enoch Sykes was naturally suspected. The two had been pals, but had quarrelled about a girl. Mary Tatham. She married Josiah Ryles later. Both Trickett and Sykes were ironworkers—fitters at Myles's Foundry. They left there when Caleb Haythornthwaite—now Sir Caleb—who was manager at Myles's, went into partnership with Luke Cross."

"Aye. Myles's Foundry never looked up again after Caleb left 'em" interposed Mr. Entwistle. "Of course, Mrs. Myles was a widow at the time and quite depended on Haythornthwaite to handle the men and generally keep the place going. Caleb and old Mrs. Myles quarrelled, it's said, but nobody got to th' bottom of what happened. Anyhow, Caleb never looked back after joining Luke Cross."

Pickersgill silenced the old man's garrulity with a look.

"Well, as I was saying, Sykes and Trickett were pals. They did a bit of poaching together in their young days. Grouse on the moor, which is preserved, and now belongs to Sir Caleb himself.

"On the night of the crime, Buller, the gamekeeper, saw first Sykes and then Trickett on the moor. You can tell how well Haythornthwaite did when, from Myles's manager in 1915, he managed to earn enough in two years to afford a shoot and a keeper. Well, Buller saw th'unlucky pair separately on the moor and heard shots, but thought they were after birds. Having followed Caleb to his new works, they were allowed free access to his preserve, so Buller thought no more about it.

"Buller had previously warned-off a tramp, known locally as Bill o' Three Fingers, about a quarter of an hour before the gunfire. We roped-in Bill at the time, but he'd nothing to say.

"Now for the girl. She'd been doing a bit of courting with Sykes and then, of a sudden, Trickett took a fancy to her and pinched her from under his pal's very nose. The men stopped speaking to one another after that, and from going everywhere together, weren't seen in each other's company again, except on the day of the crime. That was at the Horse and Jockey, a moorland pub. Sykes was having a drink there that evening after a bit of shooting and Trickett walked-in. Sykes went for him and they came to blows. The landlord chucked 'em out and heard Sykes tell Trickett he'd do for him. You can't doubt that after the murder, the first man we wanted a word with was Sykes. He'd disappeared, however, which made us more sure of his guilt. We thought he might have joined the forces and hunted in the Army and Navy after him. At last, we'd to give it up as a bad job and admit that he'd given us the slip. No wonder we were baffled, with him lying there as dead as Trickett all the time. I'd say they were killed almost together, wouldn't you?"

"Yes," answered Haworth, "I can't conceive it otherwise. Either one killed the other and then a third party did for him, or else—which is more likely—the third party shot the pair of them. Why?"

"Ah, there you're asking me! We've to find a motive first."

Old Entwistle chimed in again.

"That murder was the most excitin' thing that happened in these parts and events'll still be impressed on the memories of those who are still alive. You ought to make a start with Mary Tatham that was, and then run through the list of others that's left."

Haworth took out his notebook.

"Just let's jot down the names," he said.

Pickersgill took up the tale.

"Well, as dad says, there's Mary Ryles. She lives with her husband in Marble Street, down the town. You'll wonder, when you see her, fat and middle-aged, how two young chaps could have come to want to murder each other for her, but she was a beauty in her prime. Bill o' Three Fingers is knocking about too. So's Seth Wigley, the landlord of the Horse and Jockey, although his married daughter keeps the pub now and he lives with her and her husband. He's getting-on in years. Buller, the gamekeeper is dead. Sir Caleb is alive and lives at Spenclough Hall, about two miles from here. And old Mrs. Myles, who's getting on for eighty, is still alive, living at a little house in Moor Lane and mostly confined to her room. That's as far as I can go for the present."

Haworth looked crestfallen. They had certainly expected something more exciting than Pickersgill's half-baked account. He turned to Littlejohn.

"Any ideas on the subject, Littlejohn?"

Inspector Littlejohn removed his pipe. He had been watching old Entwistle, who seemed to have lost interest in his son-in-law's tale and was busy scratching the neck of a very tame little hen which had sidled-up to him and was pecking the eyelets of his boots. Suddenly, he raised his head. His little eyes were sparkling and he glanced humorously at his son-in-law.

"Charlie never were much of a talker," he said, "and his memory's not as good as it was. Why not ask him to lend you his old notebooks on the case and the diary we used to write up when the two of us used to discuss things together? You see, Charlie and me used to go over his problems. I was a bit useful to him in those days, havin' been Inspector here myself, and we wrote things down as we went along to get them clear, like."

Pickersgill's face lit up. He was feeling that he'd put up a very poor show in the matter and here was a readymade solution.

"I'll be right glad to do that," he answered. "We've got 'em all here and you may as well take 'em with you now, Frank."

He rose and unlocked what appeared to be his treasure-chest. It was an old bee-hive, covered in zinc-plate inside and out and as dry as a bone. A lock had been fitted and it contained what had apparently been the ex-Superintendent's private notebooks and also a number of diaries, bound in stiff board. Without much difficulty, Pickersgill selected a notebook and a diary, each carefully bearing the dates of its contents on a label.

"There you are, Frank. If you read those two together, along with such records as you'll have sent for to th' County Record Office, you'll know as much as I did about the case."

A shrill blast on a whistle startled the four men.

"Dinner's ready," said the old man and he and his son-in-law showed signs of uneasiness. Haworth, who opened the door of the shed, saw Mrs. Pickersgill's angular form disappearing indoors, after her novel way of calling the two hen-fanciers to a meal. Both were apparently scared of being a minute late.

"Thanks for your help, Charlie," said Haworth. "We'll let you have these back as soon as they've served their purpose."

"And see you come round again and let us know how you get on," interposed Entwistle, who was standing with a basket of eggs and waiting eagerly for his visitors to leave and free him for his dinner. "This is my last case, as ah've told you, and ah want to be in at the kill."

"We'll keep you informed, Mr. Entwistle."

And the two younger officers bade their elders good morning and hurried off to relieve them from anxiety.

CHAPTER V

October, 1917

O, but let me see his villain's face!
When I meet him, may God give him grace.
If he at the church-gate show his head,
With this bludgeon do I strike him dead!

HUNGARIAN FOLK SONG

FROST COVERED THE PAVEMENTS OF HATTERWORTH WITH A thin, treacherous film of ice and on the day following his visit to his predecessor, Superintendent Haworth slipped on the steps of the police-station and sprained his ankle. Littlejohn found him in his dining-room, his foot swathed in bandages and resting in an old slipper supported on a stool. He was fuming at his enforced inactivity.

"Here's a bonny kettle o' fish," growled Haworth after greetings had been exchanged. "And just as we were in the middle of a fresh case. I suppose it's been unsolved for twenty years or more and a few more days won't do it any harm, but it's damned galling, all the same. After I left you yesterday afternoon, I got the records from County Headquarters and I spent until the small hours of the morning building up a story with the help of Pickersgill's notes and diaries. Now, it looks as if I'll have to pass it on to Ross for the time being, although God knows he's up to the eyes in routine as it is..."

Littlejohn detected an invitation in his friend's tone and accepted it right away.

"Look here, Haworth, there's no point in worrying yourself to death about what can't be helped. Here you are and here you'll have to stay until the doctor gives you a clean bill. Meanwhile, I'll do the running about for you, unofficially, of course. We can discuss the results of my enquiries together afterwards and perhaps, between us, we'll have a solution before you're on your feet again."

"But this is a holiday for you, Littlejohn. It's not fair to take your time, and besides, what about your wife? She wants your company in the short time you're here..."

"She's determined to return to London with me when I go back, and has plenty to keep her occupied in the way of social calls and the like when I'm busy..."

They argued for a time and, finally, it was agreed that Littlejohn should take the investigation of the case and together the two of them would digest and compare results.

"Now that we've decided on a plan of campaign," said Littlejohn, "you can give me a picture of the old case as it happened twenty or more years ago. If, as you say, you read and compared the mass of records, you'll have some idea of the background. As a beginning, it will save me a lot of time if you can tell me what transpired."

"That's an idea, and a useful job I can perform to start with. I'll give you a paraphrase, then, of what I've gathered. Fill up your pipe and make yourself comfortable."

Haworth began his narrative and as the details unfolded themselves, Littlejohn got a picture of the scene and the incidents as they occurred in October, 1917.

He saw the great stretch of moorland, spread like a patchwork quilt in dark browns, greens and purples. Rough, trackless ground, with shrivelled heather, wimberry bushes and golden, dying bracken. Blackened stone walls dividing the holdings and mounds of peat drying beside the cuttings.

From the reservoirs of the neighbouring towns, hidden over the rim of the moor, seagulls rose, wheeling and crying. The bubbling call of the curlew. Human voices raised in hoarse chatter, quarrelling, laughing coarsely. There had been a shoot that day at the neighbouring butts, and a few of the motley crew of grouse-drivers and beaters were busy getting drunk at the Horse and Jockey, a lonely old inn, four-square to the winds, low-built of weathered local stone, which stood at the top of the road between Hatterworth and Waterfold. A haunt of wayfarers, sportsmen and their hangers-on, poachers, and those who liked to develop a thirst by travelling far to slake it.

Along the skyline, silhouetted against the flaming setting sun, a ragged series of tortured crags spread like a row of rotten teeth.

At the Horse and Jockey, the landlord, Seth Wigley, had his hands full. Enough to have a crowd of drunken beaters and loaders in the place. But here, too, was Enoch Sykes, roaring-drunk with rum, saying what he'd do to Jerry Trickett when he caught up with him. He hadn't to wait long.

Trickett entered the inn-yard with two of his pals. He had been shooting at the butts. For some reason, he and Sykes had free access to Caleb Haythornthwaite's land and where the likes of them were usually sent packing, they were tolerated, even on days when an organized shoot was arranged for Caleb's fine friends from among the local iron and woollen-masters.

Sykes spotted his one-time friend through the taproom window and, cursing, made for his gun, which he had propped in one corner, the better to handle his drink. Seth Wigley reached the weapon first.

"Nay, Enoch, yer not takin' that gun out with ye. Let it bide where it is."

The landlord was a large, fat man and the befuddled poacher seemed to see the sense in not trying conclusions with him. He staggered into the courtyard unarmed.

An expectant silence fell over the potwallopers lounging outside. They wanted the excitement of a fight but had no stomach for a shooting match. Trickett's companions whispered words of encouraging caution. They urged him to leave his gun with them and to wade-in and wipe-up the cockpit with Sykes's body. Their prudence was quite uncalled for. Trickett halted in his stride and waited for Sykes, who stood glaring, framed in the doorway of the inn. An ominous hush fell over everyone. The two cows could be heard snorting and chewing in the little byre. Seth Wigley, unperturbed, continued pumping-up a glass of ale. Slowly without a pause, he drank it off and emerged from his bar, a set expression on his good-natured, red face. He held Sykes's gun in his huge hand.

The suspense did not last long, for the tense scene ended in a ridiculous anti-climax. Sykes launched himself from the doorway, broke into a shambling trot, his arms milling, in the direction of his enemy. His heavy boots clanked on the cobbles of the yard. Trickett set himself to receive the impact. The running man caught his foot on a projecting stone, tripped, tottered on his toes and measured his length on the ground. He lay there, stunned and flabbergasted.

In two long strides Seth Wigley was on him. He picked him up by the collar of his coat, ran him out of the yard and down the road for a distance. Then he handed him his gun.

"Now be off with thee, afore ah sock thy jaw. I'm havin' no rough-houses on my property. Licences are hard enough to keep clean without the likes o' thee about th' place. So, in future, keep thy distance."

And, like a farmer driving a lively colt to grass, the landlord gestured to the drunken man to be on his road and then strolled back to his taproom. On the way, he stopped to speak to Trickett, who was enjoying the joke, not without signs of relief, among a crowd of half-drunken cronies.

"And as for thee, Jerry. Give thy old pal a wide berth if tha values thy skin. He's nursin' trouble for thee, lad."

"Don't thee bother thy head about me, Seth. Ah'm well able to tend mysel'."

Whereat, he followed the landlord indoors, drank a pint of his home-brew and went his way, carrying the birds he had bagged by their frail-looking legs.

The topers continued to guzzle, boast and guffaw. Wigley turned the worst of them out; the rest called for bread and cheese and prepared for a further session until closing-time. The war was hardly remembered amid the talk of past days and the tales of old hunting and shooting, and crude practical joking. The incident of earlier in the evening was forgotten in the din.

The landlord poked the fire, drew the curtains and lit a brass oil-lamp, which dangled from a beam in the taproom. It was almost dark outside. A carter on his way to Waterfold had stopped to wet his whistle and was telling the latest news from the town to a knot of owlish-looking, half-drunken labourers. A maid, buxom and red-cheeked, entered carrying a fresh bottle of whisky for the bar. Someone smacked her behind as she passed. There was a loud roar of laughter. The girl turned to give the libertine the length of her tongue… Across the moor a shot sounded.

A hush fell over the room as though someone had snuffed-out the noise.

"By God, somebody's keepin' th' grouse up late," said the carter, his glass poised half-way to his mouth. He drank.

"Sounds some distance away," hiccupped someone else.

"Hope it's not them two crazy devils finishin' off their rumpus..."

Seth Wigley looked uneasy. Somebody rattled a glass for a re-fill. The landlord dismissed his forebodings and walked round to attend to his customer. The clock in the passage struck six. At five minutes past, there was another shot...

At dawn the following morning, Seth Wigley rose from his wife's side, padded across the oilcloth in his bare feet, drew the blind, removed a sandbag from the junction of the two sashes, raised the bottom one, and breathed deeply. Mr. Wigley allowed as little night air to enter his bedroom from the outside as possible. He considered it injurious.

"Grand mornin', lass," he said to the buxom figure he had left behind in the bed. Mrs. Wigley grunted, turned over luxuriously, and fell asleep again.

The landlord of the Horse and Jockey suddenly thrust his head out of the open window and began to bawl loudly.

"Hey, thee! Ah've told thee before to keep out o' this place. If ah catch thee in my stables agen, Three Fingers, ah'll take a gun to thee..."

But the intruder was off round the corner of the inn, followed by a slatternly woman with a good figure and red hair.

Seth turned again to his wife.

"There's Three Fingers just taken a night's free lodgin' in my stables along with that bitch of a woman he's knockin' around with. Some time, he'll have th' place on fire and then perhaps ah'll rue not lockin'-up my buildings... Anyhow, ah'll notify th' police about this. Happen they'll warn him off and tell him to keep his distance. Ah don't trust that chap."

He slipped on his shirt and trousers without waiting for a reply and, hurrying downstairs, passed through the untidy taproom, littered with dirty glasses and reeking with last night's stale smoke, and clumped across the yard to make sure that all was well.

Meanwhile, the man and woman who had helped themselves to Seth Wigley's hospitality overnight, were hurrying down to Hatterworth. The third finger of the tramp's right hand was missing and he was therefore known as Three Fingers. A legend was attached to the missing member to the effect that, suffering from blood-poisoning in it, its owner had stoically cut it off with a pair of scissors. He was an unpleasant-looking customer. A general look of disproportion about his face. His mouth, nose and eyes seemed pushed too near the top of his head. Long, broken nose, weak, receding chin, loose mouth with yellow, broken teeth and a long, sloping upper lip. Like a grotesque tailor's dummy, constructed with freakish features to attract passers-by. Since he had picked up with the woman who accompanied him, he had shaved himself with more or less regularity.

The woman would have been a beauty had she used soap and water more and properly groomed her magnificent head of hair. The life the pair of them were leading, however, did not permit fastidiousness. She was young, of middle stature, with long legs and a broad, full breast. Her features were on the heavy side, but her complexion was flawless and exquisitely tanned beneath a coating of grime, acquired from sleeping-out and lack of toilet facilities. Every movement of her fine, muscular limbs showed through the thin dress she was wearing. How such a creature could see anything in Three Fingers sufficient to make her cast her lot with him, was a mystery. Both of them seemed satisfied with the arrangement, however, and tramped contentedly, saying little, down to town…

About half an hour after Seth Wigley had satisfied himself about the security of his property, Jethro Hamer jingled past the inn in his milk-cart. He was off to Hatterworth to deliver his wares, door-to-door, to the houses of the town. A small, moorland farmer with a few cows and a contented spirit. His little mare tittupped happily downhill, the harness chinked and rang, Jethro whistled a tune and tried to chew a bit of straw at the same time. "Mornin', Seth," he yelled as he passed the pub, "goin' to be a grand day." And he was out of earshot before Wigley could reply.

Suddenly, the little farmer flung his weight on the reins. The pony halted, almost rearing in her hind legs. Hamer's eyes were on the heather about a hundred yards from the roadside. Sprawling face downwards there, was the figure of a man. The milkman clicked his tongue at his mare, drew her gently to the verge of the road, descended, and ran to the spot, stumbling over the uneven ground as he went.

The body was cold and damp with dew. The farmer knelt and lifted the head. "My God!" he said, and turned white under his hard-baked tan. "Seth, Seth," he bawled and, as the innkeeper, hearing the cry almost a quarter of a mile away on the still air, poked his head round the side of the house, the farmer flailed the air with his arms to bid him approach.

Seth Wigley was as appalled as his companion.

"Jerry Trickett!" he said. "So that accounts for one of th' shots last neet. He must 'ave caught-up with Sykes after all…"

He gasped as he spoke. Hurrying over the rough turf and the shock on top of it had got him in the wind. In a few words he told Hamer of last night's events.

"Ah'm off for th' police right away," said the dairyman, and broke into a run back to his float. Whipping up his mare, he sped down to Hatterworth, leaving the innkeeper guarding the body.

CHAPTER VI

Superintendent Pickersgill's Solution

'But what good came of it at last?'
Quoth little Peterkin:—
'Why, that I cannot tell' said he,
'But 'twas a famous victory'.

SOUTHEY

LITTLEJOHN LISTENED WITH RAPT ATTENTION TO HAWORTH'S story. The Inspector's pipe had gone out and he had even forgotten the whisky at his elbow.

The Superintendent had a faculty for colourful narrative. A local man, he had known all the characters in the tale and briefly sketched their main features, like a black-and-white artist giving a clear impression in a few swift lines.

"You're a born spinner of yarns," said Littlejohn, as they paused to re-charge and light their pipes and fill-up the glasses.

"When you love the hills and valleys you live among, it comes easy," said Haworth simply and gathering up the threads once more, continued with his re-construction from the records before him. His colleague was soon immersed in the history of the case again.

Superintendent Pickersgill rode into his appointment as head of the Hatterworth police force on the shoulders of his wife's father. Not only that; he had the good luck to be promoted from Inspector to Super on the improvement of the status of his district, owing to the growth of the town and the absorption of several rural areas in it.

Ex-Inspector Entwistle had a good brain. Sound common sense and shrewdness made up for much he had missed in early technical training, for in his youth, the force had little of the paraphernalia of scientific detection. The notebooks which Haworth had borrowed showed how much Pickersgill owed to the old man in bringing cases to their successful endings.

The photographs of the body which accompanied the files showed it as the milkman had found it, sprawling face downwards. A tall, heavily-built corpse, clad in an old jacket, breeches of the army type, black stockings and heavy, nailed boots. A double-barrelled hammer-gun of the usual sporting model lay beside the body. The records stated that there were six undischarged cartridges in the victim's pocket, but the gun was unloaded when found. The cartridges were of the cheapest Eley make and were loaded with size 5 shots.

The police-surgeon's report showed that death had occurred about the time the reports were heard the night before. Trickett had received a full charge at close quarters, and in the back. The heart was pierced and the backbone shattered.

The first thoughts of the police were concerning Enoch Sykes. He had disappeared altogether. His mother, with whom he lived, had seen nothing of him since the morning of the grouse-shoot, when he had taken a day off work and left with his gun for the moor.

The verbatim report of the inquest was a long and detailed document.

Mr. Benjamin Butterworth, a local solicitor and county coroner, presided. A tall, slim, peppery old man, with a plentiful shock of snow-white hair, a pink complexion and a white moustache, and thick, grey eyebrows, which he raised and lowered eloquently and effectively. Piercing, grey eyes behind shining gold-rimmed glasses. In opening the proceedings the coroner made a few scathing remarks concerning the crowded state of the public-hall in which the inquest was held. In war-time, he said, it ill became people to flock to an enquiry of this kind as a form of entertainment. They would be better employed working in the national interest. He added that the least sign of disturbance or even fidgeting, would cause him to clear the court.

The police evidence was formal. Pickersgill was sure that Sykes had killed his friend and did not even ask for an adjournment. The evidence of Seth Wigley and a number of others was taken on the matter of the shots at dusk and the commotion in the yard of the inn on the memorable afternoon. It was firmly established that there was bad blood between the two former friends.

"What were they doing out of the army, two able-bodied men in their twenties?" asked Mr. Butterworth.

"Both were skilled engineers, employed by Cross and Haythornthwaite, and were exempted by the tribunal on that account," replied the police Superintendent.

Mary Tatham, the girl previously courted by Sykes and who had later transferred her affections to Trickett, was questioned. She was a dark slip of a thing, with a good figure and plump, rosy cheeks, and usually had a a ready, flashing smile for everyone. At the inquest, she was greatly distressed. She had been out with Trickett the previous week-end.

"I don't want to distress you further," said Mr. Butterworth, his glasses sparkling and his eyes in no way losing their piercing firmness, "but were you the cause of the bad feeling which existed between the two men?"

The witness burst into tears. Later, growing calmer, she was able to continue.

"They quarrelled about me."

"You were previously engaged to Sykes and broke-off the affair for Trickett?"

"Not engaged. We were just going out a bit together."

"You quarrelled?"

"Yes."

"About your change of mind, was it?"

"We had a row before Jerry… Mr. Trickett, asked me to go out with 'im."

"Now, I don't wish to probe into private matters more than is absolutely necessary, but this is perhaps important. Was this a mere lovers' squabble of a passing kind… or was it, shall we say, something more—ahem… fundamental and final?"

"Ah told Enoch ah never wanted to see 'im again."

"Why?"

The girl hesitated and seemed to grope for words.

"Ah… ah didn't love 'im any more… He'd changed from what he used to be… he were different."

"In what way?"

"Oh, ever since he got work at Haythornthwaite's and left Myles's. He'd got a better job and more money, and some'ow it made 'im cocky and… and… not like his old self. 'E spent all the time we were out together swankin' about what 'e were goin' to do and the brass… money… he'd soon be makin'. He were so lost in his dreams, that he'd no time to give me a thought. Ah just got fed-up with it."

"So you turned to his friend?"

The girl flushed and her eyes flashed.

"Nowt o' th' sort. Jerry Trickett axed me out and ah needed a bit o' persuading after wot I'd bin through."

"Very well. Did you ever see or hear the two quarrel?"

"Yes, and ah got sick of it! The first night ah went out with Jerry, Sykes was round the followin' day, threatenin' what he'd do to me and Jerry if ah didn't stop it. He begged me to come back to 'im, but ah'd had enough. Ah sent him off. Then, folk began to tell me he was drinkin' heavy. Him and Jerry had been quarrellin' and fightin' and it was all over the town that Enoch had said he'd swing one day for Jerry and th' trick he'd done on him."

The police surgeon, who had been absent hitherto on a maternity case, was none-the-less scolded for his disrespect of the court by the coroner. The doctor testified concerning the manner and time of death.

"Most unpleasant—a shot in the back. Most cowardly and contemptible, if murder can ever be anything else," said Mr. Butterworth. "I take it you extracted as many shots as possible."

"Yes. From what I can see, and after consulting a gunsmith, I'd gather that only one barrel hit him. The other must have missed. The second report was some time after the first and it looks as if the murderer stalked or chased his victim and then, coming-up with him, gave him the choke barrel."

"You are here for medical evidence only, Dr. Buckley…"

"I beg your pardon, Mr. Coroner…"

"Is the gunsmith here?"

Timothy Twigg, gunsmith, of Hatterworth, was sworn and gave his evidence.

"Is what Dr. Buckley says correct, Mr. Twigg? In other words, was the charge of shot extracted by the doctor likely to be the contents of one cartridge, or more?"

"Judging from the spread of the shots and the number, one barrel only did the trick."

Mr. Twigg was a little, cadaverous man, with a face like a wedge, and a bald head. He was enjoying his position as expert witness.

"Did Sykes purchase his cartridges from you?"

"Yes, sir. He and Trickett used the same brand and the same size of shots. Number fives, as a rule. They might have loaded a few of their own. A lot of working-men round here do that, you know."

"Yes, yes. Now, Mr. Twigg, I understand you've examined the pellets extracted from the body. What size were they?"

"They were mixed. Number fours and number fives. Some sportsmen have a theory that although fours give a smaller load, they hit harder. A good shot, therefore, is surer of a kill with fours. A mixed loading, of course, either involves a special order, or else a man must load his own cartridges."

"You have said that local sportsmen load their own cartridges. Did either Sykes or Trickett buy shots from you for such purposes?"

"No, sir. But of course, there are other gunsmiths, and often, men will place a large order with a firm out of town and then share it out among several of them. It's cheaper to buy in bulk."

"Very good, thank you, Mr. Twigg. That will do."

The remaining witness was Buller, a gamekeeper, who seems to have been the last to see the men alive. He said he met them separately, both going in the direction of Hatterworth. He spoke to neither of them, nor noticed anything unusual about them, except that Sykes seemed to have about as much liquor as he could carry.

Mr. Butterworth thereupon addressed his jury. The latter consisted of local men, shopkeepers, clerks and the like, and they took the job very seriously. The coroner explained the virtues, at that juncture, of finding a verdict against persons unknown. The police were on the track of a suspect, and, in due course, if he were apprehended, such a verdict would give him a fair chance of clearing himself, without in any way impeding the police.

The jury were headstrong, however, and returned their verdict of wilful murder against Enoch Sykes.

Mr. Butterworth was very annoyed at this disobedience and showed his disapproval by dismissing them after the fashion of unruly schoolboys, with frowns, furious contortions of his eyebrows, and not a word of thanks.

Pickersgill agreed with the verdict. He had made up his mind, and set in motion the machinery of the law for tracing the missing man. On the information lodged by the landlord of the Horse and Jockey, he laid Three Fingers and his woman by the heels, although they had, by this time, reached Sheffield. Both vehemently denied seeing either the body on the morning of its discovery, or anything of Trickett or Sykes during their prowling of the moor in search of free lodgings on the previous evening.

Meantime, every policeman in the British Isles was on the lookout for Sykes. The Army, Navy and R.F.C. recruiting offices were combed and the ranks were scrutinized. Nothing. Mrs. Sykes, the missing man's mother, was closely watched, in case he might be hiding with her connivance. One so demented, however, could hardly be guilty of such an offence. It seemed unreasonable to harry the simple, distressed widow.

At length, it was assumed that Sykes must have joined some branch of the forces and met his death incognito. The loss of so many of the town's men in the war gave people other things to think about. The files were closed and the case regarded as ended, although for a long time the search was continued unobtrusively.

Superintendent Pickersgill regarded his investigations as a triumph, and Sykes's continued absence as confirming his deductions. In time, he thought of the moorland murder, even though the criminal had vanished, as something of a successful investigation. The coroner's jury were responsible for this frame of mind. In spite of Mr. Butterworth's desire to give the suspect a chance to prove himself innocent, a jury of Sykes's peers had found him guilty and confirmed the Superintendent's own views. To him, it was a victory.

CHAPTER VII

Dry Bones

I feel like one who treads alone,
Some banquet-hall deserted,
Whose lights are fled, whose garlands dead,
And all but he departed!

TOM MOORE

"BETWEEN YOU AND ME," SAID SUPERINTENDENT HAWORTH, "Pickersgill is a better hen-fancier than a limb of the law. He doesn't seem to have investigated any angle other than the Sykes one. In this case he behaved just like a horse with blinkers on."

The two detectives had gone through all the available notes and evidence connected with the murders on the moor and were now discussing a plan of campaign.

"Perhaps we oughtn't to blame him overmuch," replied Littlejohn. "After all, the scent was so strong and, like a good hound, he kept his nose to it. That's what the real murderer intended, isn't it? And, by gad, he pulled it off, too. We've nothing left but dry bones and faded memories to work on."

"Well, we'd better make a list of the dry bones, as you call 'em, Littlejohn, and see what they can tell us. The inquest this afternoon will probably bring some more information to light, although Griffiths, the police surgeon, is no Dr. Thorndyke. He was industriously extracting pellets from the backbone last time I saw him."

They took pencil and paper and listed the characters in the case, like two producers selecting the cast of a play.

Mary Tatham. Now Mrs. Ryles, former sweetheart of both the murdered men. Living in Marble St., Hatterworth.

Bill o' Three Fingers. Alive and still haunting the locality.

Peg, his woman at the time of the murder, left him and married a labourer. Living at Waterfold.

Seth Wigley. Alive, semi-invalid, and living with his daughter at the Horse and Jockey.

Mrs. Trickett, mother of Jerry. Dead.

Mrs. Sykes, mother of Enoch. Living in same house in Hatterworth, and apparently retired.

Benjamin Butterworth, County Coroner. Dead.

Dr. Buckley, police surgeon at time of murder. Dead.

Mrs. Myles, former employer of both victims. Alive, aged, and living in Hatterworth.

Sir Caleb Haythornthwaite, last employer of victims. Still alive and flourishing.

Buller, gamekeeper on the moor at time of murder. Dead. His son Peter, who often accompanied him, keeps a café, *Peter's Pantry*, in Hatterworth.

Pickersgill, Entwistle, engaged in investigating the murder. Alive and retired.

"There we are," said Haworth, laying down his pencil and laboriously shifting his injured limb. "What can we get out of that lot that Pickersgill missed?"

"We can only do our best," replied his colleague and rose to go. "I'll be down at the inquest after lunch, and then we'll have another conference as to what line we'll take. This promises to be interesting, if only we can blow the dead embers into a bit of flame. By the way, how will Inspector Ross take my interfering? I take it, he'll be at the inquest representing the police. I wouldn't like him to be peeved, you know."

"That's all right. I've had a word with him. He's delighted that you're in at it. He'll share any kudos, being the temporary chief, and a better fellow you couldn't wish to meet."

Of the old firm of Butterworth, Coughey, Mills, Butterworth and Mills, Solicitors, only Mr. Simeon Mills survived. This was somewhat of a public relief, for previously, nobody had known which Butterworth was which in the firm's title and as for the other Mills, he might have been the invisible man; no one ever knew or saw him. Mr. Coughey, developing strange ways owing to the incessant nagging of his wife, ran away with his typist just after the death of both the Butterworths. The field was therefore left to the only visible Mills, who assumed the mantle of county coroner unopposed. He presided over the inquest on the poor bones of Enoch Sykes.

There was a great gathering in the new courthouse and this time, although there was another war on, the coroner reprimanded nobody. In fact, he relished the large audience.

Mr. Mills was a little, fat fellow, with a clean, red, negroid face, thick, shapeless lips, and a head completely bald except for a fringe behind his ears. He wore large pince-nez, heavily corded, and he had large eyes with bilious, bloodshot whites, which, somehow, reminded Littlejohn of blood oranges. The coroner was a vain, pompous man, who loved to hear himself talk. He opened the proceedings with a little homily on the mistakes which men can make. Here, he said, was a man condemned as a cowardly murderer by a bygone body of jurymen similar to those now assisting him. Now, the one who had for so long been branded with the curse of Cain, was revealed as a victim of the same foul and unknown hand. All of which proved how careful one must be and how essential it was to bring sound and unbiased judgment to a court such as this. He emphasized that his late friend and predecessor, Mr. Butterworth, (here Mr. Mills looked as though he would have bared his head if he had had his hat on it), had advised an open verdict. How wise; how prophetic, even. And he as good as assured his men that he would stand no nonsense from them this time. He then sat back as though expecting noises of approval. None were heard, and the enquiry opened.

Proof of identity came from various quarters. There was an old fracture of the tibia, for instance, which the victim's mother recollected. He had fallen in the schoolyard and done it. Then there was the ring on his finger. She identified that, too. It had been his father's, who had the same Christian name as his son. And a silver hunter watch, too. Also his father's. Mrs. Sykes had given them both to Enoch junior on his twenty-first birthday. The watch had been pierced by a shot and had stopped at 5.54. Old records showed that to be the time of the first report. Sykes must have been the first victim; Trickett followed.

Dr. Griffiths could say little, except that the bones tallied with the height and description of the dead man. Judging from the position of the pellets in the backbone and ribs, the murdered man had taken the charge full in the chest. He could not say whether or not death had been instantaneous. He had extracted some of the shots and others had been recovered from the earth around, preserved apparently by the clothing.

A ballistics expert from Leeds followed the doctor and stated that the sizes of the shots were fours and fives. Apparently a mixed charge! Two barrels of the same gun might have killed the two former friends. The shotgun unearthed beside the bones of Sykes had been unloaded when examined.

Inspector Ross gave a very able synopsis of the former crime and Mr. Simeon Mills, not to be outdone, made the solo into a duet, which prolonged the proceedings without doing much except confuse the jury. They returned a verdict of murder against person or persons unknown, without retiring. Mr. Mills told them to do so and, unlike their forefathers, who were more independent, they obeyed.

The police were not disposed to do much in the way of interrogation until after the funeral of Sykes. It was a strange affair.

Mrs. Sykes had long been sure that her son was dead. She had never believed him guilty, knowing his nature and, mother-like, refusing to permit the idea of his being a killer ever to enter her mind. She had mourned him as lost, time had taken her grief but not her pleasant memories of happier days, and she had adapted herself to circumstances with fortitude. Her friends at the Methodist Chapel had treated her kindly and never shown any change of front towards her through her son's presumed infamy. Other townsfolk, however, had been less charitable. She had, in certain quarters, been regarded as almost as abhorrent as her son, and been saddled with scorn for having brought him into the world at all. Vicariously, she had suffered much of his punishment. She had lived through it; it was almost forgotten; she could move through the streets, at length, without a single accusing head being turned to or from her. Now, the whole thing was reaped-up again. This time, however, sympathy was universal. The woman who had been ostracized, became almost a popular heroine. Anxious to make-up for the suffering once heaped upon her, her onetime detractors overdid it. They turned-up in droves at the funeral of the poor remains of her son.

Mrs. Sykes did not want it. She had forgotten her grief. The bones meant nothing to her. She was just seeing them decently put away in the grave where, thirty years before, she had left her husband. The contents of the simple coffin, behind which she followed in a cab, accompanied by the Rev. Gotobed and two or three of her friends from the Ladies' Sewing Class, did not seem to her to contain the remains of her son. Short of knowing where he was for twenty or more years, she had buried him in her heart, and there he was going to stay. Littlejohn watched her from a distance at the cemetery. She was bewildered at the public ceremony and the large audience. She was dressed in old, rather shabby black, and wore a long-outmoded hat. Her face reminded Littlejohn of those in woodcuts. Angular, with a small, sharp nose and a jutting, determined little chin. Straight-hewn lines instead of curves. She bore herself with self-possession and a calm dignity which put the superficial or sham emotions of the public to shame. The storm-tossing which the world had given her had made her the little captain of her own soul.

Two mornings later, for Sunday intervened, Littlejohn called on Mrs. Sykes. She lived at number 9, William Henry Street, a small cottage in a row of nine. He knocked on the door, which was quickly opened by the old lady herself. She must have mistaken him for a salesman of some sort for, with a "We don't want anythin' to-day," she would have closed the door in his face, had he not hastily announced the purpose of his visit.

"I'm a police-officer, Mrs. Sykes. May I have a word with you?"

"Oh. Ah've bin expectin' you. Come in."

The front door led right into the living-room. It was as neat and clean as a new pin. An iron kettle was singing on the hob of the shining, blackleaded kitchen range, with its bright steel fender and fire-irons. On the mantelpiece, two old, white china dogs and a small, black marble clock. Coconut matting on the floor and a home-made rug of pieces of old cloth. A rocking-chair and a saddleback in horsehair by the fireside, and two cheap, wooden kitchen chairs with their seats tucked under a plain kitchen table. The latter was covered in white American-leather and on it was a pint mug. The woman was apparently making herself a morning cup of tea. The sideboard was of heavy mahogany and bore two complicated ornaments with lustres dangling from them and protected from the dust by a glass shade. There was a small clock, too, and its pendulum, in the form of a little girl sitting on a swing, flew to and fro with dizzy monotony.

Mrs. Sykes was a small, wiry woman, with white hair drawn tightly back from her forehead and fixed in a small bun at the back. Her eyes were brown and, in the half-light of the dim room, looked like bright, black beads. She had small feet and hands, and her mouth was like a thin, little slit. At close quarters, she still reminded Littlejohn of one of these carved Swiss images of old people, with regular features, clean-hewn and angular and showing evidence of the carver's knife. She wore a black skirt, a home-knitted dark-blue jumper, and a white apron tied round the waist. With the apron she dusted the saddleback chair and bade the detective sit himself down.

"Will you 'ave a cup o' tea?" she asked hospitably, evidently taking a fancy to Littlejohn.

"Gladly, thank you, Mrs. Sykes." She brought out a cup and saucer, probably part of her best tea-set, brewed the tea in an earthenware pot and poured it out.

"Now, what can ah do for you, mesther?" she asked as they sipped their drinks.

"I know this is perhaps going to be a bit painful for you, Mrs. Sykes, but it's got to be done. You see the discovery of your son's body..."

"Bones," interjected Mrs. Sykes with brave realism.

"...Bones, then. The discovery has re-opened a case which has slept for a long time. In brief, your son is cleared of a suspicion which has long hung over him. Now we've to try and find who killed not only Trickett, but Enoch as well."

"Its not painful at all to me, mesther. All my pain were gone through long-since. Ah'm glad to know as my lad's innocent. Ah never believed 'im guilty, but there were some as wouldn't be told. Ah don't want revenge on anybody. Them as did it's 'ad it on their consciences and that's its own punishment. But that doesn't mean to say ah'll not give a civil answer to a civil question. So you can ask away, mesther, and ah'll try to answer."

"Well, how long had Trickett and your son been friends?"

"All their lives. Last thing eether on 'em would 'ave done was to kill th'other. Neether of them was hot-tempered."

"But, they quarrelled about a girl?"

"Aye. Perhaps it was Enoch's fault. Mary was always a nice girl, and she still is. But Enoch was so taken-up with his new job, that he neglected 'er a bit. They were working overtime and he was so busy with his own plans. Jerry was more happy-go-lucky and when Mary jilted Enoch, wasn't long in takin'-up with her himself. They'd both wanted her ever since she was a kid. Jerry's gettin' Mary seemed to wake Enoch up, but it were too late. And then him that had been T.T. all his life, started drinkin'. Nothing ah could do would stop 'im. He got that quarrelsome and moody, too. But ah will say, that whoever else he quarrelled wi', he never 'ad a wrong word for his mother."

"What was that you were saying about his job?"

"Ah never asked you if you'd 'ave a bit of oat-cake with yer tea, mesther." Littlejohn looked-up at the thin bannocks, hanging, like little dry cloths over the empty clothes-rack overhead, and declined with thanks.

"His job, you were sayin'. Oh, yes. Well, Caleb Haythornthwaite used to be manager for Mrs. Myles at the foundry, and wi' so much war work about, he wanted to start-up on his own. Old Luke Cross, who was gettin' on in years and had a foundry down th' valley, offered Caleb a partnership. So, Caleb went and took Enoch with 'im. Enoch was one of his best men at Myles's and he begged 'im to go with 'im. Enoch said he'd go if Jerry could go too. So they both of 'em went. Caleb paid our Enoch well, too. Ah were surprised when ah found out how much he'd left me when th'courts said ah could presume him dead."

"Enough to leave you comfortable?" ventured Littlejohn, knowing that he was on delicate ground, but wondering how a fellow in his late twenties had come by such a nest-egg.

Mrs. Sykes hesitated. "A pound a week for life through a post-office annuity, it brought me," she said proudly.

"That's very good. Very good indeed. I'm glad you were left free from want, at least…"

"Of course, ah'd to make-up with a bit o' cleanin', but now ah've got old-age pension, so ah'm allreet."

"Your son never talked much about his job, I suppose?"

"Well, it's a long time since, mesther. They were on shells at th'time, ah remember. But it were after the war that Caleb Haythornthwaite were thinkin' of, ah reckon, as well as during war-time. You see, both Myles and Crosses were loom-makers and they were competitors, too. Mrs. Myles would never 'ave taken Caleb into her firm. It were an old family concern with no room for outsiders. But Cross jumped at th' chance and it paid him. By gum, it did that. For, when th' war were over, and things got a bit normal agen, Crosses went ahead like wildfire and Myles went backwards, until th' old lady had to sell-up to keep her creditors quiet. She's a rare 'un is Mrs. Myles. Carried on th' business after her husband died for many a year. She'd two boys, you see, and was keepin' it goin' for them. And then they was both killed at th' war. Not much use goin' on after that. She's still alive and well-nigh on eighty."

"Well, Mrs. Sykes, I don't think I'll trespass on your time any longer. Thanks for the tea and for all you've told me. We'll do our best to find the man who committed the crimes. Your son had no enemies, I can take it?"

"No. There never were a better liked lad until he left Myles's. Then, of course, there were some jealous of his gettin'-on. There always is, isn't there? But none of 'em would a' thought o' shootin' him. No, if he'd any as wished him evil, ah never knew of it. After he got his new job, he kept more to himself and told me less."

They moved to the door. A framed photograph of a bullet-headed man with a large moustache, a white tie and an aggressive look hung over the sideboard. A memorial card "Enoch Sykes", and dates of birth and death, had been inserted under the glass. The verse caught Littlejohn's eye.

We think of you, dear father,
Your name we often call,
But there's nothing left to answer,
But your photo on the wall.

"My husband. Died when Enoch were a lad," said Mrs. Sykes simply. Littlejohn bade her good-bye and departed. On the way to Haworth's home, he puffed his pipe and thought about the points of the interview.

A struggling widow, left with a young lad who took her less and less into his confidence. The new job, which cost him his girl and his friend, and made people talk jealously about him. The change in character as well as in occupation. He did something for which he got himself killed and then left his mother enough to provide a pound a week for life. That was at the root of it all?

Mary Tatham, Sykes's old flame, could perhaps throw some light on the cause of the quarrel and the change in her old lover's nature. Littlejohn decided to call on her that afternoon.

CHAPTER VIII

The Old Love

I gang like a ghaist, and I carena to spin;
I daurna think on Jamie, for that wad be a sin;
But I'll do my best a gude wife ay to be,
For auld Robin Gray he is kind unto me.

LADY A. LINDSAY

LITTLEJOHN FELT VERY CURIOUS AND NOT A LITTLE EXCITED as he made his way to the house of Mary Ryles, the Mary Tatham who had been successively courted by the two dead men. The sweetheart they both had fancied since boyhood. The cause of their bitter quarrel. The girl whom even the mother of Enoch had defended and described as nice. The one who, six months after the murder of one and the disappearance of the other of her lovers, had wed another, Josiah Ryles!

Marble Street was a cut above William Henry Street. Its houses were in rows, but had small gardens instead of fronting starkly on the pavement. Plots of sour earth, some moss-grown, covered in sham rockery, or sprouting coarse plants, others overgrown with shrivelled grass or too fouled by the caustic attentions of cats even to yield weeds, rescued them from the title of cottage property in the books of estate agents and gave them the doubtful honour of being messuages. Cast-iron railings, mounted on low stone parapets, separated the plots from each other and from the street. The houses seemed to boast small, dark sitting-rooms at the front, too, and the outlet-pipes sprouting from the walls here and there testified to the presence of what are advertised as modern conveniences.

Littlejohn raised the stiff knocker attached to the letterbox of No. 21 and knocked. The sound of children's voices inside ceased and a silent and urgent expectancy seemed to prevail behind the closed door. Slowly it opened. A woman, with a small child clinging to her skirts, stood there eyeing the visitor suspiciously. Littlejohn took her in at a glance. Calculations put her down at about forty-two; she looked nearer fifty. Fat and ungainly, with straight bobbed hair, badly cut, as though some amateur had put a basin over her head and clipped off all not covered by it. A round face, with healthy cheeks, grown puffy, and dark, placid eyes, with a look combining innocence and ignorance. Her figure had gone altogether. Heavy limbs, protruding stomach, great breasts flopping beneath her dress. A hard-working woman, weary with child-bearing and gone to seed before her time. She had five children and her husband was a plumber.

"Mrs. Ryles?" said Littlejohn. "I'm a police officer. May I have a word with you?"

The woman still regarded him placidly and opened the door wider. She had been expecting something of this kind. News travels fast.

"Come in."

A black cat, rubbing round the child's ankles, fled down the dark passage and rushed up the dim stairs.

"Go into th' kitchen and stay with your grandma," said the mother to the child, who obediently toddled-off at her bidding.

They entered the parlour, stiff with cheap, little-used furniture in imitation green leather, with a yellow oak sideboard with a bowl of artificial fruit in the centre and a gallery of photographs of children in various stages of development, and here and there a family group. In the corner, a whatnot filled on three tiers with small knick-knacks and ornaments of every shape and size. Over the fireplace, a framed plumber's diploma.

At first, the detective was not invited to sit down. The woman was agog with curiosity and kept him standing hesitantly on the hearth-rug. When he explained briefly the purpose of his call, she offered him a chair, but remained standing herself, until she realized that he would not sit until she did. Then she flopped on the edge of the green-cushioned chesterfield, her hands picking at the folds of her apron.

At close quarters and in a lighter room, Littlejohn could see that, until domesticity and middle-age added to her weight, she had been good-looking. *Sic transit gloria*... The eyes were still bright and, beneath the nervous exterior, there seemed to be a genuine happiness.

From the back room could be heard the noises of children warming-up to their play again, and now and then the louder, querulous voice of grandma, keeping them at a deferential pitch of control on account of the visitor.

"I've called about a very old story, Mrs. Ryles," said Littlejohn, "and if it embarrasses you, please believe me, I'm not poking and prying out of idle curiosity, but out of necessity. We must, if we can, lay by the heels the murderer of Sykes and Trickett, though a lot of water's gone under the bridge since the time."

The woman nodded. She didn't seem to know what was expected of her or what to say in reply.

"You were, I gather, more or less engaged to both the dead men... ahem... in succession."

"That's right."

Mrs. Ryles smiled. At first, it was inscrutable and faint, as though she were casting back her mind to events in those past amours of twenty years ago. Then, her look became almost coquettish. The pride of a woman who had past conquests to her credit, whatever the present might hold.

"You quarrelled with Sykes. Do you mind telling me, as fully as you can, what change in his character caused you to give him up? You told the coroner years ago that he *had* changed, didn't you?"

Mrs. Ryles blushed and wrung her hands awkwardly.

"Well, it's hard to say, really. It were the way ah felt about it at the time. You can't help your feelin's, can you? Ah felt ah were takin' second place to his other love, his big ideas of makin' money an' gettin'-on. Ah'd 'ave been content with a little house and enough to manage on. But he wanted to be a fine gentleman and me a fine lady. Above our stations, like. He seemed to 'ave plenty of brass to spend, but kept sayin' there were lots more comin' his way and one day he'd be th' foundry-master himself. A partnership was what he were after, nowt less, and then we'd be rich. To tell you th' truth, mesther, ah got scared of him. Burned up with big ideas, he seemed to be."

"Did you know where the money was coming from?"

"No. That were another thing, too. Once, when he were at Myles's, we'd all in common and he told me everything. Them were our 'appiest days together. After he left there, he got close and full of his own secrets. He just shut me out of his heart."

"So you gave him up?"

"Yes. Ah knew ah'd never be happy that way."

She spoke the last words softly, as though remembering some old happiness of first love. Her voice was another charming thing about her. She spoke the plain speech of the valley, but in a low contralto key.

"Was Trickett the same about his change of job?"

"Ee, no. Jerry were more 'appy-go-lucky. He'd be content wi' a livin' wage and a home and children and now and then, a bit of shootin' when he was of a mind. 'E were a caution, were Jerry."

Again, the soft sadness, but this time, her eyes twinkled in recollection of some light-hearted incident of long ago.

"The two quarrelled about you?"

"Partly that. But they'd not bin so friendly for some time before that. Enoch were treatin' Jerry like 'e treated me. No time for his old pal, too busy with his own big ideas."

"Facts have now proved that one didn't kill the other..."

Vehemently the woman interposed.

"Neether of them 'ad it in him to murder anybody. A couple of better men never lived... until they left Myles's, and that started all the bother between them."

"You've no idea who might have borne a grudge against either or both?"

"No. Both of 'em were well liked. Mrs. Myles took it hard their leavin', specially as she'd lost Haythornthwaite, too. She wanted to make Enoch under-manager. But 'e wouldn't be persuaded. Wanted to go with Haythornthwaite. So Jerry followed him."

"Were they great friends of Haythornthwaite?"

"No. He fancied himself a toff, did Caleb, the foxy, stuck-up nobody. Bein' manager of th' foundry, he didn't mix with the likes of us outside. But at th' works, he was as thick as thieves with Enoch. They spent a lot of time together, an' if you ask me, Caleb were pickin' Enoch's brains good and proper. Ah never liked Haythornthwaite. And that was another cause of bother between Enoch and me."

"You didn't like him?"

"So you've not met owd Caleb? See if you like 'im when you come across him."

"Hm. There's nothing else you could tell me which might help me or throw any light on the subject?"

"Ah think not. It's so long since it all 'appened. Ah must be goin', too. There's my husband's tea to be got."

"Yes, I'm sorry I've worried you and kept you from your duties."

"Aye, that's all right, mesther. You're welcome. But it all 'appened so long since, didn't it?"

Looking at her, Littlejohn thought she seemed to have entered calm waters after the storm of her early years, even if her looks and circumstances had changed considerably. He bade her good day and she saw him to the door.

Dusk was falling and the workpeople were on their ways home, pouring out of factories and workshops, their shoes and clogs rattling on the flagstones, their chatter and banter ringing down the mean street. As Littlejohn closed the gate, a little man with a pleasant, ruddy face appeared on the scene and bidding him how-do, turned-in there. Apparently Mary Ryles's husband, Josiah. The one she had taken six months after the death of her ambitious and happy-go-lucky former lovers.

The little plumber had a grey moustache, wore a cloth cap and carried a workman's bag of tools, from which protruded the nozzle of a blowlamp. A short briar was wedged in his mouth and he puffed it contentedly. A good-natured chap, by the look of him. He had probably finished his day's work, unless he had returned for some forgotten tools, which was unlikely at that hour. He was evidently anticipating his tea and the company of his wife and family with eager, cheerful relish.

Looking at him there, the honest north-country working-man, Littlejohn understood the reason for Mary Ryles's placid, contented look. With a man like Joss Ryles, she was safe and wouldn't go far wrong.

CHAPTER IX

The Iron Man

O what can ail thee, wretched knight!
So haggard and so woebegone?
The squirrel's granary is full,
And the harvest's done.

KEATS

OVER THEIR PIPES AND GLASSES AND BEFORE A WARM FIRE, Littlejohn and Haworth discussed the results of the Scotland Yard man's enquiries, whilst their womenfolk, their voices rising and falling in the next room, knitted scarves and balaclavas for the forces.

"One thing's quite certain," said Littlejohn, "and that is, the sooner I interview Sir Caleb Haythornthwaite, the better. His name keeps cropping-up and the whole series of incidents leading to the quarrel between the two friends and their murders, seems to start with his leaving Myles's and taking them with him on his new venture."

"Yes, Littlejohn, and there you're up against it. Sir Caleb is a most difficult man to approach. Hard as nails and as sour as vinegar. His success has brought him no happiness, I'll tell you. There've been some unpleasant tales about him in these parts at one time or another."

"Such as…?"

"Well, in the first place, the circumstances under which he left Myles's. Years before, Jonathan Myles had died, leaving his wife with two growing boys to look after and the whole of his foundry business. A very strong-minded woman was Mrs. Myles—and still is, in spite of her years—and she ran that place like a heroine. She'd been a bit interested in it before her husband died, but afterwards, went into it heart and soul. Of course, she aimed at keeping the business together until the boys were old enough."

"But surely, a woman among all those foundrymen would find it a hard furrow to plough?"

"Oh, she was quite up to it. She could hold her own with the best of them. Sir Matthew Hardcastle's daughter, real county gentility and out of the top drawer. But, as you say, she needed a man about the place. That's where Haythornthwaite came in. He'd risen from an apprentice in the shops and knew the business from A to Z. But a mere manager's job wasn't enough for him in the end. He hankered after a share in the firm. You can guess his ability, when I tell you that at that time, he wasn't forty. It is rumoured that he asked Mrs. Myles to marry him, although she was years older than he was. Whatever the cause, they had some quarrel or other. It leaked out that she was going to haul him before the courts when he left, but the thing was hushed-up. Nobody quite got to the bottom of it."

"And Myles's business went downhill after Haythornthwaite left?"

"Not at first. There was enough business for all of them, what with war work and one thing and another, at the time. But, you see, both the Myles boys joined the army and both were killed. The bottom fell out of Mrs. Myles's world after that. Things seemed to go from bad to worse at the foundry and, whilst Haythornthwaite prospered, Mrs. Myles met her creditors and just managed to pay twenty shillings in the pound. Marvellous the way she's kept her chin up, though. She lives at a house just outside the town, with a couple of servants and I believe she's too frail to turn out now. She's well over seventy."

"Perhaps I'd better pay her a call, too, if possible, Haworth. She may be more disposed to discuss past history now."

"Even if she won't, the visit will be worth while. She's a real character… an old tartar, when she sets that way."

"And Sir Caleb…?"

"Oh yes. He made money right enough, and quickly, but somehow, troubles have come with it. He married Luke Cross's daughter. It wasn't a love match, as you can guess. They haven't seemed to hit it off for years and are never seen together. There's a saying in these parts: 'Clogs to clogs in three generations'. Well, in this case it won't be as long as that at the rate things are going. Young John Haythornthwaite, Caleb's only child, specializes in whisky, fast cars and fast women. His father's always getting him out of scrapes. The foundry belongs to Caleb altogether now and it's not likely to last long when he's gone."

"So Mrs. Myles is having her triumph, after all."

"Yes, and that's not all. Caleb's beastly temper has made him generally disliked. He's a local J.P., and quarrels with his fellow magistrates on the bench and even tries to tell the Clerk and the lawyers in court how to do their jobs. But the bitterest pill of all was when he put up as M.P. for the division. He'd given quite a lot to the party funds and got a knighthood that way and then some sycophant proposed him as parliamentary candidate. Caleb thought it was a walk-over. Local man, large employer of industry, hundreds of men dependent on him. They showed him, by jove! They pitched him out, neck and crop, with a ten thousand majority for his opponent, Tom Hoole, a Labour man. Sir Caleb never got over it. It was the culmination of a series of nasty blows. His trade's iron, his heart's iron, his hand's iron and I believe his soul's iron."

"It's some job I'm taking on, if I go to interview him."

"You're right there. But there's one thing to remember: He's a conceited chap. Flatter him, defer to him, and he'll talk. Whether he'll talk about what you want, is another matter, though."

Littlejohn made a wry face.

"Not much in my line, those tactics. Still, the end perhaps justifies the means. Provided I keep my self-respect, I'll try anything once. There are one or two things about Sir Caleb that intrigue me. First, the money that Sykes came-by just before his death. He did well for himself from some source or other. Well enough to leave his mother quite comfortably situated. Now, was that hush-money for something from Sir Caleb? Blackmail, or for services rendered? I don't suppose I'll get the old man to open his heart in that direction, though, but I'll have a try, and I think I'll make a frontal attack, too."

"I admire your nerve, Littlejohn!"

"Then again: Sir Caleb used to do a fair amount of shooting. He owned the shoot on which the men met their death. Where was he when the shots were heard? That's twenty years since, but I'm going to have the cheek to ask him where he was at the time. He can only throw me out on my neck."

Haworth burst into loud laughter, stubbed his game leg on the stool on which it was resting, and pulled up with a jerk.

"Oh, blast this leg! Double blast it! I'm missing all the fun. I can just see Sir Caleb being asked for his alibi."

"When will be the best time to call at The Hall, do you think?"

"You'll not get much satisfaction in the daytime. If you call at the foundry, you'll find your style is cramped by a hell of a row going on everywhere and Sir Caleb dealing with a continuous stream of underlings coming and going in his office. I've had some. I was there last month, after young John had knocked down the bollard in the main street here. Driving, dead-drunk, I imagine, one night and smashed the Turn Left sign to smithereens, and made scrap-iron of his car, without so much as scratching himself. Heaven seems to look after the boozers. Ross was on duty and left him to cool-off in the cells overnight. There was a devil of a row about it… but enough of that. Evening's the best time. You'll find the old man at home any night."

"It's not nine yet. What about my going now?"

"Better ring-up The Hall and see if he'll see you. You can take my car, you know."

"Right. I'll not be away long. I'll call back if I'm all in one piece when we've finished with each other…"

Spenclough Hall was built on a small scale. A square house, with a short tree-bordered drive, a large gravel sweep and a few acres of parkland surrounding it. The present owner had bought it lock, stock and barrel from a bankrupt millowner. The main gates were open and Littlejohn drove to the house without halting at the lodge. It was a dark night and he had passed the little cottage before he realized that it was there.

An elderly maid answered the door. She was portly and bad on her feet and wore a white cap and a long white apron. She reminded Littlejohn of a retainer at some provincial hotel. She ushered him into a small, cheerless room and switched-on an electric heater, which battled valiantly and vainly against the cold, damp air. The maid took Littlejohn's card and left him to examine the room. A conglomeration of furniture, suggesting that, unable through sentiment or taste to part with the humbler odds-and-ends of their less prosperous days, the occupants had mixed them higgledy-piggledy with those ready and waiting for them when they bought the Hall.

The maid returned almost at once and bade Littlejohn follow her. They passed along a cold, well-carpeted corridor to Sir Caleb's study, just as Big Ben boomed nine from a wireless-set somewhere in the region of the kitchen.

Sir Caleb Haythornthwaite was a small, portly man of sixty or thereabouts, but he looked much older. Worry had ruined his temper and digestion. His head was broad and shining-bald and was fringed with thin, grey hair. His face was round with a chalk-white complexion, but the long, pointed nose was a dyspeptic pink. Tight, thin lips, sparse grey eyebrows, firm chin, clean-shaven. "What does that face remind me of?" pondered Littlejohn momentarily to himself, and the answer came into his brain almost at once. Grock! The chalk-white ground, the red nose, the bright dabs of unhealthy colour on the cheek bones, the fringe of thin hair framing the bald pate, brought to mind the clown in make-up. But only for a flash. The pale-blue eyes met those of the detective. They were hard and steely. The chin was rocky and square and the look stubborn and aggressive. Sir Caleb assumed a pair of black-rimmed spectacles with broad sidepieces. They hid the heavy half-moon pouches beneath his eyes somewhat and accentuated the palor of his complexion. He rose and extended his hand to his visitor, but there was no smile or friendliness in his greeting.

"Well, Inspector, and what can I do for you?"

He spoke with a north-country accent, but without trace of the dialect.

"Good-evening, Sir Caleb. I've called about the Sykes case, recently re-opened by the discovery of his remains on the moor…"

"They've surely not called-in Scotland Yard on that. Sit yourself down."

"No. I've been spending Christmas with Superintendent Haworth and, as you know, he's laid-up through an accident to his leg…"

"Yes. I've heard about that…"

"I've undertaken to help him, unofficially, and I'm doing a bit of the running about for him."

"What about Ross. Can't he take charge?"

"He's fully occupied as it is. This arrangement works very well, if I can only get those concerned to co-operate."

"Meanin' me, I suppose, Inspector. But what have I to do with all this, and why bother me at this time o' night? There's nothing I can tell you, that I know of."

"Both the dead men, Trickett and Sykes, were well known to you, sir. Perhaps some incident or light you can throw on their characters might give us a lead. I grant you, it's a long time ago, but we've got to make the most of what we have left, and, if I might say so, Sir Caleb, you're part of what remains in the shape of their last employer.

"Well. What do you want of me? I'm busy as you can see, and it's no use our keeping on quizzing and fencing. Let's get to th' hosses."

There was no goodwill in his attitude. He had offered neither smokes nor drink to Littlejohn, but taking up a large pipe from his desk, struck a match and lit it. Then he pushed a box of cigarettes across the table with such a graceless gesture that Littlejohn declined. A hostile witness and to be treated as such!

"Can you throw any light on the relations between Sykes and Trickett and their fellow-workers during the time you employed them and whilst they were at Myles's along with you, Sir Caleb?" said Littlejohn, gently feeling his way.

"You must think I've a good memory, Inspector. Well it happens you're right. I have; but I don't know much about what went on in the workshops. Trickett was an ordinary mechanic, of course. Sykes was under-manager at my place and directly responsible to me."

"Who was manager, Sir Caleb?"

"I was. I was junior partner as well. So you can take it from me that the manager didn't murder Sykes out of jealousy, if that's what you're gettin' at."

"Was Sykes popular with the men?"

"He was *my* man, if you know what I mean. I brought him from Myles's because I liked him and he was a chap with brains. Now, whoever's on the boss's side isn't, as a rule, popular with the men, especially in a foundry. But that doesn't mean they'd shoot him."

Sir Caleb's tone was domineering and offensive and he seemed to be making an exhibition of showing that he was quite aware of what was going-on in Littlejohn's mind without being told.

"Sykes wasn't a trade-union man, then?" continued the Inspector unperturbed.

"No. If he had been I wouldn't have made him my assistant. I don't like folks that run with the hare and hunt with the hounds."

"Did it ever strike you, Sir Caleb, that Sykes or Trickett had enemies—outstanding ones, I mean...?"

"No. Sykes was a bit unpopular after he got his promotion, as I've already said, if you'll listen to what I'm telling you. But I can't bring to mind anybody who'd risk his neck by killing either of them."

"They left Myles's with you, I gather. Did they resign, or were they dismissed?"

"No. They both left of their own free will. Sykes came first and brought his pal with him."

Sir Caleb rose impatiently. "Look here, this is gettin' us nowhere. Why disturb me at this hour about things other people—his mother and such—can answer?"

"I wanted the views of someone of independent opinion and trustworthy judgment."

"Now, Inspector, I don't want any soft-soap..."

But Sir Caleb was pleased and mollified nevertheless. Littlejohn ventured a step further.

"I understand from the records, that the pair of them were killed on your preserve on the moor, just after your shooting-party had left the butts. Were you anywhere about at the time, sir?"

"I thought that would be comin', Inspector. So you want an alibi for me, do you?" The haggard-looking knight thrust his pale face venomously across the desk. "Well, you can go to hell," he said.

"That's not very helpful..."

"It's not intended to be. Over twenty years have passed since that day. A lot of those who were there are dead and done with. The rest are old and getting past being bothered. Why root-up all that's past? Best stop wasting your time. You'll not solve it, any more than Pickersgill did. As for my alibi: Well, I'll tell you something, just to show you. I left the butts with a keeper that's been dead for years. I parted from him and got a lift in the car of a young chap that was on leave from France. He took me home and, after that, was killed in the line. When I got home, I'd dinner with my wife and was attended to by a butler. The butler's dead and my wife's evidence won't be accepted... Now do you see? Not a ha'porth of good askin' anybody for alibis. It's just damned nonsense going-on with it."

His chalky face was flushed and his pouched eyes sparkled maliciously as he sat back in triumph.

"Hm," said Littlejohn. "That's for me to decide, isn't it?"

"You! Who are you? A stranger here. You know nowt about life and happenings in these parts. Ask Pickersgill and that old doddering father-in-law of his. They'll talk sense to you about this case."

"Just one more question then, Sir Caleb, and I'll finish."

"Well, let's be hearing it and end it."

"When Sykes died, he left his mother quite a comfortable little sum. Over a thousand pounds, I'd say. Where did so young a man gather such a nest-egg? Not in wages, surely."

"Why ask me? You can take it from me, the wages I paid him didn't allow such saving. Although towards the end, he was doing pretty well… ten pounds a week."

"Did you pay him anything else… a lump sum, as bonus or retaining fee…?"

"Or blackmail! Why don't you out with it? Who's been putting ideas in your head? Because there's nowt o' that soart in it, whatever tha might be thinkin'."

Rage broadened Sir Caleb's vowels and he lapsed temporarily into his native dialect, as he did when squabbling with the hands at his works.

"I'm suggesting nothing, Sir Caleb. You're putting your own construction on this. The money must have come from somewhere, and naturally, wages, commission and the like are the first to be thought of here."

"Well, I can't help you and I'll bid you good night."

The foundrymaster rose. Littlejohn continued, as though musing to himself, as he stretched his limbs ready to depart.

"Perhaps we can get at it through the old bank accounts of Sykes, if they're in existence…"

A cunning shot, which shook Sir Caleb visibly.

He plucked his thin under-lip, hesitated, and then changed his tune.

"It's a long time since and perhaps I've forgotten. I'll just look at my records and see. Sit you down again for a minute."

He left the room. Littlejohn was sure it was to gather his thoughts. The random-shot had found a bull's-eye. Littlejohn smiled to himself. He knew what Sir Caleb apparently didn't, that bank figures were as hard to get at as their cash-reserves, without a court order. He glanced round the room as he waited.

Heavy mahogany furniture. Chairs upholstered in horsehair. Ponderous, gilt-framed pictures on the walls. Still life, stags and cattle on Scottish moors, cows knee-deep in grass and pools. Poor stuff, for the most part, and probably acquired with the Hall. Cases of books, uniform in dark, stiff, leather bindings and little used. On the top of a massive secretaire lay a gun-case, weathered and well-polished. Littlejohn eyed it and listened. Not a sound. He crossed the deep carpet noiselessly, lifted down the case and placed it on the floor. Kneeling, he slipped the catches and raised the lid.

A couple of beautiful sporting guns lay snugly in the interior. A few hundred poundsworth, turned-out by a first-class maker! The detective did not touch them, although he was tempted by his love of such things. A cartridge-box was in its place there, too. Littlejohn did not handle it, but swiftly noted the name of the maker on an old envelope. Ashworth and Hall, Huddersfield. He closed the case, and was back in his chair when Sir Caleb returned.

Just before the ironmaster re-entered, Littlejohn heard the front-door open and slam. Footsteps approached, and the entrant seemed to meet Sir Caleb on the threshold of the study. Voices were raised in anger. Sir Caleb reviling; the newcomer answering in a lower, jaunty tone. Evidently the clogs-to-clogs son had come home from his carousing. The wretched knight rejoined the detective, his face blotched with livid patches. He sat down, paused, and then thrust his face across at Littlejohn again.

"When Sykes came with me, I find I paid him seven hundred pounds for some patents he'd been working on and which he agreed to sell me. I'd forgotten about it..."

"Patents? Were they used at Myles's, too?"

"That's nothing to do with you... and we've had quite enough for one sitting. You're just asking questions for asking's sake, now. I've had enough. There's nothing else that I can tell you that'll be of any use."

The man's nerves were on edge. Whether from the questioning or from his son's arrival, the Inspector couldn't quite decide, but he had his own ideas.

"Again that's for me to decide, Sir Caleb," he replied, feeling nettled by the tactics of the man. "Thanks for your information. I may call again as the case goes on."

"I'm a busy man, Inspector, and it'll have to be something more important than all this, or I'll not see you. I won't have my time wasted."

"If I think it necessary, I shall call again and, if you're in, you'll see me, Sir Caleb. I'm not in the habit of wasting people's time with my enquiries, any more than I'm prepared to tolerate sleeveless errands for myself. Good night."

Haythornthwaite took the rebuke lying-down, rang for the maid and grunted a good night.

As Littlejohn started-up Haworth's car, a sports model, apparently parked round the side of the house, barked into action, swooped dangerously past, and out into the darkness at the end of the drive, heedless of the black-out. The second generation of Haythornthwaites rapidly returning to its clogs!

CHAPTER X

The Betrayal of Three-Fingers

I've got no wife to worry my life,
Let fools get wed and rue the day.
Out on the road a woman's a load,
Growling and nagging all the way.

AMMON WRIGLEY

FEW MAIN CHARACTERS REMAINED OF THOSE WHO WERE ON the stage at the time of the double murder. Of these, one in particular appealed to Littlejohn on the keen, sunny morning which followed his visit to Sir Caleb Haythornthwaite. He decided to walk up to the Horse and Jockey to meet old Seth Wigley, superannuated landlord of the place.

The Horse and Jockey stands four-square to the Pennine winds, an inn of character and history. It has been known to be isolated for as much as six weeks at a time during bad winters and in Seth Wigley's hey-day, was famous locally for its home-brew and its liberal table. Ham and eggs were its speciality in days when they were plentiful and cheap, and Seth knew how to serve them. Toasted cheese, too, and succulent Wensleydale, served in a piece for you to take your cut. *Eheu fugaces*...!

The main characteristic of the Horse and Jockey was its sign. It swung with every breeze that blew, solid and weatherworn, on the windiest corner. As Littlejohn stood under it after his four-mile uphill trudge, he longed for the ham and eggs of bygone times about which Haworth had told him. He was just able to discern in the grimy paint of the inn-sign the features of St. George and the Dragon! An itinerant artist during old Wigley's reign had one time arrived and volunteered to paint the sign for a night's bed and unlimited beer. Seth had done him so well that he forgot the name of the pub, confused the horses and riders, and made an excellent job of the wrong pair before the mistake was discovered. The landlord saw the joke and the publicity in it, too. The tale spread the name of the inn far and wide and brought crowds of curious sightseers.

Mrs. Bracegirdle, the landlady, took Littlejohn into the little, stuffy parlour where sat her father before a huge fire. A brass bedstead, a mahogany clothes-chest and a heavy wardrobe crowded-out the place. Seth Wigley was propped-up in an armchair beside the fireplace, his legs and feet swathed in a rug. A fat, dropsical-looking, rosy-faced old man, with snow-white, silky hair. He was full of jollity for all his years and infirmities and eagerly waiting for spring days, when his chair could be moved out-of-doors and he could smell again the fresh moorland air that he loved, feel the clean wind and the sun on his cheeks, and hear the birds crying in the fastnesses. He listened attentively whilst Littlejohn explained the purpose of his visit.

"Don't make him laugh, Inspector," said his daughter, buxom and fifty, as she left them together. "I'm always afraid he'll bust once he gets laughin'."

Seth rumbled with good-humour, bade his visitor be seated, and shouted for a drink to be served.

A young girl entered with a glass tankard of ale and, with a bright smile for the two men, placed it before Littlejohn. She was stockily built, graceful and muscular, and was dressed in the gymnasium costume of some school or other. She moved with the ease and rhythm of a ballet-dancer, reminding Littlejohn of the figures of Degas.

"Well, grandad, I'm off," she said, and she kissed the old fellow and departed.

"My grand-daughter," said Seth with pride. "Goes to a Girls' High School in Manchester. She's on holiday and she's goin' givin' exhibitions in dancin' in Huddersfield at a Red-Cross do. Eddication's a grand thing... That lass is goin' out into th' world, mesther. No moorlan' pubs for her. Well, Inspector, you're axin' a lot, wantin' an account of what 'appened here on th' day of th' murder. It's a long while since and there were so many of 'em. When them shots sounded, we thought, after thinkin' it over a bit, that somebody were takin' a last shot at birds in the dusk. We couldn't believe that Sykes and Trickett were blazin' away at one another. Instead of which, it must 'ave bin one chap shootin' them both."

"Yes, and who might that have been, Mr. Wigley? Have you any ideas on the matter?"

"No, lad. There might have bin several people on th' road at th' time with guns, but not one of th' chaps I knew would kill another in cold blood, and ah knew 'em all pretty well, ah can tell you."

"Uhu."

"Ever since Sykes were dug-up, ah've said to myself over and over agen, 'Now, who'd want to kill either of 'em?' and always th' same answer comes back: 'Nobody!' It was dusk at th' time when it occurred. Buller, the gamekeeper,—he's dead—was on th' moor and see the pair of them just afore it 'appened, he said."

"Yes. A pity he didn't stay about a bit and see them off the preserves."

"Aye. But this has always struck me as bein' funny. If Buller saw 'em, why didn't he see whoever was out after the pair of 'em, too? They thought at that time, o' course, that Sykes had done-in Trickett. Buller's evidence seemed to bear that out. But, if both of 'em was killed together, how was it that Buller didn't see a third party on the prowl? Or if he did see anybody, why didn't he say so at th' first inquest?"

A very shrewd point, thought Littlejohn and then:

"He was working for Sir Caleb Haythornthwaite at that time, I understand, Mr. Wigley?"

"Aye. But ah don't think there were much love lost between master and man. Caleb took over Buller with the shoot, because Buller were th' best keeper for miles round here. Before that, when the moor belonged to 'er, Buller worked for Mrs. Myles, aye and 'er 'usband before 'er. It was a hard day for Buller when that shoot changed hands. You see, mesther, he'd been with the Myles family ever since he were a lad. But he'd to go where his bread and butter was, ah guess."

"Was anybody else likely to have been on the moor about that time?"

"Well, ah've never quite been able to understand why Bill o' Three-Fingers was so quiet at th' time of th' inquest. Him and his wench slept in my stables on th' night o' th' crime. They must a' been somewhere on th' moor when the killing was done. Three-Fingers was as close as a clam, however. Of late, he's bin a bit above himself, too. Two days ago, he called here as drunk as a lord, and Charlie, my son-in-law, wouldn't serve him. Where he'd got his liquor from, ah couldn't say, but Charlie said it were rum and smelled th' place out. Three-Fingers was pleased with himself, ah understand, boastin' and braggin' about his luck bein' in. What he's up to, ah don't know. Nowt good, you can take it from me."

"I think perhaps I might have a look at Three-Fingers, Mr. Wigley. Does he come here often?"

"Oh, he's like the wind—comes and goes, tha' knows. Sometimes, we'll see him two or three times a week; then he'll be missin' for months. He's evidently in th' locality agen and if he calls here, ah'll see that Charlie rings you up at th' police-station."

"Thanks."

"Another thing ah'll tell you, too. You'll think ah'm full of ideas, mesther, but ah've little else to do these days than sit an' think. That red-headed lass he used to knock about with, has got wed and settled-down in Waterfold. I'd call and see that girl, if ah were thee. She might tell you summat about what 'appened that night, you know. Ah did hear that Three-Fingers sent her packin'. He never could abide th' same woman for long at once, although that one were a bonny lass when she were younger. They stuck together like leeches at th' police enquiry, as well they might. But now she's been cast-off, or rather, *was* cast-off ten years or more since,—how time flies, doesn't it?—perhaps she'll sing a different tune."

"A good idea. You're in excellent form, Mr. Wigley! What's her married name, and where does she live now?"

"Peggy Hepworth, she was; now she's Mrs. Joe Fairbarn. Perhaps my daughter'll know where they live. Sarah… SARAH…"

"Yes, dad," said Mrs. Bracegirdle, bustling-in.

"Red-headed Peg, you know… Three-Fingers' owd flame. Where's she livin' in Waterfold?"

"King Street. Ah don't know th' number, but anybody there'll tell you. Her husband were a labourer for a long time, but now he's employed by th' Waterworks. You'll be able to find their house because there'll be a sign, 'Waterman', over th' fanlight, so's people know where to go when there's a burst and they want th' water turnin'-off."

Mrs. Bracegirdle showed a disposition to enlarge on the history of Peg after her rejection by Three-Fingers, and Littlejohn let her go on.

"It's a funny thing how that girl made good after such a bad start. Most of 'em who go wrong like that, specially with a gipsy-chap like Three-Fingers, come to a bad end, in th' gutter, as likely as not. Well, it's lucky she came across Joe Fairbarn when she did. Joe were a drunkard, who got converted by th' Salvation Army, and from being a right bad lot, he turned over a new leaf and became a regular member of th' Army. One Saturday night, after Three-Fingers had cast off Peg, she was knocked down in th' main street in Waterfold by a motor-car. Not badly hurt, you know, but bruised and dirtied a bit. Well, th' Salvation Army was marchin' past at th' time, singin' like, and Joe picked-up the girl. He must a' seen th' good in her, shows how, and she must a' taken a fancy to Joe, too. For he got her a job in one of th' factories, and then wed her. Nobody but a proper workin' Christian would a' done that for a well-known bad character like Peg. Anyhow, ah believe they're very happy, and have a nice little family, too..."

A customer, entering the bar, broke-up the harangue and Littlejohn prepared to go, too.

"I'll take a trip into Waterfold now, I think, Mr. Wigley," he said. "I'm half-way there, as it is. Are there any 'buses?"

"Let me see, what's time? Nearly eleven. There'll be one up from Hatterworth in ten minutes."

Promising to return and see the old man again, the detective thanked him, wished him well, and took his leave.

At ten minutes to twelve, Littlejohn found himself walking down the main street of Waterfold. A small town, with its principal thoroughfare built along a ridge, and with about a dozen side-streets branching off it, like ribs from a backbone. Gaunt houses of stone, three-storied, and with large windows in the attics, denoting the onetime pursuit of handloom-weaving by their occupants. A profusion of children, dogs and cats playing about, for it was Christmas holiday and the youngsters were running wild. King Street was easy to find, and Littlejohn was soon knocking at the door labelled "Waterman", as predicted by the landlady of the moorland inn. Neighbours eyed Littlejohn curiously as he stood waiting for an answer. The reputation of the waterman's wife had probably died hard, and there were some who still took a malicious interest in her. He was raising the knocker to strike it again, when the door opened and the red-haired woman stood before him.

"What do you want?"

She had put on weight since the days when she gallivanted round the countryside with her gipsy lover, but she was not too heavy, and carried her forty-odd years well. There was grey in her hair and her cheeks were a bit florid, but she held herself well and was trim and clean.

She was altogether more of a woman than many of the anæmic-looking neighbours who emerged from the cottages on each side and pretended to be sweeping pavements or cleaning windows, the better to investigate what was going-on.

Littlejohn stated that he was a police-officer and asked Mrs. Fairbarn for a word in private.

A look of fear crossed her face. She was safe out of the storm and had no desire to be thrust back into it.

"You've come about…?"

"There's nothing wrong, Mrs. Fairbarn. I only want your help in a little matter."

"Come-in, then, but you'll have to be quick. My husband's due home at half-past twelve and he'll want his dinner then."

"I won't keep you more than five minutes."

With a sign she bade him enter. She was struggling to keep calm. He followed her along the narrow lobby into the living-room. The furniture was cheap, of plain wood, but spotlessly clean and polished. The floor was covered with oilcloth. The table was laid for four on a white, American-leather cloth. Two children's mugs and two cups and saucers. A small, cold meat-pie on each of two plates; half a pie on each of the other two. A young child toddled-in from the back-yard calling "Mother". Perceiving the stranger, he hid his face in her apron and began to snivel. She led him to the back door and thrust him out.

"Go and play with Bessie in your sand, like a good boy," she said, closed the door and returned.

"You'll have to excuse me, Inspector. I wasn't expectin' you, and I've my work to do."

She spoke quite well. Evidently she'd seen better days before she met Three-Fingers. Littlejohn wondered where she had come from, originally. Tactfully, he explained the purpose of his visit. The woman flushed scarlet and looked at him in cold fury. She had won peace and respectability for herself and was going to put up a fight to preserve them.

"I want nothin' to do with you, or anything connected with you. I'm surprised at you pesterin' respectable people and I'll bid you good morning. There's the door." And she pointed to the lobby.

"I'm sorry, Mrs. Fairbarn, but it's not so easy as that. I've my duty to do, and that is the finding of a murderer. Now, I warn you that if you won't help willingly, the truth will have to be forced from you in public, probably under oath in a court of law. If you tell me, privately in your own home, I'll promise you that if I can possibly prevent it, the matter won't go further. All I want to know is, were you and Bill on the moor when the two shots were fired on the night of the murder I've mentioned and, if so, did you see anyone about? That's all. Now come, Mrs. Fairbarn."

The woman had cooled-off. She saw that it was best to be pleasant about the ordeal. She reminded Littlejohn of a tigress protecting her young and her home.

"Very well. But you've promised."

"Yes."

"Well, we were on the moor when the shots were fired. We were nearing the Horse and Jockey, where Bill said we'd find a dry and cosy bed in the barn after dark. The shots went-off behind us, somewhere in the middle of the moor."

"Did you see anything?"

"Not then. The day was closing-in fast, and it was hard seeing. 'Keep movin', sez Bill. 'We don't want to be mixed-up in anythin', even if it's only poaching'. So we kept on. But just as we turned to get round the wall of the inn, we saw a figure, set-off like, against the skyline, hurrying to the road. Just out of a dip it came, and then we turned the corner. 'I know who that is,' says Bill. 'Who?' I says. 'Never you mind. Less you're told, less you'll tell', says Bill, and there we dropped it. Next morning, when we heard about the murder, Bill makes me swear to say we'd seen nothin' or nobody. 'The police'll pull us in if they know we're about; so it's up in the mornin' early and off out o' these parts', he says. But they got us and Bill and me swore we'd never seen anybody."

"Yes. Did you know who it was that Bill saw?"

"No. I swear it. I wouldn't tell you a lie, mister. I don't want any trouble with the police, or anybody. I'm happy now and want to stay like it, not being disturbed or reminded of them days."

"Very well, Mrs. Fairbarn. Thank you for being so candid and helpful. I'll see that your confidence isn't abused. Probably you'll hear no more about this."

"Well, mister, you'll have to excuse me. I'm late as it is, and I've some chips to cook for our dinners..."

Littlejohn departed and made his way back to the Hatterworth 'bus. He was more anxious than ever to meet Three-Fingers and wring the truth from him. The meeting came before he expected it. As the 'bus passed the Horse and Jockey at the top of the road, Littlejohn spied Mrs. Bracegirdle waving to him. He asked the conductor to stop, and the landlady put her head in at the door.

"He's here, Inspector... came not long after you left. Half-drunk he is, already, so you'd better come if you want to see him," she said.

Littlejohn descended and followed the woman. He entered the taproom for the beastliest interview he had ever had in his career. Three-Fingers looked to have slept-out all night. The same silly caricature of a face, already described so well by Haworth, covered in several days beard. He was half-drunk and truculent.

"He wasn't sober when he arrived," said Mrs. Bracegirdle. "He'd an empty rum-flask with him and seemed to have drunk its contents on th' way up. We wouldn't 'ave let him in, only ah thought that this was a good chance for you to catch 'im."

Two or three lorry-drivers, their vehicles standing outside the inn, were in the taproom eating their food and drinking beer. They regarded Three-Fingers as comic entertainment and jested among themselves at his expense. Three-Fingers said nothing. Littlejohn touched him on the shoulder.

"I want a word with you; come into the bar-parlour."

Three-Fingers, slouching on a bench at the side of the fire, looked up at the detective with watery eyes.

"Wad yer want wi' me? You'll 'ave to wait until I've wet me whistle." He drummed on the table before him and ordered beer. Littlejohn nodded to the landlady, who placed a glass before the tramp. "Watsiss? A pint or a quart's wot I want. This is no good." He drank it off in two gulps and knocked for another.

Littlejohn was waiting no longer. "Either you come and talk in the parlour, or I'll haul you into Hatterworth lock-up. Coming?"

Three-Fingers broke silence again. He hiccupped and manœuvred himself upright, then staggered to his feet. He planted himself before Littlejohn and addressed him. His voice was thick and his tongue uncontrolled, and he emitted a stream of gibberish. Then, his drink seemed to take a firmer grip of him. He reeled back, struck the bench with the back of his knees and sagged into sitting posture again. Without a sigh or a word of warning, he vomited.

The landlord rushed-in and had him by the collar in a trice, slapped his dirty cloth cap on his head, and rushed him out into the yard. Both cursed furiously in the process and their arms and legs seemed to get mixed, like the tentacles of an octopus. The landlady entered with a mop and pail.

Littlejohn followed the milling procession to the door and the lorry-drivers, now serious and uttering threats concerning the disgusting interlude which had disturbed their meal, went too. Littlejohn called to the landlord.

"Where have you put him?"

"Across the yard, by the cowshed wall. He can cool-off, the dirty bloody swine!"

"Lock him in the stable. Now, see to it. I want to know where to find him. He can sleep a bit there and then, if he won't talk, I'll 'phone for the police-van from Hatterworth, and we'll take him down there and charge him with being drunk and disorderly."

Mrs. Bracegirdle, her cleaning operations finished, appeared. "Have you had onny lunch, Inspector?" she said. "Not that you'll feel like it much after that…"

"I think I might manage a sandwich, Mrs. Bracegirdle."

"Right. We've a bit of cold ham. That do? Perhaps you'll wait in th' parlour. Father's asleep, else you could 'ave had it in his company."

Everything grew quiet again. There were noises from the kitchen, which told of a meal in preparation. Littlejohn sat waiting. He was depressed with the recent scene, and hungry. A cat entered and rubbed against his legs. Absently, he bent to stroke it. A dirty head was thrust in at the open door of the inn. "Any rags or bones?" cried a husky voice. A donkey-cart stood outside, and a servant girl exchanged rubbish for rubbing-stones.

After a meal of cold ham, pickles and apple-pie, Littlejohn felt better. He filled his pipe and thought on the case. If Three-Fingers had seen someone on the moor at the time of the crime, he must be made to talk. Probably, he would say he had forgotten the incidents of so long ago, not wishing to incur a charge of lying to the police in connection with the long-closed case. His memory would have to be jogged, then.

Littlejohn rose and called for the landlord. Bracegirdle appeared, and together they went to the stables to release Three-Fingers.

The tramp was asleep on a pile of hay. By his side was a rum-flask, which he had apparently emptied after being locked-up.

"He must 'ave 'ad another in his pocket, the drunken sot," said Bracegirdle and prodded the inert form with his foot. Littlejohn bent and shook the man. Three-Fingers made no move. They carried him to the door. His breath came in wheezy gasps and with difficulty. His face was ashen. Littlejohn raised one of the tramp's eyelids and rose to his feet with an exclamation.

"Let's get him out of this. Bring him into the air and knock him about a bit. We've got to get him awake. Ask Mrs. Bracegirdle to ring-up the nearest doctor, and tell him to bring-up a stomach pump. This may be alcohol or apoplexy, but it looks more like narcotic poisoning to me."

They dashed water on their patient, paraded him about in the air, and tried the usual expedients of first-aid. The man lolled helplessly in their arms. They were unable to administer coffee or emetics; Three-Fingers just dribbled them away.

Before the doctor arrived, the pulse of the tramp grew feeble, his breathing quieter, and, in the end, Bracegirdle and Littlejohn discovered that they were dangling a dead man.

CHAPTER XI

At the Horse and Jockey

See, by the roadside a shelter bids you stay,
Where a welcome is waiting for you and a maiden looks out from the door.
Quaff your fill, clear and cool.
Give me, too, maiden, of thy flowing bowl;
Let me worship thy glowing youth!

GOETHE

MR. SIMEON MILLS DECIDED TO HOLD HIS CORONER'S COURT at the Horse and Jockey. The scene of the murder was just within the administrative boundary of Thorn, a small, moorland village, consisting of about two dozen houses clustered round a ruined woollen-mill and a Nonconformist chapel. The latter was, as a rule, the centre of such social life as prevailed in Thorn and precedent, in the shape of a tramp who died on its very doorstep in 1847, gave it the right to be used as a courthouse. Mr. Mills, however, was less fervent than the congregation which, at the time of the death of Three-Fingers, had been worshipping for four Sundays at ten degrees below freezing-point, until they could, by jumble-sales, offertories and other forms of self-denial, raise enough money to repair the heating-apparatus. The Coroner ruled that the large public-room of the inn would be a better place for an inquest, in view of the fact that snow was already appearing on the hilltops.

In the two days between the sudden death and the inquest, Littlejohn worked hard. He not only set-about getting to the bottom of the sudden demise of Three-Fingers, but kept his nose to the grindstone on the Trickett-Sykes murders as well. He paid a visit to old Mrs. Myles, the ex-foundrymistress in her gaunt old house in Hatterworth. He called at Peter's Pantry, and had a long talk with its proprietor, Peter Buller, son of the late gamekeeper of the preserve on the moor. And he had a highly technical interview with a firm of gunsmiths in Huddersfield.

Dr. Griffiths opened-up Three-Fingers at the autopsy and before putting him together again, discovered that at the time of his death from a strong dose of sleeping-tablets dissolved in rum, he was also in imminent danger of a more or less sudden end from hob-nailed liver, valvular disease of the heart, and general bodily debility and neglect. The body was in shocking condition and the surgeon was glad to pack it up and be done with it.

Inspector Ross ably assisted Littlejohn in the police-work of this new case. Ross was a tall, fair, athletic officer, with a fresh, red face and a small, sandy moustache. He was a bachelor, and many of the eligible girls of Hatterworth lived in hopes, but he seemed happy without them, and devoted himself to his duties and to training a choir of policemen, who gave concerts far and wide and carried-off prizes at musical festivals.

Haworth, Ross and Littlejohn held a conference at the police-station to which the Scotland Yard man had driven the hobbling Superintendent, who had insisted on bestirring himself against medical advice.

"We've something to put our teeth into, at last," said Littlejohn. "It's quite evident that Three-Fingers had some knowledge which was dangerous to an unknown party, and had to be silenced. The inference is, that the murderer of Trickett and Sykes is still alive. Three-Fingers knew who it was and had a hold on him and, therefore, had to be polished-off."

"That's it," added Haworth. "You say he's been reported as being very cock-a-hoop of late. That's probably due to the fact that the discovery of the second body had proved that Sykes didn't kill Trickett, and that somebody seen by Three-Fingers on the night of the first crime, when Peg says he spotted someone on the moor, probably *did*. Three-Fingers has been doing a bit of blackmailing but, having met a resolute victim, has got more that he bargained for."

"Which means," chimed-in Ross, "that we'll have to scour the neighbourhood and find-out, if we can, Bill's movements up to the time he arrived at the Horse and Jockey."

Ross and Littlejohn had already done much routine work. They had discovered that Three-Fingers had possessed two rum flasks. This led Ross to a bright deduction that perhaps the tramp was in the habit of carrying liquor about with him in this fashion in flat bottles which would easily fit his pockets. Much better than being burdened with the usual cumbersome wine bottle. Ross, therefore, set three constables to search the roadside for a larger empty rum bottle and his smartness was rewarded by the discovery of a black, unlabelled one, smelling strongly of the liquor, but empty, in a ditch about half-way between Hatterworth and the Horse and Jockey. Ross gave an account of his researches up-to-date to his senior colleagues.

"It seems to me that Three-Fingers called somewhere in Hatterworth, or in this neighbourhood, and got money and drink from somebody, probably from the one he was blackmailing. He had ten pounds in dirty notes, which we'll probably be unable to trace, and some loose change in his pockets, as well as a clasp-knife, some string, his identity-card, ration-books and a hawker's licence, with a pipe, tobacco and matches thrown in. That was all, and doesn't help us much. He probably carried the large rum bottle in his pocket until he was out of the town, and then filled his two flasks and drank what was left. There are his own fingerprints on all three bottles, and nobody else's."

"Did you have the little that was left in each bottle examined?" asked Haworth.

"Yes, sir. All of it showed the presence of the drug. The contents of the large bottle were probably doctored when he got it."

"If he drank some of it when he filled his flasks, however, wouldn't he have dropped by the roadside?" asked Haworth.

"Well, as I see it, sir, there wouldn't be much left in the big one when he'd filled the others. Not enough to knock him out, anyway. Perhaps he felt the effects coming-on but just thought he was tired, so stopped at the inn for a rest. He'd emptied his first flask on the way there, but, as Inspector Littlejohn has said, he drank a glass of beer on top of it, and vomited. That would rid him of most of the first dose, and he'd probably have slept it off and been no worse for it, only when they left him in the stable, he set about his second bottle. That did the trick. On top of what he hadn't thrown-up on the pub floor, the second dose was fatal."

"That's a reasonable statement, I think. What do you say, Littlejohn?"

"Agreed. There were about two teaspoonfuls of rum left in the second bottle. I've sent half of that off by special messenger to a friend of mine at Scotland Yard. We'll have a full report on that rum. There's a lot of difference in various types of liquor, and any peculiarities in this stuff might help us."

"Old Seth Wigley,—and what he doesn't know about drinks, apart, of course, from the intricate chemistry of 'em isn't worth knowing—says that it's good stuff and a cut above that supplied by the average pub or wine-merchant," added Ross.

"Yes," said Littlejohn. "And another point is, there was no label on the original bottle. What does that mean?"

"Either cunning removal, or else, contents of somebody's wine-cellar decanted into plain bottles from a keg," answered Haworth.

"Exactly."

"Whose?"

"That we can't say until my report comes from Scotland Yard. Then we'll have something to work on. It should be here by to-morrow morning at the latest."

Haworth struggled to his feet, solicitously hovered over by his subordinate.

"Well, we'd better be getting off to some lunch, if we're being at the inquest by two o'clock. You and your wife are eating with us to-day, and Mrs. Haworth's making a gradely meat-and-potato pie for Mrs. Littlejohn's benefit. So let's be off."

Ross's eyes sparkled at the mention of this culinary treat and Haworth grinned at him.

"You'd better come, too, Ross. I never knew such a trencherman as you, in my life!"

The Horse and Jockey was the scene of great animation when the police-officers arrived later in the day. Ordinary business had been transferred from the large parlour to the taproom and bar, and the place appropriately arranged for Mr. Simeon Mills and his jury. Seth Wigley, in great danger of bursting from excitement, was surreptitiously given a sleeping-draught in more attenuated form, of course, than that which had caused the present invasion of his premises, and snoozed blissfully through the proceedings in consequence. When he awoke later, after the tumult and shouting had died, his daughter decided that his annoyance was likely to do him more harm than if he had been present at the inquest. He was ultimately pacified by being given, against the doctor's orders, a mess of cheese and onions, made to his own specifications from the meagre stock of cheese in the pantry, after which he fell asleep, to rise the following morning full of beans and declaring that he felt better than he'd done for months past.

When Mr. Simeon Mills arrived at his strange court, he found a motley crowd of spectators drinking in the taproom and at the bar and overflowing into the yard and outbuildings. There had been a steady procession from both the Waterfold and the Hatterworth sides of the hill, and the occasion reminded one of the festivities of Good Friday or Whitsuntide. Before the official enquiry began, the crowds, lubricated by Mr. Bracegirdle's ale, had held their own inquest and arrived at a verdict. Person or persons unknown. They were disappointed; the inquest was adjourned.

Mr. Mills was not annoyed at the vast concourse. In fact, he revelled in it, and wished he had been able to relay his own speeches in the proceedings, by means of loudspeakers, to the multitude which was crowded-out of the courtroom. His jury consisted of moorland farmers, two shopkeepers, and two woollen-weavers from the village of Thorn. The natives of the latter are conservative, suspicious folk, who intermarry to keep the money in their families and who are, therefore, all related to one another. They bear signs of inbreeding, and the two men impanelled on this occasion were not exceptions in this respect. They were small, with large heads, hatchet-like faces, red-rimmed eyes, and a great economy in speech. They spoke freely to each other, but answered "foreigners" in monosyllables, as though suspecting that any friendly gestures would result in the strangers taking the liberty of marrying into their families and removing their closely-guarded building-society deposits into alien communities. They were both chewing sandwich-lunches with their gums, having removed their false-teeth the better to eat with, and probably to preserve them as well, and asked the buxom barmaid for a drink of water each afterwards. "Just like folk fro' Thorn, that is," said Bracegirdle as he charitably filled a couple of glasses from the tap. "They're all too greedy to be owt but T.T."

Mr. Simeon Mills's bell summoned his jury to their places, and the two men from Thorn solemnly inserted their dentures and entered, looking determined to bring a verdict of wilful murder against anybody but a member of their own closely-knit clan.

The jury had already inspected the body during its stay in the annexe to the chapel, which had been used for a similar purpose in 1847. They heard Dr. Griffiths give expert evidence and looked solemnly shocked at the idea of rum being used as a vehicle of death. For months afterwards, not a drop of that liquor was consumed within miles of the spot by anyone present at the Horse and Jockey that day. Evidence of identification was given by several witnesses. In fact, there had been quite a waiting-list of volunteers for the latter role, willing to be of service in exchange for a peep at the corpse. Mr. and Mrs. Bracegirdle and Littlejohn gave their accounts of the incidents leading to the death of Three-Fingers, and one of the lorry-drivers present at the time also corroborated the facts and retired disgruntled at being brought from Leeds to play little more than a walking-on part.

Superintendent Haworth had held a long conference with Mr. Mills before the proceedings opened, and they had decided on an adjournment, without any detailed questioning of the police. As little of the rum-bottle incidents as possible was, therefore, mentioned, and only the evidence concerning the two flasks was taken from Ross. Meanwhile, Haworth, whose hobbling had been observed, was the object of sympathetic glances from the audience. Littlejohn, too, was regarded with curiosity and a certain pride by the locals, for it seemed to put Hatterworth on the map when a man from Scotland Yard was involved in the machinery of its justice. The two men from Thorn eyed him as one might a confidence trickster, with suspicion and hostility.

Mr. Mills expressed his intention of adjourning the enquiry. The two men from Thorn thawed to the extent of entering into an animated conversation with the foreman of the jury, who thereupon rose and asked the coroner if the same jury would be required, as certain members of it had been compelled to absent themselves from woollen-weaving, with consequent loss of wages. Also, would there be any compensation for such losses? At this, there were murmurs in the audience concerning the characters of the people of a certain village.

Mr. Mills whipped-off his glasses, fixed the two little men with a baleful eye, and informed the world in general that he could make no promises concerning the constitution of his future jury, and that its present members would in no way be exempt from service again. As to expenses, he was surprised that citizens of this country should descend to considering public duty in terms of £. s. d. He adjourned the inquest until a future date.

The two men from Thorn, after a heated discussion with the coroner's officer, departed whence they came in dudgeon. There was great local indignation in their village when they returned with their tale, and there were comings and goings from one house to another during half the night, when the day's injustices were fully aired in even the most attenuated branches of the family. After that, the legal business of the clan passed from the firm of Butterworth,

Coughey, Mills, Butterworth and Mills, of Hatterworth, to Lemuel Harrison, Son, Swallow and Beech, of Waterfold.

After the departure of Mr. Mills at four o'clock, informal proceedings continued on the premises of the Horse and Jockey until opening time at 5.30. The beer ran out at 6 o'clock, and it was not until fresh supplies from Hatterworth arrived and were broached at 6.40, that good feeling was restored.

CHAPTER XII

The Iron Woman

But O the heavy change!—bereft
Of health, strength, friends, and kindred, see!

WORDSWORTH

WHEN LITTLEJOHN CALLED AT MRS. MYLES'S, HE WAS USHered into a large front room of the gaunt, old-fashioned house she occupied "up top of the town", which was Hatterworth's suburbia. Here the old lady had immured herself after the collapse and liquidation of the family business and she had gone less and less out of doors until now she was a recluse, attended by a housekeeper and a kitchen-maid. The latter admitted the detective.

The place was gloomy and forlorn. The room in which Littlejohn was asked to wait was fireless in spite of the time of year. It smelled of dust and neglect and sheets covered the larger pieces of furniture. The latter was of heavily-carved oak and had at one time been expensive. Apparently the salvage of a bigger house. An exquisite, long refectory table in the middle of the floor spoke of times when Mrs. Myles had entertained the best people of the locality. A dozen faded chairs, upholstered in tapestry, were pushed beneath it. Family portraits in frames on the walls; a standard-lamp with a faded pink shade; moth-eaten skin rugs; a dusty Indian carpet. A strange, sad picture of change and decay.

The maid returned and beckoned Littlejohn to follow. He was surprised to be led upstairs. At the top of the stairs, she tapped on a door and ushered him in. The first thing he saw was a large window, with a single huge pane of glass in the bottom sash. This framed a full view of the distant moorland, with a background of snow-capped hills, and brown bracken and heather in the foreground. The road ran along the moor-edge like a shelf. In the distance, the Horse and Jockey Inn was visible at the top of the pass.

The place was furnished like a bed-sitting room of the better-class Kensington variety. In one corner, a large, old-fashioned bed, with a canopy. A small table in the centre of the room; two comfortable easy-chairs; a Turkish carpet underfoot, and three striking water-colours on the walls.

A bright fire burned in the hearth and beside it, in a straight-backed chair, placed so that she could have a direct view of the scene through the window, sat Mrs. Myles. She looked very old. Her face was small and wrinkled, but her complexion was healthy and pink. She had clear, glittering, brown eyes. Her hair was white, plaited, and gathered back in a bun behind. The lips were tight, but the mouth large and generous. Broad, wrinkled forehead, serene, and with a touch of nobility about it. She had a fine, large nose, with wide, proud nostrils and a firm, rounded chin. Her voice was gentle, clear in tone, but with a trace of weariness in it. There seemed little of infirmity in her manner, but an air of sadness about it, unhappy, such as is worn by those who have no illusions left.

"I must apologize to you for bringing you up here, but I never leave this room now," she said, after the detective had introduced himself. She displayed little anxiety or curiosity concerning the purpose of his visit. "The 'phone here is my link with the outside world when I want anything, which is rare. The world has left me far behind, and I doubt if I would know it if I went out into it now.

Only the little bit visible through that window, hasn't changed since I was a girl. The stairs are too much for me these days."

They talked generalities for a minute or two. Littlejohn admired the pictures, especially one of the moorland road with which he was now so familiar, and in which the ubiquitous Horse and Jockey again appeared.

"You like them, Inspector? I call that one 'The Moorland Road'. It was done by a friend of mine… dead these forty years… the best thing he ever did, I think. He'd have gone a long way… he died at twenty-four."

The detective told Mrs. Myles why he had called.

"It's a world of twenty years ago that I'm here to consult you about, Mrs. Myles. You'll have heard, no doubt, about the rather sensational re-opening of the Trickett-Sykes murder case?"

"Yes. My housekeeper seems to have gathered all the news about it."

"I wonder, if it won't tire you, whether you'd be good enough to tell me the tale of how Haythornthwaite, Trickett and Sykes came to leave your employ and whether in doing so, they incurred the enmity of anyone in particular?"

The old lady grew stern and thrust out a quivering jaw.

"Yes," she snapped. "They incurred *my* lifelong enmity for one, and when two of that unholy trio died violently, I didn't feel a pang of regret. A pity the third and worst of 'em didn't die at the same time!"

The fire then seemed to die out of her. She gasped for breath, as though emotion had exhausted her, wiped her lips on her handkerchief, and grew very calm again. She smoothed-down the black serge dress she was wearing.

"My tale's a long one, Inspector, and covers thirty-five years or more, but it can be told briefly. My husband died young, in his forties, in 1912. I was left with two boys, both at school, and the old family foundry to keep going until they were able to take it over themselves. We specialized in woollen-weaving machinery, looms, you know. Michael, the elder, should have gone to Cambridge, but when his father died, came into the works. Patrick stayed-on at school. Micky was a born engineer and settled-in fine. There they are…"

She forlornly indicated the framed photographs of two handsome boys in khaki officers' uniforms, standing on the table.

"Micky was killed in Gallipoli in 1915; Pat, at Cambrai in 1917. They were all I'd got left and when Pat went, too, I seemed to die as well."

The old lady took a drink from a Thermos jug standing on the mantelpiece.

"By the way, Inspector, please smoke if you wish. I'm going to." She offered him a box of cigarettes. He helped himself and lighted hers and his own. She puffed away with the practised ease of a man.

"Whilst my husband was alive, he himself managed the foundry," resumed Mrs. Myles. "After his death, I asked Caleb Haythornthwaite, a young man, whom my husband had taken from the shops and trained personally to the rank of under-manager, to take charge. I followed my husband as managing-director. I knew little about the trade at first, but I soon learned. I set myself out to do so, because my first and foremost task in life thereafter was to keep the goodwill and reputation of the family concern at the high level it had reached under my husband and his father before him. Sykes was a favourite of Haythornthwaite's and he took him under his wing and trained him as his right-hand man. I didn't mind, provided it was to the good of the concern as a whole."

Mrs. Myles sat back and seemed to retire within herself for a while, as though consulting memory. Then, she took up the tale again.

"Haythornthwaite was of poor breed, however, and soon began to show his true colours. Power and authority grew to be too much for him. He began to grow familiar with me. Then... I'll never forget that morning... it was in my private room and he did such a lot of hemming and hawing before he came to the point... he suggested that in double-harness we'd make a grand partnership. In other words, would I marry him? The impudent lout... I soon brought him to earth! Had one of the men in the moulding-shop asked me to marry him, I'd have thanked him for the compliment. But Haythornthwaite... well... he might have been doing me a favour, the way he put it. Next time he came for a serious talk, he was different. He wanted a seat on the Board. That was the end, as far as I was concerned. I'd put up with enough. I told him that I regarded myself as trustee for my boys and under no circumstances would I sell one tittle of their birthright. He'd been fluttering round Luke Cross for a time, and I guessed what he'd do. He resigned and took a partnership with Luke. He left the same weekend, taking his pals, Sykes and Trickett with him. The following Monday, I got word that Micky had been killed."

Mrs. Myles's hands gripped the arms of her chair as though she were living through the ordeal all over again. Then she relaxed.

"In spite of the way I despised those three turncoats, I missed them. They were the three best men I'd got. I filled their places from the ranks, but without the thought of Mick coming back, it wasn't the same. Still, there was Pat to think of, and I had to pull myself together. We were on munitions at the time and were making good profits. Haythornthwaite soon had Cross's on the same footing and from being a more or less moribund place, Luke Cross's foundry sprang into great activity. I discovered that the trio had taken with them many of the ideas which really were the property of my company, but I couldn't put-up any fight at the time, because the law was then concerned with munitions, more munitions, and yet more munitions."

"Yes," said Littlejohn. "You'd probably have made yourself very unpopular if you'd started anything at the time."

"There was, however, a limited amount of trade on the old lines, repairs and renewals, and a bit of new stuff in the way of looms. After all, the clothing mills were hard at it making cloth for the forces. Now, it came to my notice that work on some of the looms we'd made for West Riding factories, was going to Cross's, instead of coming back to my place. I found that they were price-cutting and using our ideas, so I sent a man to investigate one of the jobs they'd done. They'd used a patent Micky had brought out during his spell at the works! I felt I'd got them at last. I sent for Haythornthwaite and told him what I knew. He'd made a bad slip and knew it. He grovelled, offered to pay, begged me to overlook it. I told him I was still trustee for my son and would make an example of him, not only on the one count, but on the way he and his two confederates had filched other rights and secrets of my place and used them against me. I told him the next thing he'd hear would be from my lawyer."

Mrs. Myles passed her hand over her forehead. She was tiring. She took another drink.

"Don't trouble with any more to-day. I'll call again, Mrs. Myles," said Littlejohn, anxious not to press his enquiry to the point of exhausting the old lady.

"There's not much more to tell, Inspector. Before my solicitor had properly taken the affair in hand, I got news of Pat's death in France. That finished it. I called the whole thing off. No use flogging a dead horse. What was the use? The foundry ceased to interest me. Peace came, I'd lost my zest for work, I neglected the place. Meanwhile, Haythornthwaite gained confidence through my not pursuing him… But, he was working alone then. You see, the death of Trickett had intervened, and Sykes was branded as his murderer. Haythornthwaite had got rid of… No, perhaps that sounds as though I were accusing him of the double murder… I can't do that, although I wouldn't put it past him. Let's say, the two men who held the evidence of the dirty work he'd done against my place were dead. Luke Cross retired and left Caleb in possession. Since when, Haythornthwaite hasn't looked back. Gradually things went from bad to worse with me. I just got out in time to pay twenty shillings in the pound. I sold-up the old home and retired here with my memories. And here I am."

They sat in silence for a while. Then, "Any more questions, Inspector?" asked Mrs. Myles.

"Just another one or two, if you feel up to them, Mrs. Myles."

"Yes?"

"I understand that Buller, the gamekeeper, the man who seems to have been the last to see the murdered pair alive, was once a family servant of yours, and remained more or less faithful to you until his death, although he worked for Sir Caleb after you sold your shoot. Did he ever tell you anything about what he saw on the fatal evening?"

"No. I saw very little of him after he left my employ. The shoot was one of the first things I sold, and Haythornthwaite bought it through an agent, otherwise he'd never have got it. I was fond of a gun in those days…"

She looked keenly at Littlejohn.

"Now don't be thinking I took a gun to that pretty pair, Inspector, because you're barking up the wrong tree there."

"The idea never entered my head, Mrs. Myles."

"I was far enough away from the moor that afternoon. I was at the Elvers', at Waterfold, taking tea with them. Old friends of mine, every one of 'em now dead. So they can't speak for me."

Littlejohn rose and bade Mrs. Myles good-bye.

"Good-bye, Inspector. I hope you'll soon lay the culprit by the heels. You'll have a tough job on, I'm thinking."

"Good-bye, Mrs. Myles, and thanks. I hope I've not tired you by all this questioning."

"No. It does me good to have company and a talk now and then, even if I do reap-up past grievances… I'm glad you like my pictures… And now, I'll have a nap before my cup of tea…"

The maid entered again in response to Mrs. Myles's ring. Littlejohn followed the girl downstairs. At the foot of the stairs, they passed a tall, masculine woman with a heavy, square face and dark, scowling eyebrows. Evidently the housekeeper. She fixed Littlejohn with a stare and eyed him up and down, but did not speak.

"Now what's bitten you?" thought Littlejohn.

The housekeeper followed the Inspector and the maid with her eyes and, as the street door closed on him, the detective imagined her still standing in the dark hall, grimly watching him off.

He was glad to be in the fresh air again, gratefully lit his pipe and strode off to attend to the next item on his agenda.

CHAPTER XIII

Peter's Pantry

The hungry sheep look up, and are not fed,
But swoln with wind...

MILTON

PETER'S PANTRY IN MARKET PLACE, HATTERWORTH, IS ONE OF those places where the appetite is never satisfied. Unable to afford the luxury of a *chef*, Peter Buller, the proprietor, compromised with sparse sandwiches, eggs-on-toast, scotch woodcocks, cornish pasties, and a dozen or more culinary frills and furbelows, a perfect geography book of unsubstantial gewgaws. And lest, after such trifling, the yawning stomach should still cry for more, there was another tour of the British Isles or the Continent available in the form of flatulent Eccles cakes, Bath buns, Bury simnels, Bakewell tarts, Banbury cakes, Swiss rolls, and meringues Chantilly. The whole topped-off with a wash of Indian, China or Russian tea. Let the trenchermen go and eat the ordinary at the commercial "Barley Mow" (R.A.C. Inn., C.T.C.,) or the more dignified "Herald Angels" (A.A.**, R.A.C.). Peter's Pantry was for the thrifty genteel, the underpaid clerk or typist, or the gastric carefree who could, without internal protest or spasm, load their stomachs with puff and weight.

It was about noon when Littlejohn entered the place on his way from Mrs. Myles's and business was just warming-up. He chose a table in a quiet corner, only to be joined, a moment later, by a nervous-looking clergyman, who, in spite of the number of empty tables scattered nearby, seemed to prefer the security of the big detective's companionship and ordered a boiled egg, lightly done, if you please. Littlejohn asked the waitress if he could see the proprietor, and was told that Mr. Buller was out at the moment, but was due to return at any time. He called for a coffee to justify his presence there meanwhile.

The place was dark and imitation candles, with feeble filaments, set in sconces in an attempt to give an olde worlde atmosphere, failed miserably to do anything but create a morgue-like feast of spectres. The only bit of cheer about the place was in the shop in front of the café, into which boys wearing the caps of some school or other, came and went and bore away quantities of doughnuts and custard tarts.

A funeral party was in progress, too, and the black-clad celebrants occupied a long table mounted on a dais at the far end of the room. Having disposed of their duties to the dead, they were, as far as rationed bake-meats would allow, discharging their dues to the living by cheering-up the widower with quips and chatter, which caused him to smile with becoming restraint. Laughter or tears did not impair his appetite, however, and he ate his way steadily through several plates of canned tongue, piles of bread, large helpings of tinned pears and innumerable sweet cakes, with sublime contempt for the Ministry of Food and greatly to the satisfaction of the other guests, who said one to another that he was "taking it well".

Enthroned among the rest of the customers sat a portly man, with a bald head, like an egg thrusting itself from a deep, stiff collar. He was the mortgagee of the premises and came regularly every day to eat two boiled eggs, which, in their white cups, looked like small replicas of him. Now and then, he would raise his eyes, which were like cloudy-grey poached eggs, from his plate and scan the place critically, as though putting the whole lot under the auctioneer's hammer then and there. On the table adjacent to Littlejohn and his parson, who by this time was chasing the underdone slime oozing out of his cracked eggshell across his plate, a crowd of men began to play dominoes and soon covered the baize cloth with strings of spots and blanks. They played with intense preoccupation and gravity, shouting with enthusiasm as they pursued their courses, and concentrating as if the whole world depended upon their being able to keep up the endless chain of black specks. The parson smiled at Littlejohn, nodded his head in the direction of the players and mumbled "Domino, dirige nos!" blushed to the roots of his hair, rushed off to pay his bill and was not seen again.

Littlejohn was relieved when the waitress arrived to inform him that Mr. Buller was in his office, and could now spare him a few minutes. The girl led him upstairs to a small room, where sat the proprietor ready to give audience. Peter Buller was a small, thick-set man with a pleasant, round, clean-shaven face and a head of thin grey hair, plastered carefully down. He had started life as a grocer's boy, but after marrying a masterful woman, had launched-out into confectionery and, then, catering. He was holding Littlejohn's card between a thick finger and thumb and looking perplexed, when the detective entered. He seemed relieved when he learned that the visit concerned only the history of his late father.

"He's been dead these ten years, Inspector," said Buller. "But, no doubt, I can help you if you'll say exactly what you're after."

"Your father was the last man to see the murdered pair alive, with the exception of the actual killer, of course..."

Mr. Buller shuddered.

"...I'm wondering whether or not he spoke to his family about events of that evening. More freely, I mean, than he did in his evidence before the coroner."

"No, he didn't, Inspector. As a matter of fact, the whole business seemed to get thoroughly on his nerves. He used to go off at the deep-end if any of us mentioned it at home."

"It made a deep impression on him, then?"

"Yes. In fact, he was never the same again after it. It struck us all that he got it into his head, that if he'd ordered the pair of them off the moor, the crime would never have been committed."

"Strange, wasn't it, Mr. Buller?"

"Yes. After the inquest, he had a sort of breakdown for a time. Got morose and… and… well, he started drinking. I'm sure it shortened his life."

"He was working for Sir Caleb Haythornthwaite at the time?"

"Yes. Not that he cared for the job. He'd been with the Myles family all his life, until the old lady sold-up, and naturally, at his age, he couldn't take-on another job. He didn't take kindly to changing bosses, I can tell you."

"Did he go back to his job as gamekeeper after his breakdown?"

"On and off. He carried on for two more seasons, and then his health began to fail. So he retired and went to live with my married sister."

"He'd enough to retire on, then?"

"No. Mrs. Myles granted him a small pension, though how she managed it in her straitened circumstances, I don't know. But that family were always good to their servants. Haythornthwaite ought to have been the man to look after him, as his last employer, but Sir Caleb hadn't got it in him to be generous."

"Just one more question, Mr. Buller, then I'll leave you to your business. Do you know what kind of cartridges your father used in his gun?"

Peter Buller looked startled.

"Here, Inspector, what are you getting at? You're surely not associating him with the crime! That's quite unthinkable. Although I say it myself, there wasn't a better, more upright man in Hatterworth than my father, and that he should have shot anyone is absolutely out of the question."

"This enquiry is a routine question, Mr. Buller, and in no way implicates your father. I'm enquiring concerning the type of cartridges used by everyone hereabouts..."

"Oh. Well, when I was a nipper, I often went out on the moor with him, and I handled his gun and his cartridges. He bought his supplies a hundred or more at a time from Huddersfield... Ashworth and Hall's."

"What kind of a load...? The size of shots, I mean."

"Mixed. Fives, with a few fours among them, specially made-up by the gunsmiths. He was very fond of a mixed load. Fours gave him hard-hitting and, well, the addition of fives gave him a larger number of shots than if they'd been all fours. You follow?"

"Yes."

"Perhaps it was a bit of a fad he had, but I think he was right. He convinced Mrs. Myles, and she had the same kind of loading, only in a better class of cartridge... and so did Sir Caleb, later."

"Is that so? The mixture seems very popular round here."

"Yes, it was. A lot of the local men, poachers included, used them. My father loaded his own for quite a long while. I used to help him do it. Then, Ashworth and Hall started to make-up a special cartridge which was almost as cheap as the home-made, and it saved time, of course, to get 'em ready-made."

"Yes. Well, I'm much obliged for your help, Mr. Buller, and sorry to take-up so much time at your rush-hour."

"That's all right, Inspector. My wife's below and keeps an eye on things, you know."

Littlejohn followed Peter downstairs and they were met at the foot by a fat, bustling little woman who looked daggers at them.

"Come along, Peter," she said to her husband. "The place is crowded... you ought to know better than sitting chattering at this time o' day. Get off to the cash-desk; there's quite a queue there, and I can't look after it with these new waitresses... never heard of such a thing..."

Sheepishly, Buller bade his visitor good-day and entered a small glass pen in the shop. Dominoes clicked incessantly, and Mrs. Buller dashed around, endeavouring to increase the tempo of the waitresses. Littlejohn extricated his overcoat from the tangled mass of clothing which dangled from the only hat-stand in the place, and made a hasty departure on the direction of a substantial lunch.

CHAPTER XIV

The Rum Flask

I often wonder what the Vintners buy
One-half so precious as the Goods they sell.

OMAR KHAYYAM

THE THREE RUM BOTTLES WHICH THREE-FINGERS HAD SCATtered on his last trail revealed nothing in the way of fingerprints but copious quantities of those of the tramp himself. They were bottles of the common type, which could be obtained from any pub, and it was impossible to trace whence they had come. Their contents, however, were a different matter. The Scotland Yard expert in alcoholic beverages grew quite lyrical about them.

"You'll not get that kind of stuff nowadays for love or money," he told Littlejohn over the telephone. "It's quality Number 1., Jamaica. It's probably been in the cask for forty years or more, and is prime, except for the lacing of drugs which some irreverent person's put in it."

"Is that so. But when you've finished rhapsodizing over it, is there anything about it which will help us in laying its original owner by the heels?"

"Oh, that's another matter, of course. But look for somebody who's bought in bulk and kept it. The average stuff you'd get from an ordinary wine-merchant, would probably be a blend of No. 1 and No. 2.

"No. 2 is inferior, and lacking in full flavour and aroma—a bit like Demerara and blended the same. If discretely mixed, can't be detected, except by the expert, but being cheaper, gives either more profit or makes the price more acceptable. Your sample, I'd say, was made in the old-fashioned small still—they rarely use 'em now, hence the deduction about the age—and comes from a spot where soil and climate make for the finest product. That's about all…"

"Thanks for the help, and if I'd a bottle of the untainted real stuff, I'd send it to you…"

"Oh, you might track it down, you know. Don't forget me if you do. Good-bye."

Superintendent Haworth, who was hobbling around with the help of a stick and chafing at being unable to rush briskly about as was his wont, listened to one end of the conversation and looked anxiously at Littlejohn as he hung-up the police-station telephone. The Inspector told his colleague what he had heard.

"We'd better send a man round to the local wine-merchants and licenced grocers, as well as the pubs, to enquire about their rum stocks, past and present, then," said Haworth.

"Yes. A sound idea. I'm beginning to think that when we discover where Three-Fingers got his rum from, we'll be getting warm concerning who killed him. Don't you agree?"

"Oh, yes. But somebody must have supplied it originally to the murderer, so best try all the retailers."

"Yes. Probably we'll find they only stock a medium quality, though, and not the small-still type. And maybe, the stuff was bought a long time ago. I suggest that as well as the local trade sources which you mention, we also have a word with the estate agents. I believe Haythornthwaite, for instance, bought Spenclough Hall lock, stock and barrel, and I take it agents would handle the sale. Did the inventory include a wine-cellar, and if so, was there rum in it?"

"Hullo. Got your eye on Sir Caleb?"

"Well, there's a nigger in the woodpile there, you know. The sums he paid to Sykes before his death are suspicious. Haythornthwaite was sheepish about them, and his excuse about their being payments for patents didn't seem convincing to me. Mrs. Myles mentioned the dirty work which went on in connection with certain of her firm's patent rights. Might not Sykes have known something, too, and been blackmailing Sir Caleb?"

"Yes, that's feasible."

"Another thing, too. Three-Fingers is reported to have been very pleased with himself after the re-opening of the case. That may have meant that, on hearing that Sykes didn't murder Trickett, but that both of them were shot by a third party, he at once remembered seeing somebody on the Moor at the time of the crime. Assume that he immediately made contact with that somebody, and found a victim for blackmail. You can imagine his satisfaction. Having called for a part of his spoils, Three-Fingers is given the doctored bottle of spirits, and has no more sense than to drink the lot practically at one sitting. Find the donor, find the triple murderer!"

"We'd better set about finding-out, then, whether Three-Fingers was seen in the region of Spenclough Hall about the day of his death, then."

"Yes. Or elsewhere. Who are the leading estate agents here?"

"Taylor and Collins, in the Market Place. They handle most of the large stuff. In fact, short of going out of town, you'll find the bulk of big property deals in these parts have gone through their hands. They've been established since before my time, and are of good reputation."

"I think I'll cover that angle myself, Haworth. Perhaps you'll put one of your men on the trade enquiries."

"Yes. Right away."

"As regards the gunshots, I'm afraid that's a forlorn hope. Ashworth and Hall's cartridges seem to have been the vogue in the days of the first crimes, and the 4. and 5. loads seem to have been pretty general. I gather that Buller favoured them and converted his employers and most of his pals to his views, too. Nearly everybody used the mixture."

"A pity, but there it is. I thought at first that we were on something there."

Later that afternoon, Littlejohn called at the offices of Taylor and Collins and was ushered into the presence of Mr. Dawson Taylor, great-grandson of the founder of the firm. Mr. Taylor was a tall, heavily-built man with a paunch so large that he seemed to be leaning backwards. He had a peculiar cast in one eye, due to being struck by a "peggy", a game at which he was an adept in his boyhood. The defect gave him the appearance of looking in two directions at once and Littlejohn, seated before the estate agent at a desk cluttered-up with dusty papers, sale bills, rent-books, and accounts in huge paper-clips shaped like hands, was frequently surprised to find that whilst one eye was looking to the left of him in the direction of the office door, the other was fixed benignly on him. In the adjoining saleroom, an auction was in progress, and the interview was punctuated by alternate bouts of loud and excited bidding and long, eloquent silences, broken by the raucous, pleading voice of Mr. Taylor's clerk, urging his audience to greater efforts and lauding to the skies each and every piece of junk placed under the hammer.

Littlejohn, after introducing himself, decided that perhaps a cautious approach was necessary. Mr. Taylor looked like a *bon-viveur* who, in his cups, might easily grow confidential to his boon companions, and betray in full the purpose of the present interview.

"We've reason to think that the local character, Bill o' Three-Fingers, either stole or was given a bottle of rum on the day of his death. This was either drugged when he got it, or he subsequently was given poison in some way or other and drank the rum just before he died. We're anxious to trace the place of origin of this spirit. Expert opinion on the rum reports it to be of exceptional quality, and it strikes me, Mr. Taylor, that it might have been from the cellar of some large house in this locality. Perhaps you could help by informing us whether or not you've handled such liquor in recent years."

Mr. Dawson Taylor swivelled his head round, the better to fix Littlejohn with his good eye.

"That's a rum question to ask," he said in a deep, rumbling voice, and seemed disappointed that Littlejohn did not laugh at his pun. He scratched his bristly, grey beard meditatively. During the silence the sound of furious auctioneering could be heard in the neighbouring salerooms.

"Wot am I bid for this lovely wash-hand-stand, ladies and gents… solid mahogany… marble top…"

"Four and six," from a shrill woman.

"Hey, missus. I wouldn't insult it by accepting yer bid. I'd rather give it yer…"

"Five bob…"

A fusillade of threepenny increases and the thing went for six-and-nine.

"Now wot am I bid for this luvely brass-knobbed, double bedstead… slep' in by Charles one, or I've bin misinformed…?"

Mr. Dawson Taylor was consulting his books and papers, but did not seem to strike any trail.

"Rum, rum, rum..." he muttered... "Most unusual thing for sale..." One of his eyes ran down the ledger; the other seemed fixed on the fireplace.

"Did you handle the sale of Spenclough Hall, Mr. Taylor?"

"It wasn't sold... it's still the property of the exors. of old Thomas Lightbody. Sir Caleb Haythornthwaite holds a long lease. I handled that... but why it should interest you, I don't know."

"Was there a wine-cellar, which went with the furniture and other stuff?"

"Oh, yes. But that's twenty years since."

"Was there any rum among the effects?"

"Now, you're asking me. I'll have to hunt-up the bill of contents. It'll be in the records in the cellar. Just a minute."

Mr. Taylor strode to the door of the general office.

"Willie!" he bawled. "Just get up the Spenclough Hall bundle from the cellar, quick, that's a good lad, and bring it in to me here."

In a very short time, a diminutive office boy, who looked as though a wash behind his ears and a holiday in the fresh air would do him a world of good, entered with a dusty parcel, swept off the dirt with a duster, and opened it for his chief's inspection. Mr. Taylor rooted among the contents for a minute or two, and then produced a lengthy inventory consisting of scores of long sheets clipped together. He consulted it rapidly.

"Garden tools... hm... hm... hm... washing-copper... laundry utensils... hm... hm... hip-bath, meat-safe... hm... hm... Here we are. Choice wines, contents of wine cellar... port, sherry, hm hm... whisky... burgundy... claret... rum... hm, hm... one and a half-dozen bottles Hot Jock Jamaica... pah, rotten stuff... no quality."

"You mean, it's of inferior grade?"

"Oh, yes. Evidently, the old chap wasn't as keen on his rums as his whiskies and his wines. He'd some fine Hocks and Clarets, but I don't know what he was thinking of when he bought his rum. Perhaps just got it as medicine."

"That's all, is it? Has Sir Caleb inherited a good taste in wines?"

Mr. Taylor cocked his sound eye, which threw the other into more frightful relief and disarray.

"Naw. Too greedy… whisky and water's about his mark… and a lot of water at that. Different from his son, who can drink most others under the table."

"H'm. Any other cellars you've disposed of, in your recollection?"

"Oh, quite a few, but not locally. The only other in the district was Botley Hall, Jonathan Myles's place, when Mrs. Myles sold-up."

Littlejohn pricked up his ears.

"They'd a good cellar then, eh?"

"Oh yes, by gad. Mr. Jonathan had a pretty taste, and so had his wife. We sold some of the wines, I recollect, but she took some with her to her house up-town."

"What, exactly?"

Patiently, Mr. Taylor rose and yelled again for the anæmic Willie, who produced another dirty bundle similar to the one he had brought in previously. The inventory was eventually unearthed and ponderously perused by the estate agent.

"Yes. Here we are. Rum… four small casks, first-class Jamaica. 'Caxton and Roberts, prime small-still', three casks to be sold, one to Mrs. Myles."

"Ah!"

"Well, that seems to be the extent of what I can remember of rum sales…"

"I'm sure I'm much obliged for your trouble, Mr. Taylor. Do you mind keeping this visit confidential? You know how people take-on if they think you're poking into their private affairs."

"Yes, I do that,... glad to help... I'll keep it under my hat."

With one eye smiling on Littlejohn in friendly fashion, and the other staring moodily into distant space, the estate agent saw the Inspector to the door and wished him good day.

Next-door bidding was going-on excitedly.

"Seventeen and ten... seventeen and elevenpence..."

"Seventeen and twelvepence," yelled a frenzied woman's voice, oblivious of all but the lust for possession.

Back at the police-station, Haworth was waiting with the reports of two policemen who had toured the town searching for good rum. As far as the first-class stuff found in Three-Fingers' flasks was concerned, they had drawn a blank. Wine merchants, hotels and inns, not to mention the few licenced grocers, whilst keeping, in some cases, good stuff, did not rise to the quality described by the Scotland Yard expert. It was not in demand. As medicine, a cheaper brand was called-for; topers—and they were few—bought standard, second-quality spirits; connoisseurs in rum were totally missing.

"So you see, Littlejohn, your theory might bring something to light."

Littlejohn told his colleague of the information he had secured at the estate agent's. Haworth whistled.

"Mrs. Myles, eh? Well, that's a corker. Still, we might be barking up the wrong tree altogether. The fact that we can't find any rum to our standard now, doesn't mean there's never been any sold in these parts. You know, folk aren't drinkers like they used to be, and the excise has made the price of first-rate drinks prohibitive."

"All the same," said Littlejohn, "it gives us another thread to follow. We'd better concentrate on that next. Don't you agree?"

"Yes. Now, what had we better do?"

Haworth thought for a minute or two.

"We'll send a 'gas-man' to inspect the meter at Mrs. Myles's to-morrow, and he can lose his way and land in the wine-cellar. How will that do?"

"A bit risky, but perhaps worth while. He'd better go when the housekeeper is out shopping, however. She's a perfect dragon of a woman, that one, and will probably smell a rat. Find out her habits first, and act accordingly. As your man calls to read the meter, I'll slip round and have a word with the kitchen-maid. She might be informative when the old dragon's out of the way."

Haworth scratched his head perplexedly.

"Mrs. Myles… phew… what a commotion and what a surprise! Yet, come to think of it… yes, come to think of it, there's more unlikely people."

CHAPTER XV

Tradesmen's Entrance

I've heard of hearts unkind, kind deeds
With coldness still returning;
Alas! the gratitude of men
Hath oftener left me mourning.

WORDSWORTH

MIRIAM DEWSNAP, KITCHEN-MAID AT MRS. MYLES'S, NURSED in her comely bosom the eternal hope that one day the dream lover she had built-up in imagination, with the assistance of certain novelettes which she devoured when the housekeeper was not about, would materialize and release her from servitude. She had visions of motor-cars, diamonds and furs, and menials to wait upon her, but had no objection to modifying the dream to the occasion. The butcher's boy, the postman, the grocer's vanman, and even the coalman had each his little day and ceased to please her. One turned out to be furiously courting his master's daughter; another accidentally disclosed, after an undue period of dalliance, that he was the father of three; the vanman joined the forces without so much as a word of farewell; and the coalman, whilst an adept at rolling his eyes when covered with the dust of his trade, disclosed a hare-lip when properly washed, and thus shattered his chances for ever.

How was she to know that the handsome new gasman, who arrived ostensibly to read the meter, was a policeman in disguise, and had a wife and twin little girls in a distant town? The constables of

Hatterworth were too well-known to pass as anyone but themselves, so Haworth had borrowed Detective-Constable Blades from another force. Miriam set about him with her fine dark eyes and swaying hips right away. The coalman had once been heard to remark to his buddy that "Mrs. Myles's bit o' stuff was too comin'-on; even trying the vamp stuff on a chap with a hundredweight o' best nuts on his hump. Lord knows what she'd be like behind the cemetery walls,"—which, by the way, was a favourite spot for local couples after dark. D.C. Blades was inclined to agree with the man from the coal merchant's. It was all, of course, part of his job, but he thanked his stars that his missus and twins were twenty miles away.

"Come to read the meter," said the bogus gasman, after seeing the housekeeper safely off on the errand of making ninepence for fourpence from the greengrocer and the fish-man.

"New recruit, eh?" said Miriam, rolling her eyes and looking him up and down with approval. "It's not a quarter since the last chap called. You're before your time."

"Oh no, I'm not."

"Oh, yes you are."

"Well, I don't blame a chap wantin' to call a bit sooner," said the constable, crossing his fingers and grinning coyly.

Miriam gave-in. "The meter's in the cellar."

Blades knew that quite well from previous information from the gas-works. Otherwise, he would have needed to play the role of a sanitary inspector or waterman hunting for a leak.

"I'll show you the way..."

"Show me the cellar-door and I'll find it myself, thanks. I don't want to cause trouble."

"No trouble." Miriam had visions of being fondled whilst hunting for the switch.

As they reached the top of the cellar steps, the door-bell rang again.

"Oh, let 'em wait," snapped the maid, determined not to be frustrated.

"Better see who it is," said the false meterman. "Might be important. I'll wait."

"See you do, then. There's other things down there besides the gas, and there'll be a row if I'm caught letting folks free about the place." And with a fetching glance and a flounce, she went again to the tradesmen's entrance. Littlejohn stood at the door.

"Did I leave my pouch in the dining-room whilst I was waiting the other day?" he asked, fingering that object in his jacket pocket. Pleasant gentleman, thought Miriam. A bit on the old side, but well-dressed, kindly, and evidently out of the top drawer. Bet he'd make a girl the apple of his eye. She rolled her eyes, bared her white, even teeth, and stuck-out her bosom.

"Come in and we'll look," she said, and forgot the gasman.

"Doesn't look as if you get many visitors here," said Littlejohn, gazing round the desolate room, whilst Miriam played a game of hunt-the-tobacco-pouch in a fashion which displayed her figure and limbs to the full, and would have earned her the sack on the spot had the housekeeper unexpectedly turned-up.

"No, not at the front door," said the girl, rising from peering beneath the table, and smiling mysteriously. "But there's plenty of callers at the side-door..."

Underneath them, Constable Blades was prowling, torch in hand, on rubber-shod soles. The beam of light fell on walls festooned with cobwebs, heaps of coal deposited by the agitated coalman, old boxes waiting to be broken for firewood. In one corner stood a contraption of sheet-metal and wire for holding wines. A few bottles remained on it, separated into three groups. All the bottles were of the same kind, except an odd brandy or two.

"Oh, cripes!" said the interloper to himself, and then he took one sample of each group, except the brandy, and placed his spoils in the large bag which he carried for the apparent purpose of holding the fruits of his penny-in-the-slot customers. He crept noiselessly to the top of the stone steps, and soon his head appeared round the dining-room door. He ignored Littlejohn.

"Hey!" he hissed at Miriam, who had reached the stage of sitting on the table and swinging her legs as shown on the cover of her latest novelette. "Hey! 'ow much longer am I to wait on the cellar-steps?"

The maid put her snub nose in the air and looked at Blades down it.

"I'm busy. Find your own way… meter's under the steps," she answered, tightening her lips and closing her eyes as she removed them from the gasman to the gentleman.

Blades vanished and could be heard floundering down below again.

"Does Mrs. Myles ever leave her room these days?" asked Littlejohn.

"Oh, she sometimes potters about upstairs, but the stairs, especially goin' up them, nearly knock her out. I'll never forget the to-do last time she came down… in a temper it was, just because me and the housekeeper was in the garden and didn't hear her bell. But, she comes down sometimes on the quiet. Thinks I don't know—but she does."

"Is that so. When?"

"Well, I know for a fact, she was down only the other day. Doin' something on the sly, I'll be bound."

"Thought you wouldn't find out, did she?"

"Yes. But she'll have to get up earlier to catch me. She sent me off just after sourpuss—the housekeeper, I mean—had gone down town to pay the bills. Told me to go get her a packet of cigarettes… smoked all hers. Smokes like a chimney, does madam. She got quite mad at me, too, when I told her it didn't seem right to leave her alone, and perhaps I'd better wait until the housekeeper came back. Ordered me, ordered, if you please. Well, I left the side-door open and the catch up, because I'd only be twenty minutes there and back, and I hadn't a key. When I got back, the door was shut and locked. Lucky the kitchen window was open, so I climbed in."

"How do you know it wasn't somebody else who'd called, found the door open, and just fastened it?"

"I thought the same at first, and felt a bit put-out. Didn't like the idea of strangers prowling round. So, I snooped about a bit. There was a trail of dirty footprints about leading from the kitchen and up the stairs!"

"Go on!"

"Yes, there was, as sure as I'm standing here. Oho! milady, thinks I, now I see why you wanted to be rid of me. Entertainin' visitors, eh? But, I kept a still tongue about it. As much as my place was worth to mention it either to the missus or Mrs. Casey, the housekeeper. They're hand-in-glove, and if I didn't get well paid, I wouldn't stop another day playing at being odd-man-out, like."

"But even then, it might have been somebody just prowling, who made off when Mrs. Myles started stirring above."

"I tell you she must have come down. Else, why did I find her handkercher' in the hall near the cellar door? It wasn't there when I left the house. No, she'd been down and dropped it, the artful old thing, and then stayed mum about anybody calling. Never a word she said, although I asked her if she'd been disturbed while I was out. 'Why should I be disturbed?' she says, lahdidah like, and glaring at me as if she'd kill me with a look. 'Oh, I was just wonderin', madam,' I said. 'You're not used to being left, and with the tradesmen knocking about.' 'Nobody's bin,' she snaps, as large as life."

"When was that?"

"Why are you so nosey?" said the girl, eyeing Littlejohn with suspicious alarm.

"Only I thought I saw you down in town on Tuesday."

"Did you?" said Miriam, perking-up again and flashing a glance like a dentifrice advertisement at him. "Well, it was Tuesday, but I didn't go right into town… where were you?"

"Coming up this way."

"Then it *would* be me… but, of course, I didn't know you then, did I? I'll not miss you next time."

"Well, it's been nice to have a talk, and I'm sorry to have bothered you. I must have left the pouch elsewhere. Shall I go out by the back door?"

"No. Come the front way, but you needn't hurry. Mrs. Casey'll be about another half-hour yet."

Miriam was hoping her visitor would ask her when she had her evening off. Instead, he bade her good day and, letting himself out by the front way, departed without more ado.

Miriam pouted, regarded herself critically in the mirror in the hall, and wondered what other girls had got that she hadn't. She sighed dramatically. "Men are all alike," she told her image in the glass. "Ungrateful beasts! Just fool about, and when you're just beginning to enjoy yourself, they give you the air."

Then, remembering her second reserve, the gasman, she hurried to the cellar, hoping to take-up the chase where she had left off. But Blades had gone. He was already knocking at the door of Spenclough Hall servants' entrance. An elderly, plain-Jane of a woman in maid's uniform answered him. She was lethargic, and merely grumbled that it wasn't long since the meter-man was there before.

"Yes. We're getting a bit ahead of ourselves at the gasworks," said Blades. "If we go on like this, we'll be meeting ourselves coming back!"

The maid didn't seem disposed to crack jokes or bandy words, but led him to the cellar door. She made no offer to accompany him, switched on the stairs-light, and left him to his own devices.

"You know where it is," she said, and returned to her task of turning-out the drawing-room without waiting for a reply.

Five minutes later, Blades clumped back up the cellar steps. The maid heard him, and let him out at the side-door. He had found more wine on shelves, but arranged in neat and orderly fashion, and it gave him little trouble. He left with another bottle in his bag.

Meanwhile, Mrs. Myles had rung for Miriam and was questioning her concerning the noise of visitors, which she had heard going on downstairs. Miriam said it was only the gasman and the gentleman who called the other day, the big, clean, good-looking one. He said he'd left his pouch. No, they didn't find it.

Mrs. Myles's eyes blazed.

"And I suppose you did a lot of talking, as usual."

"No. Just hunted for the tobacco pouch."

"You lying little slut… I heard you chattering. What was it about?"

"It was private," said the girl, her cheeks flushing in anger.

Mrs. Myles's fingers closed round her wrist in a grip remarkable for a woman of her age.

"Leave go… you're hurting me… let me go… or… I'll hit you."

The old woman gave the wrist a deft twist. "Now, out with it, you hussy. Or, it'll be my turn to talk to the police. Oh, you needn't look pained. You little fool. Do you think I don't know where the odds and ends you think I don't miss have gone? They'll search your bag, and I shan't say I've given them to you. Don't imagine because I'm tied to my room, I don't know what's been going-on…"

Miriam tore herself free. She had sold the trinkets which she thought wouldn't be missed. They'd nothing on her. Her pent-up feelings burst forth.

"That's it… that's it, you old hag!" she screamed. "Tied to your room, indeed. Tied, my foot! Whenever you're left to yourself, you're all over the place. Think I don't know that, don't yer? Well, I do. I do, see? And if you want to know, I told Mr. Littlejohn 'ow, only last Tuesday, you got rid of me so's you could start your games. I told him somebody was here, too, and that you said nobody had been… Thought you'd done one on me, didn't you? Well, you didn't. You left your handkercher' down below, clever…"

Mrs. Myles's cheeks grew red, her lips trembled in uncontrollable, senile rage. Grasping the walking stick she used to help her about, she swung it and caught Miriam a savage blow across the face. A livid weal sprang on the girl's cheek almost before the stick had fallen.

"You… you… I'll kill you for that!" yelled the girl, and catching the bright, inexorable old eye of her mistress, burst into hysterical screams. The door had silently opened, and the next thing the maid saw was Mrs. Casey, scowling, protective of her mistress, and dark in her wrath. The housekeeper strode to Miriam, and struck her a ringing blow on the other cheek with the palm of her hand.

"And now be off and pack your bag, and get out, before I do something worse to you," she hissed, and Miriam fled.

Mrs. Casey hovered over Mrs. Myles.

"Leave me… leave me… I'm all right. Go," said the old woman.

Reluctantly, the housekeeper withdrew.

Mrs. Myles sat for a moment, deep in thought and panting from her exertions. She grew calm at length, and remained awhile like a shrivelled graven image.

Then, she stretched out a trembling hand for the telephone and dialled a number.

CHAPTER XVI

The Gorse Bush

There's shouting on the mountain-side,
There's war within the blast—
Old faces look upon me,
Old forms go trooping past.

W. E. AYTOUN

IN THE POLICE-STATION AT HATTERWORTH, LITTLEJOHN, ROSS and Haworth were standing at the window examining the contents of three test-tubes. The place smelled strongly of rum, for that was the subject of their investigation and their discussion.

"As far as my inexpert eye and uncultivated palate tell me, they're all three the same," said Littlejohn. "We'll send samples off to The Yard at once for examination, but I'm afraid they'll only confirm our verdict."

The other two men grunted disconsolately.

"So that means that both Mrs. Myles and Sir Caleb have the same brand of rum in their cellars," sighed Haworth. "We're up against another blank wall."

"All the same," added Littlejohn, "our little enquiry hasn't been without results. We've found out that Mrs. Myles was downstairs about the time Three-Fingers was in the town. Why did she take such trouble to get the servants out of the house? I'd better go to her place again, and ask her what she was doing. No use skirmishing on the fringe. We can go on like this, fencing and finessing, for ever. We'd better make a proper attack and be done with it. What do you say?"

"Agreed," replied Haworth, "but, you're dealing with a wily old bird, you know. You'll not get much change out of Mrs. Myles."

The telephone bell rang and Haworth picked up the receiver.

"Yes. Yes. This is Superintendent Haworth… just a minute."

The Superintendent held his hand over the mouthpiece.

"Talk of the devil! It's Mrs. Myles. She wants a word with you, Littlejohn."

Littlejohn took the instrument, and listened.

"Yes. Certainly, Mrs. Myles. I'll come right away. Alone? Very good."

"She wants to see me right away, and alone," he said. "Now things are beginning to move." He took up his hat and prepared to leave. He was met at the door by Miriam Dewsnap, who charged in like a mad bull. She had no eyes for Littlejohn this time. She made straight for Haworth.

Miriam's once comely face was distorted with rage and much weeping. A long, angry bruise disfigured one side of it, and the outer edge of her eye was darkening ominously. She carried a shabby fibre suit-case and was dressed in a cheap, flashy coat and a neat hat which was awry on her disordered hair.

"I want to summons Mrs. Myles for assault, the old bitch!" she screamed, and burst into hysterical tears again. "After Mr. Littlejohn had left, she called me upstairs, screwed my arms up my back until I told her what I'd said to him, and then beat me up for it. I'll make her pay… What am I to do…? She's given me the sack and I daren't go 'ome. My father'll give me another good hiding for losing me job…"

Littlejohn made a hurried exit, leaving Haworth to deal with the woman and her problem, with Ross, the bachelor, hovering awkwardly around.

Mrs. Myles was waiting for him. Afternoon-tea was laid on a table at her elbow, and she poured out a cup for him and told him to make himself comfortable.

"I dare say you're wondering why I want you again, Inspector," she said as she settled back in her armchair. "Well, it's about this revived murder case, as you might guess, and also about the death of that rascal, Three-Fingers. Things have been moving a bit too fast for my old brain during the past few days. At my age, I want a bit of peace. I'm tired and can't bear upsets. I want to get something off my mind, and then be quiet again."

Littlejohn took out his notebook and pencil.

"Can you write shorthand, Inspector?"

"No, madam, I'm sorry to say."

"Well then, listen first. It'll tire me and fray my nerves if you don't listen properly. I can't have you scribbling there and making me go slow. Take a note or two, if you wish, but come back with a proper statement for me to sign afterwards. That'll be better. Jot down a point or two now and then as it strikes you, but bear with me and my foibles, please."

"Very good, madam. But I think I ought to warn you that I hold myself free to take down anything you may say, and it may be used in evidence later."

"All right. All right. Be done with the trimmings and let's get on. In the first place, you questioned my maid today, and got out of her some information concerning my movements on the day of the death of Three-Fingers. And you heard that I'd been downstairs, didn't you? No doubt, putting two and two together, you came to the conclusion that I went down to the cellar, doped a bottle of rum, admitted Three-Fingers, gave him the liquor, and sent him packing to his death. You did, didn't you? Didn't you?"

The old lady grinned craftily, and her face looked like a death's-head covered tightly with skin.

"That is your idea, not mine, Mrs. Myles."

"Don't fence with me, man! You thought all that, and perhaps more besides. And all on the evidence of a silly, sex-crazed, little strumpet of a kitchen-maid! Well, you're wrong. In the first place, I can manage downstairs *and* up... just about. But I'd never make those steep cellar steps and then to the bedroom. Heart's too weak. I did go down and I did get the servants out, but for a different reason..."

Mrs. Myles was talking fast, her cheeks were flushed, and she had to pause to take breath.

"...Those two, the maid and the woman, are robbing me. I've suspected it for a bit. They thought I'd never get downstairs again, so they could strip the place clean. There's God knows how many ornaments, pictures and miniatures gone from down below. That's what I was after when I was down. Well, I've sacked Miriam, and I'm after a new housekeeper. When I get one, Mrs. Casey goes, but not before she's restored all she's taken! I gave that little rotter something to remember me by, too, I'll tell you. She's probably got a lovely black eye by now. I couldn't keep my hands off her."

The old woman chuckled, sipped her tea, and passed cigarettes to her visitor.

"But that's not all the tale, by any means. You bobbies also sent somebody disguised as a gasman, who carried-off some of my best bottles of rum... A pretty trick to play on a helpless old woman. How you can sit there puffing my cigarettes and look me in the eye, I don't know! I suppose you were out to prove that the rum that killed Three-Fingers was the same brand as mine. There's not much of that kind about these days. Most modern rum's like modern ways. Shoddy. Well, I'll forgive you, because you're only doing your duty.

Not only that, I'll tell you something that'll make your hair curl. You'll probably find that my rum and that which Three-Fingers drank himself into eternity with, are the same stuff."

Littlejohn smiled. "You're right, Mrs. Myles. We've done that already."

"I thought so. A fast worker, aren't you? That's why I want to tell you my tale, and be left in peace. Can't stand being buzzed around and quizzed by anybody. Now, tell me one other thing. Did the gasman go to read Sir Caleb's meter and rifle his wine-cellar at the same time, like he did here?"

"Yes."

"Aha. Then you probably found the same brand of rum there, too. Eh? Don't look surprised… He bought some of our stock of rum… Clarets and Hocks, too, for that matter, damn him, when we sold out at the Hall. He did it through an agent, you can be sure. Otherwise, I'd have poured the lot down the sink rather than let a drop of that good stuff pass down his ugly, ignorant throat. Doesn't know the difference between Liebfraumilch and Milk-Stout! But let's be getting on."

She rose and took from a drawer a pair of field glasses. Then she moved to the window of the room. Dusk was falling, but the distant moorland, with the winding ledge of a road, was still visible. "Come here."

She gave Littlejohn the glasses. She pointed to a spot on the road, which could be seen dipping from the moor on its way to the outskirts of the town. "See that house…? Know it?"

"Yes, I think so, Mrs. Myles. I was there the other night. Spenclough Hall."

"Right. That's where Three-Fingers got his rum, Inspector. I saw him leaving there on the morning he was killed. I spend a lot of time at the window, watching things coming and going on the moor and the road. I've seen you and your gang hovering about Sykes's remains several times. I've watched the spot where he was buried for over twenty years… I knew he was there, and when those volunteers, Home Guard you call 'em, don't you…? When they dug him up under my very eyes, so to speak, I knew that the burden of my conscience was soon to be lifted. It had to come, you know. Murder will out, won't it?"

She moved back to her chair and sat heavily down. Littlejohn was flabbergasted, not only at the mine which she had so suddenly sprung, but at the matter-of-fact way in which she had done it.

"I suppose you think I'm callous, talking about it so easily, Inspector. Believe me, I'm not. But, when you're my age and have been through what I've suffered, you'll take a lot to excite you. I didn't kill Sykes myself. But, I know who did… and his pal, Trickett, too. Sykes was murdered in cold blood. Trickett was shot in defence of me by a very faithful servant of mine, now dead. Buller, the gamekeeper. Haythornthwaite killed Sykes. And now you know…"

Littlejohn took down the confession itself in his notebook. He was not missing that at any cost. The old lady seemed to regard her story as told, however, and was busy gathering tea-things on the tray ready for their removal by the housekeeper.

"That's not all, is it, Mrs. Myles?"

"Surely, that's enough, Inspector!"

"Can't you give me more details than that? I want to know how it all occurred."

"I'm very tired, and it's getting my bedtime, man. I'll just give you another five minutes, and then you'd better be off. And think yourself lucky to have heard what you have… I might have died without speaking of it… Which reminds me of a play of my heyday… East Lynne. Let's get on, then."

"On the day of the murder, I'd been at the Elvers' at Waterfold. They'd some rough shooting and I had my gun with me. I was alone in the car, and coming home along the road you saw through the window. It was dusk as I passed the Horse and Jockey. The place was busy; there'd been a party on Haythornthwaite's shoot that day, and the beaters and other hangers-on were finishing-off the event properly. I drove on, and in less than three minutes passed another car, nose pointing towards Hatterworth, parked by the roadside. I'd got some distance past before I realized that it was Haythornthwaite's. I pulled-in, got out and strolled back. I wanted a word or two with Caleb. You remember, I told you I was thinking of instituting proceedings against him for stealing patent-rights. I thought I'd tell him so. I felt quarrelsome, and just ripe for a row."

Mrs. Myles licked her dry lips, almost with relish.

"There was nobody about, so I stepped on to the moor, peering about to see if Haythornthwaite was anywhere near. I'd hardly set foot on the turf, than a shot was fired. As you've no doubt heard, it was too dark for potting at birds. I thought there'd been an accident, so set-off in the direction of the noise. Just as I was getting near the scene of the tragedy, a man rose to his feet. Apparently, he'd been kneeling over the body. It was Haythornthwaite. I'd know his figure anywhere. He bolted for his car and, before I'd decided what to do, the engine was going and he was off with the wind to Hatterworth. 'At last I've got you, my beauty,' I thought, and rushed to the place where he'd risen from. There was Sykes, sprawling, dead, his blood all over the wimberry bushes."

The old lady paused, her eyes glassy, her lips twitching, as though, in memory, she were once again on the ghastly spot.

"But, somebody else had heard the shot as well. Jerry Trickett lumbered over the turf, his gun under his arm, and the worse for drink. He stood there, snorting for a minute, taking in the scene in the dying light, and then bellowed with rage at me. I was unarmed, but he must have thought that Sykes's gun, which was lying there, was mine. 'So, you've caught-up with him at last, have you, you bitch?' he snarled. 'Well, you're not goin' to get away with it. He was my pal and, by God, I'll make you pay.' He raised his gun, probably with the idea of holding me up and taking me down to the lock-up or something. I didn't like the look in his eye. I'd no idea that the gun wasn't loaded, as it proved afterwards. 'Look here, Trickett,' I said, 'I've not done this. He was dead when I found him. But, I know who did do it.' Jerry was too befuddled to listen to reason. He thrust his gun-barrels at my chest. I wasn't going to stand that. I just got hold of them and twisted them away. We tussled for a second or two, and then a third visitor arrived. Trickett broke away from me and raised his gun again. The newcomer fired, and down went Jerry like a ninepin. It was Buller, my old gamekeeper, who'd fired the shot."

Littlejohn listened spellbound, not uttering a word. The scene on the darkening moor unfolded itself before his imagination. Mrs. Myles poured out a cup of the cold tea and wetted her lips with it.

"We faced each other there, appalled. I told Buller what had happened. At first, we thought of fetching help, and telling the police the full story. Then, we realized what it would mean. It was obvious that Sykes must have been blackmailing Haythornthwaite, and that meeting him alone, Sir Caleb had taken the bull by the horns and removed him. I was known to have a grudge against all three of them. In fact, I'd made a public parade of my feelings. How was I to fare if accused of the crime? Haythornthwaite might deny it, and accuse me of trying to saddle him with it. Besides, however timely Buller's arrival might have been, he'd no justification for shooting my assailant, even if his tale were believed. He'd get gaol for manslaughter, if he missed the rope for murder. It seemed hours before we decided what to do, although it must have been merely a matter of minutes. I had a sudden brainwave. The quarrel between the two dead men was the talk of the town. Buller had come from the Horse and Jockey, and said they'd just had a row there. Suppose we buried one; the odds were that the other would be suspected and be thought to have fled after the crime. I told Buller and he fell-in with the scheme at once. In the boot of my car was a small spade, which Micky used to use. He was a bit of an antiquary, and used to go hunting for flints and other stuff on the moor. Buller set about digging a grave in the dark…"

Mrs. Myles's eyes were fixed stonily ahead, as though she were living through that awful night once more. Outside, darkness had fallen, and the view through the great window was cut-off as though by a deep blue curtain. A dead coal fell into the hearth with a tinkle.

"Draw the blind and put on the light…"

Littlejohn did as he was bidden.

"In less than half-an-hour, we'd buried Sykes. Trickett we left as he was. I'd a pocket torch, and we shaded it to a mere pin-point of light and carefully obliterated all our tracks, wiping my fingerprints from Trickett's gun, too. No doubt, you and your modern ways would have seen through it all. But Pickersgill was on the case and not too bright. Good job he didn't bring in his father-in-law, Inspector Entwistle. He's as sharp as a bunch of needles. We tucked Sykes away under an old gorse bush, about a yard down. I've watched that bush ever since, from the Hall and from here. When it shed its green and its blooms with the autumn, I shuddered, lest, laying bare the soil beneath, it might betray my secret. And then, with the Spring, came foliage and flowers again, throwing a blanket over the dead. So, it's gone on for more than twenty years. I'm glad it's over. I'm tired…"

Littlejohn was in a quandary. The old lady was exhausted, but at her age one couldn't leave a statement like that unrecorded and unsigned overnight.

"Suppose I write out briefly what you've told me now; would you sign a statement to-night, Mrs. Myles?" he asked.

"Yes. Do it downstairs in the dining-room, though. Mrs. Casey will find you pen and paper, I'm almost dead with weariness. I'll be getting in bed meanwhile, and I'll sign it there. Mind you, I expect you to bring this home to Haythornthwaite. Poor Buller, rest his soul, is past caring. Never got over that night. Turned to drink to forget it, and drank himself away."

She rang the bell for Mrs. Casey, and when that grim woman arrived, issued brief instructions concerning the provision of writing materials. Littlejohn followed the housekeeper down the dark stairs, which seemed to descend into the pit itself.

Mrs. Myles rose when she was alone. Wearily, she made a tottering tour of the stuffy room. She smiled at the family portraits, her husband and boys, and stood for a moment before the picture of the moor, so much admired by Littlejohn. Regaining her chair, she sat thinking awhile, and finally seemed to make up her mind. Taking a pencil from a drawer in the table, which she unlocked with a key from her pocket, she wrote a brief note and tucked it under the pink tape of a bundle of papers marked "Copy Will", also in the drawer. Then, she took out a large pill-box, bearing the label of a chemist and a description in her own hand. "Capsules for destroying dogs." Years old, she mused. Cocker spaniels, setters, a fox-terrier, a bobtail sheep-dog... they'd all taken release from weariness and old-age from that box. And now, their mistress, too. She extracted two capsules, slipped them in her mouth, swallowed them with a draught of cold tea and composed herself, her hands gently folded in her lap...

CHAPTER XVII

Council of War

Their winding-sheet the bluidy clay,
Their graves are growing green to see:
Now wae to thee, thou cruel lord,
A bluidy man I trow thou be.

BURNS

SNOW WAS FALLING AS LITTLEJOHN, HAWORTH AND ROSS arrived back at the police-station after their investigations into the death of Mrs. Myles. There was no mystery about it. The old lady, apparently weary of existence, disturbed in her mind concerning the outcome of her confession, and overcome by the rapid rate of developments in the case, had taken a dose of prussic acid, which she had apparently been holding against an event such as this. She now awaited an inquest; another victim of the series of evil events set in train by Haythornthwaite.

"We must work quickly," said Haworth, shaking the snow from his greatcoat and swishing the water from his hat into the fireplace of the charge-room. He was still hobbling a bit, but now wore a shoe, split down the toe-cap, over his damaged foot. Ross did not remove his overcoat at once, but stood musing on the hearthrug, his thumbs tucked in his pockets and his face a study in depression. Littlejohn's pipe was hissing from a catch of snow. His face was ruddy and his nose red. His hat was on the back of his head. He removed his coat and hat, shook them violently in the corridor, and hung them on a hook behind the door.

"We must get something before the inquest, Littlejohn," continued Haworth, lighting a cigarette and ejecting jets of smoke down his nostrils. "You're the chief witness here, and by the time it comes out that the suicide occurred after your visit, we must have nailed Haythornthwaite in one way or another. If your evidence before the coroner gets around, which it's bound to do, Mrs. Myles will probably be branded as the murderess. It's all round the town what you're here about now, Littlejohn, and it'll be said that she took the short way out when liable to arrest. We don't want that. It's not fair to the old woman and, what's more important, it'll hamper our movements in roping-in Haythornthwaite."

"Yes," butted-in Ross. "But how are we to get him, sir? Inspector Littlejohn was alone with her when she confessed. She signed no statement; whatever she did say might simply be smashed by a good lawyer, as the ramblings of an old woman in her dotage, and the evidence of one police-officer without witness, no matter how reputable he may be, will hardly pass as convincing. Looks to me as if we're in a jam, unless we can trap Sir Caleb into a confession."

Littlejohn puffed away at his pipe with undisturbed good humour.

"That's what we aim at doing, Ross," he said. "We'd better settle down and cudgel our brains as to ways and means. I believe what Mrs. Myles told me. She was a perfectly lucid woman, with a keen mind, in spite of her years, and I'd stake my reputation on her telling the truth. The point now is, whether to face Haythornthwaite with the visit of Three-Fingers and the death of Sykes, or continue our search for someone who saw the tramp near Sir Caleb's place or coming and going there..."

The outer door opened, admitting a blast of the east wind, which swept through the building like a hunted ghost. There was a sound of footsteps along the passage accompanied by grunts and snorts, and Ex-Inspector Entwistle entered the room.

The old police-officer's beard was covered in snow and his breath came and went in brief gasps. His face glowed from his exertions, but his lips were blue. He stood for a moment recovering his breath, removed his hat and flicked off the snow, and unbuttoned his overcoat, which he shook all over the floor, dog-fashion, without taking it off. Finally, he unwound a thick woollen scarf from round his ears and throat, and smiled sadly on the three officers.

"Evenin'," he said briefly, and flopped in the nearest chair.

Haworth hurried to a cupboard, poured a tot of brandy into a glass, and passed it to the visitor.

"Here, get that into you, Inspector," he said. "This is a bad night for you to be abroad. Let's all go in my office. It's cosier, and we'll get this cold properly out of our bones."

"Ah couldn't stop indoors to-night," said Entwistle as they adjourned to the smaller room. "Ah've just heard about Mrs. Myles, and feel I must come and talk to you about it. Charlie and his wife have gone to th' pictures, which makes it easier for me to slip out. What my daughter'd say if she knew ah was away from th' fireside on a neet like this, I don't know. Ah thought maybe ah could help a bit. You see, ah knew Mrs. Myles very well. We grew up together from children. Ah came from the village where she lived. Her father was th' squire."

The old man did not tell them how, as a young constable, he had fallen in love with the daughter of the lord of the manor. He remembered how in schooldays they had bird-nested together and gathered wimberries on the moor. He'd never fancied his chances with one so much above his station, but none the less, she'd been his first love. Whenever he had met her on the roads—and a fine figure she had cut on a horse, daredevil rider, too—they'd stopped for a word. When, at length, she had come as Mrs. Myles to Hatterworth, where he was later to rise to chief of police, they'd resumed their old friendship and he'd watched her happy home life, her fine growing boys, and the increasing prosperity of her husband's firm with a secret joy, for he never wished her anything but well. Then, the decline of her fortunes, the loss of her boys, the end of Myles's foundry, all came as blows to his spirit and he had stood helplessly by, unable to interfere. For twenty years or more, she'd shut herself up in the house up-town. Every Christmas he'd called to wish her the compliments of the season, and take her a few of his own eggs, and each time he'd found her more aged, but as vigorous in mind as ever. She was still his oldest and best friend. All that remained of the happier world he'd known long ago. Hearing of her tragic death, he made up his mind to get to the bottom of it and what had caused it, and to see that she was honourably acquitted of any sin which might be associated with it.

"Ah thought maybe ah could help a bit," he said again, looking at his three companions pathetically, his eyes asking a hundred and one urgent questions.

"Good of you to take all the trouble, Inspector," said Haworth. "We're just about to hold a conference on the very matter, and you may as well join-in. The background your experience will bring, will be invaluable, I've no doubt. You probably don't know it yet,—it hasn't gone beyond the three of us—that Mrs. Myles's death is intimately connected with those of Sykes and Trickett more than twenty years ago..."

"Ah guessed somethin' o' th' sort, but I'd be glad of some light on the subject."

"Well, I suggest that Littlejohn, who's been in charge of the investigations—and thank goodness he *was* on the spot—gives us all an outline of the case, and leads up to the state of affairs as they stand at present. The narrative'll clarify our minds, as well as giving you a full picture of what's happened."

Littlejohn's admiration for Haworth increased. His courtesy and respect for the long superannuated police-officer were exemplary. But, Haworth knew his man, too. Old Entwistle was no fool. He still had a shrewd brain and a huge fund of local knowledge. He was an invaluable ally in the forthcoming fight with Sir Caleb.

Littlejohn began his tale.

"The case begins really with the death of Mrs. Myles's husband. She was left with the business to preserve until her two boys were old enough to take over. Meanwhile, Caleb Haythornthwaite became manager. The promotion went to his head. Soon, he fancied himself the be-all and end-all of the business, grew too big for his shoes, proposed to Mrs. Myles, and came a cropper for his pains."

Old Entwistle omitted a throaty growl, like a good dog dreaming of evil things or hearing them prowling around.

"We know that Mrs. Myles and Haythornthwaite quarrelled and parted company, and that he joined a rival concern in the town. He also took his two hirelings with him, Sykes and Trickett, and other things as well, including certain patents belonging to Mrs. Myles. Goodness knows what else they carried away, too. Maybe, it was portions of the plant, tools, patterns of machinery. Anyway, there was something disreputable about the whole business, because as far as we can gather, Sykes began to blackmail Caleb when he became prosperous enough to pay-up. We've evidence of the amount Sykes accumulated from the fact that he left enough to make his mother comfortable for life. He didn't do that on a mechanic's wage. Haythornthwaite, when faced with the large sums he'd paid out to Sykes, said they were for patent rights. You know better than I do, and I've found it out from his old workmates, that whilst Sykes was an excellent man at his job, and one well worth his place in any foundry, he hadn't an ounce of inventive genius in him."

"That's right," muttered Entwistle, deeply interested in the narrative and sitting gazing intently at a spot on the floor, his beard resting on his ready-made tie.

"Haythornthwaite was running for local honours. He couldn't do with a man like Sykes for ever round his neck, with his blackmail and his impudence. Haythornthwaite was going places, as the Americans have it, and Sykes wasn't going to bear him company, if he could help it. Especially, as by this time, Enoch had quarrelled with his girl, who'd jilted him in favour of his bosom pal, and he'd taken to drink. Trickett, of course, was just a faithful hound to Sykes until they quarrelled, and even then, was ready to make it up, retaining a measure of his old loyalty, as we'll see later."

"A decent chap, was Jerry. Nowt much wrong with him, except that he backed the wrong horse…" interposed the old man.

"Well, Caleb was after a knighthood and had bought Spenclough Hall. Time to be rid of Sykes, he thought. He perhaps tried to buy him off. We don't know. But Sykes was sticking where he was. He was on a good thing, apparently. So Caleb must have contemplated killing him at a favourable opportunity. There may have been plenty of chances in a foundry, with so much dangerous machinery and material about, but perhaps Sykes was too wary…"

"He was lucky, you mean. Come to think of it, there was a mysterious accident there, when a pig of iron, being unloaded, fell from the first floor and just missed Sykes by inches. Lamed the chap standing next to him for life," cut-in Entwistle, looking-up bright-eyed. "Caleb was blamed for that. The men said he'd been messing around when they were unloadin', and interfering in things he knew nowt about. Very likely, he pushed-off that lump of iron."

"There you are, you see," continued Littlejohn. "But, at last, his chance came. Haythornthwaite was returning from shooting and, crossing the moor with, as he thought, nobody about, he met Sykes, drunk and floundering his way home in the fading light. He let him have it with his sporting-gun. Whether or not they quarrelled, we don't know, but no doubt, Caleb was getting ready to make it look like an accident, when suddenly he was disturbed. Mrs. Myles, who had discovered that certain of her firm's patents were being infringed by Caleb's company, was after his blood, and, finding his car parked in a lonely part of the moorland road, stepped out to find him. Caleb fled with her approach, leaving obvious signs of murder.

"But there were others on the moor that evening, as well. There was Trickett, with whom Sykes had just had a public brawl at the Horse and Jockey. He was following his friend, perhaps to try to make peace, who knows? Jerry was a harmless sort of fellow, and seemed anxious to shake hands and be friends again. He must have heard the shot, and hurried to the spot to find Mrs. Myles bending over the dead body of Sykes."

Littlejohn eased his body in the hard chair, stretched out his long legs, and re-lit his pipe.

"Mrs. Myles was the sworn enemy of the whole unholy trio of renegades. What more likely than that Trickett should think she'd killed Sykes? At any rate, he acted accordingly and accused her of it. He'd plenty of drink in him, and was too stupid to listen to explanations. He poked his gun at her, she resented it, and tried to push it aside. There must have been something of a tussle between them.

"Then number five arrives on the scene. This time, it's Buller, the gamekeeper, an old servant of Mrs. Myles's, who, from what I can gather, worshipped the ground she walked-on..."

"Not the only one," muttered Entwistle in his beard.

"Beg pardon?" said Littlejohn.

"All right, all right, go on, go on..."

"Things must have looked desperate for Mrs. Myles when Buller appeared. Trickett's gun wasn't loaded, but he was making movements as if to fire at her. Buller up with his gun, and shot Trickett on the spot. You can imagine what Mrs. Myles and Buller felt like when the heat of battle had died down. Two corpses on their hands. Should they call in the police, explain what had occurred, and accuse Haythornthwaite? Sitting here, conducting an inquest in cold blood, I ask you, gentlemen, can you believe such a fantastic tale? I'd find it hard to swallow, myself, had not a dying woman with nothing much to gain from lying about it, told it to me."

"If Mrs. Myles said it was so, it was so," said Entwistle, and Haworth nodded. "What we've to do, I take it, is to tear the truth out of Haythornthwaite."

"Yes. But to go on with my account... Mrs. Myles had a spade in her car. Buller buried Sykes. They removed all traces of their intervention, and left it looking as though Sykes had killed his former pal and bolted."

"Pah!" grumbled Entwistle. "I remember Charlie Pickersgill sayin' to me, 'You keep out o' this, dad. You're on the retired list. It's as plain as the nose on yer face, and I don't need any help'. He was too clever in his own eyes, was Charlie. All right for keepin' law and order, but not much good at owt else. To anybody who knew that moor properly, it was impossible, in the dry weather we were havin' then, to miss anybody's tracks, try as they would to wipe 'em out. But no, Charlie was so sure that Sykes had done it that he couldn't see any farther than his nose-end. Go on, Mr. Littlejohn, don't mind me. Only a rude old chap butting-in."

"So," continued Littlejohn, "the case rested, apparently solved, but with the killer missing, until the Home Guard dug-up Sykes. Then, Three-Fingers came into the picture. He was number six on the moor on the day of the crime. We know he'd been warned-off the preserves by Buller just before. The girl who was with him that night told me, too, that he recognized somebody—she herself didn't know who it was and Three-Fingers wouldn't tell her—prowling about. That must have been Caleb, for, no sooner was it noised abroad that Sykes and Trickett had both apparently been murdered together by a third party, than Three-Fingers was heard boasting about his turn of luck. He'd remembered whom he'd seen on the moor at the time of the crime, and was getting ready to cash-in on it. Not that his evidence would have been a hanging matter for anybody, but it might have caused embarrassing questions and brought to light goodness knows what. He called on his victim, was paid-off, and at the same time given a bottle of doped rum. The bottle was unidentifiable—the sort one might pick-up anywhere. The murderer forgot, however, that the rum was very special stuff. In fact, he probably didn't know himself, that it was special. He's reputed to have execrable taste in liquor! Mrs. Myles saw Three-Fingers leaving Spenclough Hall shortly before his death. I guess that Haythornthwaite hoped that the tramp would go on the moor, drink himself blind in the heather, and die there. Instead, he died on my hands and, luckily, we were able to rescue some of the rum. That's the story, gentlemen. We can take it or leave it. It's *probably* true, although we've no actual proof."

"In other words, we've to wring it out of Sir Caleb," said Haworth. "That's a tough proposition, and no mistake. We're not allowed third-degree methods here. In fact, we've overstepped our powers considerably in taking samples of rum from Myles's and Haythornthwaite's cellars."

"You don't mean to say you've been burgling wine-cellars," chuckled Entwistle. "Well! That beats the band."

"We had to do something desperate, Mr. Entwistle," replied Haworth. "It was a long chance and probably our reputations were at stake. But it's come off, and yielded results."

"Oh, aye," said the ex-Inspector. "But you've still the worst to face. Caleb's goin' to be a tough nut to crack. He's landed where he is by bein' unscrupulous and wily. It's a problem how to trip him up, and no mistake."

"Yes. That's our next big job."

Entwistle thought a moment.

"Ah remember telling the pair of you, when you came to see us that day in my hen-pen, that ah wanted this to be my last case. Ah'll take on th' job of laying Caleb by the ears. Ah know him better than any of you, and none of his ways are foreign to me. I've got a plan at the back of my mind, and want a bit of time to think it out. Ah'm an old man and ah've no reputation to lose. Ah'll take all th' responsibility for this job, if you'll both trust me."

Haworth looked at Littlejohn and Ross. Both nodded agreement.

"Right, then, but we'll want to know all about it before we set to work," he said.

"Good," said Entwistle and rose to put on his outdoor clothes. They helped him into his overcoat and swathed him in his scarf. "Ah'll just be back home in time. The pictures 'll be out in quarter of an hour, and they'll find me where they left me, by th' fireside.

Ah want no questions, and Charlie Pickersgill's to know nothing of this. Ah'll teach him to push my nose out of cases. Well, I'll bid you good night, and ah'll see you all in the morning at ten o'clock. Ah'll have to tell my daughter ah'm going out to change my library-book. Ah daren't make a move these days without a full account of my doings. Good night."

And the lively old man of eighty plunged out into the snow.

CHAPTER XVIII

Inspector Entwistle Takes a Hand

Give ample room and verge enough
The characters of hell to trace.

THOS. GRAY

PROMPTLY AT TEN O'CLOCK THE FOLLOWING MORNING, EX-Inspector Entwistle, otherwise the Emeritus Inspector, as Mrs. Littlejohn dubbed him, arrived at Hatterworth police-station. He was dressed-up to the nines for the occasion, which was probably a high-spot of his declining days, and how he had got past his inquisitive daughter was a subsidiary mystery. He wore a new cloth cap set squarely on his head, a smart dark-blue overcoat of pilot cloth, and a suit of grey homespuns. These were set-off by a new pair of fur-lined, suède gloves, and a hand-knitted scarf, which swathed his neck and ears, hiding a new, ready-made tie. He was smoking a cigar with the band still round it. Evidently the Emeritus Inspector had done well in the way of Christmas presents from his granddaughters! He took the helm immediately, greatly to the secret amusement of Littlejohn. His torpedo beard protruded aggressively, his eyes shone with the light of battle, and he rubbed his hands together, more from relish of the chase than to restore circulation.

He placed a bottle on Haworth's desk. The Superintendent picked it up, looked in astonishment at the old man, and passed on the object to Littlejohn.

"Well. What are they?" chuckled Entwistle.

"Sleeping tablets," replied Haworth.

The Emeritus Inspector had already been to Spenclough Hall, for he knew that at that time Sir Caleb would be at the foundry and his lady probably in the town among the shops. The elderly parlour-maid at the Hall was the widow of the son of a second-cousin of Inspector Entwistle, and hence was one of the family. Entwistle rang the front-door bell and his remote relative appeared.

"Well, Clara, compliments of the season, lass."

"Same to you and many of them, cousin Will. What brings you here so early in the morning?"

Clara Uttley was a lethargic woman of well over forty, and not too contented with her lot and the blows fate had dealt her in robbing her of her husband six weeks after they were married. She it was with whom the pseudo-gasman had made such heavy weather, but with her present visitor she thawed considerably. He was one of the family, so that was different! Besides, he'd always been good to her and treated her like a daughter. She owed him a good turn.

"Ah've come to see thee on a bit o' business, lass."

"Come in, then. What is it, cousin Will?"

"Now, Clara, ah want the truth. Ah want to know whether Three-Fingers was here last week on the day he died."

Clara Uttley's face was anæmic to begin with, but it turned a good deal paler at the question. She wrung her hands and fumbled with her apron. Emeritus fixed her with an innocuous paternal eye.

"Well…? Come on, lass. He was, wasn't he?"

"If I tell you, cousin Will, you'll not noise it abroad, will you?"

"Ah'll see that you come to no harm by tellin' me, if that's what you're after, Clara."

"Well, he was here. He came to the side-door, as large as life, and asked for the master, as cheeky as you please. He arrived hoity-toity at the back, and went-off cock-a-hoop by the front door. And then Sir Caleb had me in his study after, if you please, and gave me a good dressin'-down for not tellin' Three-Fingers he wasn't at home. As if he hadn't said he'd see him, mind you, when I said he was there axing for him. And then the boss says to me, 'Clara,' he says, 'you're not to tell a soul about this visit. If you do, or if I hear of it, you're out of a job and no references given.' Proper upset he was and jumping and twitching about just like he'd got St. Vitus' Dance, or somethin'. Well, after that, ah had to keep my mouth shut. At my age, jobs are hard to come-by, cousin Will. So I kept mum. Sir Caleb must have been afraid of bein' seen associatin' with such riff-raff, and I'm not surprised eether."

"Did Three-Fingers take anything with him?"

"Not that I saw."

"Not a bottle, or such-like?"

"If he did, it was in his pocket. Sir Caleb did go down the cellar, though, and brought up a bottle, but I thought they'd just be having a tot together, like. He might perhaps have given Bill the bottle. He was a proper old scrounger, was Bill, but the boss doesn't often part with somethin' for nothin', ah can tell you."

"Did Sir Caleb go right back to Three-Fingers when he came up from getting the bottle?"

"Ah can't rightly say. When he got up from the cellar, the boss said he'd left the light on below, and I was to go down and put it out. When I got back, he was upstairs doing something in his bed-room. Then, after about a couple of minutes, he came down and let Three-Fingers out at the front door. Let him out himself, too."

"Now, Clara, can I see Sir Caleb's room?"

"Eeh, for goodness' sake, cousin Will! Do you *want* to get me the sack? There's only cook and the girl in just now, but if the missus or Sir Caleb returns, ah'm done-for."

"Just for a minute or two, Clara. If you get caught, I'll say you didn't know I'd gone up. Ah'll take all th' blame. Which is the room? You stay dusting in the hall and, if anybody comes, start to sing *Beautiful Zion*, and leave the rest to me."

"All right. But ah'm warnin' you, cousin Will... It's first room on th' left. If anybody hears me singin', they'll think ah've gone potty with religious mania or some such like... Hymns isn't my strong point."

Ex-Inspector Entwistle mounted the stairs with measured tread. Five minutes later, still unperturbed, he descended them. In his pocket was a bottle he had found in one of the legs of a pair of winter pants under a pile of clothing in a drawer. It bore a local chemist's name.

"Thanks, Clara lass. You can trust me. Ah'll see you come to no harm."

"Ah know that, cousin Will. You're a proper caution! What are you up-to again? Ah thought you'd finished snoopin' thirty years since."

"Them that asks no questions, gets told no lies, lass. Be good."

"Be good, cousin Will, and take care o' yourself."

On his way to the police-station, Entwistle called at the chemist's mentioned on the bottle, and obtained the formula of the sleeping-tablets. Barbiturate group and tallying with that found in the rum bottle.

"Well. That's my share," said the Emeritus Inspector. "And ah hope it hangs him."

"We're very grateful indeed, Inspector, for your help. This is an invaluable contribution. In fact, this is going to finish Sir Caleb, I'm thinking."

Littlejohn nodded. "We'd better be seeing that gentleman and ask him a few questions again, I think..."

"And ah'll be gettin' along home," said Entwistle. "Ah've a lot to do in th' hen-pen. This cold weather keeps 'em indoors, and plays Old Harry with their layin'. Let me know what happens, won't you?"

"We certainly will, Inspector, and again very many thanks. We're going your way to the foundry. We'd better call right away on Sir Caleb, so we'll see you that far," said Haworth, slipping-on his great-coat. They bundled-up the aged one in his scarves and cap and coat again, and turned-out. The wind was in the east and cut like a whip. There were about four inches of snow on the ground. The air was crisp and clear, the snowfall had ceased, but the sky foretold more to come. The distant moors and hills looked like a vast white counterpane which some giant had heaved about on rising. Already men were abroad in the streets, shovelling the snow from the pavements and piling it up in the gutters, whence carts picked it up and bore it off to heaven knew where. Other workmen were throwing salt in the roadway. Footsteps were deadened and an eerie silence hung over the place. Passers-by, their heads down to the wind, bustled past, intent on getting indoors again.

Emeritus led his little party to the foundry gates. Beyond, a scattered lot of buildings, some new, some ramshackle. No order about the construction of the place. It had apparently started with a small nucleus, and additions had been flung round it as required. Inside, bedlam seemed to reign. Above all other sounds, the dull, metallic thud-thud of some great machine, beating rhythmically, and shaking the whole neighbourhood. Then a subsidiary racket, composed of innumerable ingredients, the howling of drills, the whine of lathes, the click of ratchets, the hum of gears, the steady blows of hammers of all sizes, the monotone of dynamos, the bark of riveting machines, and the hiss of steam. Two great chimney stacks and a battery of smaller chimneys vomited forth smoke. The air reeked with chemicals. In the yard beyond the gates, lorries were being loaded with great packing-cases filled with munitions of war. Crate after crate in endless succession. This was the hive which Sir Caleb Haythornthwaite had built-up almost from scratch. And probably his drunken son would pull it down in half the time, when the old man went.

There was a small gatehouse at the entrance to the yard. The lower halves of the windows were covered with gauze screens, marked "Cross and Haythornthwaite, Ltd.," in gilt lettering, but the door was panelled in plain glass. Through this could be seen a man, who looked like the traditional Chinaman, with a yellow face, slanting almond eyes, and a drooping black moustache. One almost expected that he was concealing a pigtail under the greasy cloth cap he wore. He was telephoning, and seemed to be browbeating someone. He was standing aggressively pawing the air, thumping the desk, and grimacing as though the person at the other end of the line were in his very presence. His eyes bulged and his putty-like cheeks grew red. The conversation ended, the Chinaman groped for the telephone stand, missed it a time or two, and then hung-up. He was still muttering to himself when Entwistle rapped on the glass panel. The man came to the door and immediately shed his bad temper.

"Well, if it isn't Mr. Entwistle," he said with a grin, which made his slits of eyes vanish completely into his head. "Ah were just havin' a row with a bookie about a football pool he's bin runnin'. We don't think we're gettin' enough for our brass... Eeh, Superintendent Haworth. Ah didn't see thee. Ah'd better be keepin' me mouth shut about bettin' and such like. What can ah do for you, Mr. Entwistle?"

"These two gentlemen want to see Sir Caleb, John Willie. Is he in?"

"Aye, go straight through. You know wheer th' offices are, doan't you, Mr. Haworth?" The Superintendent nodded. They bade the ex-Inspector good-bye and he went on his way home.

They passed through the yard, and entered the offices. There was a general office first, with rows of desks, walls filled with box-files, with a large staff busily writing and rooting among them. Then came the drawing-office. Desks, blue-prints, green-shaded lights, drawing-boards, T-squares, and men in their shirt-sleeves and wearing eye-shades. Somewhere in the vicinity was a typists'-room, emitting the sharp, crackling, machine-gun noises of batteries of typewriters going like mad, the tinkling of little bells, and the thud-thud of carriages being hurled back. Nobody interfered with the progress of the officers. Once past the keen scrutiny of the man at the gatehouse, their path to the managing-director's suite was clear. Curious eyes followed them, and now and then, someone who knew Haworth would greet him.

The private offices consisted of an entrance-hall, with the doors of Sir Caleb's room and that of his secretary to right and to left, and the board-room straight ahead. The door of the latter stood open, revealing a sumptuous carpet and a small board-table with four chairs, which testified to the limited control of the establishment. The waiting-room was opulently furnished, too. Mahogany easy-chairs, a round table, and a Wilton carpet on the floor. Hanging on one wall, a photograph of the works, apparently taken from the air. Over the fireplace, a heavy portrait in oils of a stern-looking, elderly man with a heavy face, clear blue eyes, and mutton-chop whiskers, and a very high white collar, over which he appeared to be straining to see. "Luke Cross, Esq., 1858-1924," said a plaque screwed to the frame...

Haworth sent in their names by the typist who, patting her blonde permanent waves, approached them leisurely from her room and asked them their business. They were admitted to the presence of Sir Caleb almost at once.

The cold weather had not improved the appearance of the ironmaster. His long nose was red, his complexion was like dough, and he looked as if he had been up all night.

"Good morning, gentlemen," he said. "What do you want with me? I'm surprised at this second visit, and haven't much time to spare. Can you be brief?"

He bade them be seated, and sitting down at his own desk, began to shuffle his papers. He was obviously nervous, not knowing the purpose of the call, but was trying to behave like a cock in his own barn-yard.

"Sorry to intrude, Sir Caleb, but Inspector Littlejohn has another urgent question or two to ask you, and I came with him to pilot him safely into your presence," said Haworth.

"Well, what is it, then?"

Littlejohn took up the cudgels. He went straight in to the attack.

"Sir Caleb, I understand that on the day of his death, the tramp known locally as Three-Fingers, called on you at your home. What was the purpose of that visit?"

Two bright pink spots appeared on the cheeks of Sir Caleb and slowly grew until they suffused his whole head and neck.

"He… he… called begging… I showed him the door," he said at length. "I can't help you. I don't know where he went after that."

"But you gave him a bottle of rum as he left…"

"Where did you get that tale from? I've something better to do than give every tramp that calls my liquor."

"Please don't try to deny it, Sir Caleb. Although you gave Three-Fingers the rum in a plain bottle, you forget that it was a special brand which has been traced to you."

The blood drained from Sir Caleb's face, leaving his complexion a greenish hue, like that of one who has had a bad channel-crossing. He looked wildly round, and then seemed to gather his thoughts again.

"Well. If I did give him the rum, what of it? I'm free to do what I like with my own, aren't I?"

"Funny behaviour towards a tramp to whom you're showing the door, isn't it? Do you recognize this?"

Littlejohn took from his pocket the bottle of sleeping-tablets and put it on the table before the foundry-master.

"Where d'you get those?"

"They're yours, Sir Caleb. A dose of the same medicine was found in the dregs of Three-Fingers' rum bottle…"

That ought to have taken the wind out of Sir Caleb's sails, but he still showed fight.

"Pah! Anybody can get that stuff from the chemist's. If Three-Fingers wanted to commit suicide, he could have got it."

"Not without a prescription. Besides, tramps with tendencies to suicide aren't, as a rule, so pettifogging in their way of taking their lives. Three-Fingers called on you shortly before his death; you saw him and gave him a bottle of rum; you were then in possession of sleeping-tablets identical with the drug which killed him. You were upstairs for a time before giving him the bottle, and these tablets were found upstairs. Now, what have you to say, Sir Caleb?"

The knight licked his dry, blue lips, opened his mouth as though to speak, and then Littlejohn spoke again.

"I suggest that Three-Fingers knew something about your movements on the day—more than twenty years ago—when Sykes was killed. On hearing that the case had re-opened by the discovery of Sykes's body, he came to blackmail you. So you had to get rid of him..."

"All lies, all lies!" yelled Sir Caleb, rising to his feet. There was foam on his lips and his face twitched with emotion.

"Let me continue, Sir Caleb," said Littlejohn relentlessly. "Before Mrs. Myles died, she told me everything that happened on that fatal evening. After you'd killed Sykes, you heard someone coming, you didn't know who, so you bolted. You thought later, that it was Three-Fingers. Actually, it was Mrs. Myles, and she saw everything. She was in at the death of Trickett, however, and that sealed her lips. Now, why did you kill Sykes?"

The last question came like the shot from a gun. For years, waking and sleeping, Caleb Haythornthwaite had imagined such a situation as this. Faced by the police, driven into a corner, he was asked, why did you kill Sykes? In nightmares, he saw the body which he had seen dead at his feet and which had strangely disappeared, suddenly brought to the light of day, and then the question. Why? He had turned it over and over and fled from it. It had pursued him to the verge of madness, and in the throes of nervous terror, he had confessed to his wife, rather than bear the burden alone. Then, in a saner moment, he had threatened what he would do if she breathed a word of it. Since then, they had lived separate lives. She was terrified of him!

As Littlejohn was speaking, Sir Caleb's brain was active and, in a strange detached way, he reproached himself for a fool. If he'd only kept his head when Three-Fingers called with his oily threats! The tramp couldn't have proved a thing. The word of a vagrant against that of Sir Caleb Haythornthwaite! But the incessant nagging of his conscience, and his fears had carried him away into a mad act. Murder will out! Your sins will find you out! Bury them deep or throw them into the depths of the sea, they'll rise to accuse you! Thus said his conscience. Like a gramophone in his brain. Only when at work among the noise and turmoil of his great machines, could he stifle the voices, and forget. Over twenty years all his resistance had been worn away, his restraint had been slowly undermined.

"Why did you kill Sykes?" asked Littlejohn.

And like an automaton Sir Caleb spoke the words which, in imagination, he had so long uttered as his excuse…

"It was self-defence…"

No sooner were the words out of his mouth, than he realized what he had said. His hand flew to his lips, as if to capture their fatal message and replace it before it reached other ears. His eyes sought those of Littlejohn, fear deeply in them, like those of a rabbit faced by a stoat.

Haworth's voice broke-in.

"In that case, Sir Caleb, perhaps you'd care to make a statement, but I must warn you that anything you say will be taken down and may be used in evidence later."

"There's not much to tell," replied the distressed man, now resigned to his fate. "I met Sykes on the moor. He'd been getting above himself at the works, and I wanted a quiet word with him. I was passing in my car on the way home from the shoot, when I saw him."

"He'd been blackmailing you?" interposed Haworth, his pencil poised, for he was taking down the statement in shorthand.

"When he left Myles's, he took with him some secret designs and patterns, which he said were his own. I bought them from him. It turned out they were young Myles's work. After I'd paid him, Sykes never left me alone. Said I'd not finished paying him his dues, and if I didn't make it worth his while, he'd go back to Mrs. Myles and tell her the tale. I hadn't covered myself properly over the deal, and it looked as if I'd stolen the designs myself. The old lady was out for my blood, and I couldn't afford to let Sykes go into the enemy's camp. He knew several other things, too."

Haythornthwaite placed his hands to his temples as though trying to still the pulses hammering there. Outside, in the yard, the noises of loading and the hoarse shouts of men could be heard. Somewhere in the neighbouring offices a telephone rang rhythmically... Sir Caleb looked over his glasses at Haworth. His eyes told of the dirty work that had gone-on when he changed horses and left Mrs. Myles to fend for herself.

"Yes?" said Littlejohn.

"I intended to sack Sykes and be done with it. I couldn't stand it any longer. When I saw him on the moor, I was going to tell him I'd done with him, and he could do his damnedest. He threatened me with his gun. Mine was loaded and in my hand, and before I knew what I was doing, I'd fired and killed him. Then, I heard somebody coming, and I ran off in panic. I didn't know who it was. I never knew it was Mrs. Myles. I thought it was Three-Fingers. I'd seen him about before that day. I was utterly bewildered when I heard that Trickett and not Sykes, was found. I didn't know what to make of it. So I kept quiet..."

"So you killed Three-Fingers after Sykes's remains were found, because he said he knew?"

"No... no..."

He persisted in denying it in spite of the evidence. Haworth rose.

"I'm afraid you'll have to accompany us to the police-station, Sir Caleb... In other words, I'm arresting you in connection with the deaths of Enoch Sykes and William Peters, known as Three-Fingers, and I must warn you that anything you say will be taken down and used in evidence…"

Sir Caleb Haythornthwaite tottered to his feet. To be tried in the summary court where he had been accustomed to preside! And to be led off under arrest through rows of watching workpeople, past the works he'd built-up, out through the gates never to come back… He clutched the desk.

"I… I… I…" he gasped and then fell to the ground.

His face was the colour of lead, his lips were mauve and drawn back in a hideous grimace. His eyes bulged and were full of frantic appeal. He fought for breath and feebly pawed at his watch pocket. Littlejohn knelt beside him, raised his head and thrust his fingers in the pocket, producing a pillbox full of small glass ampules, such as are broken and inhaled by sufferers from angina pectoris. He smashed one and thrust it under the twitching nostrils, but it was too late. The rigid body grew slack, the eyes rolled, grew glassy and remained staring at the ceiling. The hands flopped limply to the floor.

Haworth was busily telephoning for a doctor. When at length the surgeon arrived, he could do nothing but close the glazed eyes, and order the removal of the great man to the public morgue.

CHAPTER XIX

The End of Many Things

And those who husbanded the golden Grain,
And those who flung it to the Winds like Rain,
Alike to no such aureate Earth are turned,
As, buried once, Men want dug up again.

OMAR KHAYYAM

ALTHOUGH HE DESERVES NO MORE OF OUR CONSIDERATION, we cannot leave Sir Caleb Haythornthwaite on the cold slab of the Hatterworth mortuary. Mr. Simeon Mills is waiting for him, and then, the undertakers.

The coroner thoroughly enjoyed a double event, in the form of consecutive inquests on the ironmaster and his victim, Three-Fingers, the tramp. In pursuance of the powers vested in him, Mr. Mills transferred the proceedings connected with the latter from the country pub to the larger urban centre, greatly to the disgust of old Seth Wigley, who talked of being on his feet and about for the replay, as he called it.

Lady Haythornthwaite was by far the most dramatic of the witnesses called. She was a little, shrivelled woman, who had shared none of her husband's public life. She had been almost as much a recluse as the late Mrs. Myles, whom Mr. Mills had found, on the day before the greater double event, committed suicide whilst the balance of her mind was disturbed. Her Ladyship had long ago divorced herself from Sir Caleb in her heart, and had, for many years, resorted to very eccentric behaviour as a result. This had principally been manifest in the form of scuttering from shop to shop in the town, armed with a string bag, buying-in the following day's dinner. In the humbler days of her dear father, Lady Haythornthwaite, then Deborah Cross, had been entrusted with his entire domestic economy. For a time after her marriage to Sir Caleb, she had abandoned her shopping, but later resumed it, endeavouring to live the happy past over again. She made no bones about telling Mr. Simeon Mills that for the past twenty years, she had known who killed Sykes. Her late husband had, during a brain-storm, insisted on sharing with her his awful secret. Later, on recovering his poise, he had enumerated all the horrible things he would do to her if she breathed a word of what he had said, and he had clinched the argument by stating that a wife could not bear witness against her husband.

The end of Haythornthwaite brought relief to many people. Young Haythornthwaite, for example, abandoned his drinking habits and joined the R.A.F. He has been over the Ruhr on several occasions and whenever there is a foundry to bomb, he is in his element. His mother, although the recipient of gestures of sympathy and goodwill on every hand, fled from the valley of her fear, and settled down in a small village in Sussex.

The half-finished Haythornthwaite Gardens, which Sir Caleb had been subsiding as a memorial park to himself, was turned into allotments by the embarrassed local council. Emeritus-Inspector Entwistle, now a local celebrity for his share in bringing to book the viper in Hatterworth's bosom, was elected nem. con., as president of the Hatterworth Fur and Feather Club, an honour which he seemed to appreciate all the more by its being vacated through the decease of Haythornthwaite, who was patron to most institutions in the valley, whether he knew about their objects or not.

The foundry was bought, lock, stock and barrel, by a syndicate, and somehow, the absence of the bilious, conscience-ridden knight from its offices and workshops created a new atmosphere about the place. Even the lifetime sycophants of the late boss, whose funeral they had not attended—it was conducted without fuss and in a humble grave—were heard publicly to declare that the new management was streets ahead of the old, and that it was a pleasure to work for them.

The excitement of events in Hatterworth passed quickly. Anybody travelling through, early in January 1941, would have been greatly surprised if he'd been told that that quiet little place had recently been shaken by bloodshed and scandals. But people were too busy on war work, digging for victory, sorrowing for their lost ones, wondering about the progress of the conflict which was shaking the world, to bother about past history. Time had brought other cares, joys, sorrows and labour.

Littlejohn and his wife departed quietly for London shortly after the end of the case. The train arrived at Waterfold more than two hours late, after battling through drifts and staggering across frozen points. More and more snow had fallen in those last days, and from the platform of the station at Waterfold, which is like a terrace, they had their last view of the lovely expanse of Pennine hills covered in their deep mantle of white. Littlejohn carried a large parcel presented to him by Mr. Simeon Mills on the day before his departure. The last letter written by Mrs. Myles before she took her life, gave instructions to her lawyer that the detective was to inherit the picture "The Moorland Road", which hung on the wall of her room. Littlejohn's first task on arriving at their renovated flat in Hampstead, was to hang it in the dining-room. Besides giving him intense pleasure as a work of art, the picture reminds him of a very gallant old lady, and one of the strangest cases he has ever handled.

THE MURDER OF A QUACK

"With the help of a surgeon he might recover and prove an ass."

SHAKESPEARE'S *A MIDSUMMER NIGHT'S DREAM*,
from which the quotations heading the following chapters are taken.

"Never excuse; for when the players are all dead,
there need none to be blamed."

ACT V. SC. II.

CHAPTER I

Policeman

"Gentles, perchance you wonder at this show;
But wonder on, till truth make all things plain!"

ACT V. SC. I.

P.C. MELLALIEU, REPRESENTATIVE OF LAW AND ORDER IN THE village of Stalden, sat with his stockinged feet resting on the mantelpiece of the living-room of his cottage and gravely pored over the daily paper. He had a pair of steel-rimmed spectacles half-way down his large, bulbous nose and a short briar pipe, which he puffed enjoyably, between his teeth. The light of the summer evening was fading and he gradually drew the newspaper nearer and nearer to his eyes. Now and then, he gave a contented grunt, not quite knowing why he did it, but expressing his happiness thereby and from time to time he took a draught from the glass of beer at his elbow. After each drink, he gathered his moustache into his mouth with a large underlip and sucked the drops from it. He was a tall, heavily-built man and every time he moved, the arm-chair which held him creaked ominously. In his shirt sleeves, bootless, his pipe burning beautifully and his beer nice and mellow, the bobby had been granted the very circumstances in which to enjoy his liberty. His wife had gone with her sister to the nearest town, Olstead, to have a good weep at the pictures and his three kids had gone with a tribe of others and a teacher to pick foxgloves for the war effort. Like a small boy in mischief, P.C. Mellalieu counted the precious minutes of peace yet to go. In half an hour, all the family would be back. Better be in uniform and his boots on by then, otherwise Mrs. M. would have something to say.

The constable's wife was as proud as could be of the exalted position of her husband, William Arthur, but prouder still of the new police-house. Up to twelve months ago, it had been a small cottage hardly capable of holding their growing family, to say nothing of temporary prisoners. Then, the County Authorities had decided to erect a brand new home for the policeman. It had three bedrooms, a kitchen and a parlour, a cell, a greenhouse, a bathroom and hot and cold. Mrs. Mellalieu could only be persuaded with great difficulty ever to leave the place. She seemed to think that once she was out of sight, some jealous neighbour might squat in it with her family, or else remove it on a magic carpet. Also, she expected her husband to be as trim and spry as the house and he was rarely allowed even to unfasten the collar of his tunic. She would, had she dared, have insisted on William Arthur wearing his helmet, that symbol of his office, all the time! He was only allowed to relax when doing his garden. There seemed acres of it to the sweating constable as he dug his potato and bean rows and hoed his flower borders.

To-night, Mrs. Mellalieu's more masterful sister from the next village had called and whisked her off, protesting, to a most pathetic film in town. In departing, his wife had given the P.C. a last word.

"Don't forget them potatoes want rakin' up a bit, Will. They'll all be green when we get 'em else. You'll jest mannige it afore I get 'ome."

"Oh cripes!" groaned the bobby, who had been hoping for an hour or two of perfect peace. The only thing was to get a move-on over the job; and move he did. Rushing hither and thither down the potato rows like someone demented, P.C. Mellalieu did the work in half the scheduled time and here he was, gently cooling-off, sipping his beer and priming himself with the strategy of the war ready to tell the folk he met on the morrow a thing or two.

"The grand strategy of the war…" said he, without taking his pipe from his mouth. Then he removed it. "The *grand strategy* of the war." He rolled it on his tongue sonorously. Somebody was going to get it on the morrow. He sipped his beer.

"Ah… ahhhhhhh…" and he gave a sharp intake of breath and a sweep of his nether lip, whereat his moustache leapt into his mouth as into some strange vacuum cleaner. Like a great comfortable cat the policeman wriggled his body in the cushions and flexed and relaxed his feet and toes in his heavy grey socks… Then the telephone bell rang!

P.C. Mellalieu's eyes flashed fire.

"Oh 'ell," he groaned and the bell persisted. "Sharrup! Sharrup! I'm comin'… wot the 'ell…" And still muttering and grumbling he walked softly across the room and took up the instrument. Why couldn't they leave him alone on a night like this! With every prospect pleasing and then this…

"'Ello. Yus, perlice. Yus. 'Oo? O Yus, Mrs. Elliott and wot can I do for you?"

An excited voice quacked in his ear at great speed.

"'E has? Can't you make 'im 'ear? Can you see anythin' through the window?… Haven't you got another key to the room? Well, I'd better come round. Right. I'm on me way, Mrs. Elliott."

The constable slowly replaced the receiver and reached for his boots and tunic.

"Bet the old cock's not in the room at all," he muttered as he dressed himself properly.

As the constable hurried heavily down the village street to his destination, heads bobbed over garden walls and hedges following his progress with inquisitive eyes. Women seeing the bobby pass, peeped round curtains or came to the doors of their cottages and then compared notes with their neighbours, for it was unusual to see Mellalieu hurrying, especially at this time in the evening. The village main street was a secondary road, macadammed, with causeways of moss-grown cobblestones. Houses lined it, small dwellings for the most part, until eventually it widened into a small square, bordered by a few shops and several large, old houses, sedate and well preserved. There also stood the village inn, *The Mortal Man*, the doctor's house, and the village hall. Behind the latter and well off the main thoroughfare, were the village green, the market-cross, the vicarage and finally the church.

The house to which the constable was making his way was the last of the larger dwellings in the square. It had no front garden, but gave boldly on to the cobbles of the footpath. Small beds under its wall held tiny bushes, lichens and other rock plants. The building itself was three-storeyed, with sash windows dotted in its red-brick façade. The main door had a bright brass knocker and was painted cream and very clean. The whole place belonged to a gracious past, when builders had time to pursue their trade with care and solid materials. The date over the graceful fanlight was 1787.

Let in the wall to the right of the door was a large brass bell-knob. The policeman heaved at this and could hear the jangle of the bell indoors. Mellalieu whistled tunelessly to himself as he waited and cast his eye down the three brass plates which adorned the door. The first of these was scarcely legible, so well had time and metal polish done their work.

THEODORE WALL

FARRIER

The next in succession was also weathered but easily made out.

SAMUEL WALL

BONE SETTER

Finally, bright and comparatively new,

NATHANIEL AND MARTIN WALL

BONE SETTERS

The three plaques, one beneath the other, constituted the family tree of the Walls since their arrival in Stalden years ago.

The door opened and an elderly lady, Nathaniel Wall's housekeeper, appeared. A small, wiry, trim woman of sixty or thereabouts, with bright eyes, now anxious, a healthy wrinkled face with a small nose and pointed chin. Her hair was white and gathered straight back, in old-fashioned style from her brow to a knob on the crown of her head. Her dress was black and voluminous in an out-of-date fashion. She was evidently in a fearful stew about something as she greeted her visitor.

"Come in, constable. I'm sure there's something wrong with Mr. Wall. The surgery-door's locked and I can't get any answer. He must have had a seizure or something, for I'm certain he's inside."

"Now, now, calm yourself, Mrs. Elliott," said Mellalieu heavily, raising his great hand as if in blessing. "Everything's probably h'allright. 'Ow long 's this bin goin' on?"

"Well, constable, I was away last night. I went over to Sleeby to see my sister yesterday afternoon and they asked me to stay. I said I couldn't on account of the master, though I'd left his supper on a tray and all he needed was to open his bottle of ale. They pressed and, in the end, my brother-in-law telephoned the master to ask if it would be in order for me to stay overnight and come back this morning, like. Mr. Wall said certainly. If I got back in time to-night to make his bed, I could stop all day there to-day as well. It was a bit since I'd had a change and he'd go for his meals to *The Mortal Man*. I was very pleased. Very nice of the master. I got back at eight o'clock to-night, cleaned up the supper dishes, made the bed, and then went to tidy up the surgery, thinking Mr. Wall had probably gone out, me not having heard anything of him moving about. The door was locked. The master never locks that door… I thought a bit and the more I thought the more anxious I got. I banged on the door and tried to peep through the window from the front. Then I found the blind was down, which I hadn't noticed before. So, I rang you up."

"Quite right, too, Mrs. Elliott. Quite the right thing to 'a done. Probably it's h'allright. I'll jest knock on the door fust."

The bobby solemnly approached the offending article and smote it with his closed fist.

"Anyone in?" he asked timidly at first and then more boldly. "H'anyone in?"

There was a chilling silence, punctuated by the steady ticking of the great case-clock in the hall.

Mellalieu applied his eye to the keyhole, after removing his helmet, without which he looked almost naked.

"Carn't see a thing, Mrs. H'Elliott." He shook the door with increasing vigour, first with one hand, then with the other and lastly with both. "Hey! hey…!" he grunted, as though expecting to make the occupant relent and speak-up. Finally, he dropped his hands to his sides in a hopeless gesture.

"No good," he panted. "Sure Mr. Wall didn't lock it and go out?"

"Why should he lock it? There's nothing in there to lock it for. I don't like it. I think you ought to force it."

It was gradually dawning on the brain of the constable, which ground slowly but exceedingly small, that force the door was what he ought to have done from the start. Instead, he had dilly-dallied and talked all round it when a man's life might be in danger. Suppose old Wall had had a stroke or something... Beads of sweat broke out on the officer's brow and bald head and he reacted vigorously.

"Right oh, Mrs. Elliott, provided you say so... provided you say so."

"I do," replied the woman wringing her hands.

Mellalieu gathered himself together in a mighty effort, coiled his body grotesquely and then unwound himself in a mighty heave. There followed a terrible anti-climax, in that the old screws which held the lock gave at once and precipitated the policeman full length into the room. The blind was drawn and no light showed within. Mrs. Elliott switched on the electric light, screamed and fell in a dead faint on the floor. The bobby recovered himself, seized his helmet with one hand, and still on one knee like a worshipper genuflecting, raised his head to see what Mrs. Elliott was doing. Instead, he saw something which made his blue eyes pop almost from their sockets. He gave a strangled cry and sprang to his feet with remarkable agility.

Dangling from a rope passed over a pulley in one of the beams of the ceiling was the stiff body of a man. As Mellalieu looked at it, the draught from the open door caused it to turn and face him. It was the livid-faced corpse of Nathaniel Wall!

CHAPTER II

Victim

"And, being done, thus Wall away doth go."

ACT V. SC. I.

THE USUALLY QUIET HOUSE IN THE SQUARE WAS, LESS THAN half an hour after the discovery of the body of the dead bone-setter, over-run by an army of police officials. Headed by Inspector Gillibrand of the Olstead Force, they sought for fingerprints, clues and anything else which might enable them to solve the crime. For Dr. McArthy, the police surgeon had provisionally stated that the victim had been murdered.

"Strangled first and then slung-up, I should think," said the doctor, after a preliminary examination. "A rope wouldn't make marks like that on a man's neck. Although whether or not he was dead when the murderer hoisted him aloft, is another matter. The autopsy will throw more light on that."

Inspector Gillibrand examined the marks on the neck of the corpse and grunted. He was a tall, thin, fresh-complexioned man, with dark hair and eyes and a very persistent beard which he shaved off only to leave himself with a blue chin and upper-lip which he had to deal with twice a day sometimes to keep well-groomed. There was something Wellingtonian about his nose, a fine handsome organ. His broad brow denoted intelligence and breadth of outlook. He was well-liked by his subordinates and respected by his chiefs.

"How long would you say he's been dead, doctor?" asked Gillibrand, gently prodding one of the limbs of the corpse, now decently laid out on the couch.

"Since last night, probably twenty-four hours ago. That's as near as I can get now. He ate his supper, presumably at the usual time, which the housekeeper says was ten-thirty. That being so, when I've opened-up the stomach we may be able to get a bit nearer. Rigor's set-in pretty furiously and hanging there hasn't improved matters. I've finished if you care to ship him off to the mortuary."

So, P.C. Mellalieu, who had by his excited and incoherent telephonings, let loose the full force of the law on the little village, was called from the kitchen where he had been taking refreshment and sent to obtain the ambulance, which in Stalden was a dairyman's motor-van convertible in a few minutes into an A.R.P. casualty conveyance. As the village bobby trod the high street looking busy and important, small knots of villagers tried to intercept him and obtain fuller particulars of the event which had mysteriously become news in record time. The contents of the snug and bar-parlour of *The Mortal Man* teemed into the road to meet him. Some had darts in their hands; others carried out their beer-pots as though prepared to settle down for a long interview. But Mellalieu brushed them all aside with a comprehensive sweep of his huge hand.

"I ain't in any position to make a statement and I'm just engaged in important business. Let me pass…"

There had never been murder in Stalden before and the new event bewildered and baffled everybody. The constable's sealed lips did not improve his popularity and there were murmurs against him as the crowd parted to let him proceed on his way.

"Wot the 'ell's come over Bill Mellalieu," said Sam Mutters as he led his team back to their pots and darts. "Wot's the use o' havin' a bobby in the place if you carn't get the latest news out of 'im? T'ain't nachurall or fair we should 'ave to wait for the mornin' papers like the rest of the world. It's our village it's 'appened in, ain't it?"

There were sympathetic murmurs again. Meanwhile, the converted milk-van had been requisitioned and with Mellalieu sitting portentously at the driver's side, set-out with its burden for Olstead.

Gillibrand closely questioned Mrs. Elliott before finally leaving the house. She repeated the tale she had previously told the village constable.

"...And Mr. Wall seemed quite as usual when you left him yesterday?"

"Oh yes. He was very cheerful and told me to have a good time."

"You found him quite a good master, Mrs. Elliott?"

"Oh yes, sir. None better..." The woman's eyes filled with tears. "There's many round here will miss him."

"In what way?"

"Well, although he wasn't what you would call a qualified doctor, he was just as good as one. He could do anything except operate with the knife, you know..."

"Did he give medicine, too?"

"Yes. Homœopathics. In the old days, when Doctor Taylor was in the village, the two of them pretty well had equal practices with Dr. Taylor being called-in when Mr. Wall's patients looked like dying. And the old doctor not liking it, but putting-up with it. The Taylors had been doctors here as long, if not longer than the Walls. Father to son, like, and although one family couldn't mix with the other on account of the Taylors being qualified and the Walls what some folk called quack-doctors, yet the one respected the other. You had to respect the Walls, sir."

"And who's in practice here now?"

"Oh, Dr. Keating. That's another matter. He hated Mr. Wall. *And* Mr. Wall knew it and laughed about it. It wasn't any wonder he hated him. You see, when old Dr. Taylor died and the practice passed to a stranger, a lot of the patients started coming here. Mr. Wall used to say that he'd captured the main part of the goodwill of the old Taylors' practice, and no wonder Dr. Keating was sore. Added to that, the two of them had a quarrel and all the village knew about it. Little Mary Selby who'd been climbing on the table when her mother's back was turned, fell off and broke her collar-bone. They took her to Dr. Keating, who didn't seem to find out that it was broken. Well, when the child didn't seem better, her father brought her here. 'Who's been treating this,' says Mr. Wall after examining her. 'Dr. Keating,' says the father, a bit sheepish-like. 'Well, this collar-bone's broken and if it'd gone on for another week, this child would have been a cripple for life.' And he broke it and set it again. It got all round the village and Dr. Keating came here and kicked-up a fearful row. Didn't do the doctor any good, that, and brought more of his patients here."

"I see. Had Mr. Wall any particular enemies about the district?"

"Not what you'd call enemies. He was thoroughly detested by the doctors about here, of course. People came from places miles away. They've even been from London. In the days of the first and second Mr. Wall, they came from all over the country, but nowadays there are more osteopaths and such-like and people can get treatment nearer home. Also, Mr. Wall, like his father and grandfather before him, had a biting tongue when he chose to use it. Didn't wrap things up when he was annoyed. But, of course, people were hurt at the time and forgot about it when they were cured. He never suffered fools gladly, sir."

"When you were away, he attended to his own surgery, eh?"

"Yes. As a rule, the patients sat in the little room across the hall, which had a side-door. That door was loose and they came that way. Then, when the master had finished with them, he'd let them out at the front and put his head in the waiting-room and call 'Next' as he passed."

"The side-door was locked when you came back today?"

"Yes, sir."

"The key isn't in it, though."

"No. It's on the nail above the door. It's a bit loose and with people coming and going used to fall out, so we put it there."

She showed the detective the spot and then uttered an exclamation. "Well! Here's the key we couldn't find. The one for the consulting-room."

Examination of the shattered lock of the death-room had revealed no key and it had been presumed that the murderer had taken it away with him. Gillibrand took the key in his hand.

"You're sure the side-door was locked, Mrs. Elliott, when you returned?"

"Quite sure."

"The murderer must have been in the waiting-room after he killed Mr. Wall. Then he must have gone out by the front way and snapped the lock behind him..."

"Will you be wanting anything more, sir? I can't stay here to-night and I've got to get the last 'bus to my sister's at Sleeby."

"No, I think that'll be all for the time being, thank you, Mrs. Elliott. By the way. You've informed Mr. Wall's relatives of this? Had he any relatives?"

"Only one. A nephew. Dr. John Wall, in practice somewhere in London. We've wired him to come."

"So there is at least one of the Walls who's not a quack, eh?"

"Yes. When Mr. Martin Wall—that was the master's brother who died three years since—when Mr. Martin was in partnership here, he said he wasn't going to have his son hounded about by the profession, so he sent him to the hospital to get his degrees. A good man is Mr. John. He's an orthopædic surgeon. The skill runs in the family, sir."

"You seem to know all their history, Mrs. Elliott."

"I've been with them so long. Ever since I lost my husband in the Boer War."

"No wonder you know all about them!"

"Yes. Rare men they were to work for. I guess I'll be retiring now… I've got an annuity, you see. When I was sixty, Mr. Nathaniel gave it to me. 'No need to wait for my will now, Mrs. Elliott,' he said, 'although I hope you'll stay on with me till my time comes to go.' Very kind and considerate always, he was. I never heard of any other master doing such a thoughtful thing…"

"Nor did I, Mrs. Elliott. Well, you go for your 'bus and I'll lock-up here. Good night."

When the housekeeper had departed, Gillibrand lit his pipe and strolled about the ground-floor rooms of the great empty house. Whoever could have wished to put an old man, who, if accounts were true, was a public benefactor, so cruelly to death? True, an old bachelor living alone can harbour strange secrets, especially one to whose consulting-room queer cases are continually coming and going.

On the morrow, he would go through the locked desk and safe with the dead man's lawyer. Goodness knew what secrets they held. If the old chap had kept case-books, they should prove interesting. His diary and his pass-books, too, would bear close scrutiny.

This was going to be a ticklish case, not only that there was so little to go on, but also it might lead into strange situations. For example, several doctors might be involved, men who had become the sworn enemies of old Wall through his unorthodoxy. He'd better talk to the chief about it. Maybe they'd better have an outsider in. One who could ask questions without causing local resentment after the crime had been solved. Besides, Scotland Yard were better equipped for tackling a murder of this kind. Personally, he wouldn't mind working with a decent colleague from London. They took none of the glory and were men who got a move on and cut through local red-tape and prejudice.

It was quite dark when Gillibrand opened the front door to let himself out. As he prepared to close it, the telephone bell rang. Now what? Gillibrand hurried back and took up the instrument.

"Is that Mr. Wall?"

"No. Who are you?"

"Mr. Slocombe, Red Dyke Farm. Ask Mr. Wall to come over right away. My daughter's tumbled downstairs and it seems serious..."

"Sorry... Mr. Wall died yesterday. You'll have to try someone else." There was a gasp and a groan of anxiety at the other end and then the line grew dead.

As he replaced the receiver, Gillibrand thought that many people hereabouts had lost a good friend at the hand of a cunning killer.

CHAPTER III

Littlejohn

"A very good piece of work, I assure you, and a merry."

ACT I. SC. II.

GILLIBRAND MET THE LONDON TRAIN AT OLSTEAD WITH certain feelings of anxiety, for he had no idea what kind of a colleague was arriving from Scotland Yard. However, when Detective-Inspector Littlejohn jumped from his compartment, singled-out his uniformed collaborator and shook him heartily by the hand, his troubles seemed to vanish and a happy partnership was established from the first. Good humoured, efficient, unofficious, thought Inspector Gillibrand and he was right.

The two men talked generalities until they reached the police station, where over a cup of tea, the local officer briefly outlined the affair to Littlejohn.

"This is a queer case," he began passing his tobacco pouch over to his new friend. "It concerns the death of Nathaniel Wall, a bone-setter of considerable local reputation, who was found murdered last night in his consulting-room. He'd been half-strangled first and then, according to the medical evidence, finished-off by being hanged on a contrivance of ropes and pulleys which he used for his job. Judging from the contents of the stomach and the time it's assumed he had his supper, he was killed about eleven on the previous night."

"I suppose he took his evening meal as regular as clockwork, eh?" interposed Littlejohn.

"Yes. He was a bachelor and lived with an elderly housekeeper. Normally, they had a young girl, too, who acted as a day maid, but she's joined the A.T.S., and they haven't been able to get another to take her place yet. Mrs. Elliott, the housekeeper, went to visit a sister on the morning of the crime, stayed overnight and when she returned last evening, found the consulting-room door locked. This was most unusual and she got apprehensive, so called in the local constable, who broke-in. The blind was drawn and there, hanging to his bonesetting gadget, was old Wall, stiff and dead."

"How old was he, Gillibrand?"

"Seventy-two and a bit and well preserved. The key of the locked door was hanging from a nail over a side entrance. Why it was put there, I don't know. The murderer must have let himself out by the front door which has a spring lock; the other door was fastened on the inside."

"Mr. Wall was unqualified?"

"Yes. The qualified men called him a quack, but that's hardly fair, considering that they call cheapjacks at fairs the same. Wall was a first class bonesetter. Quite a lot of first division footballers have been under him for treatment and he has a wide reputation for the cures he's brought about. In addition, he practised a bit of homœopathy with a measure of success. As a matter of fact, many local folk consulted him instead of the orthodox practitioners. He was wise enough to send them off to qualified men in serious cases. He couldn't issue a death certificate, of course, and his prudence has resulted in a perfectly clean sheet hitherto. He's never been involved in any scandal."

"A good record."

"Yes. He belongs to a family of high standing in the district. As a matter of fact, Littlejohn, I'd like you to meet the old vicar of Stalden, Mr. John Thorp, who can tell you the full history of the Walls since they settled in these parts. It will give you some background besides making interesting hearing. We'll call on the old chap one day."

"I'll be staying in the village?"

"Well, I've provisionally booked you a room at the inn there, *The Mortal Man*. Quite a good place. There's none better in this town. The village is about three miles down the Cambridge Road from here. A pretty place. At one time, I believe, it was almost like a miniature spa, teeming with invalids visiting the Stalden Doctors, as the Walls were called in the old days. There wasn't a room to be had anywhere then. The doctors took-in about seven or eight patients themselves and the rest spread themselves in the pub and cottages round. That was, of course, before the orthodox profession improved so much. The records show some remarkable cures, if they're true."

"This is all very interesting. Whoever would want to kill a man of that type?"

"You never know, do you? Perhaps he'd found out somebody's secret. Strange folk called at The Corner House—that's what the Walls' house was called..."

"Reminds me of home...!"

"Yes. Well, you'll see what a problem faces us. But we'll get at it right away. Pettyflower, the lawyer, has promised to call here about the will and a search in the deceased's personal effects. He's in the court next door at present defending poachers, but should be free any time. Then we'll go over to Stalden and you can help us in the search."

"I gather nothing has come to light to help us on the way? Local feuds, or gossip, or such like..."

"No. So far, we haven't combed the neighbourhood. You see, our inquiries may possibly involve the delicate task of probing among the medicos round about. You'll agree that's a ticklish job and will call for every ounce of tact we can muster. Our Chief's a terror for quick results, too. Hence, we've called in Scotland Yard at once. So far, we've hardly scratched the surface of the case, although how far we'll have to dig and what crops it'll yield are in the lap of the gods. Here's a copy of the medical report for you."

Gillibrand handed over a typed sheet of technicalities to his colleague.

"Thanks," said Littlejohn. "I'll have to study this carefully. When's the inquest?"

"To-morrow, Inspector, and it'll be purely formal. We've a good coroner here and he'll work hand-in-glove with us. It will be an adjournment… indefinitely. By the way, there's one peculiarity about the doctor's report. Wall was strangled and… well, you might call it frenziedly, as though he put up some resistance and his murderer exerted every ounce to render him unconscious and then, suddenly recovering himself, shall we say, felt repugnance at killing him that way, so finished the job with a rope. But the strange thing is the marks on the throat. Our surgeon's had them photographed for records. The finger marks on each side of the windpipe have bitten deep and left heavy bruises, and these show that the man was stronger in the left hand than in the right. He must have been partially or wholly left-handed."

"What exactly do you mean by that, Gillibrand?"

"Some men write with their right hands, but might bowl at cricket or bat with their lefts. Just depends on training, doesn't it? So we can't definitely start hunting for an obviously left-handed man. That's all."

"A good point."

At this the expected visitor entered the room.

Mr. Edward Pettyflower of the old firm of Pettyflower, Mobbs, Parker and Begg, principal lawyers of the district. A small, middle-aged man and apparently in the process of putting-on weight. He had a clean, round, red face with innocent-looking blue eyes, which had many times been responsible for leading forensic opponents into a fatal trap and bringing off his cases triumphantly. He was almost bald and wore horn-rimmed spectacles on the bridge of his nose. A habit of looking over these made one wonder why he had them at all. He tripped into the room smiling and in the best of tempers, for he had just got his clients off with a caution.

"Well now, gentlemen. I'm at your disposal…"

Gillibrand introduced him to Littlejohn.

"Let's get off to The Corner House, then," said the solicitor. "There's nothing to sit talking about in the will. All the estate of the deceased goes to his nephew, Dr. John Wall of London, who is joint executor with me. Mrs. Elliott has already been provided for, so after death duties and an honorarium for me, the doctor gets Corner House and all the rest. He probably travelled on your train, Littlejohn, and is at present, according to programme, at our office, making some arrangements with my partner, Mr. Begg, with whom he went to school and with whom he'll stay whilst settling things up. My car's outside, so let's get going."

Whereat the lawyer ushered the police officers to the door and penned them together in the back seat of his prosperous-looking car.

At The Corner House, the three investigators were joined by Dr. John Wall. He was a tall, heavily-built man, in his middle forties and more like a farmer than a surgeon. In that, he showed his physical inheritance from a race of blacksmiths, farriers and bonesetters, countrymen all. He had clear grey eyes, a heavy open countenance, with a small dark moustache, thick grey eyebrows, and a fine head of greying hair to crown the lot. He seemed somewhat bewildered by the events into which his uncle's death had drawn him. He was obviously relieved to see the lawyer, who introduced him to the two Inspectors.

"I'm glad to see you here, Ted," he said to Pettyflower. "This legal work and clearing-up baffles me and it's good to have you as joint executor. I'll be the sleeping partner in this job."

The quartet set about going through the papers and records left behind by the murdered man.

Nothing unusual in the way of monies paid in or drawn out of the bank over a long number of years.

"Did you expect it?" asked Dr. Wall, after Gillibrand had spent a lot of time over several pass-books. "My uncle was a steady-living chap. Hardly likely to be a victim of blackmail or to be keeping other establishments. I could have told you that from the start."

"We just have to be sure, don't we, sir?" replied the Inspector pleasantly. "We mustn't overlook anything."

They continued their labours. Bills neatly filed away. A day-book, showing names of patients and amounts paid. Consultation fees were reasonable and in many cases a tick in the cash column showed that someone who couldn't afford it had been charged nothing. There was a fat address book, too. All these were contained in the drawers of a large, old-fashioned secretaire. The safe was opened next. This held more valuable and confidential documents. For example, there was a file of threatening and scurrilous letters from this and that infuriated doctor or layman. There was a large scrap-book, too, which held newspaper reports of cures effected and other items of interest connected with the family. Interviews with journalists, paragraphs of history and the like.

Lastly, came eleven fine, leather-bound volumes of closely-written records. The case-books of the whole family of "doctors" since its inception in Stalden.

Dr. John opened his eyes wide as he fondly handled the books.

"By gad!" he muttered. "What a gold-mine! Officially, I'm supposed, as a qualified man, to be in the opposition camp, but blood's thicker than water and I *know* how skilled all the old chaps were. These records are invaluable, especially to me in my job. I'll take them back with me... I can hardly wait to be getting at them!"

Littlejohn interposed.

"You don't mind leaving them with us for the time being, however, Doctor...?"

"Whatever for? They're of no interest to the layman."

"All the same, I'm afraid we'll have to keep them until the case is solved one way or another. You see, they may contain something which will throw valuable light on our problems."

"Very well... although it's a bit disappointing. You'll want the scrap-book, too, then?"

"Decidedly, sir. That's of equal importance."

"Right. But don't forget, I'm anxious to have them as soon as possible, will you?"

Their work finished for the time being, the party broke-up.

Before they parted, however, Littlejohn took Dr. Wall aside.

"I hope you don't mind my asking what might seem to you an undiplomatic question, but were you in London on the night of the murder, sir?"

The doctor laughed.

"Suspect number one, am I? Well, I suppose as the old man's heir, I might have good cause for hurrying the processes of nature. But, as regards killing him… I was too fond of him for that; I'd like to get my hands on whoever did."

He meant it, too.

"However, you want an alibi, not a scene. No, I wasn't in London. I was in Cheltenham, operating. It was an emergency. I got there at nine in the evening, by road, and left the hospital just before twelve, midnight. I dined with the head surgeon there and he'll confirm that. Here's his address."

The doctor scribbled a name and address on the back of one of his own cards and handed it to the detective, who thanked him.

Gillibrand, having made a parcel of the records and scrap-book, tucked them under his arm and then offered to take his colleague to *The Mortal Man* and see him comfortably installed. They made their way to the inn and, over glasses of beer, discussed the case again.

"We've a job on with the case-books, Littlejohn. They cover a period of a hundred or more years," grumbled the local man.

"Yes. But all we're concerned with is those of the murdered man, I should say. But first, I suggest we start with the scrap-book. Then if it yields anything, amplify it by the case-book. If nothing comes from it, then we'll both have to tackle the case-books. Of course, they may have no bearing on this business at all. I propose to make a first move by trying to trace all who visited the 'doctor' on the night of his death and also I'll comb the place for anyone who's seen strangers around. Then, there'll be the old man's movements before he was killed. Lastly, your vicar for a talk about family history. I think that'll do for a beginning."

Gillibrand nodded and smiled. Littlejohn's easy, unperturbed manner gave him confidence and relief. Murder didn't often visit those parts.

"Well, I'll be off, Littlejohn. Got a lot to do. Routine, you know and it's the inquest to-morrow."

"Care to leave the scrap-book with me, Inspector?" asked Littlejohn and, with this mine of information at his elbow, he bade Gillibrand good-bye and began to watch with interest the preparations they were making to provide him with a substantial meal.

CHAPTER IV

Midwife

"The wisest aunt, telling the saddest tale."

ACT II. SC. I.

IN LEAVING THE CORNER HOUSE, LITTLEJOHN HAD NOTICED A small cottage, the only one of its kind, tucked among the more imposing dwellings of the square. Luckily, it also overlooked the bonesetter's house and the detective was struck by the idea that perhaps here, if it were tenanted by some old gossip, he might get more news than from the more formidable householders around. His hopes were not in vain, for, after having done justice to a heavy high tea, he asked the landlord of *The Mortal Man* concerning the cottage and was given a satisfying answer.

"Oh, that be occupied by Martha Harris, the local midwife and district nurse. A proper old chatterbox, she be, though wonderful handy at a lying-in. So, having to choose between being talked about or havin' an easy time, the women take the lesser evil and suffer her tongue."

Littlejohn therefore made Woodbine Cottage his first port of call.

The door opened almost before he had ceased knocking and a large woman with a figure like an old-fashioned cottage loaf confronted him. She had billowing black skirts, a black blouse, decorated with a cameo brooch and a watch hanging from an imitation bow made in gold or gilt. Her grey hair was divided in the middle and elevated by two invisible pads into an edifice resembling two large blunt horns and she wore a massive comb to keep the lot together. Her face was red, smooth and fat and her eyes were green, inquisitive and shrewd.

"Mrs. Harris?" said Littlejohn.

"Yes," said the woman, summing-up her visitor without much success. He seemed far too confident and carefree for a client anxious to bespeak her services at a future accouchement or to want her to sit up all night with an ailing wife. Perhaps a traveller for something! That would be it.

"I don't want anything to-day," said the midwife and was making as if to shut him out.

"My name is Littlejohn, Inspector Littlejohn. May I have a word or two with you, Mrs. Harris?"

The woman's face became anxious and the blood drained from it, leaving it hot and mottled. Sometimes, she gave confidential advice to clients in difficulties. Had one of them…?

"Come inside," she said, dithering.

When she heard the purpose of Littlejohn's visit, she was so relieved that she impulsively asked him to stay for tea, an honour which the detective declined.

"Oh, I can't help seein', bein' right in the middle of the square, what's goin' on round me," said Mrs. Harris, having recovered her composure and straightened out her stiff dress. "I cannot say what went on at Mr. Wall's for most of the time, me havin' 'ad four patients to clean up before me dinner, a confinement which tuck four hours in the afternoon, and two after-cares in the evenin'. So, all I see was the old man goin' over for his mid-day to *The Mortal Man* and then a few evenin' patients arrivin' as I set out after tea. When I got back about eight, there was one or two comin' and goin' at the surgery and then as I went off to Mrs. Bargery, at Marsh Farm. Terrible bad she's been and the child's life despaired of, and the 'usband drinkin' to fergit his misfortunes, bad luck never comin' singly, he sez. Well, as I went off there about ten, the last of the patients seemed to a' gone, becos I saw the old man goin' across to the inn for his nightcap."

Littlejohn had the greatest difficulty in halting this spate of information.

"You saw no strangers about, then?" he interposed with difficulty.

"No. Never a one. Not that I'd much chance, seein' I wasn't in all day, was I?"

The Inspector beat a somewhat hasty retreat towards the door, as the woman seemed to be loading up for another volley of gossip.

"Who was the last patient you saw there, Mrs. Harris?"

"Old Goodchild, the cobbler. Sprained ankle… fell off his own doorstep, if you please. In the dark… that's what comes of spendin' the generous profits he makes out of our mendin' on drink instead of on his family, which is too large as it is…"

"Many thanks, Mrs. 'Arris, and good evening," said Littlejohn. The woman did not notice the unconsciously dropped aspirate with which her visitor linked her to her more famous counterpart. The detective remembered his mistake as he closed the gate and later put it on record in a letter to his wife, to whom he made reports almost as full and frequent as those he sent to The Yard.

The cobbler's shop was not far off. It was tucked away in a corner just where the main street opened out from its bottleneck to form the square. The sign which swung over the door was plainly visible from Mrs. Harris's garden-gate.

JEREMY GOODCHILD

Bespoke Bootmaker.

Repairs.

Littlejohn made for the place and entered. The building was old and dark and a door, divided in two horizontally, stable-fashion, gave access to it. There, amid a welter of lasts, tools and old footwear sat the shoemaker slapping rivets into a shoe which looked long past repairing. A middle-aged man, flabby from lack of exercise, pale from indoor work, rheumy-eyed from drink. A bald head with a few stray hairs here and there, round fat face, and heavy ungainly body. As he rose to inspect the newcomer, Goodchild reminded Littlejohn of those little bedside lamps, which, weighted at their bases, will totter here and there if agitated but never fall down, rooted on their feet but gyrating, leaning, shuffling all over the shop. The cobbler leaned on the counter. If he was not leaning on one thing it was on another. Chair-backs, cupboards, walls, all received his weight.

"Evenin'," said Goodchild, vomiting a mouthful of shoemaker's nails into the palm of his hand and transferring the sticky mass into their appropriate receptacle.

The noise from the dim living-quarters behind the shop was appalling. A large family of children seemed to be indulging in all forms of sport. Someone was strumming on a twanging piano. Two boys were quarrelling fiercely. A child, probably teething, was yelling its head off. A parrot made bubbling noises like a bottle being emptied and from time to time shouted its name. "Pretty Poll, Pretty Poll! I know something about you! Pretty Poll!" In the doorway leading to the inner room sat a dog, busy with his fleas. And amid the welter, Mrs. Goodchild, suckling a tiny infant, rocked placidly to and fro, fat, lazy, apparently soothed by the pandemonium going on around her.

Littlejohn sucked hard at his pipe and surrounded himself by a fragrant smoke-screen to keep out the stale smells of the interior.

"Good evening," he said to the sly-looking cobbler.

"Well?"

"I'm a police-inspector. I'd like a word with you about the events of the evening of Mr. Wall's death."

"Me? I'd nothin' to dew with it…"

At this point the noise became so deafening that the shoemaker was stirred from his lethargy. Hastily seizing a large awl by the metal end, he rolled like a tidal wave into the living-room, kicking the cur before him, and could be heard cracking the pates of his offspring, like a grotesque xylophonist executing a tuneless solo. A unison of outraged yelling followed, whereat the instrumentalist waddled back to his bench, slamming the connecting door on the way and making satisfied snorts at the good work he had accomplished.

"Now; Whatsis murder to do wi'me?"

He elided his words; almost too lazy to speak.

"You were Mr. Wall's last patient, I gather, that night."

"Aw, that. Yis a waz. Sprained me ankle. Mr. Wall was betternany doctor. Cheaper too. Put me right. Yis. About quarter'fan hour after he lemmeout of the house, he followed me, locked-up and wenover to th'pub ferris nightcap."

"What time would that be?"

"Tennish. Just before closingtime."

"How long were you in the waiting-room?"

"Nearly two hours, onanoff. Lot o' patients there that night."

"On and off?"

"Yis. Went fust round eightish. Waited abit. Then, wenfuradrink to the pub. Got thirsty sittinthere. Told them as waz there to save my place while I nipped out."

"Was there anyone among the patients you didn't know? Any strangers?"

"Naw. All villagers and countryfolk from hereabout. Folk from outside mostly come afternoon."

"There was nobody in The Corner House, then, when you left Mr. Wall there and went for your final drink?"

"Noboddy. Place was empty."

"H'm. Did you see Mr. Wall return?"

"'E left *Mortal Man* as I did. Hapast ten. Went straight across 'ome, unlocked door and went in. Shuttit after 'im."

"Right. Thanks, Mr. Goodchild. That's all for the time being."

"Right. Musbe gettin' on. Promised these shoes for to-night."

More likely getting thirsty again, thought Littlejohn. He bade the cobbler good-night and the man turned to his last again, as he did so flinging a fistful of nails in his mouth, like an urchin feeding on peanuts.

Behind the closed door the piano started again and the dog, apparently finished with his livestock, began to howl a dismal accompaniment. "Pretty Poll! I know something about you, Pretty Poll!" The shoemaker furiously drove his nails into the tattered boot and drowned the tumult in his own noise.

Littlejohn looked to left and to right down the village street. The shops were closed. Knots of women had gathered at the gates of their cottage gardens and eyed him curiously. On the strip of green round the war memorial the youths of the village swaggered before groups of tittering girls. A party of men were talking at the door of the saddler's shop. Now and then, someone or other would cross the road to *The Mortal Man* and enter for his evening pint. A very old man with a long beard of dirty white shambled across to the inn, scarce able to crawl, but not missing his nightcap and gossip.

So, someone had either gained access to the bonesetter's empty house during his absence or been quietly let-in after the cobbler had seen the old man enter for the night. Littlejohn thought that he had better have a look at the interior of The Corner House again. Gillibrand had left a key with him. He strode across the square, followed by staring, curious eyes and, unlocking the front door, entered.

All was silent inside, save for the heavy ticking of the grandfather clock in the hall. This wheezily worked itself up for an effort, struck eight and sank into exhausted quietness once more. The Inspector passed from one room to another. All the windows were closed and the catches thrust home. The housekeeper had told Gillibrand that all the windows on the downstairs floor were fastened. They were never opened, except during cleaning time. The noise of passing traffic in the road annoyed Mr. Wall.

Littlejohn examined all the fastenings carefully. No sign of recent disturbance. In fact, the dust on the ledges had not been moved for days. Upstairs, the window of the dead man's room was ajar. Only that. There was no easy access to the first floor from back or front. He passed into the dining-room which overlooked a long garden from a french window. Thick hedges on two sides of the lawn and flower beds. A smaller yew hedge at the bottom of the garden, over which could be seen a wide stretch of country with an allotment in the foreground. In this vegetable patch a tall man, like a scarecrow, was feverishly at work, apparently weeding.

The french window had been recently opened, for there was earth on the mat just on the inside of it. Littlejohn examined this closely for footmarks. There was no key in the lock of the casement but Littlejohn soon found this among a litter of clock and drawer keys in an ornament on the mantelpiece. He opened the window and stepped out. Rain in the night had washed away any traces of intrusion from behind. The outside of the lock, however, bore recent scratches as though someone, in unsteady haste, had lately used it. He made a note of this for when he next interviewed Mrs. Elliott, who was returning on the morrow for the inquest.

Enough for one day.

The detective locked-up the house again and crossed the road to *The Mortal Man*. He might gather something from the gossips over their evening ale. Besides, he was thirsty himself.

Suddenly, he halted in his stride. One thing more. Perhaps the scarecrow in the market-garden at the back had seen something. Better ask him at once and then call it a day.

So, turning on his heel, Littlejohn made for the lane which led from the village street to the country behind.

CHAPTER V

Smallholder

"This man, with lanthorn, dog, and bush of thorn, presenteth Moonshine."

ACT V. SC. I.

THE HUMAN SCARECROW TOILING AMONG HIS CABBAGES AND cauliflowers did not even look round to greet his visitor. Instead he remained bent, grubbing about among his plants, chattering to himself and now and then half-straightening himself to inspect something he held between his finger and thumb and which he then dropped into a large tin at his side. The light was fading, but that did not deter him. A thin mongrel dog sleeping on the grass verge, growled, opened one eye and dozed off again without challenging the newcomer.

"Late to be working here," said Littlejohn for want of something else to say to attract the man's attention.

The tall, bony frame uncurled itself, revealing an emaciated body, arms and legs like drumsticks, large hands like shovels and covered with mud from rooting in the wet earth. The face was long, thin and with cadaverous cheeks. The fellow had a dark, unkempt moustache, burning black eyes and his dirty clothing was covered by a dirtier raincoat. A shapeless hat topped the lot, too large and held in position by its wearer's ears.

"Late!" piped the scarecrow. "Never too late for this job! Slugs and leatherjackets in millions. Here's me, huntin' slugs with me torch o' nights and leatherjackets every hour God spares me by day."

A bit dotty, thought Littlejohn. Better humour him and get him calmer before questioning.

"A pity that. How's it come about?"

"Somebody put 'em 'ere to spite me. Last year, I won first prize at Stalden Show with me caulies and me marrers. Somebody borne it agen me. Put a blight on me, that's wot they done. Evil eye, that's wot it is. Never been no slugs or leatherjackets on this plot afore. Now look at 'em."

He thrust the tin, half-filled with seething insects, under the detective's nose.

"Look at me caulies... look at 'em..."

They certainly looked motheaten.

"Slugs is best caught after dark. Hunt 'em with a lamp, I do. Squash 'em to a jelly! A pulp!"

He eyed Littlejohn suspiciously.

"Wot you want? If yer from the landlord, you'll get no rent. Land wi' a blight on it ain't gettin' no rent o' mine. You jest shift these slugs and leatherjackets fust..."

"I'm a police officer and I'd like a word with you about what happened on the night Mr. Wall died..."

"I don't know nuthin'. Too busy. Ain't time fer botherin' in other folk's troubles. Too many o' me own... A detective, are yer? The very man I want... Look at that..."

He thrust a horny hand among his rags and produced a dirty piece of paper which he brandished at the Inspector.

Littlejohn could hardly decipher the uncouth handwriting in pencil amid the surrounding filth.

> "Six little collyflowers
> Swanking on their own,

Up come six letherjackets,
Give a dog a bone."

Evidently a joke played by some rival or spiteful trickster. The man had taken it to heart.

"Detective… eh? Tell me who wrote that and I'll tell yer who done this."

"Well, suppose I finish what I'm on at present and then we'll talk."

"Ain't got no time for talkin'. Got to get on with this. Show's in three weeks… and look at 'em."

The man was almost weeping.

"Just tell me one thing. Were you here the night before last?"

"Night it rained so 'ard? Yes. I'm 'ere every night. Can't let these get better o' me afore the show."

"Before the rain came, I mean."

"Before and after, I waz 'ere."

"Did you see anybody prowling about the back of Mr. Wall's place just before black-out?"

"Too busy wi' me own devices to be noseying in other folk's. But I did see somebody."

"Who?"

"Dunno. Too busy. Chap came along that back road there. Stopped by the gate, got over and went in Wall's by the back way."

"Sure?"

"Course, I'm sure! Thought it was the landlord comin' for rent he's not goin' to get. But it wasn't."

"What kind of a man?"

"Dunno… didn't notice. Had a raincoat and hat pulled over his eyes."

"He came round the field-road; not through the village?"

"I said so, didn't I? I dunno any more and haven't time to talk..."

"Would that be after ten, sure?"

"I said so, didn't I? What yer botherin' me for? Clock struck hal'past-ten as I looked up..."

"Sure you heard it?"

"Googodamighty... caren't you believe wot I sez? I heard the clock 'cos I wuz listenin', see? I got to fasten up the 'ens. Foxes about as well as slugs 'n leatherjackets. Fasten up the 'ens and get me supper jest afore black-out, so I won't need to draw me curtains, see? Otherwise, that blasted Mellalieu 'll be on me and I got enough troubles without 'im. Now leave me in peace, mister..."

"Very well. Thanks, and I hope you win the prize."

The scarecrow growled and resumed his hunting with grunts and cries of hatred for his victims. Before Littlejohn turned to go, the poor fellow had forgotten his presence in the heat of the chase.

The detective followed the road indicated by the smallholder as being the one along which Mr. Wall's late visitor had arrived on the night of the crime. Not far past the market-garden, it diminished into a mere earth track, passed through a field and a spinney and then by thick woods, which apparently surrounded some old house or other. Leaving the woods, the path again took to the fields and finally joined the main road through the village before the houses began. An excellent way of arriving at The Corner House unseen, for the track passed no dwellings and at dusk, when the intruder had used it, he was most unlikely to have passed anyone. Added to this, he had worn a hat shielding his face and presumably had taken care not to be seen by any chance strollers, lovers and the like, on the way. If he were one of the villagers, he had merely needed to make his way out of the village until he reached the beginning of the path and then follow it in its semi-circular detour, skirting all the houses, to the back of the bonesetter's.

Littlejohn pondered the case as he returned to the High Street.

Motive as yet unknown. Opportunity, however, had arisen through the absence of the housekeeper. Had old Wall made an appointment with his visitor? Had he let him in by the back way himself. Or, had the unidentified man heard of Mrs. Elliott's absence, gained entrance in some way and been waiting for the old man when he returned from his evening drink? There were many questions awaiting Mrs. Elliott on the morrow.

The Inspector reached the main street just in time to see the barrel-like form of Goodchild disappearing into *The Mortal Man*. Mrs. Harris, too, bustled along the street with a monstrosity of a hat on top of her head, apparently off on some errand of mercy or gossip. From the house of Dr. Keating a hatless man emerged. Idlers standing in the square greeted him. "Evenin', doctor." Presumably the local representative of the orthodox school. Littlejohn didn't much like the look of him. He was small and plump, with a receding forehead and a long nose. Shabbily dressed in tweeds with a disordered soft collar and a rambling tie. His thin hair blew over his eyes in the evening breeze.

The doctor strutted to the gate, started his car and tore away out of the village.

"Off on another spree," chuckled a yokel, propping up the window of the saddler's shop.

Littlejohn nodded to the man who had addressed him.

"That so?" he said. "Is he a bit of a wild 'un then?"

"Not 'arf, 'e ain't. Never see such a chap fer moppin' up the whisky!"

"By the way, who's the old man on the allotment behind the Walls' house?"

"Oh, Daft Dick, you mean. Aye, thinks somebody's filled 'is plot with weeds and plaguey pests to stop him winnin' prizes at the show. Dick Pottinger, that is. Lost his wife last summer, poor devil, and it's turned his brain a bit, that has. Lives alone, and that don't do 'im no good."

An old gaffer, more ancient even than the one previously swallowed-up by the village inn and with his face completely lost in a foaming white beard, emerged from a cottage and crossed for his nightcap at *The Mortal Man*. He was more nimble on his feet, however, and seemed in a tearing hurry to be getting to his destination.

"Hey, grandpa, ye'll be meetin' yerself comin' back if ye bustle like that," shouted one of the idlers.

The ancient was too intent on the matter in hand to heed his tormentor. He was under the thumb of his masterful daughter-in-law and she'd just granted him half an hour's leave. Almost trembling with eagerness, he entered the dark portals of *The Mortal Man*.

Littlejohn followed him in.

CHAPTER VI

Mortal Man

"What hempen homespuns have we swaggering here?
... I'll be an auditor;
An actor too, if I see cause."

ACT III. SC. I.

LITTLEJOHN ENTERED THE BAR-PARLOUR ALMOST UNNOTICED, for a diversion was going on. It was the nightly pleasure of certain regulars of *The Mortal Man* to bait the two oldest inhabitants of Stalden as they took their nightcaps. The detective walked right into such a bout.

The ancient of days who had just preceded him held the floor and was pitching into his opponent, the one with the long beard whom Littlejohn had encountered earlier in the evening.

"And who told you, Ben Beales, as moi insides weren't so good? You made it up, you did, to disgrace me. My insides is better'n yours any day, in spite o' the fac' as Oi can give 'ee ten years."

The old one's voice emerged from his froth of whiskers, shrill, sibilant, telling of no teeth.

"Oi on'y sez as yore Mary sez to my Jane, as yore innards waz on'y pretty middlin'..."

"Troi to disgrace me be'ind me back, Ben Beales. Jealous, that's wot you be..."

"Oi bain't, Sam, Oi bain't..."

The elder of the two thrust forth his foaming beard until it almost touched the dirty grey one of his rival. They tottered at each other as if about to execute some senile polka.

"Oo be the oldest o' we two?" quavered Sam Meads.

"You be, Sam, you be…" muttered Ben with some reluctance.

"Then don't argew," hissed the winner triumphantly.

"Oh, that'll do," grumbled a dark man, drinking quietly in a corner. With a wooden leg and a patch over one eye he would have looked like Long John Silver.

It was said in Stalden that in his nightly prayers to his Maker, Ben Beales asked for the speedy death of his rival, Sam Meads. Ben was eighty-five; Sam ninety-four, and Ben had long felt that his rival was hanging-on to life out of sheer cussedness and for the pleasure of doing him out of the honours of being oldest inhabitant and taking the drinks that go therewith. Sam had sworn to outlive his would-be supplanter.

"Ale bain't wot it woz," said Ninety-four, lowering half a pint. "Now when I fust started drinkin' ale, about ten I'd be, Ben there wasn't born then…"

"'Ow do you know, Sam Meads?" protested his opponent whose hand trembled so much with age and rage that he poured his beer down his beard.

"Wuz fergettin'. You'm a forriner an' not o' these parts o' Norfolk, Ben," retorted Sam, his temper restored by this bright sally.

"Bin 'ere seventy-noine year, man and boy!" shouted Eighty-five querulously.

"Fer God's sake put a sock in it, you two," snarled Long John, a local gamekeeper. "Dammit, we come 'ere fer a bit o' peace and pleasant company. Wot do we get? Two potty old curmudgeons argufyin'! Two as ought to know better and be settin' an example to the rest. Go 'ome, the pair of yer, an' get yer datters to tuck yer in yer little beds…"

There was a loud burst of laughter and the mention of their daughters seemed to remind the two ancients that they were out on ticket-of-leave and had better be off. Leaving someone else to pay for their drinks, they shambled out together, glaring at each other, presumably intent on renewing the contest on their way home. Had one died that night, the other would speedily have followed him. Each constituted the other's sole interest in life!

This comic prelude gave Littlejohn a chance to get settled in the company and his share in the laughter broke down any barrier which might have arisen against a stranger. They were a sociable and merry lot in the inn that night.

Once the old boys had cleared the stage, the more serious business of discussing the murder began.

"Who'd a thought of anybody wantin' to do fer old Wall," said a little weasel-like fellow, wiping the froth from his moustache on the back of his hand.

"And why not?" roared Long John aggressively. "Knew all the secrets of these parts and the folk in 'em, didn't 'e? Like as not, somebody told 'im too much, thinkin' they waz dyin' like, and then got better and were sorry for it."

"Oh, come, come," said Weazel. "Secrets o' these parts ain't as bad as all that."

"That's roight," said a tall, lean man, whose face seemed carved in melancholy lines from granite.

"I bet all of you's got some secret or other ye'd nearly rather kill somebody than yer wife, children, or parson, or neighbours should know. An', like as not, if you waz at death's door and got somebody like old Wall, kindly, friendly, one-of-ourselves sort o' doctor, you'd tell 'im yer sins 'stead o' to the vicar, 'oping to eaze yer conscience. Then you gets better, see? Wotyer feel like?"

"Oh, come off it, Steve," said the cobbler, apparently coming out of a trance and joining in. "Your job's killin', ain't it? But yer shouldn't think killin' a yewman bein's as easy as killin' a stoat or somebody's cat as is pinchin' yer pheasants."

"Thasright," ejaculated Granite.

"An' when they found the old chap hung up there, o' course, Doctor Keating wasn't in. Never is when he's wanted. I hear they 'ad to send to Olstead fer a doctor," grumbled a little, bilious-looking fellow, with red hair, disgustedly thrusting his nose into his pint pot.

"Oh, like as not, wenching all over the countryside," said Long John with an oracular sweep of a large dirty paw.

"Maybe it'll turn out to be suicide, after all," said a meek man, baring his yellow teeth in a smile and patting his bald pate as though either blessing himself or stimulating his brains to activity.

"It'll *wot*?" said Weazel. "Not on yer loife, Mr. Toft, not on yer loife. Wot would Mr. Wall be wantin' 'anging himself for? And, if wot I 'ears is k'rect, strangling hisself afore he slings hisself up..."

Subdued laughter greeted this ironic gem and Weazel, with a nod in Littlejohn's direction, added:

"Bet 'e could tell us a thing or two."

To which Littlejohn replied that he couldn't, that he was a new arrival, and that he didn't believe in combining duty with relaxation.

"I'd say the doctor... Keatin', I mean. I'd say he done it," boldly said the cobbler, now well in liquor and therefore throwing caution to the winds.

"An' why?" asked the mellifluous Toft.

"Remember the row they 'ad 'bout little Molly Selby's collar-bone? 'Ad Keating found it was broke? Not 'e. Remember 'ow Keating lost patients and respec' o' half the village through it? I say Keatin' done it afore he lost all his practice to Wall."

"Get away!" grumbled red-head. "That rate we'd all be killin' one another. Yer don't kill a chap because he pinches a bit of business from yer."

Red-head was doing a bit of boot repairing as a sideline in his spare time!

"S'right," intoned Granite.

"P'raps Mr. Wall hanged himself because Miss Cockayne's goin' to marry Rider," persisted the pacific Toft. "He was fond of Betty Cockayne, you know. Folk did say…"

"Now, now, now," rumbled Long John, whose special function seemed to be to keep the party clean and orderly. "Old Wall was a particular friend o' Miss Cockayne's, granted. But more like a father, that's all. If she were weddin' a good chap, nobody'd be more pleased than Wall. Some might like Rider. I don't know whether Wall liked 'im. I *don't*. Too sarcastic fer me. A deep 'un. Still, Wall might a' liked 'im. But get it out of yer 'ead, Mr. Toft, as Mr. Wall done fer himself. Remember, strangulation 'appened before he was hung. Keep on rememberin' it and don't be so persistent with yer suicide!"

Mr. Toft subsided, squashed, but goodwill reasserting itself, he ordered and paid for a pint for Long John to show there was no ill-feeling.

"S'right," muttered Granite, who by this time was in no condition to differentiate between right and wrong.

"Waddabout Dr. John from London? Inherits all the old man's wealth, as like as not," said Weazel. "'E might a' got tired waitin' and done 'is uncle in."

"A proper gentleman is Dr. John. If you must 'ave a doctor fer a murderer, 'ave old Keating. Come to that, 'e is one already, judgin' from number o' folk he's sided off into churchyard," said red-head, and almost yelled his head off with laughter at his own wit.

"Well, who could 'ave done it then if it's not suicide?" whispered Mr. Toft.

"Don't ask me," replied Weazel. "Ask the perlice." And he gave Littlejohn a dirty look as though resenting his silence.

"Time, gentlemen, please," said the landlord, bustling in.

"Thasright," said Granite, and without another word staggered out into the night.

Littlejohn ate his supper and retired to bed. Before he turned-in he wrote in his notebook the names which had been bandied about in the parlour, just to keep them in mind:—

Dr. John Wall.
Dr. Keating.
Miss Cockayne.
Mr. Rider.

Then he climbed into his old-fashioned four-poster with its sweet-smelling sheets.

To-morrow, the inquest, Mrs. Elliott, the vicar, John Wall, Cockayne, Keating, Rider...

He fell asleep.

CHAPTER VII

Parson

"This man doth present Wall."

ACT V. SC. I.

AFTER BREAKFAST AND AS HE WAITED FOR THE ARRIVAL OF Wall's housekeeper in the village, Littlejohn turned over the pages of the scrap-book which Gillibrand had left with him the previous day. It consisted almost entirely of newspaper cuttings, neatly pasted in chronological order, with here and there a few leaves apparently cut from some local guide book or history and dealing with the Stalden "doctors".

There were accounts of visits by persons of moderate eminence to the unqualified consultants. Such extracts came from the *Olstead Sentinel*, a local organ, and were obviously not "news" enough for the great dailies. Now and then, however, some instance did crop-up where wide publicity had been given to the doings of one or another of the Walls. One was a court case in which some doctor had brought an unsuccessful libel action. That had been years ago, against Old Samuel Wall, now, Littlejohn hoped, with God. One of the Taylors, too, had evidently overstepped the bounds of professional etiquette by taking over a case from one of the so-called quacks and been hauled before the medical powers-that-be. Escaped with a telling-off instead of being removed from the register.

Then came a number of pages extracted from unorthodox journals on new health, bonesetting, osteopathy, homœopathy and the like. Articles in which the work of the Walls was recorded and acclaimed. A club foot healed, long standing lesions relieved, paralysed limbs brought into service again. A regular gold mine for the specialist like Dr. John, but of little use in the investigation of murder. Littlejohn turned over the remaining blank pages, having merely scanned those concerned with technicalities. It was like reading a medical dictionary. Made one aware of the flesh and the ills it was heir to… Wonder if the old chap would have been any good for the cartilage I got kicked off at football thirty years ago and which bothers me a bit now and again? thought Littlejohn.

After the intervening blank pages, came another batch of clippings, which seemed for the most part to concern odds and ends, off the main track, of family history. The yellowed estate-agent's handbill extolling *The Corner House*. Scraps concerning the wills and monies left by certain local bigwigs. An article on local medicinal herbs by a field naturalist. Even a column on the husband of Mrs. Elliott, with details of his death at Mafeking and certain functions in his posthumous honour. Finally, Littlejohn took up a bunch of cuttings fastened carefully together by a paper clip. Here was something more in his line.

First came a column from the *Morning News* of ten years ago.

BANK ROBBERY IN GRAY'S INN ROAD

THIEF GETS CLEAN AWAY

CASHIER SHOT

"A daring hold-up occurred yesterday afternoon at the Gray's Inn Road Branch of the Southern Bank…"

Briefly, just as the bank was about to close for the day, a bearded man, evidently disguised, entered and at the point of a pistol forced the cashier to fill a bag which he carried with notes. Unfortunately, there were no other customers in at the time and of the staff of four, three only were on the premises. The fourth was out clearing a cheque. Upon the cashier showing fight, the intruder shot him and forced the manager, who entered from his room, to fill the bag instead. The remaining lady clerk he told to come round to the counter and hold up her hands. It was a job of five minutes and the thief then escaped by car, which he had left down the side street. On leaving the premises, the robber locked the door behind him, thus, although the alarm was immediately given, making sure of a fair start. The cashier was not seriously injured, the bullet fortunately passing just below the collar-bone. The car in question was later found in a car-park near Holborn Viaduct. No proper description could be given of the man, but the police were following certain clues… The manager, however, stated that the intruder seemed to suffer from some infirmity in his right hand and arm. He held his gun with the left hand and, on taking the bag of cash, transferred the weapon to his right and seemed to hold it with more difficulty. The proceeds of the robbery were said to be well over six thousand pounds.

Then followed a cutting of a few days later.

BANK GUNMAN STILL AT LARGE
CAR FOUND ABANDONED
THOUGHT STILL TO BE IN LONDON

Littlejohn rubbed his chin. What in the world was an out-of-the-way quack doctor doing with cuttings of hold-ups in London?

At the bottom of the file was yet another cutting. Just a mere scrap of less than an inch. It bore a date a year after the rest, nine years ago.

"Harold Greenlees, whose death sentence was later commuted to one for life, in connection with the Redstead Murder in 1922, was to-day released from prison."

What the…? Surely, old Wall wasn't interested in crime as well as broken bones. Yet, if so, why only the three cuttings? Perhaps they had some bearing on present events. At any rate full details of each would do no harm.

Littlejohn made his way to the telephone, rang up Scotland Yard and asked for full particulars of each of the cases mentioned in the cuttings. He then put the latter in his pocket-book, parcelled-up the scrap-book and locked it in his bag. It was time to call on Mrs. Elliott.

Mrs. Elliott reminded Littlejohn of the Cockroaches in Capek's *Insect Play*. In next to no time, she had had executed a special mourning order and was decked out in funereal black from head to foot. Gloves and stockings, too. Gillibrand was already at The Corner House and introduced the Scotland Yard man to the black woman. She had recovered from her shock somewhat and was very anxious to talk now, so filled with avenging spirits had she become.

"Nothin', nothin', I'd stop at nothin' to bring the brute who did that cruel thing to the master to the scaffold," she said and burst into tears.

"Well, let's get strictly to business, if you don't mind, Mrs. Elliott," said Littlejohn after a pause, during which the housekeeper sniffed herself back to a composed state.

"In the first place, did anyone know you were going away for the night when the crime occurred?"

"Not exactly, sir. But, of course, it would get all round the village after Mr. Wall took his meal at *The Mortal Man*; in fact, I know it did.

He told the landlord after his tea that I'd gone visitin' and wouldn't be back till the morrow."

"Another thing; were all the windows fastened when you left?"

"All except Mr. Wall's bedroom. He didn't like those downstairs to be open. They let-in too much noise from the road."

"Quite sure, Mrs. Elliott?"

"Certain. I did the rounds before I left."

"The french window, too?"

"Yes. The key was kept in the ornament on the mantelpiece."

"Was the window often opened?"

"Sometimes. Mr. Wall liked to sit on the lawn now and then, or even take a meal there when it was nice weather."

"Were there many comings and goings through the window? I mean were private patients admitted that way?"

"Never, sir. They'd always use the front door. The tradesmen used the side-door, that was used for the waiting-room entrance during consulting hours."

"I see. Would you be surprised to know that someone came in by the french window just before Mr. Wall's death?"

"I would that… I've *never* known it."

"I gather that at one time some of Mr. Wall's patients boarded here. Kind of nursing-home. Is that right?"

"Yes, sir."

"Were these guests under your care, Mrs. Elliott?"

"Yes, always. I saw to their comforts and food and Mr. Wall treated them."

"What kind of patients were they as a rule?"

"Well, sir… there'd be footballers having ligaments put right or muscles attended to. And perhaps somebody who didn't want to or couldn't travel long distances for treatment, so stayed here. Or else, sometimes people with plenty of money came for consultation, liked the village and the house, and stayed until the master had finished with them."

"Any queer characters among them?"

"Oh, plenty, sir. One old gentleman wouldn't use the bath. Never been used to anything but an old fashioned tub, he said. So I had to go to town and get one for him and carry up cans of water every morning. A colonel, he was, with a stiff leg. Mr. Wall did him a lot of good, too."

"H'm. Any patients who came on the quiet? I mean, who didn't want the world to know they were here?"

"Quite a number o' those, too, sir. One was a bishop, who had a son a doctor. And he'd neuritis that bad and the son not able to do him a ha'porth o' good. Mr. Wall set him right. But the bishop didn't want it thought his son was no good and he'd had to come to an unqualified man. We even had a doctor here once. Came in the dark for treatment, and went away in the dark. Spinal, I think."

"Very well, Mrs. Elliott. I think that's all for the time being. But I'm sure to want to see you again later. I'll be able to get to you easily?"

"Yes, sir. I'll be at my sister's for a week or two and Mr. Gillibrand has the address. They're on the 'phone."

Littlejohn talked over the case briefly with his colleague and then Gillibrand suggested the visit to the vicar.

"There's time before the inquest, if you've nothing more urgent, Littlejohn. This is a good time to catch the old chap at home."

They found the Rev. John Thorp snoozing in a chair on the delightful lawn of his vicarage, a gracious old place set amid trees and with a peaceful walled garden. The vicar was very old. He reminded Littlejohn of the Venerable Bede, for he had a long, snow-white beard, silky white hair with a tonsure of baldness at the crown, and placid blue eyes. He was in clerical attire and had an air of drowsy saintliness about him, such as often surrounds good old men. He would long ago have retired from Stalden, but the villagers wouldn't let him. So he paid a curate good money to do most of the work and himself became the patron saint of the place, to whom his flock brought their troubles and therein found much relief and consolation.

The old priest greeted his callers and Gillibrand, having introduced his friend, made excuses on the strength of the forthcoming inquest and took his leave. Mr. Thorp called for a chair and a bottle of beer for his guest and they settled down for a chat.

"I suppose you've called to discuss this shocking affair of Mr. Wall. Nothing of the kind has ever happened in this village before in my time or on the records of which I'm so fond," said the vicar. "I'm not only grieved at the loss of an old friend, but hurt and horrified beyond measure at the manner of his passing. I suppose there's no doubt that it's murder?"

"None whatever, sir. Medical evidence puts that beyond question."

"What baffles me, Inspector, is who should want to do such a dastardly thing to a public benefactor. For Mr. Wall was one. Not only by profession, but by his philanthropy in our own village. Many a one will have cause to mourn his passing."

"So I gather, sir. The family has long connections here, I understand."

"Yes. A hundred and thirty years exactly since this village saw Theodore Wall for the first time. He arrived one evening in 1812 with nothing but a few clothes tied up in a bundle. He was then thirty years of age. He came from Cumberland and said he was a blacksmith. Old Isaac Small, village blacksmith at the time and an aged man, took him on as assistant. When Isaac died five years later, Theodore took over the smithy. By that time he had earned quite a local reputation as a farrier. In fact, there wasn't much that young man didn't know about things on four legs. Horses, cattle, sheep and domestic animals... what he didn't know he learned from books and commonsense. It was not a long step to human ailments, which, in these parts are mainly surgical except in the old. Broken bones, cuts, poisoning of wounds, sprains, muscles and the like going wrong, and joints and such. Dr. Taylor, the local sawbones of the time, was away at the wars. People began to call in the horse doctor. Thus was established the family of Stalden 'doctors'."

The old man paused and his gentle, but remarkably searching blue eyes looked into those of his guest.

"I hope I'm not boring you, Inspector. I'm sure you've not called for a lesson in local history."

"Continue by all means, sir. This is most interesting. You have a remarkable memory."

"Interest, Inspector, interest. I've been here for more than sixty years and this is my world now... I don't remember Theodore, of course. I wish I did. I knew Samuel, his son, however, A fine man, who inherited his father's skill. He died in 1907 and I buried him. He it was who moved from the house by the old smithy and took The Corner House, then known as Patchings after the family who had just left it. Then there was Nathaniel. Born 1870 and now one must add, alas, died 1942. Samuel had two sons, Nat and Martin. Martin was three years older than Nathaniel and died in 1937. Nat was a bachelor. His fiancée, a nice girl from Olstead, died from a riding accident which all the poor fellow's skill couldn't repair. I don't think he ever thought of a woman after that. Martin married and his son, John, took his degree and set up in practice in the south. Every one of them good fellows of sound character and undoubted skill, although none was professionally qualified except young Jack. Funnily enough, it's only comparatively recently that they've got across the qualified fraternity. The Taylors, surgeons from father to son for nearly two hundred years, were most tolerant of them. Broadminded, charitable men they were. Keating here, however, has been most unpleasant, Perhaps he thought he'd cause for it. After all, it must be galling to have to undergo a long and costly training and then find that the bulk of the custom goes to what is called a quack, and, as if to add insult to injury, the hopeless cases are passed on for a death certificate. Nevertheless, there's work for both if they can only agree. I hardly dare to hope that Dr. Jack will come to take over the family practice, buy out the disgruntled Keating and amalgamate the two under a proper orthodoxy… May I offer you a cigar?"

The good man called for his cigar box, which was brought by a manservant. Littlejohn took advantage of the lull to turn the conversation in the direction he wished.

"I hear, sir, that The Corner House was something of a hospital at one time."

"Oh yes, Inspector, until quite recently. In fact, it overflowed into the village. I was a frequent caller there and one day I saw a bishop hiding in the private drawing-room. Yes, I did. I knew him well, but pretended not to see him."

The priest burst into hearty laughter at the thought of it.

"I've been wondering, Mr. Thorp, if at some time or other Mr. Wall discovered something about one of his patients which later recoiled on him in the tragic fashion we know."

"That I can't tell you. There have been some strange cases there, of course, but I can't discriminate. I often called after hours to smoke a pipe with Nathaniel and Martin, *and* with old Sam before them, but I saw little of the patients, of course. No, I can't help you there."

"I must confess to listening to gossip in the local inn last night, sir, and I overheard the names of Mr. Wall and Miss Betty Cockayne mentioned, as well as that of a Mr. Rider. Can you throw any light on the relationships?"

"Yes, Inspector, certainly. Betty Cockayne, who is twenty-eight—I christened her, so I know—was the adopted daughter of Miss Martlett, her aunt, who died last year. Miss Martlett took her when her parents were killed in a French railway accident during holidays. They lived here. The child was unfortunately left penniless, for whilst her mother, also a Martlett, had inherited quite a small fortune from her parents, she had invested it in her husband's business which, owing to his poor handling, was insolvent at his death. The surviving sister was comfortably off and when she died last year, left her niece and adopted daughter about thirty thousand pounds. I know that, too, because I was executor."

Littlejohn wondered what, in the family lives of his people, the old vicar was not connected with.

"When Betty was about fifteen she became very ill indeed. In fact, she began to lose the use of her lower limbs and the local doctors were baffled by the case. Finally, in desperation, Miss Martlett turned to Nathaniel Wall. He discovered, I believe—I'm no expert on these things, of course—that one of the spinal vertebrae had been displaced through the girl trying to crank-up her aunt's little car and was in some way pressing on the cord. He manipulated it into position again. That's just an example of what the Wall family was always doing. During that affair he became very fond of young Betty. In fact, I think he'd have adopted her then and there if her aunt would have agreed. At any rate, he was like a father to her and she thought the world of him."

"And now she's become engaged to a local man, I understand."

"Yes, Charles Rider. He lives at the last cottage in the village, a very pretty place and hardly a cottage. Evidently a man of means, who was struck by the locality and settled down here. He's been with us about ten years and, although he never comes to church, he's quite interested in the life of the village. A very close man, though. In all the ten years he's been here, I've learned little about him either directly or from gossip. He's said to be a writer. I've never read any of his books as I understand he writes novels under a pseudonym. A bit artistic-looking, Vandyke beard and all that. Nothing much wrong about him, though, although poor Mr. Wall was terribly upset when Betty Cockayne got engaged to Rider about a month ago. He said the fellow was fortune-hunting and had suddenly begun to take an interest in the girl after she'd inherited her aunt's money. I think he spoke to Betty about it, but you know what lovers are. They're certainly fond of each other..."

The old man stared at Littlejohn keenly.

"You're surely not connecting those two with the crime, are you? I do assure you, Inspector, that neither would think of such a thing. Mr. Rider had the greatest admiration for Nathaniel and has been heard publicly to say that he hoped to know more of the old man through his marriage with Betty."

"Didn't Mr. Wall like Rider before the engagement business, sir?"

"That I can't say, although I'm sure Nat would have told me. He frequently opened his heart to me, as, of course, he should. He just seemed indifferent to the man."

Littlejohn felt that he had trespassed enough on the vicar's time and rose to go. Quite apart from its business aspect, Littlejohn felt that the interview had done him good. There was a restfulness and a steadying calm about the old priest which seemed to convey itself to the spirit of those who enjoyed the privilege of his company. Stalden was indeed lucky in possessing such a man. Apparently from the first, when he arrived as a young clergyman new to the ministry, he had known what he wanted and stuck to it…

"Come again, Inspector. If I can help in any way, be sure I will and, if I'm no further use to you in the case you have in hand, come as a friend whenever you've a few minutes to spare."

"I certainly will, sir, and I'm very grateful for your help and interest."

"And now I must be getting along, too, Inspector," said the parson. "I've a call to make to take a very old and very aggressive lady a bottle of my port. Otherwise, I'd have asked you to lunch. If you're staying in the village, I shall expect you at church next Sunday, you know."

Littlejohn was there.

CHAPTER VIII

Coroner

"I will roar, that I will do any man's heart good to hear me;
I will roar, that I will make the duke say 'Let him roar again, Let him roar again.'"

ACT I. SC. II.

ON THE NIGHT BEFORE THE INQUEST, P.C. MELLALIEU OILED his boots well, for at his last appearance on such an occasion, he had, by the creakings and squeakings of his footwear, brought down ridicule on his head.

"Thank you, officer," the coroner had said after hearing him out. "Thank you, and next time, ahem, see that your boots are paid for..." And the whole court had rocked with laughter.

A proper one for a sarcastic joke at somebody else's expense was Mr. Timothy Shearwater and if he could come out like that at the inquest of such small fry as a bashful farm labourer, father of four, who had put a milkmaid in the family way and rather than face the music, had thrown himself into the local reservoir greatly to the consternation of the consumers, if Mr. Shearwater could come out like that, then, what might he do on the all-important morrow.

This involved thought passed many times through the bobby's mind in the course of the day, with the result that he set about his number elevens with neatsfoot oil until there wasn't a sound in them.

"I don't mind owld Shearwater bein' sarcastical with others, but on a chap wot's only doin' his dooty and not expected to be toffed-up to the nines in glassy kid or patent leathers, well, it's a bit thick, Ma, it's a bit thick," he confided to his wife.

"Well, don't you go makin' a fool of yerself again, that's all, disgracin' me and the children in the eyes of all the village..." was all the sympathy he received from his masterful spouse.

"He'd be better if he didn't shout so... People in the next village can 'ear 'im when he starts," said P.C. Mellalieu, this time to the boot on his fist.

Mr. Shearwater certainly had a good voice and knew how to use it. He roared his way through an inquest like a lion in the jungle. His inquiries were always short and sweet and anyone who wilfully or accidentally tried to prolong them got the full blast of the coroner's lungs and the whole edge of his sarcastic wit. He was a huge man with a thick black beard, shoulders like an ox and a keen intelligence. At one time, he had been the best pleader in Olstead and in defending malefactors, terrified not only his own clients but the rest of the advocates and the bench. Some shrewd local official had finally struck upon a good idea for giving the Olstead petty sessions a chance, by having Mr. Shearwater appointed county coroner. Since then, his milder partner had done the court work and the ferocious solicitor had had a court to himself to bellow in.

Mr. Timothy Shearwater arrived at the Women's Institute at Stalden, where he proposed to pitch his tent, in a pony and trap. Since the first day of the war, he had abandoned his car and put the rest of the local petrol-consuming gentry to shame by his example and whipping tongue.

Inspector Gillibrand and the coroner got on well together, for the police officer always rode a bicycle. No sooner had Gillibrand suggested an adjournment than Shearwater agreed. He contented himself by hearing the police, the doctor and Mrs. Elliott. The jury, dressed in their best and having seen the body, were a mere box of puppets and filed-out, disappointed and chagrined like the rest of the audience which crowded the hall. The whole place smelled of jam, for the women of the institute had been boiling and bottling furiously for over a week.

"Don't be nervous, man," thundered the coroner at the constable, who had rehearsed a pithy statement of his part in the affair so thoroughly, that he couldn't remember anything else and then forgot his lines at a crucial point. P.C. Mellalieu assumed the colour of his own beetroots, stammered, coughed, abandoned his script and launched into a long and involved account.

Mr. Shearwater took off his gold-rimmed spectacles, polished them meticulously on a silk handkerchief and took a deep breath. The constable felt himself shrinking like Alice in *Through the Looking Glass* and waited for the storm to break.

"Thank you, constable, that will do," thundered Mr. Shearwater. "You behaved with promptitude and good sense... That will do."

Mellalieu somehow stumbled from the box and as he went on his rounds for many days to come, he trod air. His wife, to mark her approval, gave the police house an extra spring-cleaning, although it was well past midsummer, and made her husband a succession of his favourite apple dumplings, which, by giving his digestion too much to do, counteracted to some extent the lightness of his heart and spirits.

Mrs. Elliott was the next on the list and entered the box darkly. In spite of her attire, she cast no gloom over the coroner nor caused him to pitch his voice in a funereal key. He questioned her with gusto and received her replies with obvious relish. Her evidence consisted of a more or less embellished repetition of what she had told the constable in the presence of the corpse. She recited in a flat voice a summary of events leading to the discovery of the body and gave her opinion concerning the state of mind of the deceased just before she last saw him.

"Did anyone suggest that you should take a day's holiday visiting your sister?" boomed Mr. Shearwater.

"It was my sister herself, sir," came the response, all the more feeble and plaintive following the questioner.

"Did anyone know that in advance?"

"Plenty of people, sir."

"WHO EXACTLY?"

"Well, sir, I should think Mr. Wall told most of those he met during evening surgery and as he was eating his evening meal at the inn or having his drink."

"I see. Medical evidence mentions something about his supper. Did he have that at home?"

"Yes, sir. Half-past ten every night like clockwork. I left it ready on a tray, just biscuits and the dish of cheese, with a bottle of beer for him to open…"

"So, he must have had it between returning from *The Mortal Man* and meeting his death, for the biscuits had been eaten and the bottle opened."

The coroner dismissed the housekeeper.

"I offer you my sympathy, Mrs. Elliott. You have lost a good master and presumably a good post."

Whereupon the witness burst into tears and was assisted from the box by her attendant sister, also dressed in complete mourning for the occasion.

Dr. John Wall followed, gave evidence of identification, expressed his emphatic opinion that his uncle's state of mind and the medical evidence precluded suicide and was thunderously scolded by Mr. Shearwater for anticipating the police surgeon, who followed him and gave a technical account of the cause of death.

"Please translate that into everyday terms for the benefit of ignoramuses like myself and the jury," roared the coroner, benevolently baring his teeth and showing his red lips through his huge beard.

The resulting simple statement of physiological facts caused a stir in court something like a mixture of a deep groan and the murmurs of sympathetic endearment made by certain women in the presence of infants and pet dogs. This noise was really a mass exhibition of grief and condolence and caused Mr. Shearwater to look over the top of his glasses at the packed house and take a deep breath as though preparing to blow them all out of the place. Instead, he uttered a long sigh like the wind in the willows and went on with his writing. He next raised his head and announced an adjournment.

That was all the inquest the villagers got that day. A deaf old man whose daughter had been keeping him posted in a stage whisper was heard to remark in a loud voice that "Crowner be playin' about to make things last longer and tantalize the folk", and Beales and Meads, who had been glaring at each other across the room throughout the proceedings, now opened noisy hostilities concerning what happened at an inquest on a man who was brained whilst bell-ringing in 1872. Beales, the youngster, finally fled from the field and could be heard in another part of the room telling a juvenile of sixty-eight what happened to Samuel Wall in 1899.

"Flung from his pony-cart he was and broke both his legs. Ted Harrows, the roadman, found 'im in the ditch and swearin' loike a trooper. Could swear wi' the best, could old doctor. 'Nobody's goin' to set moi bloody legs but me,' says Mr. Samuel. 'So you can put me in that barrow o' yours and wheel me to me blasted surgery.' An' he swore somethin' 'orrible as Ted lifted 'im, as best 'e could, sayin' as he were makin' of 'em worse... hee... hee... hee..."

His mirth was short-lived, however, for from his elbow came the voice of his familiar spirit.

"You'm all wrong agen, there, Ben Beales, as usual... That were Master Theodore in 1852... that's moi toime, but long afore you was thought of. My old father told me that tale..."

The villagers were sore about the curtailment of their pleasure and some looked ready to throw brickbats at the coroner, who mounted his trap with a vigorous bound and bowled-off to an inquiry in a neighbouring hamlet, where an old man had died of a surfeit of mushrooms and beer before the doctor could get at him. On the way he passed a number of cars parked in front of the pub and muttered "HOWLING CADS" to himself in a roar which swept the village from end to end.

Returning to the inn, Littlejohn found the post awaiting him.

There was a packet from The Yard giving full details of the crimes reported in the yellowed newspaper cuttings he had unearthed.

The Gray's Inn bank-robber had never been laid by the heels, but his identity was known. He was Percival Bates, who had already served a term of imprisonment for making counterfeit money. He had evidently found a better way of securing banknotes later.

The identity of Bates had, more or less, been established from the bank manager's description. Then followed particulars of the man. His right arm had been partially paralysed and his nose broken and turned awry after an explosion which had wrecked a laboratory in which he had worked prior to turning to bad ways. A chemist originally, he had shown an aptitude for metal processing and engraving which had led him astray. The police thought he had slipped through their net and gone abroad. No trace of him had been found since the bank crime. He had served his first term in Dartmoor prison from 1924 to 1930. His record had there been exemplary and he had finished up as a librarian.

As regards the murderer at Redstead, there was little to report.

He had lived peaceably on a smallholding near Truro since his release from Dartmoor. The police knew his exact whereabouts. His sister, of whom he had been very fond, had got herself in trouble with a local man, who had treated her badly. She apparently broke down under the strain and drowned herself. Harold Greenlees had thereupon visited the seducer and mercilessly thrashed him; to such an extent that he had died in hospital three days later. He had been found guilty of murder but the jury had made strong recommendations to mercy. Condemned to death, however, Greenlees had found sympathetic support in his own neighbourhood and a monster petition for reprieve had been signed. At the last minute, the sentence had been commuted to life imprisonment. Good behaviour, combined with official broadening of views had resulted in his premature release.

Littlejohn thought hard and studied the records carefully for a long time and then, having made up his mind, telephoned Detective-Sergeant Cromwell at Scotland Yard, giving him detailed instructions concerning certain lines of inquiry he wished him to pursue. Then he took out his notebook, entered certain points in it and studied the whole again.

"What time are Dr. Keating's surgery hours?" he asked the waitress who cleared away the remnants of his meal.

"Six-thirty to eight," said the girl, eyeing him critically and wondering what was wrong with the ham and eggs.

Littlejohn laughed.

"I'm not ill, girl. It's a private matter I want to talk about and I've just time before he sees his patients."

Greatly relieved, the maid burst into a fit of uncontrolled giggling, rolled her bright eyes at the Inspector, knocked over a dish of pineapple chunks on the table and retired in confusion, backing her way to the door like someone exiled from a royal presence.

CHAPTER IX

Doctor

"Out, loathèd medicine! Hated potion, hence!"

ACT III. SC. II.

ALEXANDER KEATING, M.B., CH.B., WAS STANDING IN HIS consulting-room drinking whisky when Littlejohn rang his door bell. The doctor had lately ceased from drinking in his wife's presence; the reproach in her eyes took away half the pleasure of it.

After an undistinguished school career, Keating drifted into medicine mainly through lack of enthusiasm for anything else and through the efforts of a forceful mother, who had a fancy for putting her round-peg in a square hole as a "healer", as she called him. He failed several times both in inters and finals, but at length scraped through. He lived riotously among the worst sets in the medical school. This was the man whom the examiners and the faculty launched into the world to heal the sick. He soon began to hate the job he had so irresponsibly chosen.

Keating was quite unable to behave with due professional decorum. His former wildness remained dormant in his blood for a time and then burst out again under the strain of holding down a country practice, bought with the money of the girl he had married as soon as he graduated. The sense of frustration caused through competition with his only local rival, a quack, whose unqualified skill and prestige far exceeded his own, was more than he could bear. He had bought the practice from the executors of the last of the Taylors for about £4,000. At first, it yielded a fair return, but the newcomer's reputation soon spread. His personality and his professional failures were not conducive to retaining what he had inherited from the old and eminent family of country physicians he followed. There was the story of the child and her collar-bone, too, following him everywhere. He chose to blame this incident entirely on Wall, dubbed him a charlatan and thus roused the ire of almost the whole of the area, which was rather proud of its bonesetter. Unable in any legal way to assail his rival or discredit him, the thwarted Keating took to drink. He had taken too much liquor when the maid brought in Littlejohn's card.

The girl was saucy. She was too young and pretty for her master to resist and Mrs. Keating had given her notice. The doctor's wife was contemplating handing-in her own notice as well and retiring to her parents' home.

"What's *he* want?" growled Keating.

"Search me!" said the maid with impudent familiarity.

The doctor leered at her over his glass.

"Show him in."

"Well, Inspector. Am I a suspect then? I didn't kill him, you know, although I'd damn well have liked to."

"As you apparently already know, doctor, I'm here investigating the death of Mr. Wall and, as the only doctor in the place, I thought you might be able to throw some light on his activities from a fresh angle."

"Have a drink!"

"No thanks, sir."

"Well, if I tell you that, thanks to Wall's activities, filching my patients and good name—an outsider can do it; a qualified man can't—he's reduced the value of this practice to next to nil. Almost ruined me. Now that he's gone, thank God, it'll perhaps buck-up. Might just as well have poured my money down the drain as invested it in this one-eyed hole..."

"Yes?"

"Yes. Of course, my predecessor, Dr. Taylor, belonged to a family of local gentry who'd been here since the year One! They had immense local influence and you know what that is. Wall battered himself against that without any effect. But I came in as a stranger and had to make my way. Hell! It makes my blood boil to think of what I've stood from Wall."

Littlejohn, looking at the shaking hands and shifty eyes of the doctor, added his own inward commentary to the sorry tale. He also noticed that the doctor smoked and drank with the help of his left hand.

"You quarrelled with the bonesetter, I understand?"

"Like hell I did. Gave him the full length of my tongue a time or two. Wouldn't *you* if a quack had the bloody impudence to take your patients, treat 'em till they were at death's door, and then sling 'em back at you for a death certificate that he couldn't give? Or else because I could perform operations that would land him in quod if he tried 'em?"

The Inspector remembered the collar-bone, but did not mention it!

"So you had a row or two, then?"

"Yes—as I've already said. Why keep laying it on? I didn't string-up the old chap or throttle him, if that's what you're at. But I told him where he got off and what I'd do if I ever got a chance, through the police-courts, I meant, not taking the law into my own hands..."

Littlejohn could imagine Keating brawling with his neighbour after lacing himself with courage from a bottle. He could imagine the frigid reaction of Wall, too.

"No, doctor, I didn't think you'd go to the extent of killing."

"I don't know... I felt that way sometimes. You know how you get? I wouldn't have strangled him, though. Shooting's more in my line..."

"Where were you between ten and eleven on the night of the crime, Dr. Keating?"

Littlejohn fired the question suddenly, quietly watching the man's reactions. Keating didn't like it at all. A queer look came over his features, a sort of tightening of the muscles of his eyelids and a sly sidelong glance.

Keating pretended to think hard. His response was not convincing and bore the hall-mark of a trumped-up tale.

"Ah yes. I was at Marsh Farm. Mrs. Bargery had had a bad passage with her first child the night before and I had to call again then. I was there at the time you mention. You can confirm it if you like."

"Thanks, doctor. I think that's all. You weren't in when the body was found, otherwise I'd have been asking you a lot more perhaps."

"No. Dammit, I can't be expected to stay indoors on the strength of people being likely to need me when they get themselves done-in. Now, can I? It was my night off, too. Long past usual surgery hours when it happened. It would have been damned ironical and like my luck to be called-in to bring-round the chap who'd ruined me, wouldn't it? However, I seem to have missed the boat this time... to my advantage, eh?"

Keating poured out more whisky and drank again.

Outside, the waiting-room seemed to be filling-up with patients.

"Sounds like surgery time, Inspector. Hear 'em? Panel patients coming for their money's worth. Nothing wrong with them, but just want their dose of physic and the doctor's time… Hell! Why did I ever become a doctor? Never liked it. Tied hand and foot by etiquette when I want to be free to enjoy life. Surgery hours, calls, up all times of the day and night. And old Wall never called-out in the dark, of course. Sleeping snug in his little bed while the M.B. does the rounds of the quack's daytime following. I wish I'd joined the police myself!"

"It's just as difficult getting the truth out of people in the police as it is dragging out information and diagnosing symptoms by the doctor," answered Littlejohn.

"Meaning…?" said Keating, alternately maudlin and nasty under his drink. His patients were in for a good time without a doubt.

"Nothing, doctor. Good evening and thanks."

Keating let Littlejohn depart and then emptied his glass. Before calling in his first patient, he reached for the telephone, dialled a number and began a long, detailed conversation with whoever came on at the other end.

CHAPTER X

Beloved

"O dainty duck! O dear!"

ACT V. SC. I.

MISS BETTY COCKAYNE HERSELF ANSWERED THE DOOR TO Littlejohn. She was a good-looking girl, with large, wide-set brown eyes, high cheek bones, small straight nose, firm pointed chin and black hair which shone with a blue sheen like gunmetal. She was wearing black-rimmed spectacles as she faced the detective. She removed these as she listened to him explaining the purpose of his visit, and her eyes looked deeper-set and misty as is often the case with those who wear glasses regularly. Littlejohn judged that she would be about thirty.

The mistress of Green Hedges waited until the Inspector had finished his introduction and then bade him enter.

The house was small, cosy and well-furnished. The room they entered had large windows overlooking a well-kept lawn and flower-garden. A pleasant place.

Miss Cockayne put on her glasses again and offered Littlejohn a seat and a cigarette. A cursory glance round the room told Littlejohn of good taste in furniture and pictures and the many books on shelves and scattered here and there suggested an owner of more than average intelligence and of catholic interests.

"So you want to hear my tale about Mr. Wall, do you, Inspector? I'm afraid I can't help you much in your investigation. He was an old dear and a very good old friend of mine. I haven't got over the horrible end he's come to. Who could want to murder an inoffensive benefactor of all who came in contact with him, I can't imagine."

"You've known him since you were a child, Miss Cockayne?"

"Yes. Ever since I could toddle. But only since he cured me from a serious illness when I was in my 'teens, have we been intimate. He visited me so often then, that we became firm friends. I called him uncle, and he liked it."

Littlejohn could well imagine the old bachelor finding joy in the company of this vivacious girl. Her manner of speech and the firmness of her chin convinced him, however, that neither Wall nor anybody else would make her do what she didn't want to do, or turn her from doing what she wanted.

"I hear though, that Mr. Wall combined benevolence with a certain forthrightness of speech and a stubbornness—arising no doubt, from a strong and upright character—which might have caused certain people to dislike him. Was that so?"

"Oh, yes. He knew his own mind and stuck to his opinions like glue. He and I often had friendly wrangles about things he thought I ought or ought not to do. But we always ended friends."

"Not quite such good friends, though, at the time of his death were you, Miss Cockayne?"

The woman's mouth tightened and she looked the Inspector straight in the eye.

"What exactly do you mean by that, Inspector?" she said testily.

Littlejohn was gradually gathering the impression that Miss Cockayne had been used to getting her own way from most people with whom she came in contact. Her aunt, old Wall and the folk of the village had, no doubt, humoured her and spoiled her as a child and she had carried her expectations of homage into later life. Probably, too, what charm and the fact that she was an orphan had won for her in childhood, had become the dues to her beauty in later life.

"I mean exactly what I say, Miss Cockayne," replied the detective. "To tell you the truth, I learn from talk in the village that there's been a coldness between you and your old friend of late."

"How stupid, Inspector. Do detectives place reliance on idle chatter of gossips then? If so, it's a poor look-out for the innocents of the world."

"Your rebuke is quite uncalled-for, Miss Cockayne. It's the duty of one investigating a dastardly crime of this type to search everywhere for help, rejecting nothing until it's been proved irrelevant or untrue. This story has come to me from more than one source, reliable sources, too. Come now, Miss Cockayne, for the sake of your affection for your late friend, you owe me a straight answer, to say nothing of furthering the ends of justice."

"I've nothing to say about it. I regard your question as an unwarrantable intrusion in my private affairs, Inspector."

"Very well, then, Miss Cockayne. I must tell *you* then why you and Mr. Wall weren't such good friends as formerly in the days just before his death. He objected to your marriage… or rather your engagement to Mr. Rider, didn't he?"

The girl flushed scarlet and rose to ring the bell for the maid to show out her visitor.

"Before you ring," said Littlejohn, "just one more word, Miss Cockayne. I'm giving you a chance to tell me informally what was the trouble between you and Mr. Wall and why he objected to your engagement. If you refuse, I shall use every official means in my power to get the information from other sources. That may result in some unpleasant publicity… in fact, you and Mr. Rider will be brought forward as witnesses at the resumed coroner's enquiry and asked under oath the questions I'm now putting to you in private and in the quietness of your own home."

"You cad!... No, I didn't mean that, Inspector. I'm sorry. I suppose you're only doing your duty, as the stock detectives always say..."

"Have it your own way, Miss Cockayne," said Littlejohn rising. He had had quite enough of the woman's impudence.

"Don't go, Inspector Littlejohn. Perhaps I'd better tell you. Mr. Wall did object to our engagement."

"Why?"

"I suppose you know that not long ago, I inherited quite a considerable fortune on the death of my aunt. I'd been friendly with Mr. Rider for long before that... In fact, I've known him ever since he settled here eight or more years ago."

"Mr. Wall thought Mr. Rider was after your money, then?" continued Littlejohn relentlessly.

"Yes, he did. He was quite wrong, but he stuck to his guns, like a stubborn mule. I tried to convince him. He was just prejudiced against my fiancé. In fact, I don't think he ever liked him. Why, I can't imagine. They lived in separate worlds, of course. Mr. Wall was an excellent practical man with little or no interest in art and letters; whereas Mr. Rider's an artist and scholar to his fingertips."

Littlejohn felt that he had an idea whence the taste for D. H. Lawrence, Proust, Barbellion, Joyce and others whose works were prominent on Miss Cockayne's shelves, had been derived. He had never read any of them, but Mrs. Littlejohn had...

"Were Mr. Wall and Mr. Rider well known to each other, then?"

"Well, they *did* live in the same village, you know! Mr. Rider's is the last house on the main road. They probably met almost every day, but avoided each other. To tell you the truth, Mr. Rider regarded

Mr. Wall as an old fossil. Bourgeois respectability and morality, Victorian stuffiness and all that. And Mr. Wall, in turn, thought Mr. Rider an adventurer and a good-for-nothing dilettante. Funny, isn't it? I knew them better than they knew each other and I liked them both. When we'd been married a bit and Mr. Wall had been persuaded to visit our home, I'm sure they'd have found a lot in common and grown to like each other immensely…"

Littlejohn wondered.

"…Just like men, though, Inspector. Like great boys, all of them. So anxious to be cocking it over each other, like roosters. You're married of course? I'm sure your wife would agree with me if she were candid."

Littlejohn wished his wife, Letty, could have heard this nonsense. She had a way of dealing with prigs like Miss Cockayne.

It was now becoming quite plain that this good-looking girl had somehow completely fallen under the spell of Rider, whoever he might be, had lapped-up a crowd of cranky notions from him and had been completely spoiled thereby. There was an air of stupid sophistication about Miss Cockayne, probably the result of Rider's influence on her. Mr. Rider was on Littlejohn's visiting list and the detective rather looked forward to seeing him.

"So, Mr. Wall objected strongly to Mr. Rider as your future husband?"

"*Most* strongly. I naturally told him one of the first, on account of our long friendship. He also regarded himself, more or less, as my unofficial guardian and I often went to him for advice and sometimes to open my heart about problems and troubles. You know how it is?"

"Quite. And he objected to his place being taken by another."

"Not half. I've never seen him in such a rage. In fact, bad temper was quite alien to Mr. Wall's nature, but when I told him of our engagement, he went right off at the deep-end. Said Mr. Rider was a good-for-nothing and after my money, and that he'd never loved anybody but himself all his life. Well, seeing that Mr. Wall had never given Mr. Rider a chance to show himself in his real colours, I thought that most unfair and prejudiced. I told him so, rather heatedly."

"And what did he say?"

"Oh, that a girl like me was no good at reading character. As if that counts when you're in love! He also said that I knew nothing at all about Mr. Rider and his family and antecedents."

"Did *he*?"

"He hinted that he did, but I couldn't get anything out of him on that score. I told him that *I'd* known my fiancé long enough to know my own mind, and that I was old enough, too. I wasn't concerned with ancestors or family. I'd known him long enough to be quite content to marry him…"

"Yes?"

"Well, uncle, that is, Mr. Wall, said it was just a temporary infatuation and would soon pass off. Then, he went on to say that I didn't want to throw myself away on the first man that came along with a proposal. He knew that Mr. Rider wasn't the first, but he was just being nasty. I told him so and I went off right away and stayed away, just to show him that he couldn't treat me like a kid in short frocks any more."

"And that was the last of your friendship?"

"No, not really. Uncle got me on the 'phone the same night and asked if that was my last word. Begged me to be careful and all that… I told him I was old enough to look after myself and live my own life."

"Then?"

"He called here and we quarrelled again."

"Mr. Wall must have been terribly keen on preventing your marriage to Mr. Rider, Miss Cockayne."

"Awfully. And just out of pure pig-headedness, I think. He'd made up his mind and nothing would budge him. I determined to be the same."

"Did Mr. Wall tackle Rider about it, too?"

"Yes. He called on him and played hell with him. Accused him of marrying me for my money. Mr. Rider showed him the door..."

"That is Mr. Rider's account, of course?"

"Yes. Why?"

"Nothing."

"And what did Mr. Rider think of Mr. Wall?"

"Oh, he was very tolerant and humoured him, but, dash it all, it did get a bit thick towards the end. Half the village had got to know about it and if it hadn't been for the past, I'd have kicked up a frightful row about it. As it was, I said I was going to marry Mr. Rider whatever uncle said and he'd see that he'd have to eat his words when he found out how happily things went."

Now that Miss Cockayne had started on the topic, there seemed to be no stopping her. Littlejohn decided to change the angle.

"What does Mr. Rider do, by the way?"

"He's a publisher's reader."

"Very interesting. Does he do a lot of it?"

"Not a great deal. He has enough private income to live on comfortably."

"Novels, I take it he reads, eh?"

"Yes and poetry. It's a bit hush-hush, you know. I never see the manuscripts about or get a chance to read them. Part of the etiquette of the profession, Mr. Rider tells me. Secrecy, you know, in case the thing is turned down. They don't want it making public. Natural, isn't it?"

Littlejohn knew more about publishing than Miss Cockayne thought, and guessed that Rider had been stuffing her with a lot of bunkum to avoid too much investigation of his real job. Probably an arty scrounger, a good-for-nothing, as Wall had shrewdly surmised, and setting his cap at Miss Cockayne as an easy source of wealth.

"Which publishers does he read for? I know quite a lot of them in London."

"That I can't say, Inspector, but they think very highly of him. I've seen letters just gushing thanks to him for choosing best-sellers. No, the nearest I've been to his precious manuscripts is seeing them sent-off to London by registered post."

"From Stalden?"

"Yes. Why?"

"Nothing really. I wondered if there were a proper post-office here… I haven't seen it. Bought my stamps from the landlord of *The Mortal Man.*"

"Oh, yes. The post-office is Miss Mullins's, the general store just along the main road to the right from here…"

Littlejohn knew it quite well.

"Oh, thanks," he said.

"And now I really must go, Miss Cockayne. Thank you very much for being so candid about your private affairs. I promise you to be discreet…"

"And do please find out who murdered uncle, quickly. I may have had rows with him of late and perhaps we'd both been beasts to each other, but I was fond of him and he of me. I'm so sorry we didn't make it up…"

Then and there Miss Cockayne burst into tears. A strange mixture of Riderian nonsense superimposed on a very decent nature. Perhaps a bit spoiled before Rider took her in hand, but worthy of a good, straightforward chap for a husband instead of a half-baked adventurer. Although he had not yet come across Rider, Littlejohn felt he knew him quite well. He imagined him to be a feeble, posing noodle of an emasculated Bloomsbury type, beard, corduroy trousers, half washed, dirty-nailed, shoddy thinking… He was in for a shock.

As Littlejohn bade Miss Cockayne good-bye in the hall, the garden gate clanged and steps were heard approaching the front door. Without knocking or ringing, the newcomer turned the knob and entered the house.

Miss Cockayne introduced the two men.

Nothing of the flabby half-washed poet here. True, the beard was vandyke and curly. The hair was thick, auburn and grey, the brow high and narrow, the lips long, thin and firm and the nose formidable. The eyes behind slightly smoked spectacles, probably Crookes's lenses, were hooded and hard. The hands large and strong and the body sinuous and apparently in first-class trim. In the late forties probably.

The Inspector was not surprised that Rider had failed to impress Wall. How he could have captured the heart of Miss Cockayne was a puzzle! Perhaps a good talker or, in his better moments, possessed of a certain amount of virile charm. Whatever it was, Littlejohn felt sorry for Miss Cockayne, for when the bloom had worn off the fruit, there would be some bitterness to follow. No wonder old Wall objected! The fellow was a cross between Mr. Murdstone and Mr. Carker! Here he was, greeting Littlejohn pleasantly, but with a challenging look of inquiry in his eye.

"Glad to meet you I'm sure, Inspector. Hope you soon run the blighter to earth... You must pay me a call when you're at a loose end. I spend a lot of time gardening and if you're interested I've rather a nice show now."

"Thanks, I'll be delighted. In fact, I'd planned to call on you in connection with the death of Mr. Wall..."

Rider gave Littlejohn a quizzical look, one eyebrow cocked.

"I understand you and he have met lately under not too pleasant circumstances."

"Ah, I see someone's been telling tales."

Rider glanced inquiringly in the direction of his fiancée, who did not speak, however.

"You know where to find me, then, Inspector?"

"Yes... Miss Cockayne has told me where you live."

"Ah... She has, has she? Very informative this afternoon, Betty, aren't we?"

Miss Cockayne smiled at her lover. Littlejohn felt like shaking her. She was completely under Rider's domination. And with a chin like that, too! If she'd cared to assert herself...

"Well, good-bye, Inspector. Glad to have met you. Looking forward to seeing you at my place," said the newcomer and with that Littlejohn departed.

As he made his way down the garden path, he could see Rider watching him off and then turning to meet Miss Cockayne as she entered the room.

The young lady was in for another cross-examination, probably less pleasant than the last.

CHAPTER XI

Reveller

"I can no further crawl, no further go;
My legs can keep no pace with my desires.
Here will I rest me till the break of day."

ACT III. SC. II.

After leaving Green Hedges, Littlejohn decided to call at Marsh Farm to confirm the doctor's alibi, which he mistrusted. He was casting around for someone from whom to inquire the direction, when P.C. Mellalieu hove in sight, pursuing his stately course in a round of the village. The constable saluted and the Inspector asked his way from him.

"I'm goin' part the road myself, sir," said the bobby. "And then I'll put you on the right track."

Together they took the highway and tramped out beyond the village boundaries. Littlejohn tried to make conversation with his companion, but the poor fellow was completely tongue-tied and overawed at having one so famous at his side. Poor Mellalieu didn't get much practice in conversation. He didn't believe in being too familiar with the villagers. After all, the law must not be seen gossiping and back-slapping with every Tom, Dick and Harry in the place. And at home, Mrs. Mellalieu did all the talking. To tell the truth in justification of the P.C., he was a shy man, without a gift of tongues. He hid this defect beneath a veneer of silent self-sufficiency. His eldest son, Joseph, (called after his mother's father, of course,) was Mellalieu's safety-valve, his particular favourite and buddy. Every Sunday, wet or fine, the pair went for a long walk and then Mellalieu chattered all the way; the full spate of all the past week's experiences. Like many men who have nothing to say or who can't express what they have to say coherently, Mellalieu earned a local reputation for depth and great wisdom hidden under a bushel, and hence was respected.

Clump, clump, clump. That and his heavy breathing was most of the noise Littlejohn's companion made all the way. The Inspector tried to plumb his knowledge, experience and hobbies, but it was no use. The bobby answered in monosyllables, or if he did try to expand, poor chap, he grew involved and incoherent and gave up the ghost half-way in confusion. Littlejohn felt as though he were being silently marched to the lock-up, and no familiarity!

"'Ere we are, sir," said Mellalieu at length and in the longest speech of the session, he put the Inspector on his way. "'Ere's the path. You follers this lane, crosses the first stile to the right, then, there in front of yer, is the farm. Marsh Farm. There ain't no marsh and never was as far as I know."

And with a salute, he bade his superior good-day, blushed, shuffled his feet and stumped off on his business without more ado. When Littlejohn had disappeared, the constable removed his helmet, which released a flood of pent-up perspiration down his face, and solemnly mopped himself up with a red handkerchief. All cause for repression having gone, he began to chatter volubly to himself.

Marsh Farm was small, compact and cosy looking, with buildings of red brick and roof-tiles to match. Bargery, the farmer, was in the first field apparently inspecting his stock and Littlejohn bade him good-morning. The man looked under the weather, as was natural if what Mrs. Harris had said about his either celebrating or lamenting the arrival of his first-born, with the help of the bottle, was true. He gave Littlejohn a hearty good-day, but eyed him with a mixture of fear and suspicion. The Inspector noticed the telephone wire leading to the farm and guessed that Dr. Keating had already arranged for his alibi to be confirmed.

"How's your wife, Mr. Bargery? I hear from the village that she hasn't been having too good a time."

The man looked surprised.

"Goin' on nicely, thank 'ee, sir. Child, too. A fine bouncing boy, sir."

"Good. I'm glad to hear it. Touch-and-go for a time with Mrs. Bargery, I gather."

"Yes, sir. Fair put me out it did..."

"By the way, was the doctor here the other night?"

"Yes, sir. Night that Mr. Wall died in the village, doctor was here from ten until nearly midnight."

"Sure?"

"Yes, sir."

The poor fellow lied without much conviction. Probably felt under a great obligation to the doctor for pulling his wife through and was doing his best to do him a good turn.

"Right, thanks, Mr. Bargery. Good day."

Back in the village, Littlejohn met Mrs. Harris pursuing her somewhat uncertain way on a bicycle. Her black bag was strapped ostentatiously on the carrier. He gestured to her and she dismounted, wheeling her bike to join him with an unwilling air, as though suggesting that at any moment something might happen in the family way to one of her clients and she couldn't waste any time in idle chatter.

"Mrs. Harris, you told me the other day that you were at the Bargery's when Mr. Wall was killed. Was the doctor there with you?"

"No! I can mannige quite well without 'im. Breathin' his whisky on the newly born! Disgustin', I calls it. He was there at the birth. I *had* to send for him through no fault of mine, mind you. Much good he was when he *did* arrive. After that, I manniged myself. Most of the children in this village are mine with no medical 'elp needed..."

With this scandalous assertion, the midwife mounted again, wobbled dangerously for about fifty yards and then sped off, treading the pedals heavily. Nothing but an imminent accouchement could have thus saved Littlejohn from a long spate of woe and gossip and he couldn't help feeling grateful to someone unknown for the relief. He made straight for the doctor's house and rang the bell. The cheeky maid admitted him.

"What, you again!" said Keating, who was just in for lunch and was sitting writing up his account book with a glass at his elbow.

"Yes, doctor. I won't take up much of your time. All I want to ask is why you gave me a false alibi for your movements of the other night."

Keating sprang to his feet in an effort to bluff himself out of his difficulties.

"What the hell! Bargery told you I was there, didn't he?"

"Oh yes, doctor. Almost before I asked him. He'd learned the piece you taught him over the 'phone properly, but spoke it a bit too fluently and prematurely."

"Look here, Inspector. I won't stand for any third degree. I told you where I was and it's been confirmed. That's all there is to it. You've got a suspicious mind. I tell you, I had nothing to do with Wall's death."

"Perhaps you didn't. But you weren't at Bargery's, you know. The nurse happened to be there at the time and confirms what I suspected, that you've concocted an alibi!"

Dr. Keating slumped down in his chair and tossed-off half a glass of whisky at a gulp.

"So what?" he said, uneasy fear showing through the bluff.

"Let me have a proper tale, doctor. That's all. Lying won't do any good and only focuses suspicion on you."

By this time, the man couldn't meet Littlejohn's eye. He talked to a paper-knife which he held in his left hand.

"Oh, very well then. If you must have it, you must. Though you'll believe this less than the first tale. Blast Bargery!"

"Blast nobody. Don't in future try to involve decent people in deceit of the police. Now, doctor, where were you?"

"I slept the night in my car in the road through Hanbury Wood."

It came out like the confession of a small boy caught stealing apples.

"You what?"

"There you are! I knew you wouldn't believe it. But it's the truth this time. I went to see friends at Talby and I got too much drink. I was in the car and when I left, the air must have taken hold of me. I couldn't drive straight. There were a lot of army lorries about and I didn't fancy trying conclusions with them. So, I turned off the main road into a side road through Hanbury Wood. I sat there for a time, trying to collect myself and then, before I knew what I was doing, I'd fallen asleep. I must have slept for two or three hours. I didn't get home until past three."

"What time did you leave Talby?"

"Ten o'clock. We'd been at a road-house until closing-time. I'd a call to make, so didn't go back with my friends."

"So, you slept through the important time, doctor?"

"Yes... You won't believe it, I know. But it's not a trumped-up tale this time."

"Can your friends confirm where you were until ten?"

"Yes. But for God's sake don't go dragging-in what happened to me after."

"I shall do what I think fit, doctor. You're lucky I don't take you off to the lock-up on suspicion. Give me the names of your friends, please."

Sheepishly, Keating gave the names and addresses of another man and two women.

"Thank you, doctor. And in future, please don't try to deceive the police. It comes out, you know. You've had me on a wild-goose chase this morning and I'm very annoyed about it."

The doctor remained staring at his empty glass. He made no apology or effort to rise.

"You'll probably see more of me, doctor, and I do hope that your tale holds water this time."

Littlejohn left the place without another word. He hadn't patience left even for courtesies and found himself hoping that Mrs. Keating had a brother or even a lover who one day might give the bounder a good hiding. The thought of such a man practising medicine almost made Littlejohn sick himself.

CHAPTER XII

Anonymous

"Extremely stretch'd and conn'd with cruel pain."

ACT V. SC. I.

LITTLEJOHN WAS STRUCK BY THE IDEA THAT THE LATE MR. Wall's case-books of ten years ago might prove interesting. Perhaps a perusal would disclose some link between the bonesetter and the newspaper reports of the bank robbery. He therefore telephoned to Gillibrand who sent the records in question to Stalden by special messenger.

The Inspector, having made himself comfortable in the quiet summer-house in the pretty back garden of *The Mortal Man*, lit his pipe, called for a pint and settled down to work. He soon found himself against a formidable obstacle, however. The case-book he was examining was a well-kept affair and done in the small, neat handwriting of Mr. Wall. Its entries ran in date order and were copious and they dealt fully with the patients and their treatment, the whole case-history in each instance being linked together by a carefully compiled cross-index. A meticulous man, Mr. Wall, but difficult to follow. His narratives were couched in highly technical terms, the language of anatomy, and the old man seemed to have a wide knowledge of the orthodox terminology and methods of description. To Littlejohn, who could read the handwriting without any trouble, the subject matter was double-Dutch.

One case, however, particularly attracted the detective's attention. It was that of one Joseph Bollington, who first presented himself to Mr. Wall on the very day of the bank crime, ten years ago. "J.B.", as he was called after the first entry, seemed to be a patient of some importance, for his treatment persisted over several months. Littlejohn could not follow what had happened and waded in vain through a maze of technical jargon, much of it rendered more difficult by drastic abbreviation. The many expressions of satisfaction in the text, however, seemed to indicate that Wall had been highly pleased by the progress of his experiments and operations.

The Inspector felt the need of a doctor to translate the entries into everyday language. Keating was quite out of the question. It would probably take some time if he got a police-surgeon on the job and he was anxious for immediate guidance. Suddenly, he thought of Dr. John Wall. The very man! One particularly interested in this branch of surgery and, as a member of the family, likely to bring a personal touch to the matter, too. Littlejohn sought the telephone directory and rang up the home of the Olstead lawyer with whom the surgeon was staying.

Yes, Mr. Wall was in. The maid brought him to the telephone and he fell-in with the detective's suggestion with such gusto that he motored over to Stalden forthwith and half an hour later, joined Littlejohn in the summerhouse. Together they got to work.

Mr. Wall became so immersed in the case of "J.B.", that he seemed to forget his companion and only awoke to his presence again when he had reached the end of the record.

"Well!" said the surgeon. "That's a very interesting and useful account and a veritable triumph for the old man. At one and the same time, he gave a patient with a nasty disfigurement—a broken nose—a new and presentable organ, but what is more important, and much more daring, he cured by manipulation an almost useless elbow joint, which had seriously impaired the use of the forearm and hand."

Littlejohn sprang to his feet with excitement.

"Light at last, doctor!" he said and in answer to the astonished looks of his companion, he told him of the case of the bank-robber who according to records supplied, had a paralysed right arm.

"It seems to me, Dr. Wall, that your uncle received as a patient a fugitive from justice and by treatment eliminated two of the main features by which the police hoped to trace him and run him to earth. A paralysed arm and a broken nose. By curing him of his defects, your uncle disguised him more effectively than if he'd changed the colour of his eyes and hair! Could you give me a brief outline in simple terms of what the late Mr. Wall wrote in his records?"

"Gladly, Inspector. In a few words. Over a period of a little more than six weeks, 'J.B.' went through a terrible ordeal. A most painful course of treatment involved the use of various mechanical devices on the nose; and a method of treatment by manipulation, stretching, pulleys, wrenching and the like on the elbow-joint which only a desperate man would undergo. The result seems to have surpassed my uncle's most sanguine expectations. The man recovered the use of his hand and arm and his appearance was changed for the better by a straight and presentable nose. Very interesting and a matter for congratulation to the old man. The last entry says that 'J.B.' was making splendid progress with the right hand. Hitherto, he had written with his left; now he was doing well with the right."

"Tell me, doctor, would the right grow as strong as the left? Or would it lag a bit behind?"

"Probably the left would always be the better. You see, the man had trained himself to use the left and during the time the right was out of commission, naturally the active member was gaining strength and dexterity. It would probably maintain this, unless, of course, the patient so re-educated the right hand as to be able to put the left voluntarily out of action and thus give the right first place again. But ordinarily, the left would probably continue to be used and keep its strength. There'd always be a slight weakness in the right, although for writing it would be as good as the other. Heavy work would bring the left into play more."

"I see. Well, I'm very grateful indeed for your help, doctor. It's been a most interesting conversation and one which, I hope, will bring us much nearer the solution of our case. Sorry, I can't say more at the moment, but I'll give you a full account later after I've tried one or two theories out."

Dr. Wall smiled shrewdly.

"Are you thinking that the patient returned and strangled his benefactor, then? That seems a good line to follow, seeing that the marks on the throat showed an excess of strength in the left hand!"

And with that and a knowing nod, he bade Littlejohn good-day and departed.

The doctor had hit the nail on the head. Littlejohn's interest in the mysterious "J.B." had been furiously aroused. Where had he stayed during his treatment? He would need to lie low whilst he changed his appearance. The police were after him and it would be dangerous for him even to show his nose out of doors. His nose! Surely, that would be a pretty sight during alterations! Then, Littlejohn remembered that The Corner House had taken in patients like a nursing-home. Probably Bollington, as he called himself, had become an inmate. What better way of hiding away until the hue and cry had died down, than in an out-of-the-way Norfolk village in the home of an old bonesetter? And then to emerge a different man, with a new nose and a perfectly good hand and arm. Mrs. Elliott was probably there at the time. She was the next person for interview.

Littlejohn was lucky enough to catch the infrequent 'bus to the nearby village where Mrs. Elliott was staying with her sister. She was surprised to see him again.

"Bollington, Bollington," she said with a grave show of jogging her memory in response to the detective's question. "No. I can't remember any Bollington."

"I know it's a long time ago, but, if as you say, you were then working for Mr. Wall, how could you have missed this patient, who seems to have stayed with your late master for about two months whilst he underwent treatment for a paralysed arm and a broken nose?"

"Wait a minute, sir… wait… a… minute. I *do* remember the arm and nose. I recollect Mr. Wall telling me about them after the man had left us. Very pleased he was, the master, about that. Rubbed his hands over what he'd done. But I never knew him as Bollington. In fact, I never knew 'is name at all, come to that, sir."

"Sounds a queer tale to me," said Littlejohn.

"It was a queer business, now that I bring it to mind. The man arrived late one night and from that day until the night he left, I never see his face. A mystery to me that the master should be so secretive. Usually such an open man. He gave him treatment in his room and in the surgery and rare hard treatment it must have been. I've heard patients yell and groan at what's been done to them, but this one seemed to go through it every night. Not that he raised the roof, of course, but the groans was terrible sometimes. I'll never forget that case, although you mentioning Bollington didn't bring any recollection. I didn't know his name, you see."

"Who gave him his food and cleaned his room and such, then?"

"I did that whilst he was in the surgery for his treatment. He wasn't always in bed, of course. I took up his meals on a tray, too. The master said I wasn't to go in on no account. Just leave the food on the table by the door and go. I didn't try to spy on the patient. All I thought was that perhaps he was such an 'orrible mess from some accident or through the treatment, that he wasn't fit to be seen. Then, one day, the room was empty and the patient gone. Mr. Wall said he was cured and a good cure, too."

"Is that all you can tell me, Mrs. Elliott? You're sure you never saw Bollington."

"Sure, sir. Honour bright, I didn't. I wouldn't tell you I didn't if I did..."

"All right, Mrs. Elliott. Thank you very much."

On the return journey in the bus, Littlejohn asked himself a string of puzzling questions.

Why did Wall take such pains to hide "J.B."?

Why, having seen the account of the bank robbery, with violence, had Wall taken in "J.B."? Or, if he had only discovered the crime after the patient had settled-in, why hadn't Wall handed him over to the police, or, at least, turned him out?

Was "J.B." really the bank-robber? The answer to that was the easiest. It was extremely likely that Wall had harboured a criminal and known that he was doing so. Why?

Had the thief some hold over Wall? This seemed likely, for why make for Stalden at all, and above all, the house of the very man who not only took him in in spite of his crime, but altered his appearance in a fashion which enabled him to evade the police?

It was all very baffling and the trail had grown cold by the lapse of time. Cromwell, his assistant, was pursuing certain inquiries which might throw some light on the matter. Better wait for his report which should arrive at any time.

Meanwhile, Littlejohn felt that a visit to the masterful Mr. Rider would not be amiss. In the course of interviewing the local notables, he could not afford to overlook the man whom the late Mr. Wall had disliked and tried to frustrate in matters of the heart. The 'bus halted near Rider's cottage and the Inspector could see the occupant vigorously clipping the box hedge which sheltered it. Littlejohn descended and crossed the road to his quarry.

Rider eyed the newcomer without enthusiasm, did not ask him to enter, but held the conversation in the open air and on the public footpath which passed his gate.

CHAPTER XIII

Lover

"We shall be dogged with company, and our devices known!"

ACT I. SC. II.

RIDER SNIPPED RUDELY AWAY AT THE HEDGE WHILST Littlejohn endeavoured to engage him in conversation. Watching him as he talked, the Inspector was puzzled to know why a good-looking and eligible girl like Betty Cockayne should decide to throw in her lot with the eccentric-looking artist—or pseudo artist—now so obviously making a show of insolence.

On closer examination Rider's appearance did not improve. He resembled certain oddities who, a number of years ago, could be found in Bloomsbury writing formless poetry and biographies and essays for eccentric and short-lived periodicals which sprang-up like exotic plants and as quickly perished. His curly auburn beard mingled with his foulard bow-tie. His face was long and pasty, with heavy ears. His forehead was narrow, wrinkled and bald and then came thick, brown, lifeless-looking hair, worn fairly long and untidily spreading over the collar of his jacket. The colour of his small eyes was hidden behind Crookes's lenses in round gold frames. He was tall, well-built and his shoulders had a tired, scholarly stoop. He wore a baggy tweed suit and had sandals on his feet.

Littlejohn decided to leave to the gossips the matter of the origins of the Cockayne-Rider affair. His main purpose at present was to sum-up the character of the rude man before him and to find out, if possible, whether he had any connection with the crime.

"I'd like a word or two with you about the recent tragic happenings at The Corner House, Mr. Rider, *if you can spare me the time*," said Littlejohn pointedly, for Rider had answered his greeting amid a tornado of box-clippings and shear-snapping.

Rider turned and faced him, lowering his implements as he did so.

"And what might I have to do with that, pray? I might also add, I don't like your tone, Inspector."

"I might reply that I don't like your manners, Mr. Rider," answered Littlejohn bluntly. "I'm not tramping the village in this hot sun for the benefit of my health. I'm investigating a crime, and I look for co-operation from everybody interested in bringing the criminal to justice. I would be glad if you'd answer a few routine questions, sir, and it's impossible to carry on a conversation if you persist in turning your back and creating as much noise as you can."

Rider looked ready to impale Littlejohn on his hedge-clippers and then his mood seemed to change. He bared his long yellow teeth and showed his red lips through his beard.

"What have I to do with the murder, may I ask?" he said superciliously. "I know old Wall objected to my marrying Miss Cockayne, but that's no reason for my wanting to string him up in his surgery. He'd always been a bit sweet on her himself and resented my intrusion. Neither of us cared a hoot what he thought about our getting engaged. More likely *he* wanted to murder *me*, not *me* murder *him*. I was the lucky man."

The sight of the fellow nauseated Littlejohn. He struggled to turn the conversation into different channels.

"I'm not suggesting for a moment that you had any wish to kill Mr. Wall. But I gather that, of late, you have seen more of him than formerly. I hear that you and Mr. Wall have called on each other…"

"Been sounding the local gossips and gasbags, eh? What a way of collecting evidence! I could have spared you that, Inspector. The old chap and I did see each other more than usual after my engagement to Miss Cockayne. He asked me to call on him and tried to persuade me that we weren't suited. How's that for a bit of cheek? I told him to go to hell."

"You don't seem very fond of Mr. Wall."

"As a matter of fact, I wasn't interested in him much until he started meddling in my affairs. I didn't want much truck with a quack who earned his keep from superstitious or gullible country ignoramuses…"

"According to my information quite a number of intelligent people were glad to be patients of Mr. Wall, Mr. Rider. *And* derived a lot of benefit from his treatment."

"That's as may be, Inspector. I wasn't much interested. As I said, I never bothered my head about him until he started trying to teach me my business. After I'd told him in plain language what I thought of him, he wouldn't let the thing rest. Called on me for further conversations. I showed him the door."

"H'm. Did he tackle Miss Cockayne, too?"

"You know that already, so why ask me?"

Littlejohn ignored the snub.

"Where were you at the time of the murder, Mr. Rider?" he asked.

"Ah, I thought that was coming. I've been waiting for it."

"Will you kindly answer it, then?"

"Under protest. The question's offensive. I was with Miss Cockayne all the evening. She'll confirm that. We're not married yet, so legally her evidence will be allowed. We're both interested in music and there was a concert being broadcast we particularly wanted to hear. I arrived at Miss Cockayne's at nine, heard the news and the postscript. The concert began at 9.30 and went on until 10.45. We settled down and remained together from start to finish."

"Thank you, Mr. Rider. That seems all right. I'll just check-up on it as a matter of course..."

"I can even give you the programme, Inspector, although I don't know why I'm bothering to do so. Overture: Ruy Blas. Then, Harty's arrangement of Handel's Water-Music; Elgar's Enigma Variations and Strauss's Don Juan. Then God Save the King, a cup of coffee and home to bed about eleven thirty."

"Good. Just one more question, Mr. Rider. Did you know of any reason why Mr. Wall should be murdered?"

"Haven't I told you, I wasn't interested in the old chap? How was I to know anything about him or other people's feelings towards him? I rarely met him about the village. I don't listen to gossip. My only encounter with him was when he started meddling in my affairs. Then I told him where he got off... Now, if there's nothing more, I'll get on with my work. The weather might break at any time and there's a lot to be done; so I'll bid you good-bye."

Littlejohn left Rider without more ado. As he passed the wrought-iron gate which broke the thick hedge on which the man was working, Littlejohn saw a well laid-out garden, with close-clipped lawns and gaudy flowers in beds surrounding them. A pretty spot for such an uncouth owner.

On his way home to his lodgings, the detective stopped at Miss Cockayne's place and received a full confirmation of Rider's alibi. The lady seemed amused at being asked to corroborate, but replied to the Inspector's questions without hesitation and in a candid manner which seemed to preclude deceit or collusion. Nevertheless, Littlejohn, when he reached *The Mortal Man* used the telephone again, this time to ask Scotland Yard to check up the B.B.C. programme on the night of the murder and also to confirm the timing of the items and report on anything else which might be of interest in them. Then he went in the bar in search of gossip more than liquid refreshment before his lunch.

Goodchild the cobbler was the only occupant of the place and his face was buried in a pint pot as the detective entered.

"Hullo," said Goodchild. "Still snoopin' around, Inspector. Foundout 'oo did it yet?"

"No, Mr. Goodchild. Solutions to crimes don't grow on trees. They call for hard work."

"Pursuin' line of inquiry, then, as the newspapers 'aveit. Wish I'd been a policeman. Easy life."

"I was just thinking the same about cobbling, myself," retorted Littlejohn.

"One up on me, sir. One up on me. Well, well, we all think t'other chap's job's the best, eh? Now look at Mr. Rider, the one you was talkin' to as I came in fer me refresher. He's got an easy life, if you ask me. Writer or somethin'. Lovely 'ome, any amount o' time on 'is 'ands and no kids to bother the life outof 'im and spoil 'is peace o' mind. And to crown all, he's goin' to marry a girl with a fortune and good looks in the bargain. Some fellows 'as all the luck. Nice bit o' stuff, Miss Cockayne..."

Goodchild leered and then drowned his sorrows in ale.

"Quite a romance, eh?" said Littlejohn. "Have they been lovers long?"

"Romance, did you say? Come off it! She's perhaps fancying she's got a romance, though I doubt it. She's never lived far away from this village and she's flattered at bein' asked by the great author. Wot he's the author of, nobody seems to know. Writes under another name. Suppose some of us'd get a shock if we knew wot 'e wrote, eh? At any rate, he's regarded as *somebody* in the village. A bit of a mystery, I'd say. Normally, Miss Cockayne wouldn't a' looked at him. But having been sweet on Squire Deverel's son for a long time and havin' done a bit of courting with him until we all expected 'em makin' a match of it. And then young Mr. Deverel goin' off and marryin' a chorus girl... well... she just tuck Rider to show she didn't care wot Deverel did. That's my way o' thinkin' at any rate and there's many more thinks the same. As for Rider, he know which side his bread's buttered. Marryin' money. Some folk 'as all the luck."

Whereat Mr. Goodchild banged down his empty pot and made a morose exit, mumbling something about a matrimonial lucky-bag and not having picked a winner.

So that was it! Allowing for the exaggerations of gossip, Littlejohn could well imagine Rider's head and not his heart choosing the girl with the money. And she, jilted by a local youngster she fancied, was prepared to make a martyr of herself by marrying a freak just to show the faithless one she didn't care a rap about him or his choice of the chorus.

Rider's occupation intrigued the detective. Author, publisher's reader. Nobody seemed to know what he wrote or what he read. He kept his business to himself and didn't even enlighten his fiancée. Yet, all the village seemed to take him at his own valuation. He would bear closer investigation, even if he had no connection whatever with the crime.

Perhaps the post-office could throw some light on the matter. Littlejohn had heard that the postmistress was somewhat of a gossip and once in full cry was difficult to hold back. Nevertheless, the ordeal must be faced. After lunch then, he'd buy some stamps and turn on yet another flow of scandal.

The perky maidservant announced that lunch was ready.

"There's pork to-day. 'Ome-fed in the village, sir," she said, flashing her eyes at him.

"Lead-on, Macduff," said Littlejohn and followed her to the dining-room.

CHAPTER XIV

Postmistress

"Make mouths upon me when I turn my back;
Wink at each other; hold the sweet jest up:"

ACT III. SC. II.

STALDEN POST OFFICE, WITH THE FIRST WORD, A MERE GHOST of it, peeping through the streamer of white paint with which it had been obliterated in the national interest when invasion was expected. Beneath the headline in smaller lettering: "Agatha Mullins, licensed to sell tobacco." The licensee was also the postmistress of the village. Had not war broken out, demanding all government officials to stay put, Miss Mullins would have fled the place. As it was, she stuck it out, bravely living down the ridicule heaped on her by jocular or spiteful natives. For Miss Mullins had made history, a perfect *opera bouffe* of it, in the Spring of 1939.

In July 1931, Miss Mullins went to Paris and Dinard with her uncle, Felix Potts, F.R.G.S., who earned his money by trailing conducted parties round English-speaking parts of the Continent in summer and autumn and lecturing, with the aid of lantern-slides, on the glories of the departed season to anyone who would listen and pay during the winter. Paris affected Miss Mullins so much, that she wished she were French herself. She even tried to alter the pronunciation of her name to Moulin and was jealous of the local bobby for possessing a better version of a corrupt French surname than her own. Whenever the buds began to burst in Stalden, her eyes grew dim thinking of the boulevards and the *dear* Champs Elysées; the smell of drains or cabbage water reminded her delicately of the Impasse S. Didier, where had once been the selected *pension*, the *dear* Pension Didier, of Felix Potts, F.R.G.S. She always ate a French breakfast of home-made *croissants* and french coffee and she had several times unsuccessfully tried to shop by post with the *Samaritaine.*

The better to promote her nostalgia, Miss Mullins attended French classes at the Olstead Technical Institute for five years. At the end of that time, she began to teach the language herself. Meanwhile, she interlarded her talk with French as far as the locals would stand it. With the exception of the curate, there was only Tommy Mather in the village capable of sustaining a hundred per cent Gallic conversation. To tell the truth, Tommy's efforts were about in the ratio of 40–60: Bad French; Frenchified English. He had served in Rouen throughout the last war and chaffered in the market there for the company's rations.

In May, 1939, Miss Mullins herself took a party to Paris. There were fourteen of them, consisting of three pupils (advanced), five pupils (elementary), three parents and three hangers-on, one of whom was Tommy Mather. Preparations lasted eight months and nearly broke down at length, for uncle Felix had died from a surfeit of stale *langouste* at St. Malo during the previous summer. At last the great day arrived. Half the village saw the party off at the 'bus-stop. They departed in triumph led by Miss Mullins and returned in dudgeon shepherded by Tommy Mather. The Parisians apparently didn't speak French, for Miss Mullins had been unable to make them understand a word! But for Tommy, who rose vociferously and ungrammatically to the occasion, the tour would have been a complete and tragic flop. Heaven knows what would have happened to the ladies in that wicked city had not Tommy pidginned-in to the rescue!

The village was still very hot about Miss Mullins and her French when war broke out and she was already looking round for another business far away, perhaps in *dear* Dinard…

But enough. Miss Mullins was weighing rice at the counter when Littlejohn entered the stores. She was a little, thin woman, with untidy grey hair, quiet grey eyes, pink faded cheeks and a nose and mouth so small that a caricaturist would have passed them off with a tick and a dot of his pencil. A lonely woman, used to no work until her father, a wine merchant, had died when she was forty. He left her like a fish out of water, floundering among his debts. Only the vicar of Stalden knew what she had gone through in fifteen years. As if fate had not played scurvily enough with her, there was added the last ironical joke of the Paris fiasco… Nay, the *patron* of the *dear* Pension Didier had even presented Miss Mullins with an unpaid account forgotten in death by her uncle Felix!

"Good morning," said Miss Mullins to Littlejohn and she bolted swiftly in and out of the back quarters of the shop to turn-off the wireless which was playing Debussy's *En Bateau.*

"Good morning, madam," said Littlejohn. He had heard part of Miss Mullins's tale from the tipsy ignoramuses of *The Mortal Man*, but he knew when he saw her that he could trust her. He told her what he wanted right away.

"I suppose it's all right, Inspector, giving you the information, although as a civil servant I'm sworn to secrecy. *Sous le manteau de la cheminée*, of course… I mean, confidentially, you understand?"

"Quite… *sous le manteau.*"

"You speak French?"

"A little, but let's continue in English."

Littlejohn knew French well. The neighbours in the next flat at Hampstead were French and during bridge evenings had taught him quite a lot. All the same, no sense in conducting inquiries in a foreign tongue. He held Miss Mullins on the rails.

"I'll just get the counterfoils of the registered letters that Mr. Rider used to send to his publishers, Inspector. Quite small parcels, of course. *Naturellement*, manuscripts aren't so bulky, are they? Let me see now..."

She bustled into the back room again and brought out her records. Nervously Miss Mullins fingered her way through the slips, her lips moving as she read the names.

"Here we are, Inspector. About once a month, the packet went to: Messrs. Grimes and Wills, Publishers, 44b, Seven Sisters Road, Stockwell, S.W.9."

Littlejohn noted the address. A funny locality for publishers! Better look into that.

"Did Mr. Rider ever get parcels through you for delivery at his place, Miss Mullins?"

"Oh, yes. Parcels of about the same size as those he sent away used to come from time to time. Probably the manuscripts he had to read or correct, *n'est-ce-pas*?"

"Very likely. Has there been any of this coming and going lately?"

"No. Not since... well... here's the last counterfoil. Not since the fall of France..."

Miss Mullins's voice trailed-off tragically.

"...dear, *dear* France," whispered Miss Mullins and burst into tears. Littlejohn fled into the telephone box and put through a call to Scotland Yard about the address on Rider's registered letters. As he waited, he saw the postmistress composing herself with the help of a large handkerchief. A woman entered and cashed a pay-warrant at the post-office counter, and two children came to buy bars of chocolate which were unearthed from some hiding-place among the jumble of groceries and drapery which littered the shelves. The scents of coffee, cheese and aniseed even penetrated the closed telephone-box.

"So sorry, Inspector," said Miss Mullins, as Littlejohn re-entered the shop. "I do get upset when I think of what has happened to that place of such *happy* memories."

She'd evidently forgiven and forgotten the indignities.

"Don't worry, Miss Mullins. Let's hope it'll soon be over and then you can see it all as it was before, all the better for having to wait, eh?"

"Yes, yes, Inspector. You really think it will all be the same. All this bombing and those horrid Germans in the dear place makes one wonder… By the way, Inspector. I've just thought of something. Probably it's of no importance, but I feel I must tell you. I think some of the parcels which came to Mr. Rider had metal in them. Would it be the plates for illustrations of books, perhaps? Anyway, one arrived which sounded quite coppery… you know the sound produced by jingling pennies together or something perhaps larger than that. The contents seemed to have come loose inside. I remember Viggars, the postman, mentioned it to Mr. Rider, who was quite annoyed and rude about it. Told him to mind his own business, or something like that."

"Thank you very much, Miss Mullins. I'm very grateful for your help and you can rely on me to keep the information confidential."

"Always ready to help, Inspector. *Au 'voir*, monsieur."

"Au 'voir, madame," answered Littlejohn with a flourish.

CHAPTER XV

Cromwell

"A proper man, as one shall see in a summer's day; a most lovely gentlemanlike man."

ACT I. SC. II.

"ANY SPECIAL KINDS OF BIRDS ABOUT HERE?" ASKED Detective-Sergeant Cromwell of a porter on Truro station.

He ought to have known better. Everybody is not as keen on watching feathered life through binoculars as is Cromwell, who spends all his spare time at it.

The porter's face lit up. He regarded his questioner with admiration. Here was a man after his own heart. One who knew what he wanted without any messing about. Came to the point as soon as he got out of the train.

"Birds? Not 'arf."

The porter rubbed his hands, grinned lasciviously and almost put his arm through that of Cromwell.

"Truro's famous for its pretty girls," he chuckled.

"I said BIRDS…" repeated the sergeant with greater emphasis, "not *birds.*"

The way he spat out the last word clearly expressed his meaning.

"Oh, birds," replied the man in a flat voice. And without more ado picked up a truck and wheeled it away, not deigning to reply.

It was already dusk when Cromwell, having waited an hour and a half for the 'bus, reached Swinford, half an hour's rocky journey out of Truro, where Harold Greenlees, released murderer, now lived in seclusion on his smallholding. The detective decided to find lodgings for the night and start fresh on the job the day after. He therefore entered the only inn in the village, *The Royal Oak*, a clean, whitewashed place which, he had been informed by the 'bus conductor, would find him bed and board.

On entering the inn, Cromwell received a shock. He was a confirmed bachelor and the jests of his colleagues of The Yard on that subject had worn thin and stale. He had his own ideas about the girl he wanted to marry and nobody else would do. A strong-minded man, Cromwell, and not likely to be deflected from his course by any siren who might come along.

Emerging from the bar parlour as Cromwell entered was the identical woman of his dreams!

Tall, long legged, with a fine figure. Deep breasted and carrying herself well, with a dainty chin tipped upwards as though she feared to look nobody in the face. Auburn hair, grey eyes set well apart, and a nose which combined Roman and Greek fashions in just the right proportions. Her mouth was rather large and she had full, generous lips. She told Cromwell, in response to a startled inquiry, that she was the landlady of *The Royal Oak*. Cromwell had noticed her name over the door. He judged at once that she was a widow, for the Christian name of the landlord, Robert, had been painted over but was dimly visible, and that of Jane substituted. The surname was Ireton! Cromwell regarded this as a favourable omen. And so it proved. We are not concerned here with the love and courtship of Detective-Sergeant Cromwell of Scotland Yard, but his well-wishers may like to know that after secretly scuttering between London and Truro for six months—everybody except Littlejohn, who on two occasions found auburn hairs adhering to his subordinate's clothing and politely removed them, thought Cromwell was bird-watching!—he persuaded Mrs. Ireton to change her name to Cromwell and leave *The Royal Oak* in favour of a flat in Shepherd Market. There, judging from her husband's changed appearance and anxiety to get home after duty, they lived happily ever after.

But to return to serious business. Cromwell, whose emotions were in a turmoil, securely locked them in a logic-tight compartment and went off to interview Harold Greenlees, the Redstead murderer. He found him emptying swill into the feeding-trough of the largest pig he had ever seen.

Greenlees was a tall, heavily built, grey-headed man, sunburned from exposure to the country sun and air and with remarkably calm blue eyes for one who had served a term for homicide. He didn't seem to resent the intrusion at all and talked civilly to his visitor. They leaned against the wall of the pigsty and the occupant, known as Eliza, punctuated the conversation by loud sucking and gobbling noises whilst her feed lasted and then by contented grunts and squeals for the rest.

"Nice place you've got here, Greenlees," said Cromwell by way of opening gambit and he scratched the back of the pig with his umbrella and marvelled at her girth.

"Yes, I reckon it's quite a presentable little holding and I'm so attached to that pig that I'll have to arrange my holidays to coincide with her time for becoming bacon. Else, I'll never be able to let the butcher get on with the job. She's had four litters already and likely to have more before her end comes. But that's not what you're here for, is it? What can I do for you? I'm busy, you know, although you mightn't think it."

"I just want to know whether you made a pal of a chap called Bates, who was doing a stretch for counterfeiting when you were on The Moor."

"Yes. Why?"

"Oh, he's been disturbing us again and I'm after a bit of background to help us through…"

"Bit unusual, isn't it?"

"Yes. The case is unusual. Sorry, I can't give you full details, I don't know them myself, but anything you can tell me about him will be taken as a very friendly gesture."

"It's a long time ago and I've not exactly kept that part of my life evergreen, but I do recollect that Bates was supposed to be an exemplary prisoner and on account of his being a cut above the average, he did a spell in the library. That's where I met him. We talked a bit, you know, and exchanged reminiscences. One gets lonely in a spot like that and tends to take anybody of one's own kind who'll listen, into one's confidence. I guess I told Bates the story of my life at one time or another."

"That's just it. What did you tell him, Greenlees?"

"What a question! What exactly do *you* tell a fellow-traveller in the train during a long journey when you get swapping experiences? You'd need a bit of time to make a catalogue, I guess. You can hardly expect me to reel off full details of scores of conversations which happened years since, can you?"

"Hardly. But I'll try to jog your memory. Did you ever talk about a man called Wall?"

Greenlees's jaw hardened and he gave Cromwell a searching, almost unfriendly look.

"What are you getting at, Mr. Cromwell?"

"Only that my visit is what might be called a by-product of a murder in which an old chap called Wall, a bonesetter in Norfolk, has been murdered."

"And Bates is suspect?"

"Well, hardly. Only... and this is in confidence... among Wall's papers was found newspaper-cuttings dealing with your own trial and also the case of Bates, who after his release, seems to have turned bank-robber. He shot a cashier, not fatally, thank goodness, pinched his money and then vanished into the blue. He's not been heard of since. We're anxious to know what interest Wall could have had in a man like that."

"Perhaps he cured Bates. You'll probably know as well as I do, that Bates had a damaged hand and arm, due, I think, to a laboratory accident. Could Wall have repaired the damage?"

"Maybe, but why? We know that at the time of the bank robbery, Bates was still deformed. And after it, with a hue and cry for him and all the papers giving his description, how could a peaceful, law-abiding country leech like old Wall treat one whom he must have known was a criminal. More likely, he'd have sent for the police instead of performing an operation to make him more nimble in wrongdoing. Unless, of course, Bates had some hold over Wall. That's where we fancied you might help. Did Bates, in a burst of confidence, ever tell you of Wall?"

The grim features of Greenlees had been gradually assuming an expression of surprise mingled with disgust. He now turned indignantly to his companion.

"I told Bates about Wall. The dirty little swine must have used my information for his own rotten ends when he got free. If that's the case, and I can't see it otherwise in view of what you say, I'm ready to talk."

Cromwell offered Greenlees a cigarette, but the latter preferred a pipe. During the rest of the interview an outsider, seeing them hanging over Eliza's sty, would have thought they were expertly appraising the pig instead of bringing the halter one step nearer to a more unwholesome animal.

"First let me tell you, it wasn't about Old Wall, as you call him, that I mainly told Bates. The Wall I knew best was a young doctor, John Wall. I did hear of Old Wall from the nephew, though. Dr. John seemed proud of him and talked about him when we got friendly."

"I see."

"Dr. John Wall was the finest man I've ever met and the thought of Bates mixing him up in his dirty work makes me see red."

He punctuated the last statement by emphatic thrusts at Eliza's back with his stick, producing a volley of contented squeals and rumblings which both men ignored in the heat of their interest in the conversation.

"Had Dr. John Wall any connection with the crime for which you were convicted, Greenlees? By the way, you'll excuse my reaping up a part of the past which must be painful to you, but you'll understand…"

"I quite understand. I've served my sentence and squared my accounts. I've had long enough to forget whatever pains I've suffered. The present's what matters to me. But if anyone has done anything against Dr. John Wall, I'm on the side of whoever is presenting the bill."

"That's the way to talk, Greenlees. What I want to know is, how did you come to be mixed up with Dr. Wall?"

Greenlees faced Cromwell and looked him in the eyes.

"Now, if I tell you, understand it's not to be made public property. It's dead and done with and I'm not reviving it if Dr. Wall's going to suffer thereby…"

"You have my assurance that what you tell me will be used with the utmost discretion. More I can't say. You must remember we're on a murder case…"

"Very well. You know that I killed a man years ago for his treatment of my sister. He was a married man, although she didn't know it, and when she told him there was a baby coming, he bolted and left her to face the music alone. She and I were living together at the time and you can guess what I felt like. I searched everywhere for the rat, but he'd gone to ground somewhere. Then, unknown to me, some old woman in the vicinity persuaded my sister to have an illegal operation performed. It was done by a young doctor of the neighbourhood who'd gone to the dogs through drink. When I arrived home from work one night, my sister was at death's door. Shortly after, the doctor called. He was scared to death at his failure, as well he might be. If my sister died, it meant gaol for him. I could hardly keep my hands off him… As it was, I took him and told him what I'd do to him if my sister didn't pull through. He said he was at his wits' end and couldn't do any more. And he daren't call in a brother doctor for consultation because what he'd done was illegal…"

Cromwell made sympathetic noises and passed a cigarette to his companion.

"'Damn you and your scruples *and* your future *and* your own damned skin,' I told him," went on Greenlees after lighting his cigarette. "'I'm off for the nearest doctor whether you like it or not,' and I pushed him aside and ran out. The man I got was Dr. John Wall. Thank God he was doing some locum work for a chap just round the corner… He came and took charge. He pulled my sister round and never breathed a word of the scandal. Shielded the other doctor, too, which, I knew, was irregular. The poor girl killed herself six months later. Couldn't somehow lift her head again. And I met the chap who was responsible for it shortly after that, with the result you know. But Dr. Wall was an inspiration throughout the whole sordid episode and I've never forgotten the debt I owe him. He's a big man now, I understand, and so he ought to be."

"You told Bates all this?" asked Cromwell.

"Yes, I guess I did. A chap gets lonely in gaol, you know. Turns his troubles over and over, you see. But as well as his troubles, he has time to think about the good turns people have done him, if he's that type. I remembered Dr. Wall quite a lot in prison, I can tell you."

"Well, I'm very grateful for your help, Greenlees, and don't worry about the consequences of your confidences. I'll see that Dr. Wall in no way suffers. And now I wish you jolly good luck and I hope you do well at your landed venture and that Eliza has a record litter next time."

And with that they shook hands and parted.

Cromwell wasted no time in getting back to *The Royal Oak*, where he wrote out his report and posted it at once to Littlejohn at Stalden. Then he made a careful toilet and set out in search of the landlady, for besides being very hungry, Cromwell, unknown to himself as yet, was in love, and craved the company of the lady of the inn even more than meat and drink.

CHAPTER XVI

Logician

"Here are your parts, and I am to entreat you,
Request you and desire you to con them..."

ACT I. SC. II.

A SPATE OF INFORMATION REACHED LITTLEJOHN IN HIS retreat on the day following Cromwell's visit to Truro. There was, of course, the Detective-Sergeant's report on his inquiries and his comments thereon, but Scotland Yard, too, had forwarded another budget of facts and figures.

Littlejohn shut himself in his bedroom, which was a cosy, old-fashioned den of a place, and after lighting his pipe set about studying his data and comparing and connecting it.

The Yard had enclosed, together with quite a considerable dossier of other things, a photograph of Bates, the bank-robber, taken when he was imprisoned for forgery. It was not prepossessing. A dark, scowling man, with a broken nose and hollow cheeks. The head and brow, however, spoke of intelligence above the average. A fellow with brains, apparently, and an acquisition to any gang of crooks. The detective studied it carefully, grunted and laid it aside for later study.

Next came a card bearing facsimile fingerprints of Bates.

Then, a report on Grimes and Wills, publishers, of Stockwell. This made Littlejohn whistle. Rider had been sending his parcels and receiving those in return from what appeared to be merely an accommodation address. Grimes and Wills were pettifogging little newsagents in Seven Sisters Road! Further, they had fallen under suspicion in connection with the affairs of a gang of forgers, which had suddenly melted away on the declaration of war. They were suspected in connection with spurious continental notes and war-time restrictions had apparently closed their export trade and its loopholes. Probably national registration and military service, too, had broken up the party.

Littlejohn left the mass of papers on the table, took off his shoes, luxuriously stretched his feet and then laid himself on the bed in a meditative pose, his pipe burning furiously.

Now, to take the facts in hand, carefully arrange them, dwell upon them and deduce a solution of the case from the lot!

Many years ago, just after a bank robbery by one Percival Bates, an unknown patient arrived at the house of Wall the bonesetter. He hid in the house apparently whilst an operation was performed which made a useful member of a previously deformed right arm. At the same time, a badly broken nose was given a straight twist again and the hitherto repulsive appearance of its owner made normal.

Bates had both a damaged right arm and a crooked nose. Therefore, it was likely that the patient was Bates.

Surely, the bonesetter must have known, however, that he was harbouring and hiding a criminal, for the newspapers of the time had published details and photographs of the bank affair. Why had old Wall remained silent?

Cromwell's report disclosed that Bates during a spell on Dartmoor before his bank crime, had come-by information concerning the connection of Dr. John Wall, nephew of the murdered man, with an illegal operation. Had he used this as a lever to force the bonesetter to hide him and change his appearance?

Dr. John himself had better be consulted on that score again and Littlejohn made a mental note about it.

Finally, there was Rider, who presumably had been mixed-up with a gang of forgers. The metallic noises, heard by the postmistress in the parcels he received, might easily have been engraved note-plates. Was Rider doing the job of engraving in a hideout in Stalden and were the plates passing to and from London by post? Bates had served a term for counterfeiting! Could Rider and Bates be one and the same?

If so, why in the world had he remained on the very doorstep of the man who had changed his appearance and who was probably the only one who knew his identity? Had he continued to blackmail the bonesetter and then had the old man, on hearing of Rider's forthcoming marriage to a girl of whom he himself was very fond in a paternal way, threatened to disclose his secret and got himself murdered for his indiscretion?

Littlejohn sprang to his feet.

What he needed now was an immediate talk with Dr. John Wall, and the fingerprints of Rider.

He hurried down to the telephone and arranged an appointment with the doctor right away and then rang-up the local police-station and gave the startled Mellalieu instructions.

Dr. John Wall was not long in arriving.

"I want to ask you a rather delicate question, doctor," said Littlejohn when they had settled down to business.

"Fire away, then, Inspector," replied Wall and his eyes twinkled.

"Have you ever been mixed up with an illegal operation? In particular, that performed on the sister of Harold Greenlees, the Redstead murderer, who served a term of imprisonment for murdering the man responsible for his sister's trouble?"

"Yes, Inspector."

Dr. Wall replied candidly and without hesitation.

"I was called-in for consultation by a man who had been a fellow student with me at the hospital and had gone downhill. He'd landed himself in a proper jam. The least I could do was to make the best of a bad job. I operated and saved the life of the girl. There was nothing unprofessional in my conduct, except perhaps, that I didn't make a scandal of the affair. The doctor concerned went abroad after it and is now dead."

"Yet, doctor, I've reason to believe that that incident was used as a lever by a bank-robber fleeing from justice to make your uncle perform an operation, which changed the appearance of the criminal so much that it threw the police off his track and enabled him to get away with the crime."

Littlejohn then told the surgeon what he knew and what he deduced from the facts in hand.

"You mean to say that to preserve my good name, my uncle did what this scoundrel asked without resistance?"

"So it seems to me, doctor."

"But Bates had already tried it on me, Inspector. After his release from gaol, he called on me at my rooms in London and openly asked for what he called help to set him on his feet again. Otherwise, he'd make public certain facts about the Greenlees case which hadn't hitherto been known by the world at large, to say nothing of the police and the Medical Council. I showed him the door and told him that if I'd any more of his pestering, I'd turn him over to the police."

"Then, why in the world did he manage to work his tricks on your uncle, Dr. Wall?"

"I think I can tell you that, too, Inspector. When Bates called at my place, I was just packing for a sea trip. I'd some post-graduate study to do, which involved a lot of reading and quiet thought. What better way than to sign on as a ship's surgeon on a vessel with not too many passengers? I'd get pay, a healthy life and plenty of time to call my own for study and reflection. I joined an eastern-bound boat, which wouldn't be back in Britain for a year or more."

"So your uncle couldn't get hold of you to confirm the tale and he didn't dare to write about it lest somebody else got hold of the letter?"

"That's about it. And I wouldn't put it past Bates to have spotted the labels on my kit, which was scattered all over the place when he called, and made use of the knowledge when he was in a corner."

"And did your uncle never mention it to you?"

"No. It was quite typical of him to say nothing. Probably thought it would upset me or something. Anyway, the job was long over and done-with by the time I got back and Bates probably swallowed-up somewhere out of harm's way..."

"I wonder, doctor. I wonder."

"Why? What are you getting at?"

"It wouldn't surprise me at all if Bates hadn't something to do with your uncle's death, doctor. You mustn't forget that Mr. Wall knew something incriminating about Bates as well."

"So Bates, the scoundrel, silenced him, eh?"

"Quite likely."

"Well, what are you doing about it?"

"Leave that to us, doctor. I can assure you that we're hot on the trail and no stone will be left unturned to bring Bates to book. By the way, wasn't your father alive at the time of the operation on Bates?"

"Yes. But father came on the round-the-world trip with me. He was a passenger, you see."

"Bates *was* in luck and no mistake. All the cards were set for him at the time."

"Well, if you don't want anything more from me, Inspector, I'll be off. But I hope you'll soon get your man, I can't bear to think of his being at large..."

"Trust us, doctor..."

But Littlejohn was in for a disappointment.

In some way or another, Mellalieu had secured a pair of garden-shears used by Rider and these were found to bear an excellent set of prints from each hand on their handles. The village bobby was quite proud of his effort and was prouder still under Littlejohn's praise and pleasure. The thrill was short-lived.

Later in the day, the fingerprint expert at Olstead, to whom the shears and the facsimile prints of Bates had been forwarded, reported in a voice so jocular that it sounded as though he were delighted with his destructive labours, that in no single respect was one set like the others!

"Oh hell!" muttered Littlejohn and turned disconsolately to two more letters which the postman had just delivered for him.

One was from Scotland Yard and confirmed the radio programme involved in Rider's alibi. The other was from Mrs. Littlejohn, a friendly, warm, connubial affair, in reply to Littlejohn's report on the case and his share in solving it. He always told his wife as much as he could about his cases. It did him good and put his thoughts in better shape.

"...For what it's worth, Tom," wrote Mrs. Littlejohn among other things of a domestic nature, "I listened myself to the wireless programme you mention as being a part of an alibi. There was a technical hitch right in the middle of the Enigma Variations. The whole of 'Nimrod' was missed as a result. I was very annoyed, I'll tell you. I always look forward to 'Nimrod'…"

Scotland Yard had mentioned nothing of the breakdown in their report.

"Good old Letty… good old Letty," muttered Littlejohn as he crushed on his hat and made for the door, and to remind him not to forget it, he wrote "Box of chocolates for L." on the back of an old envelope and put it in his pocket.

CHAPTER XVII

Nimrod

"What dreadful dole is here!"

ACT V. SC. I.

LITTLEJOHN'S FIRST PORT OF CALL WAS THE VILLAGE POLICE-station. The tight-lipped bobby's wife answered the door and was immediately thrown into confusion, for her husband was stripped to the waist and washing himself in the scullery. Mrs. Mellalieu never allowed William Arthur to use the bathroom except on very special occasions and then only after repeating a list of injunctions as long as your arm. She installed Littlejohn in the best arm-chair in her small sitting-room, which, judging from the atmosphere and stiff, unused feeling about it, was also a sacred spot, and then bustled off to warn the constable. From where he was sitting, the Inspector could hear her ordering William Arthur about in a stage-whisper full of asperity. The P.C. arrived sheepishly on the scene shortly afterwards. His red ears looked as if they had been well-pulled and his face shone as though recently and vigorously polished with furniture cream.

"Sorry not to be 'andy when you arrived, sir," he stammered self-consciously. "Jest bin gardenin' and was washing-off the dirt."

There was a snort from the lobby outside the room, where Mrs. Mellalieu seemed to be furiously dusting the umbrella stand. P.C. Mellalieu portentously closed the door of the parlour. Whatever else his better half might regard as her rights, he was not having her listening-in to the business of the law, or standing in the offing like a prompter in the wings at a play.

Heavy, angry footsteps were heard retreating to an inner room. Mellalieu knew he was in for it when his visitor departed.

Littlejohn came to the point.

"I may as well tell you, Mellalieu, that I asked you to get a sample of Mr. Rider's fingerprints because I wanted to compare them with some on record at Scotland Yard..."

Mellalieu's jaw dropped in surprise.

"Oh... ah..." was all he could find to say.

"I'm afraid we've drawn a blank, however. They don't tally at all. In view of some deductions I'd made and which are therefore disproved, I'm a bit disappointed."

Mellalieu made noises with his mouth in an effort to indicate that he was sympathetic. He sounded like a melancholy woodpecker.

"Where did you get the garden-shears, Mellalieu?"

"Out o' the tool-shed, sir. Seen 'im use 'em regular, I have. Mr. Rider was out at the time. Saw him headin' for Olstead, so I knew I was safe in borrerin' the things. Door was unlocked."

Littlejohn handed the shears, which he had brought with him, back to the constable.

"Think you can replace them without any trouble now?" he said.

"Oh yes. There's a path through the fields leads to the back o' Mr. Rider's place. I could nip round and never be seen. Matter o' fact, now's a good time. I see Mr. Rider catchin' the Olstead 'bus again about half an 'our since. I'll go right away."

"In that case, I might as well come with you."

So they set out together, followed by the eyes of Mrs. Mellalieu from an upper window. Littlejohn could almost feel the gaze of the busy constable's wife boring into the back of his head.

Mellalieu made great play of the secret excursion. He executed the last hundred yards of the deserted field-path, which led to the back wicket-gate of Rider's garden, on tiptoe. It reminded Littlejohn of a grotesque dance and he chuckled inwardly. He almost expected the village bobby at any time to burst into the policeman's song from *The Pirates of Penzance.*

"'Ere we are," said his guide at length and conspiratorially ushered his superior into Rider's back-garden. The place was neat and well-kept. A secluded spot with trim beds of vegetables and flowers rioting in the summer weather.

The constable singled out a small wooden shed and, opening the door, slipped the garden-shears inside. The place contained an orderly array of tools of all kinds, plant-pots, a potting-bench and little else. Next door was a more substantial erection. The door was locked and by peeping in through the window, the Inspector was able to make out a small laboratory. Bottles of chemicals and tins of insecticide and fertilizer were visible.

Littlejohn tried the door. It resisted his pressure. He took from his pocket a small instrument which he kept concealed from the bobby's eyes, inserted it in the lock and tried the door again. This time it opened. The pair of them entered, Mellalieu looking anxious, as though pondering whether or not to run-in his companion for breaking and entering.

The detective looked carefully round the little room. A neat chemical workshop. He examined the bottles, test-tubes and cans, opened the drawers of a cabinet and a work-table, using his handkerchief to keep off the fingerprints. An object reposing in one of the drawers of the bench caused him to whistle under his breath. He took it in his handkerchief and dropped it in his pocket. Under the work-table was a small white receptacle for refuse. Littlejohn raised the lid of this by pressing the toe of his shoe on a small projecting pedal which did the job automatically. There was little inside. A few pieces of wrapping paper, some knotted string apparently cut from a parcel and then two broken cigarettes. The Inspector picked out the latter, sniffed them and slipped them in an envelope which he also pocketed. Mellalieu, breathing heavily, watched all this with popping eyes.

At a sign from Littlejohn, they made their exit and the door was again locked as easily as it had been opened.

"You 'ot on the trail o' something, sir?" said Mellalieu in a hoarse whisper as they made their way back to the road.

"Not exactly hot, Mellalieu, but getting warmer..."

And that was the extent of the inside information which the village constable was given for the time being.

After disposing of his companion, Littlejohn made for Green Hedges again. Miss Cockayne was at home and received him without cordiality.

"You still snooping around on the murder case, Inspector?" she said impudently as the detective entered the house on her rather frigid invitation.

"Yes, Miss Cockayne. I won't bore you with it, as you're not interested in bringing your old friend's murderer to justice..."

Betty Cockayne's face flushed angrily.

"I didn't say so. I think you're a horrible man, Inspector."

"Let's leave recriminations for the present, Miss Cockayne, shall we? It's about the alibi you and Mr. Rider gave for the night of Mr. Wall's murder. You were listening to a symphony concert, I understand?"

"Yes. We've already told you that."

"Were you smoking?"

"Yes. What has that to do with it?"

Littlejohn ignored the counter-question.

"Your own cigarettes, Miss Cockayne?"

"Not all the time. I smoked some of Mr. Rider's from his case and he smoked some of mine from that box on the table. Why?"

"You heard the concert through?"

"Yes..."

"Including the Enigma Variations?"

"Yes. What's all this about?"

"Please let *me* do the questioning, Miss Cockayne. I assure you I'm not being flippant. Did you hear 'Nimrod' in the variations?"

"Yes."

"Sure?"

"YES. I never heard anything so stupid as this silly cross-examination."

"One thing is perhaps sillier, Miss Cockayne. 'Nimrod' was not played that night! A technical hitch occurred at the end of the preceding variation and continued through 'Nimrod' until half-way into the next section!"

Betty Cockayne's mouth opened and her eyes grew wide. She looked anything but pretty and self-possessed in her astonishment.

"But I'm sure I heard it..."

"And *I'm* sure you didn't. Take my word for it, it didn't come over the air. I suggest that what happened was, you fell asleep during the concert. Perhaps you heard the beginning of the Enigma Variations, dozed off, and fancied you'd heard it through. After all, they *are* variations and the theme is constantly repeated..."

Miss Cockayne's self-assurance had vanished. Littlejohn liked her better thus. She was more herself and less of Rider.

"I could have sworn I heard it all through, Inspector. I know I did get drowsy. The fire was warm and the Water Music is so comfortable, it almost puts you to sleep. I remember the start of the Enigma quite well. I was sleepy, but the music seemed to go on and on without a pause…"

"Did Mr. Rider say anything to you about the breakdown in transmission?"

"No. He seemed drowsy, too."

"Well, many thanks, Miss Cockayne. I won't trouble you further."

"But what's it all about, officer?"

"That I'm afraid I can't tell you at present, but it's all on behalf of your old friend Mr. Wall, I can assure you."

And with that Littlejohn took his leave.

He had not travelled far down the village street before Mellalieu appeared again, this time running and dishevelled.

"Ah, there you are, sir… glad I found you…" gasped the constable his face streaming with perspiration, the veins of his forehead bulging like knotted cords and his helmet rakishly awry.

"Can you come with me at once, sir? We jest found another dead body."

Without more ado or waiting for a reply from the Inspector, Mellalieu bustled him round a corner, along a road and to the smallholding of poor Daft Dick, the man at constant war against leatherjackets and the rival gardeners of the village in general.

Daft Dick was standing in his holding surrounded by a knot of men. He was shouting abuse and flailing the air with his long bony arms.

Mellalieu had by this time recovered his breath and was able to give a brief explanation to Littlejohn.

"It seems, like, that Daft Dick kept his money and other valuables in a water-tight box which he hid down a well at the bottom of his allotment. Well, this afternoon he must a' been pokin' down that well, fishin' his box up with a 'ook on the end of a pole, which he uses for such like. Instead of the box, he gets 'is 'ook entangled-like in somethin' else and what does 'e pull up but a body. Yelled the place down, he did. Like as not, it's driven him properly potty now. Always been a bit light in the top storey, but this'll 'ave finished him off proper..."

They had reached the group by this time. The men gave ground to let the constable and Littlejohn to the fore. A special constable and Dr. Keating were standing importantly beside a wet human bundle which Daft Dick had brought to light instead of his treasure. A smallish, thin man, pale, horrible and slimy in death. Littlejohn felt queasy at the sight of him, but bent down to examine the corpse more closely. He whistled and grunted and then rose to his feet again.

"Anybody know this chap?" he asked of the group.

There were murmurs in the negative from everyone.

The nose gave the victim away, however. The job had not been so well done as Littlejohn had gathered from Mr. Wall's case-book. The detective had no doubt as to the identity of the sodden mass at his feet.

It was all that was left of "J.B.", alias Bates, the bank-robber!

CHAPTER XVIII

Corpse

"Nay, but you must name his name, and half his face must be seen."

ACT III. SC. I.

A TORNADO OF WORK BROKE OVER LITTLEJOHN ON THE DAY following the discovery of the body in the well.

From records, especially fingerprints, it was established beyond doubt that the corpse was that of Bates, the missing bank-robber. This establishment of identity came as rather a relief to Littlejohn. For want of a better theory, he had tried the assumption that Rider and Bates might be one and the same person and had never felt easy about it in his mind. The discovery of Bates's body disposed of an incubus and, although bringing the Inspector no nearer a solution of the first crime, seemed to clear the decks of a case which was getting cluttered-up with a mass of disorderly detail.

One thing was clear, however, Bates had probably had something to do with the murder of Wall. That part of Littlejohn's theory had been confirmed. Then, someone had killed Bates! He had been stunned by a blow from a heavy stone inserted in an old sock for better handling and fished from the well along with Daft Dick's box. Littlejohn had the sock dried and retained it. The ultimate cause of death, however, had been drowning according to the surgeon's report. Thus, the two murders had a feature in common. Each victim had been rendered insensible—one by choking and the other by a blow on the head—and then finished-off in another fashion. Was this by design or a mere coincidence?

The police doctor who followed Keating in inspecting the corpse, was unable definitely to state when the death of Bates had occurred, for his body had for several days been immersed in the well, which contained enough water to cover it entirely. In one of the pockets, however, was a sodden daily paper, bearing the date of Wall's death, so it was assumed that the unlucky pair had died somewhere about the same time. Bates's wrist-watch, a cheap nickel affair, had stopped at 10.43. He had not been long in following Wall.

Gillibrand took over the formalities in connection with the new corpse and freed Littlejohn for further researches. There was little in the way of clues on or about the body of Bates. No letters in the pockets; nothing of importance in the soaked wallet found in his jacket; not even an identity-card. The purpose of his return to Stalden was a mystery.

On the other hand, Scotland Yard had been copious in their information concerning the Seven Sisters gang. Apparently someone had been given the job of finding out all there was to know from the past files and had done it pretty thoroughly. A number of arrests had been made before the gang finally disappeared. The results had merely been the bringing of a few small fish into the net. It had been obvious from the timid behaviour of such petty crooks when questioned that they were serving some boss of whom they were greatly afraid, but who kept himself well in the background. One and another of these underlings had been sent down for stretches in gaol, but none had been able to disclose the identity of the chief of the gang. He had, it appeared, established his contacts through a deputy, a kind of "runner", who alone knew him and who kept his name and whereabouts strictly to himself.

Then came a piece of news. Hitherto, the minor members of the gang in police hands had been unable to describe even the lieutenant, who had also transacted business by parcels through the Stockwell accommodation address. The police, however, had finally succeeded in tracing the newsagent who had owned the shop in Seven Sisters Road. He was a nasty little bit of work, but perfectly on the right side of the law, for the exchange of parcels was, he insisted, a perfectly legitimate part of his business. He never knew what was in them or inquired into the credentials of those who came and went for them, provided they paid his fee, and therefore the cops had nothing on him. Which was perfectly true.

But the police found Mr. Heggs, the ex-newsagent, more friendly in their recent visit to him. He and his missus had been buried under tons of debris in a cellar during the bombing of London, and the London bobbies had dug them out and saved them from slow death. He owed them a good turn and he paid his dues. He told how one night, when a house opposite his shop in Seven Sisters Road had caught fire and it looked as though the whole street was going to go up in smoke, a little man, apparently anxious to obtain his parcels before the flames spread across to them, had arrived and demanded them. He had produced the grubby piece of cardboard bearing a number which Mr. Heggs had been in the habit of issuing as a sort of passport to his postal system, and had therefore been allowed to take away the packets waiting to be re-addressed to him or to someone connected with him. This stranger had made every effort to hide his face by pulling-up his collar and turning-down the brim of his hat and remaining outside in the dark whilst Heggs got his stuff. But the flames from the opposite side of the street, suddenly flaring up with the collapse of the interior of the house, had caught the customer unawares and just before he shrank like a snail into his shell, Heggs had got a glimpse of his face. The description tallied with that of Bates, nose, and all!

Now, thought Littlejohn, after perusing this somewhat wordy dossier, was Bates the ringleader, or merely the lieutenant? Probably the latter. True, he had himself been a skilled engraver and might easily have started again to run a show of his own. He had not been without brains, either. All the same, Littlejohn could not reconcile the idea of the wretched little bank snatch-and-grabber, wanted by the police for a number of years, suddenly launching out in command of an almost international racket. More likely Bates had been sheltered from the law by someone bigger than himself, whom he had served and whom perhaps he had double-crossed and thus been pitched down Daft Dick's well as a piece of encumbrance.

Surrounded by his papers in the secluded summer-house at the bottom of the garden at *The Mortal Man*, Littlejohn lit his pipe and began mentally to review the case and try to formulate some solution to fit in with the facts. Bees, wasps, two cats and a colony of ants went about their business around him, but he did not notice them.

At length, he had gathered many of the pieces of the complicated jigsaw into something like order. There were bits missing here and there and the picture itself was very much awry, but it provided a working basis for further investigation.

Briefly, Littlejohn's provisional pattern worked-out somewhat as follows.

For some reason or other, Bates had returned to Stalden and probably visited his former benefactor Wall. Perhaps it would never be truly known why Wall had sheltered him when he was fleeing from the police after his bank-robbery with violence. Besides giving him a hide-out in his house, the bonesetter had performed operations which partially hid the identity of Bates. The bank-robber must have had some hold over Wall. This may have been possession of information concerning young Dr. Wall, which owing to the absence from England of the youngster and his father, could not be confirmed. The quack-doctor had very likely made an impulsive promise to keep Bates quiet and then, becoming involved in sheltering a criminal, had been forced to carry it through.

It had been established that Bates was connected with the Seven Sisters gang. The break-up of this group had probably deprived Bates of his source of income and, finding himself on his beam-ends, he had returned to Stalden, presumably to blackmail old Wall. It might be that the bonesetter had turned the tables and threatened to expose Bates, thereby getting himself murdered.

But there was someone else in the background, who had, in turn, murdered Bates. This unknown one had apparently followed the ex-bank-robber to The Corner House and stunned and thrown him down Daft Dick's well. Was this second murderer a native of Stalden or had he followed Bates from elsewhere, seeking a suitable place in which to finish him and finding it in the lonely garden behind the bonesetter's home?

Littlejohn's thoughts again turned to Rider. Not only had the postmistress connected him with the Seven Sisters address and told of parcels received which sounded to contain what might be metal counterfeiter's engraved plates, but further suspicious evidence had come to light as a result of the intrusion by Littlejohn and Mellalieu in the workshop behind Rider's cottage.

Littlejohn turned to the report he had just received from the county analyst at Olstead. He had submitted the broken cigarettes found in Rider's refuse-bin for examination. They had been found to contain a drug—a morphine salt—in sufficient quantity to produce a light sleep when smoked. Apparently, Rider had experimented until he made a presentable cigarette and thrown away his failures. The tobacco was Egyptian, the better to conceal the taste of the drug, which had been introduced into the cigarettes by means of a hypodermic syringe. This Littlejohn had borrowed during his inspection of the little laboratory and it also contained the same salt of morphine.

To his report the analyst had added "this drug need not be bought from a pharmacy. A chemist could prepare it from poppies. (*Papaver Somniferum.*)"

There was sufficient evidence in the laboratory itself and its equipment of retorts, test-tubes, re-agents and the like to show that Rider was at least an amateur chemist. He had evidently used his skill in preparing a doped cigarette to ensure that his fiancée slept whilst he slipped out and made a rendezvous with Bates. Littlejohn had by this made up his mind that Rider was involved in the death of the crooked-nosed bank-robber, if not in that of Wall himself.

Thus Rider's alibi covering the time of Wall's death was a fabrication.

It next behoved Littlejohn to have another conversation with the man. There were one or two i's to dot and t's to cross, however.

In all probability, Rider was the missing leader of the Seven Sisters counterfeiters. Had he put Bates out of the way to stop his mouth?

Another point which would give satisfaction would be the discovery of poppies in Rider's garden. Littlejohn hadn't noticed any during his visit, but would soon find out. He rose, gathered together his papers and knocked out his pipe. He had made up his mind. He was going to see Rider again, but first there was the matter of the sock which had contained the stone used against Bates. The village woman who "did" for Rider might help there. Mellalieu would probably know who she was. The bobby could also do a routine job for him by hunting for poppies in Rider's garden.

P.C. Mellalieu was again in a state of deshabille when Littlejohn called at the police-station. It was his off-hour and he was in his shirt and trousers and with his heavy leather braces displayed, digging his early potatoes. His wife was the first to spot the Inspector's approach and was unable to open the window and give the alarm before Littlejohn was down on her spouse. She stood behind the casement, fumbling with the catch, rapping on the pane and mouthing at the bobby, whose face was a study as he tried lip-reading without any success. The catch finally yielding to force and persuasion, the window flew open and the tail-end of Mrs. Mellalieu's harangue shot out.

"...yew gret fool, you..."

The policeman turned and saw Littlejohn, sniggered and became the colour of his scarlet-runners. Littlejohn burst into laughter and the window closed with a bang which shook the whole neighbourhood.

"I've got a job for you, Mellalieu. Another trip to Mr. Rider's house. This time in search of *papaver somniferum.*"

"Ah! Poppies..." said Mellalieu, his face glowing with pride and satisfaction at his thus being able to register extreme erudition.

"You recognize the name, then?" replied Littlejohn somewhat taken aback at this sudden brilliance on the part of the rustic officer.

"Oh yes, sir. Know the names and properties o' most o' they common flowers and herbs. Moi father was a gardener you see *and* a field naturalist, too. Not much 'e didn't know about they plants. *And* never went to school, either. Taught 'imself from books and observation o' nature did my dad..."

Mellalieu was evidently on a topic with which he felt at home and Littlejohn out of the kindness of his heart would have been glad to let him expand on the qualities and idiosyncrasies of his ancestor, but he hadn't the time.

"I'd like you to go right away, if you will."

"Certainly, sir. Leave the *papavers* to me, sir."

Mellalieu apologetically made his way to a potting-shed, where his clean service-boots were reposing, and changed out of his muddy gardening shoes. He washed his dirty hands in a bucket of water there, too, and as if in answer to a prayer, another and easier-fitting casement flew open and someone unseen flung out a towel at which the bobby made a clumsy leap and caught in mid-air, instead of with his head as was apparently intended by the invisible watcher.

After arranging to meet him later, Littlejohn made as if to leave the constable.

"I'm comin' part o' your way, sir," said Mellalieu, with a pleading look in his eye. He was thanking his stars that he'd hung his helmet, tunic and belt in the potting-shed, for he knew what was waiting for him indoors, if he ventured there!

"Right-o. Come on then," replied Littlejohn mercifully.

Mellalieu sighed with relief, gave the bedroom curtain, which was moving suspiciously, a glance which combined apprehension with defiance, and accompanied his superior officer in search of his poppies.

"Who's Mr. Rider's daily help, Mellalieu?" asked Littlejohn as they closed the garden gate of the police-house.

"Mrs. Congreve, sir. Lives the first o' the little cottages just afore *The Mortal Man.*"

"Right. I'll call to see her. I want a word or two with her. See you later, Mellalieu."

With that the pair of them parted and went about their respective tasks in opposite directions.

CHAPTER XIX

Snooper

"Fetch me this herb; and be thou here again ere the leviathan can swim a league."

ACT II. SC. II.

POLICE CONSTABLE MELLALIEU, HOWEVER UNINSPIRING HIS other endowments, was a first-rate snooper. His ability to follow his prey unseen, to conceal himself from its view in fields, hedges and ditches, and to draw within striking distance of it with stealthy, soundless tread arose out of domestic necessity. He was fond of taking out his gun in his spare time and, for the most part, he potted sitting targets, which required a cunning approach and closeness of range. He was not an unsporting fellow, but he could never manage to bowl-over a moving quarry without filling it from head to foot with lead. His wife's searing comments as they sorted-out the cooked flesh from the shots gave him dyspepsia for weeks after his contribution to her larder and made him prefer careful stalking and a few pellets in the head of a stationary rabbit.

He employed his technique with the fullest skill in his mission to Rider's garden. On the way there, he talked to himself as was his custom.

"Am I bein' made a mug of, or am I not?" he asked himself.

He liked Littlejohn, but was fed-up with his presence in Stalden. Not that Mellalieu minded playing second fiddle to a greater than he; but his wife had given him a hell of a time since the arrival of the great man from London. Extra shine on his buttons; extra polish on his boots. Brush his clothes ten times a day. Don't be seen in the garden "in his shirt", as if a chap could help getting dirty among his celery and potato rows. Don't shuffle yer feet, Arthur. Don't talk so vulgar; be hoity-toity like. Regular round of parades and inspections by the missus. As if the Londoner had come down to try him out for a job in Scotland Yard itself! He knew his wife was ambitious for herself and him. But after all, there are limits...

"Am I bein' made a mug of?" he asked himself, "becos nobody makes a mug of William Arthur Mellalieu... not if he knows it... not if he knows it."

And so on, along the field-path which led to the back of Rider's cottage. Then, applying the closure to his soliloquy, P.C. Mellalieu took to the hedge as he did when nearing a colony of rabbits. In due course, he reached the bottom of the writer's back garden. The bobby had removed his helmet and looked a different man, almost another person, like a judge without his wig and robes or a beefeater in mufti. All that could eventually be seen of him among the hazel bushes was a pair of large, slightly protuberant, blue eyes, taking-in all that was going on. For Mr. Rider was digging earnestly in his flower plots.

No need to seek far for *papaver*. There he was, *Rhoeas, Argemone, Dubium* in profusion of scarlet, growing wildly round the compost heap, generated from the refuse of the more orderly beds nearby. There were white poppies, too, with purple eyes. *Papaver Somniferum*, but Mellalieu did not recognize them at the time. He identified them from his gardening encyclopædia, when he got home. Meanwhile, he was realizing that there were several different kinds of poppy and memorizing their colours and shapes. He was also intently watching the occupant of the garden.

Rider was busy with a fork in a bed containing tall, blue-flowered plants. He uprooted several of them, examined them, appeared satisfied and chopped-off the flowers and foliage. The remaining roots he bore-off to the small workshop which Mellalieu had already visited.

The policeman watched all the operations intently, his mouth open, his brows contracted in concentration. He remained deep in thought whilst Rider locked the laboratory again, washed his hands indoors and then made-off for the village, apparently on some errand or other. At length, a great truth seemed to dawn on the mind of the watcher. He caught his breath, made whistling noises to himself and said "By gor!" He pondered again, heavily and profoundly, and seemed to make up his mind. First he felt in his trousers pocket and took out an instrument which he had made from a metal meat-skewer in the secrecy of his tool-shed last evening when his wife was out. If the London chap could use a pick-lock, why shouldn't he? Carefully he reconnoitred the premises. There was nobody about.

Mellalieu took a final furtive look around and then moved rapidly towards the workshop…

Meanwhile, Littlejohn halted outside Mrs. Congreve's cottage. There was a notice in the window: WASHING DONE HERE. He knocked and the door was opened after sounds of bumping and scuffling behind it. A blast of hot, steamy air met Littlejohn, and Mrs. Congreve followed it.

The professional daily-help and washerwoman was small and fat with a figure like a sack tied in the middle. She seemed to roll rather than walk and had a pleasant round red face with twinkling eyes. As good-humoured a woman as you could wish to meet on a day's march. And that with a husband who'd hardly done a day's work since he married her. He was supposed to be ailing, but nobody knew the nature of his complaint. He hung about the village centre all day, propping-up the front of *The Mortal Man* or watching the goings-on of the place with little crafty eyes. But at night he would return and threaten to do all kinds of horrible things to Mrs. Congreve for no reason whatever. Her insurance lay, however, in being the goose that laid the golden eggs for him.

"Come in," said Mrs. Congreve wheezily, for her labours combined with the tightness of her corsage impeded her respiration. She did not at first ask Littlejohn his business. She assumed that he had called to bespeak her for next week's washing. She continued ironing during most of the interview, for that was the principal thing she knew about and it kept fully occupied what bit of brain she owned. She knew nothing about the war, politics or the national effort, but she *could* wash linens white and iron better than any laundry with its fancy new-fangled machinery!

Mrs. Congreve raised various articles of intimate lingerie from a large clothes-basket and spread them on her operating table with shameless abandon. It was obvious that they belonged to somebody else! She was using a flat-iron and two more were heating on the glowing embers in the grate. Each time she took up a fresh iron, she rubbed it on the hearthrug and spat on it. The spittle hissed, formed a bead, and rolled-off on to the floor. Whereat, she seemed technically content and with a flourish and a bump, set about her pressing, groaning as she laid her weight on the delicate silks and linens.

Littlejohn took from his pocket the sock which had been fished-out of Daft Dick's well with Bates. It was of fine navy-blue wool with a white clock on the outer side of it.

"Ever seen that before, Mrs. Congreve?" he asked.

"Where you get that there from?" demanded the woman and with a pair of silk pyjama-trousers dangling on her fat arm, she approached and took up the sock.

"Do you know whose it is, Mrs. Congreve?"

"Certainly I do. I got the partner to it in me rag-bag. Brought it away with a lot of cast-offs from Mr. Rider's. I darns 'is socks for 'im and them 'at's past mendin' he let me keep for floorcloths..."

Judging from the good condition of the particular sock in hand, it looked as if Mrs. Congreve rather hurried the natural course of wearing-out.

"...But Congreve can wear socks 'at's long past Mr. Rider's tastes. Was I mad when I finds-out that one of the pair as I'd throwed out 'ad vanished? Was I mad? 'Unted high and low but couldn't find it nowhere, search as I might. Couldn't ask Mr. Rider if he'd seen it, o' course, him not bein' interested."

Under normal conditions, Rider would probably have been very interested to learn how socks were transferred from his own feet to those of Congreve!

"Where's this other sock then, I'd like to borrow it?"

The truth seemed to dawn suddenly on the daily-help.

"Where you got that there sock from?" she said with undue ferocity. Then without waiting for an answer she continued.

"Borrer an old sock! Wot next? Excuse me keeping on ironin'. Promised these things to Miss Cockayne before tea..."

And she set about the pyjama jacket with a will.

"The other sock was found down the well with the body of the dead man in Daft Dick's allotment. I want the other of the pair. Find it, please. I'm the police officer in charge of the case."

"Perlice!" whispered Mrs. Congreve, turned pale and clutched her ironing-table for support. "I didn't steal them socks, mister.

They were given to me… only yesterday… that is, only yesterday I brought away the one for a cleanin' rag. Couldn't find the other. I'm an honest woman, I am. Anybody in the village'll give me me character…"

"All right, calm yourself. Nobody's accusing you of anything. I only want to get this matter clear. You put aside a pair of socks—of which this I have here was one—at Mr. Rider's to bring home. Later, when you went for them, one was missing and you couldn't find it. So you brought one only for a floor-rag or something. That it?"

"Yes, mister, that's it without a word of a lie and strike me dead if I'm not tellin' the truth."

"Well then, please find me the sock you brought home with you."

Mrs. Congreve rolled to a cupboard, brought out a large canvas bag and turned-out its contents on the oak settle. Pieces of old cloth, rags, string, coloured bits of wool, a mangled pair of corsets… Mrs. Congreve rummaged feverishly among them. No sock came to light.

"I know I 'ad it… good for nothing but me rag-bag, not havin' a marrer one to make a pair. Where is it now…?"

She was almost in tears. She pondered heavily in a bothered fashion.

"Surely Congreve's not got it on…! surely…!" she said at length.

"Where is he? Hurry please, Mrs. Congreve. This is most important."

"He'll be in the square sunnin' himself, like as not…"

Littlejohn waited no longer. He didn't know Congreve from Adam, but inquiries brought the man to light. We will not waste time on the idle good-for-nothing. He isn't worth it. But he had on Rider's old sock. On the other foot, a grey plus-four stocking from somewhere! Congreve didn't care. He was no dandy. Suffice to say that he was persuaded with the help of half-a-crown to retire behind the yard-door of *The Mortal Man* and remove the hose from a foot which didn't seem to have seen soap and water since its creation.

Littlejohn compared the sock he had in his pocket with that he had obtained from the disgusting Congreve, who ran like a hare to drink away his spoils after shedding it.

The two articles made a pair. The clock of the one from the well was on the outside-left; the other was on the outside-right.

Littlejohn decided forthwith to go to Olstead, pick up Gillibrand and a warrant, and then visit Rider at once.

On the way to the 'bus, he met Mellalieu, returning, well-satisfied from his snooping exhibition. The constable became very loquacious, for a change, and poured out a long tale in Littlejohn's ear.

"I'm just off to see Inspector Gillibrand at Olstead, Mellalieu, so keep an eye on Rider whilst I'm away. I'll not be long," said Littlejohn.

Mellalieu felt that he had something to do at last. Very elated, he returned to his cottage for a drink of tea before resuming his vigil.

"Wot you been at again?" asked his wife in her usual fashion as he entered looking very pleased with himself.

"Ask no questions, missis, and you'll be told no lies. It's official business. Confidential. 'Ighly confidential."

Mellalieu was surprised at his own audacity. So was his wife. She threw him a momentary glance full of respect. It is a pity he didn't see it, otherwise he might have followed it up with a still more masterly attack and established himself as domestic boss once and for all.

CHAPTER XX

Deductions

"You shall see, it will fall pat as I told you."

ACT V. SC. I.

At the police headquarters in Olstead, Littlejohn met Gillibrand and together they interviewed the Chief Constable, Colonel Twiss.

The latter had at one time been a colonial administrator and during his period of office, had allowed a native to be wrongly sentenced for a crime which, it turned out later, he had never done. So, Colonel Twiss was inclined to be ultra-cautious.

"Mustn't do anythin' rash and bring the damned whirlwind round our ears," he said. "Better have it cast-iron before we act."

"I think we can trust Littlejohn for that, sir," said Gillibrand loyally. He had been putting-up with this sort of thing for years and sometimes it affected him like a strange nightmare in which for every step he took forward, his feet slipped two back. "Let's hear what he has to say."

Littlejohn stretched his legs and began.

"The preamble to this case is pure surmise…"

"Tcha, tcha, tcha," said Colonel Twiss and made gestures across his face as though trying to wash it with one hand.

"…The facts come later to clinch the theory. First, the Bates affair. Bates having robbed a London bank makes for cover in the country and arrives at Stalden. He's heard of the place as the home of a famous unorthodox bonesetter, whose technique has done wonders. The newspapers have been full of it at times. Squabbles with the orthodox school; certain bold practitioners being choked off by their colleagues for aiding and abetting Wall: celebrities cured of complaints the rest couldn't touch. It's all been in the news. Bates has an idea. Why not change in himself the principal means of his identification given by the police? A deformed arm and a broken nose."

The Chief Constable blew out his cheeks and Gillibrand winked encouragingly at his colleague.

"How to persuade Wall to harbour him, an escaping criminal, however? Bates is in luck. In gaol he's heard from a buddy who's given him chapter and verse of an illegal operation with which Wall's nephew is connected. This relative is a qualified man and Wall is as proud of him as if he'd been his own son. Bates makes the most of this in persuading the old fellow to do as he wishes. And here again, he's lucky. Young Dr. Wall and his father, Nathaniel Wall's partner, are on a cruise somewhere and can't be contacted. Perhaps on the other hand, Old Wall was so out of it in his little village immersed in his work, that he didn't know who Bates was, or not until he'd become too far involved in harbouring him or in performing an operation on him. He did the job; not very successful in the case of the nose, but almost a complete cure of the arm. The surgeon who examined the dead body will tell you that. The result seems to have been that Bates was given a new lease of life and freedom and the police didn't nab him.

"We know that Bates was mixed-up in a counterfeiting racket before his spell in gaol. He was a skilled engraver. Probably when released, he was so hard-up that bank-raiding was all he could think of. After he'd finished with Wall, he managed to make contact with another gang of forgers, this time on an international scale. The head man kept himself in the background. He eventually hid himself in Stalden, whether at Bates's recommendation or not, we can't say. He took a cottage and there, posing as a writer, engraved the plates which were sent to London for use, by way of an accommodation address at Seven Sisters Road. That man was Rider."

The Chief Constable cleared his throat noisily, thrust his hands deep into his pockets and paced about the room like a caged tiger.

"Pure surmise, Littlejohn. Pure surmise!" he said explosively.

"Not quite, sir. We've traced parcels, presumably containing engraved plates, passing between Rider and the Seven Sisters address. The postmistress at Stalden has produced the records to bear it out. Furthermore, Bates was the go-between for Rider and the gang and picked up the parcels at Seven Sisters Road. The proprietor of the newsagency which constituted the accommodation address there, has given a recognizable description of him. The police laid hands on several of the small fry of the gang, but the big fish, Rider and Bates, kept clear of the net. And whilst they were free, the rest wouldn't talk; so you can guess the fear they'd instilled into them. The war and the cutting of continental communications, as well as the tightening of regulations, finally put them out of business."

"Urumph, urumph… still a bit vague, eh?"

"Now let's get down to more tangible matters."

"Rider became engaged to Miss Cockayne, of whom old Mr. Wall was very fond. In fact, he was almost her self-appointed guardian. Wall, probably rightly, imagined that the seemingly lackadaisical Rider was after Miss Cockayne's money. He instinctively distrusted Rider and didn't hesitate to say so. At first, we suspected that Rider and Wall had quarrelled fiercely and that Rider had grown violent and killed him. The medical report indicated an assailant stronger in the left than in the right hand. I suspected that Rider might be Bates. But that was soon disposed of by testing his fingerprints and the discovery of the body of Bates later.

"Now, had the well on Daft Dick's allotment not been used by the eccentric owner for keeping his valuables in, and belonged to somebody who used a bank or a bottom drawer, probably Bates's weighted body would never have been found. As it was, it came to light. Also, the stone in the sock, which someone had used to stun his victim before throwing him down. The sock has been identified as Rider's property. I hold the other one of the pair and I've evidence to show that the incriminating article vanished whilst actually in Rider's cottage. Who else but Rider could have taken it?"

"Hurumph… sounds better, sounds a deal better. Brass tacks, down to brass tacks at last! Who's the witness about the sock?"

"Mrs. Congreve, Rider's daily help."

"Good gad… a charwoman!!"

"Why not, sir? An honest woman, respectable, and remembers every detail, because she was planning to use the cast-off socks for her own husband. Another thing. At first, Rider said he'd an alibi for the time of the murder: he'd been with Miss Cockayne all the evening until past eleven. Now, it turns out that she was asleep part of the time during a concert on the radio and the odds are that she was lightly drugged by being given a doped cigarette. We found evidence that Rider, who's quite a chemist in his way, had been working on cigarettes with opium in his little lab. in the garden…"

"The fellow's a damned cad… blasted outsider… Go on, then, anythin' more?"

"Well, as I see it, the gang had been broken up and Bates was on his beam-ends. So he turned up to touch Rider for some help.

Whether or not he tried blackmail, we don't know, but he seems to have gone to Wall as well. Perhaps he tried to get something out of the bonesetter on the strength of past history—a ghost from the unpleasant past in whose crime the old man made himself an accessory. Old Wall must have turned on him and threatened to hand him over to the police. I think Bates must have got violent, attacked the old man and left him, half-strangled into unconsciousness. On his way out of The Corner House by the back window—of which we found a key in the well with Bates, probably stolen for future use years before when he lodged there—Bates was struck down by Rider. He wasn't dead, just like old Wall, so Rider weighted the body with stones and sank him in Daft Dick's well. Then, he returned to Wall and found him lying unconscious. What had Bates told Wall? You can imagine Rider seeing Wall with a case to convince Miss Cockayne and do him out of his expectations or even to put the police on his track. But Rider was a fastidious man. He couldn't go on with the throttling where Bates had left off, any more than he could have beat out Bates's brains with a stone in a sock. So, he slung Wall up on the rope and pulley in the surgery and left him to choke. Then, he crept off the way he and Bates had come, through the fields behind the town, throwing the window-key down the well. Daft Dick saw Bates arrive, but had gone home for his supper when Rider came sneaking in his tracks."

Gillibrand now broke in.

"I think on the strength of this, sir, we'd better call and see Rider at once and question him further about the sock and his movements on the night of the crime. If he can't give a satisfactory answer, we'd better have a warrant ready and haul him in."

"Oh, all right," said the Chief Constable, still a bit timid about taking the plunge. "Swear one out, but go carefully."

The two detectives, having obtained their warrant, set out for Stalden, after a bite of refreshment, for it was well past tea time. As they passed through the centre of the village, a knot of men, hanging about outside *The Mortal Man* gazed curiously after them. Among the loungers was Congreve and he was half-drunk. As Littlejohn drew level with him, he whistled impudently and when the Inspector turned his head, he hitched up his shabby trousers by lifting his pockets, and laid bare four inches of hose above his battered shoes. He had replaced the sock which Littlejohn had purchased from him by another of exactly the same pattern!

CHAPTER XXI

Murderer

"I see their knavery; this is to make an ass of me; to fright me if they could. But I will not stir from this place, do what they can..."

ACT III. SC. I.

LITTLEJOHN WAS FLABBERGASTED AT CONGREVE'S SHOW OF finery! If, as appeared to be the case, this type of hose with the fatal identification marks, was common all over the place, then the bottom fell out of the theory incriminating Rider. In the present case, however, Congreve was wearing a pair which matched each other and Littlejohn hastened to him to investigate the new phenomenon.

"Where d'you get those socks, Congreve?" he said not too politely, for the idler seemed delighted with the situation. "I thought the one you gave me was the only one you'd got."

"Sell 'em to yer fer half a dollar apiece," leered Congreve impudently.

"Now, none of that. Answer the question and be quick about it."

"All right, sir, all right. No offence intended or taken. I 'ad 'em among me other clothes an' changed into 'em after I give you the other."

"Where did they come from?"

"Missus got 'em from one of the places she works at."

"Which?"

"Dunno... better ask 'er. She'll tell yer."

Followed by Gillibrand, Littlejohn hurried to the washerwoman's cottage. Mrs. Congreve was still ironing. This time it was somebody else's smalls. She seemed surprised to see the Inspector again. He told her the purpose of his visit.

"Oh, them!" she said. "An' 'as 'e put on 'is best socks? The artful one that 'e is. Came 'ome and said he'd sold a sock and was puttin' on another. Them's his best. Miss Cockayne give them to me last Christmas, she did. Bought a pair for 'er young man, Mr. Rider—them as you know of—and another fer Mr. Wall, God rest 'im. Pore Mr. Wall's feet was too big for those socks, so she gave 'em to me. Got them from London she did."

Considerably relieved, Littlejohn thanked the good woman and he and his colleague now made straight for Rider's house. The man was at home, regarded them with an ill-grace as they arrived and, with a show of reluctance, asked them in. A half-filled glass of whisky and soda stood on his desk, but he did not invite his visitors to join him in a drink. The room was low and old-fashioned, with a french window giving on to the lawn and another overlooking the road across the garden gate.

"Well, what is it now?" asked Rider. "I thought I'd told you policemen all I know about your infernal case..."

"Not quite," said Littlejohn. "There are still one or two questions we'd like to ask you about your connection with it, Mr. Rider."

"Mine?"

"Yes. To begin with, your alibi for the time of Mr. Wall's murder has lost its confirmation..."

"Miss Cockayne was with me and has said as much. What more do you want?"

"Unfortunately, Miss Cockayne was asleep at the time."

"What nonsense is this? Has she told you so?"

"Yes. And I think you know more about that than you have told us. I suggest, Mr. Rider, that she smoked a drugged cigarette which you gave her…"

"Look here, I'm busy. I haven't time to sit here listening to your preposterous nonsense. Drugged cigarette, indeed! What next? This isn't a scene from the latest spy-thriller."

Littlejohn took the two drugged cigarettes which had been returned to him by the official chemist after examination, from his pocket and put them on the table.

"Those were found in your workshop, Mr. Rider. They've been drugged. Just before Miss Cockayne fell asleep on the night in question, she smoked a cigarette from your case…"

"By gad, I'll make you pay for this," shouted Rider now flushed with anger. "Not content with making insinuations, you have to break and enter my premises collecting evidence and then concoct a grotesque tale. The police'll hear from my lawyer about it."

"Let that pass for the time being, Mr. Rider. We're quite prepared to face any accusations in due course. For the present, we're concerned with the night of the crime. When last I interviewed you, you kindly gave me the programme of a broadcast concert covering the fatal hour. In particular, we're interested in whether or not you heard Elgar's *Enigma Variations*. Did you?"

"Of course. I did. Dammit, I've already told you."

"All through…? You're a musical man, Mr. Rider?"

"Yes. I like good music and know quite a bit about it. I heard the piece all through. Where the hell is this getting us, because I'm fed up with it all and I'll be glad to see the last of you?"

"Forgive my pressing the point, but did you hear the Nimrod variation, too?"

"For the last time, YES. I heard the whole damn lot and now let the matter drop. I've work to be getting on with."

"How comes it that you heard Nimrod, Mr. Rider, when there was a technical break in the broadcast that night, which cut the whole of that variation and a part of the following one off the air? I suggest that you weren't indoors at all and that you left Miss Cockayne asleep whilst you left her place."

"Suggest what you damn well like. It's all the same to me. Are you trying to say that I slipped out and murdered Wall. What should I want to kill the old chap for?"

"Did you ever know a man named Bates?"

Hitherto, Rider had managed to keep-up his bluff. The mention of Bates shook him for a moment, but he was soon back on form again.

"No. Who the hell's Bates?"

"A member of a defunct gang of counterfeiters who once haunted Seven Sisters Road, Stockwell. Know the address?"

"No. Why should I?"

"You used to send parcels to that address. Publishers, they were described as. Actually an accommodation address. Bates used to call for those parcels, Mr. Rider."

"Look here. What are you getting at? Murderer, counterfeiter, cigarette-doper. What next are you going to try on me? Get out. I've had enough."

"Just one more question, Mr. Rider. Is this yours?"

Littlejohn took the sock he had obtained from Congreve from his pocket and threw it on the table.

Rider's control was wonderful. He looked at the sock and then at Littlejohn without turning a hair.

"How the blazes should I know. Why? You pinched that from

here, too? I've scores of pairs of socks. And, I suppose there are scores like that about..."

"This one was yours all right, Mr. Rider. I got it from Mrs. Congreve, your daily-help, who took it, as past wearing by you, from your mending and gave it to her husband."

"Well, what about it?"

Littlejohn took the other sock from his pocket and threw it beside the one already on the table.

"*That* one was used with a stone inside it, to knock out Bates prior to his being thrown into the well behind Mr. Wall's house and drowned."

"Are you trying to say that Mrs. Congreve did the murder, or that she provided the weapon?"

"No. Mrs. Congreve never had the second sock. She only took away one of the pair. The other was taken from her rag-bag here before she could take it home and as you're the only one who has access to the place besides her, I think you know something about it."

"Good God! Another crime to my credit! How many more?"

Rider laughed shrilly. Too shrilly. Then he picked up his glass of whisky and soda and balanced it between his fingers. He looked boldly at Littlejohn.

"Well?" he said. "What next?"

Littlejohn decided to answer boldness with boldness. If it didn't come-off, he must take the consequences. But he was sure in his mind that the murderer was sitting before him and that nothing short of drastic measures would shake his complacency.

"I don't know how you came to live in Stalden, in the first place, Mr. Rider, but I suspect that your old confederate Bates... don't interrupt, I'll let you have your say later... I suspect that Bates told you it might prove a quiet hide-out when things were getting too hot in London. As head of the Seven Sisters gang, you found it convenient to prepare your plates for printing forged banknotes here and sent them to London, to an accommodation address, for Bates to pick up. Correct me if I'm wrong."

"Like hell I will. The whole thing's just a crazy fairytale. I've no time for such nonsense..."

"Well, for a time all goes well. Then the war arrives, the gang breaks-up, restrictions stop you from shipping off your dud notes to the continent and your income ceases from that source. You seek another. There's an heiress in the village. Miss Cockayne. She'll do."

Rider was on his feet in an instant and made for Littlejohn.

"Why you... you swine. I'll make you sit up for this. Nobody's bringing her into this..."

He made a lunge at the Inspector, who deftly avoided the blow and with an easy gesture swept Rider back into his chair.

"Now, Mr. Rider, that'll do. Be quiet, and listen to the rest."

Gillibrand began to look anxious. He sensed the beginning of a third-degree and he didn't relish it. He had never worked with Littlejohn before or he wouldn't have shown apprehension on that score.

"Mr. Wall resisted your engagement, but you both carried the day and defied him. Unfortunately, the old man's dislike was instinctive, and he'd none of your past history to guide him. However, your old colleague, Bates arrived here stealthily, in the nick of time. He, too, was feeling the effects of the slump in your trade and came to try to wring something from you by fair means or foul. Probably foul. That sealed his fate, for you cleared him out of the way before he began to talk."

Rider licked his lips and glared.

"I don't know what the devil you're talking about. But go on, you haven't got anything on me and I've got a devil of a lot on you. Gillibrand's a witness, even if he is on your side now. The law'll soon alter that, however, when I take you up for slander and assault."

"Bates and Wall had met before, Mr. Rider, in the capacity as doctor and patient and Mr. Wall had usefully altered Bates's features somewhat at a time when he didn't want to be recognized, and restored a disabled right arm to almost normal use. Bates called on Wall, as you knew he would, just at dusk so that he wouldn't be seen. You gave yourself an alibi by gently putting your companion to sleep, racing out to follow Bates and killing him before she awoke. Then you pretended you'd been listening to a piece which hadn't been broadcast at all. Bates had quarrelled with Wall and half-killed him in a struggle when you appeared. You had a very innocent-looking and handy portable weapon in your pocket. An old sock into which you slipped a large stone. When Bates emerged from the back of Wall's house, you let him have it with your cosh and dropped him unconscious down the well on the other side of the fence. Then you returned to the still unconscious Wall and afraid of what he might have learned from Bates about you and how he'd use it to separate you from Miss Cockayne, you finished him off by hanging him on a rope in the surgery."

"All a lot of poppycock, and you can't prove a word of it," cried Rider, having recovered some of his poise.

"No? The weapon is enough. I think your sock will hang you, Mr. Rider, and I'm prepared to back my judgment there."

Littlejohn nodded to Gillibrand, who rose and approached Rider.

"Charles Rider," said the local Inspector, "I arrest you in connection with the murder of Percival Bates and I have here a warrant for this purpose. I must warn you that anything you say may be taken down and used in evidence."

Rider sighed heavily, stretched his legs and arms and yawned.

"Really," he said, pondered for a moment, and then drank off his glass of whisky and soda. As he gulped it down he made a wry face and then again regarded Littlejohn with a mixture of admiration and triumph.

"Has the recital finished, Inspector, because it's my turn now?" he almost shouted.

"Yes. But remember, anything you say will be taken down..."

"Oh, don't say it again, man. Why make it like a twopenny shocker. Oh, Lord. Here come the *real* police."

Treading portentously up the front path was P.C. William Arthur Mellalieu, looking, in his anxiety to communicate with his superiors, like a hen wishing to lay an egg. He knocked boldly on the front door and Littlejohn rose to open it for him.

"I got somethin' I think I ought to tell you, sir," said the bobby when the Inspector appeared. And in a low, hoarse voice, Mellalieu unburdened himself of a strange tale.

CHAPTER XXII

Hangman

"Approach, ye Furies fell!
O Fates, come, come,
Cut thread and thrum;
Quail, crush, conclude and quell!"

ACT V. SC. I.

RIDER SHOWED SIGNS OF IMPATIENCE WHEN LITTLEJOHN returned from his palaver with Mellalieu. Otherwise, he was sitting undisturbed by the accusations just levelled at him.

"Come, Inspector," he said as though inviting Littlejohn to an interview for a job, "I can only give you a few minutes and I've a lot to say."

Gillibrand's eyebrows shot upwards in surprise at the cool effrontery of the fellow, but his colleague seated himself, unmoved.

"As a detective story your account of what you've discovered by investigation backed up by surmise, would make very poor reading if it were published," continued Rider. "For example, Bates's forcing Wall to alter his features and restore the use of his arm on the strength of some cock-and-bull story about an illegal operation performed by his nephew. Come, come Inspector! I'm surprised at you. A man of old Wall's strength of mind wouldn't for a moment submit to such blackmail. No. Bates heard of Wall's *skill* from his prison-mate, the murderer, and made up his mind when he got free to become a patient. But he'd more sense than to try blackmail there, even if he'd had the grounds for it. The truth was, according to Bates, Old

Wall simply didn't know who Bates was. That's all. The bonesetter didn't bother himself with reading crime reports in newspapers. He was too busy and immersed in his job. He took-on Bates as a very interesting patient and Bates, in his desperation, was willing to submit to drastic treatment. A guinea-pig for an experiment. Wall found out who he was later, however. Somebody spotted Bates leaving at the end and gave Wall some old newspaper cuttings. The old chap showed them to Miss Cockayne and was upset about it, but Bates having gone God knows where by that time, the matter seemed to drop and whoever told Wall doesn't seem to have pursued it further. Probably didn't want to get the old man in trouble with the police.

"You were right about Bates recommending Stalden to me as a quiet hide-out. A good guess on your part, for you can't possibly have found it out by investigation."

Here Rider paused and winced, as though in pain. He gripped the arms of this chair convulsively and beads of sweat sprang from his forehead. Gillibrand rose anxiously from his seat, but Littlejohn laid a big restraining hand on his arm, and answered his look of questioning astonishment by a shake of the head. Rider seemed to recover from the passing spasm and resumed his narrative a little wearily.

"I daresay you wonder why I'm being so damned communicative. In the first place, I was training as a barrister before I discovered that my true talents lay in the direction of chemistry with a spot of engraving thrown in. So I turned them to good account instead of waiting for problematical briefs. Now, my view as one trained in the law is that the sock in your pocket is enough to hang me, Littlejohn, wriggle as I may. Just the thing to carry a jury. Your bulldog of an average man doesn't want a lot of airy pros and cons by lawyers. He wants something to get his teeth into, and there he has it. You'll discover later in the tale that I've also other motives for my confessions."

He winced again and put his hands to his midriff. Littlejohn again restrained Gillibrand.

"Are you all right?" said the latter anxiously to Rider.

"Yes. Just a touch of indigestion. I'm a martyr to it."

He sat-up again, white and shaken.

"I must get this off my chest. You made a mistake, Littlejohn, about Miss Cockayne. I love her. It's not her money I'm after. I intended to marry her and settle down to a peaceable country life. To-day, she sent me packing. She, too, found out about the drugged cigarettes, after you'd raised the point, of course. And I gather Mrs. Congreve told her about the sock, too, when she delivered her washing earlier to-day. Miss Cockayne bought those socks for me. So, when I called an hour ago, she told me plainly, she thought I'd killed Wall and never wanted to see my face again. I could have killed *her*, of course. But what's the use…? I can't go on killing people. I'd an account to settle with that wretched little doctor across the way. He saw Bates arriving here after dark on the night before the murder. Picked him up in his headlamps as he passed my cottage, saw him enter, and then identified him again when he was called to see his corpse after they'd hauled it out of the well. He didn't go to the police, but came here. He's hard-up through drinking all his earnings away and was prepared to sell his silence. I couldn't have that over my head. So, I'd a rod in pickle for him. I was going to give him a glass of doctored whisky when he called and then take him for a ride in the woods and leave him there. Candidly, I'm in a mess. I used to be an expert at extricating myself. But this breach with Miss Cockayne has dulled my faculties, robbed me of my desire to get out of trouble…"

He paused again, a curious look on his face as though anticipating a further spasm of pain, but nothing seemed to happen. He went on with his tale, but appeared to be gradually losing his nerve and powers of concentration. He passed his handkerchief across his lips and forehead with a trembling hand.

"I must hurry. Can't go on all day. Time's limited… I was getting along very comfortably here and settling down. I'd even planned to get married and retire. I'd made enough money out of my trade… you know what it was, it seems, Littlejohn… and I looked forward to a peaceful existence pottering in my garden and playing at chemistry, which is my hobby. Old Wall objected to my marrying Miss Cockayne. He never liked me from the start. Thought me an idler and a dilettante, I guess. An instinctive antipathy.

"Then, Bates came on the scene. He was penniless and in a nasty frame of mind. He'd had his share of our profits in the past, but had spent it and then seemed to think that I'd had more than I ought to have had and that more was due to him. He evidently intended to live on me for the rest of his days. I wasn't going to have that. I decided to settle him once and for all. He'd arrived after dark and I thought nobody could possibly have seen him enter my place. Just my luck for the blasted doctor to be passing at the time! I decided to kill Bates and dispose of his body. I fancied poison. I'd means of getting it without being traced. I'm a bit of a toxicologist as well as a chemist, so it was easy."

Gillibrand again showed signs of excitement and apprehension and when Littlejohn tried to quieten his fears, he looked at his colleague as if suspecting he had taken leave of his senses.

"Bates told me in cold blood what he expected," went on Rider. "He wanted a sum down in cash—a ridiculous sum—and so much a month after. I told him it wasn't possible. He said he'd have it or make it hot for me. I said I'd have to think it out, hoping to keep him until I'd a chance to give him a doped drink. I'd preparations to make, too, and couldn't just kill him then and there. He stayed overnight. I was ready to finish him off and drive him away to the woods when it got dark the following evening. Just as I was bracing myself for it, Bates said he'd another errand to do. I knew where he was going. Apprehensive lest anyone should see him, I told him to wait until dusk and then take the quiet field-path to Wall's. He grinned, that nasty, crooked grin of his. 'So you guessed where I was going, eh?' he said. 'That's another who's going to pay me a pension. Harbouring a criminal's a punishable offence. I'll have to tell him, that if he doesn't hand me enough to live on, I'll have to give myself up to the police and get them to keep me for a year or two. I've got a few years' lodgings still owing to me.' Even as he cackled at his own joke, I saw a better way of killing him. He'd a key to Wall's place and was going to let himself in by the back french window and face the old man. I knew the existence of the old well behind The Corner House. If I caught Bates on his way back, I'd only to knock him out and sink him down the well and the job was done. I thought the well was never used. That was my mistake. How was I to know that a daft old gardener was using it to hide his money in and rooting down it with a hook on the end of a pole?

"There's little else to tell. I followed Bates. Having no sandbag or loaded stick handy, I just found an old stocking, put a round sizeable stone in it, and used that as a weapon. But things didn't quite turn out as I'd hoped. Wall wasn't in when Bates got in the house. So Bates waited for him. He calmly put the light on and I could see Wall enter by the dining-room door. Then Wall drew the curtains and I could see no more. Soon Bates emerged in a hurry but furtively. I clouted him good and hard before he could get his bearings and dumped him down the well. He'd left the french window open, so I went back to take a peep at what he'd been at. Very foolish of me, but quite natural. I found Wall on the ground. Apparently they quarrelled and a struggle had ensued. Wall was in a terrible state, for Bates had almost throttled him to death. He was just recovering consciousness when an awful idea dawned on me. If he survived, he'd be sure to ask what had happened to Bates. Even if nothing could be pinned on me, there was a big risk. Besides, what had Bates already told Wall in his truculence? I'd got to silence Wall, too. I didn't like it, but it was to save my own neck. I'd no weapon… I'd thrown my own down the well with Bates. So, I hanged Wall on his own limb-stretching device. That's all. Except that I locked the french window and threw the key down the well."

Littlejohn rose. Gillibrand did the same, feeling utterly at a loss.

"Well, if that's all, you'd better accompany us to Olstead police-station, Mr. Rider, where you can sign a statement…" began Littlejohn.

Rider burst into harsh laughter.

"Not on your life, Inspector. Why do you think I've kept you here so long? The whisky I drank contains a deadly poison. I was expecting you, so had it handy. Given a quarter of an hour—and it's that since I took it—nothing on earth can save me. Any moment now and the pangs will be on me. No hangman for me… And you can thank Miss Cockayne for this… I might have given you a run for your money otherwise. *And* you can thank the whisky-sodden doctor opposite, too. Because I prepared this poison for him."

Gillibrand took up the 'phone hastily, but Littlejohn stayed his hand again.

"I guessed all along he'd taken something," Gillibrand was saying. "But I thought…"

Rider looked hard at Littlejohn. The Scotland Yard man didn't seem in the least bit perturbed. Something had gone wrong somewhere, for instead of an atmosphere of tension prevailing, there seemed to be an anti-climax in the offing.

Littlejohn crossed to Rider and snapped a pair of handcuffs on his wrists.

"Now, Mr. Rider, come along and no more prevaricating. What you thought was aconitine, was merely a strong dose of horse-radish. Fortunately P. C. Mellalieu, who called round here on another matter this morning, saw you digging up monkshood root. He's a naturalist and recognized the plant. Contact with me and the investigation over the past few days has made the constable suspicious of you, Rider. He suspects you're up to no good. So whilst your back was turned, he substituted horse-radish root, which is almost identical with that of monkshood, or wolf's-bane, as Mellalieu calls it. He just came to tell me his tale. Your pains are merely tummy-ache."

Gillibrand had no time to register relief, for as soon as the hoax dawned on Rider, he became like one possessed. He fought like a madman, flailing the air with his manacled hands and giving with his feet, the best exhibition of *la savatte* that Littlejohn had ever come across. He and his two captors struggled and heaved about the room, the Inspectors hanging on his arms like bulldogs, Rider almost lifting them from their feet in his demoniac frenzy. The face of P.C. Mellalieu appeared at the window. Two eyes grew round as saucers and a moustache bristled. The front door opened and in trod the bobby, truncheon in hand. With the light of one set purpose in his eyes, William Arthur Mellalieu relentlessly advanced on the milling mass of arms and legs which constituted his two superiors and their captive. Carefully the village constable selected the head of Rider from the heaving group and, raising his staff, he gave it a precise, but telling swipe. The bottom seemed to drop completely out of the struggle and all that remained was to transport Mellalieu's victim to the lock-up.

*

The dairyman's motor-van having been requisitioned again and the bemused Rider, with Gillibrand and Mellalieu supporting him hustled off to the Olstead gaol, Littlejohn crossed the road to Dr. Keating's surgery. The doctor was exasperated at the sight of the Inspector, for he had an appointment at a bottle-party that evening and had been bustling his patients about with a view to an early finish.

"When am I going to see the last of you policemen?" he asked trying to muster his professional dignity and failing miserably. "I can't get on with my daily duties for your pestering."

"I won't keep you long this time, doctor, if you'll answer a couple of straight questions."

"Well, get on with them, then..."

Keating's eyes grew shifty.

"You were sent-for when Bates's body was found in the well on the allotment behind Wall's place?"

"Yes. You know I was."

"Right. Had you ever seen Bates before that?"

"No. Why should I? He was a stranger here, wasn't he?"

Littlejohn raised his eyebrows and looked Keating full in the face.

"Sure you never saw him before?"

"No, I tell you. What are you driving at?"

"Where were you on the night before Bates's death, doctor?"

"Oh hell, is this beginning all over again. I suppose you think *I* killed Bates now. Well, I didn't. I was out on my rounds until well after dark that night. You can see my case-book and follow my tracks for alibis if you like."

"That won't be necessary. Did you pass Rider's place after dark?"

"Of course I did. How else could I have got home?"

"See anybody going in there by the light of your headlamps?"

Keating turned the colour of putty.

"I may have done. What of it?"

"You *may* have done, eh? Then, why did you tell Rider you saw Bates entering his place that night?"

"I might have said I... I... saw somebody like Bates. I was chaffing Rider a bit the other day..."

"Funny sort of joke, doctor. Why didn't you tell that to the police when they arrived at the well?"

"I wasn't sure... you see..."

"I see nothing. I only know that you suppressed evidence and demanded from Rider a price for your silence."

"It's a damned lie. I never..."

"Rider has been arrested to-day on suspicion of murder, doctor. You are involved in it. An accessory, in fact. Now are you going to make a clean breast of it and give me a statement, or are you coming with me to Olstead under arrest?"

Half an hour later, Littlejohn left with a statement in his pocket and the doctor remained to get blind drunk alone in his surgery.

As Rider had prophesied, the jury fastened on to the sock and hung to it like bulldogs. All the efforts of defending Counsel could not shake them. It was stated that Rider had made his confession under pressure and in a confused state of mind. It was even denied that he said certain things. Counsel poured scorn on the tale about the horse-radish and the attempted suicide. A tissue of theory which wouldn't hold water, he said. But the jury hung on to the sock and the shamefaced and faltering evidence of Dr. Keating, who put up a shocking show under the withering cross-fire of the prosecuting lawyer.

Throughout, Rider behaved as though he cared little for the result. One way or the other seemed all the same to him. Relentlessly the structure of his past life was erected, his connection with Bates, his movements at the time of the crimes, his false alibis and, ever and again, his socks. He was sentenced to death; he took it calmly. His appeal failed; he didn't seem to care. He told the prison chaplain that he'd gambled and lost and would take his medicine without spiritual assistance. He played draughts with his warders and his cold-bloodedness gave the pair of them nerves.

"Never see a chap like 'im before," said one of them. "You might think his feelings 'ad left 'is body. A proper cold fish…"

Rider made no further confession, but his last remark to Epicurus Smayle, the hangman, was full of significance.

"If I'd been as good a botanist as I am chemist," he said as the pair of them met for the last time, "I'd have saved you a job."

The matter bothered Epicurus for a long while after the event.

Had he known of it, Old Wall would have been mighty pleased with the ultimate results of his violent passing.

Dr. Keating was removed from the register by an indignant Medical Council, and ceased to trouble the sick of Stalden as a result. His practice being put up for sale by a trustee in bankruptcy, and Mrs. Keating removing herself and her private money to her mother's, people wondered anxiously who was to be their next doctor. To their delight there came another Wall. This time, Dr. John, who made a real job of it by amalgamating the two practices—quack and orthodox under one roof at The Corner House.

Perhaps you saw the notice in *The Times* to the effect that Dr. John Wall had been married to Miss Betty Cockayne…

Littlejohn attended the wedding. He's always letting himself in for functions of that kind. It was widely rumoured that he was the match-maker, but that remains an unsolved mystery.

Dear Reader,

We want to tell you about George Bellairs, the forgotten hero of British crime writing.

George Bellairs wrote over fifty novels in his spare time (his day job being a bank manager). They were published by the Thriller Book Club run by Christina Foyle, manager of the world famous Foyle's bookshop, and who became a friend. His books are set at a time when the real-life British Scotland Yard would send their most brilliant of sleuths out to the rest of the country to solve their most insolvable of murders. Bellairs' hero, gruff, pipe-smoking Inspector Littlejohn appears in all of them. Though his world might have moved on, what drove people to murder—jealousies, greed, fear—is what drives them now. George Bellairs' books are timeless.

If you liked this one, why don't you sign up to the George Bellairs mailing list? On signing you will receive exclusive material. From time to time we'll also send you exclusive information and news.

So join us in forming a George Bellairs community. I look forward to hearing from you.

www.georgebellairs.com
George Bellairs Literary Estate